BECCA BILBO DORRIS

Disgruntled Joy

First edition

This book was professionally typeset on Reedsy.
Find out more at reedsy.com

Representation of race, disabilities, health issues– both physical and mental, lgtbqtia+, and many more are all important and it matters in all forms of art. I wanted to respectfully include a group that is dear to my heart, and gut – my celiacs & GF peeps. Here is a MC with Celiac Disease! Might not be a main plot point, but she exists, she matters, as do you.
This is also for everyone who's ever been on high doses of prednisone and unable to sleep in the middle of the night!
I see you. <3

"Dreams drift and change all the time... It doesn't make any of them less valid if you chase them for a lifetime or a day. They're dreams. Giving up a dream is it's own form of grief. Rediscovering a forgotten dream can be incredibly painful or incredibly soothing. Don't let fear of pain, of grief, of loss stop ever you from dreaming."

-a famous person, eventually

Contents

Foreword

My Dear Readers,

I started writing this shortly after I was diagnosed with two autoimmune conditions in 2016 that severely impacted my life. I found myself working most often during the quiet hours of the 2 AM high doses of prednisone rush. It's been a hot minute since, and I am finally able to publish a book that I never thought I'd complete.

While being a romance - and having plenty of sweet, silly, and sensual moments, the main character has faced significant challenges related to loss and grief, which are important themes in this book. I will not be offended if this book is not for you. Your mental health is much more important to me. Please check the content warnings for your mental health and well-being, and read this at your discretion.

Content warnings

- Death- spousal and child loss
- Mental Health issues- depression, grief, panic attacks, PTSD from a car accident, reference to suicide contemplation
- Renovation issues- termites, mold, lead, etc.

No matter how introverted or alone you feel, we all need community in order to thrive.
A non-toxic, encouraging, and helpful community comes in varying forms- a friend who shows up at the right time, a helpline, a meme, or a moment. However, it can take a lot of work, time, and energy to build your village -work, time, and energy that you may not have. Here is a non-exhaustive list of resources that may be of help. Please look into what is available in your area, when you can. To my knowledge, these were up to date in the USA at the time of publishing the first edition of this book.

- Suicide prevention hotline- 988
- The TED talk: Nora McInerny's - "The messy truth about grief"
- Anxiety and Depression Association of America (ADAA)
- Crisis Text Line- Text HOME to 741-741 in the U.S.
- Hospicefoundation.org has helpful articles on dealing with grief and how to support someone else who is grieving in addition to knowledge of support groups and grief counselors in your area

-Much love,
Becca

Acknowledgement

I could never have accomplished this without all my support from all my IRL friends and family to my online friends and support community. I cannot express how much it means to me that you believe in me.

Erin Brosey. What can I say that you don't already know? Without you, I probably would've never finished this. Our friendship has been such a huge blessing to me. I love you dearly. I'm so grateful you're still in my life despite you living so gosh darn far away. Miss you so much!

Julia Biagi, making you laugh is one of the biggest JOYS of my life. Thank you so much for all your help during this painful process of editing and all the other things. You bless me with your friend ship.

My body doubling online community, Work Buddies, for your help with concentration and focus and for all the encouragement to keep going and finish the thing. Jamie, my love, my leader host extraordinaire. You may have been a fast friend. But you are a soul sister. My savior - who swept in at the eleventh hour to my dear work buddy, Jessica - thank you for breathe some life into the last bit of proofreading. Your notes gave me the push I needed to get this thing completed.

1. but first, Joy

A lot of good that UV protection is today, Joy thought as she cringed, feeling her skin burning through her long sleeve athletic shirt.

"It's because you don't wash your clothes correctly." Her friend Jessica's voice seeped into her thoughts. *Ugh, yes I do. Different doesn't mean WRONG.* The disagreement they'd repeated throughout the years was down to a script. *It does sometimes.* She shook her head trying to quiet the other voices seeping back in with her friend's.

The traffic was terrible—per usual. She needed to focus. So many cars were pulling into the bike lane to see if they could get a better view, turn around, or to just be dicks. If it wasn't so hot and still so far from her destination, she may have been petty enough to stop and photograph every car, including license plates, that was making her journey that much more hazardous. Not that she would do anything with it, she just wanted them to think about why some crazy woman on a bike was yelling at them while taking their picture.

Rocky the fudge road, no. She didn't have time to be petty. She had to keep moving and get out of this heat. *Why am I doing this to myself?!* She sighed audibly, knowing all too well why she wouldn't drive to work. *Just focus on the heat, Joy, or rather, why the actual fudge monkeys does it feel like I'm riding a bike through chicken noodle soup before it's even 8 am.*

After managing to maneuver through all the craziness, she made it to the intersection she longed for. Didn't matter if she went straight or right; either way, she would be just a few minutes back to downtown, back to her shop, back to the only place that felt remotely safe anymore. But the light changed and she turned left. *Welp, as long as I beat him there, this works too,*she thought, remembering the frantic phone call she received this morning from Jessica, her best friend and best employee until she'd hired Benny. She really needed to train him how to open.

It was normally her day to sleep in, the one day a week when she wasn't the one to open the store. But unfortunately, Jessica had had car trouble and had her hubs and children's logistics to juggle.

"I am so incredibly sorry to call you like this" Jessica emphatically moaned, the rest of it flying from her mouth, "but we're getting that delivery today and I know I'm supposed to handle it, and it's such a big deal and I just don't want to miss it and have to deal with it cause I KNOW we need it and it's almost the anniversary and THIS IS A BIG DEAL and I don't want to let you down!"

"Hey, hey, it's fine. It's totally fine. Deep breaths." Joy inhaled and exhaled audibly to encourage Jessica to take a breath, too "Take care of you and yours and we'll figure it out. It's really fine; I'll get there on time. Just—if he calls you, tell him I am around the corner." Joy did her best to calm her friend down knowing full well it would take a miracle to get there before he left. Blast needing signatures on deliveries of things she needs for the store. Blast they can't trust people to not steal things. Blast this friggin heat.

"I promise I will be there as soon as I can," said Jessica as her husband yelled to her that the tow truck was arriving.

"Go. Really, I got this. You'll just owe me a giant coffee, and a girls' night margarita from Rose Pepper."

"Kk, cool cool, totally all the coffee and the good Lord knows I could use that margarita, too. Gotta go, I love you, byeeee!" said Jessica in her normal, chipper voice, all dramatics disappearing from her tone.

Joy had a creeping sensation crawl up her neck. It was going to be a strange day.

"Finally." She breathed a sigh of relief as a gust of wind cooled her sweaty brow. She had arrived at her store. Her little adorable Studio Ghibli-esque store, a small, old renovated home at the corner of a street just around the corner from the main strip. Home to so many unique local treasures, she loved being able to give back to her community while still appealing to the vast amount of tourists that flocked to the area. One of the best perks of owning a store, and living in one of the cutest towns outside of Nashville. Joy never got used to the idea that this was hers. It was still so surreal. "Oh bless it, I didn't miss him," she muttered seeing the delivery truck still in front of her store.

"Ah, there she is! What a Joyful morning I'll have now." The delivery man flashed her a toothy grin. "Cutting it close this morning, aren't we?" he asked with a smirk as he stepped down, tipping his hat in her direction.

"Well," Joy replied slightly out of breath. "Well, hello to you too! What can I say? I like sharp objects." Joy scrunched her eyebrows together, not really even knowing what she meant by that.

"Don't worry, I'd wait all day for a hint of Joy." He winked.

"Hah, thanks." She nodded and turned away to unlock the front door, rolling her eyes at herself, completely oblivious to his lingering stare. The store keys slipped through her finger as she pulled them from the bottom of her oversized work bag. Somehow she managed to catch them in midair, somehow grab the correct key then open the door in one sweep. "Still got it," she triumphed—only to trip and stumble in, knocking her shin on the edge of the door. "Son of peanut butter rocky road fruit cake," she said as she reached for the lights and punched in the alarm code.

"Nice catch, where would you like these?" the delivery man asked while gesturing to the load of packages on his dolly and ever so subtly taking in all that she was. Her long hair stuck to her forehead, flat from wearing her helmet, the rest tied in a low bun at the nape of her neck. Her dark eyes searched for an answer to his question, her breathing still a little rapid.

"Oh, um. Over by the register would be perfect if you don't mind," Joy replied after glancing around "Thank you so much...!" Well, shit. *What was his name again? I should know this by now. I have seen him at least weekly for the last year!* Her mind was blank. She searched for a nametag and only caught a glimpse. *C. Chad? Charles? Cary? Who names their kids Cary? Is he British? I wonder if his parents were Carey Elwes fans. Oh, it's been a while since I've watched Robin Hood: Men in Tights. I should do that. Speaking of tights, David Bowie in Labyrinth. Adding that to the rewatch asap list. Do I even have that? Is that streaming? What was I trying to think of? Oh, that's right, his name,* se reminded herself as he started walking back towards her. She saw his eyes travel down and up her body. And he was smirking. Again. *Do I have something stuck on me? I know I'm a hot sweaty mess, I must smell or something.* She turned her head to the side as she yanked her bun out of his ponytail holder and did a quick sniff check. *Rank. That must be it. Note to self, use extra deodorant when I go change in a minute.*

"I think that's everything today. Unless you have something for me to pick up, or is there something else I can help you with?" he asked, one eyebrow raised. "I'd be happy to serve you in any way possible."

"No, no, I think that's everything. Thank you..." She pinned her elbows to her sides as she glanced at his nametag finally

5

in view. "CHUCK!" she overemphasized. "I hope you have a good rest of your route!"

"Always a pleasure to see you, Joy." He lingered, smirking still.

"Bye!" Joy said with her wide-eyed 'I have no idea what is going on' smile. Wondering why he wasn't leaving, her phone buzzed loudly in the awkward silence, prompting her to ask, "Is there something wrong?"

He leaned forward and whispered, "You're blocking the exit."

"Oh! My bad!" She stepped aside and high-tailed it to the register, pulling out her phone.

So... how about I just realized that my store keys are in the car that is already gone and on the tow truck? Leave the door unlocked for me! I'll be there eventually!

Again, I am so sorry! I promise I'll let you sleep in on Monday!

Joy rolled her eyes. They were closed on Mondays. *Jessica is such a sarcastic ass.* But she was her sarcastic ass, and she wouldn't have it any other way.

Whatever just bring me coffee!

Joy quickly cleaned herself up and changed out of her sweaty athletic wear and into her preferred personal work uniform: lightweight black pants with usable pockets, a simple white shirt, flats, and her rings, one on at least three fingers of each hand. Hair up. Lip gloss on. Deodorant on. Quick. Simple. Easy. Comfortable. Plus her butt looked so good in these pants... no, the pants looked great on her. "I wear clothes, they don't wear me," she said to her reflection. Body positivity, reframe these thoughts. She fist-pumped the air and started her 'get shit done' playlist: a mix of female empowerment ballads and light, happy, hopeful, pop-rock. She was ready to attack the day, and those damn boxes.

Stepping back into the main room, she could feel her massive mental to-do list growing by the second. "Whelp." She flared her nostrils and put her hand on her hips as she circled in place, stopping when she faced the registers. "No sense in opening the doors until you can take people's money, let's wake up the sleeping cash monsters."

As she waited on the beasts to purr, she opened the first box and pulled out one of the stacks of personalized reusable bags, tracing her finger over her logo. *It's beautiful.* A wave of nostalgia and incredulity hit her senses. She'd really done it.

This place had been her dream for years, to open her own store. The bell over the heavy original front door led to beautifully crafted shelves displaying all the knick-knacks and paddy whacks that wove a meandering maze, enticing her customers to come in a little further... The checkout area was simple but obvious with a huge gold-framed vintage mirror leaning on the wall behind helping to throw the soft light of various vintage chandeliers on the seating area in the center. A heavy blush curtain across the way both served as a backdrop for special events like book and poetry readings, and also hid the changing areas. Two luxurious velvet couches, one deep peacock blue, the other an emerald green, faced each other in the middle; both supported and enveloped you, enticing customers to sit longer, and feel welcomed. Clothing and linens softened the back. Everything was locally made—clothing, trinkets, books, art, essential oils, soaps, jewelry—anything that she approved of aesthetically and thought would sell. It was a safe, warm place to gather, to be a part of the community, to give back at least a little.

Had it really been another year since she opened her doors for the first time? It must be, they were getting ready for the second-anniversary sale and party next week. *It's still new but established, and it's real.* It was tangibly hers, unlike other memories that slipped through her fingers like a freezing mist, biting but never solid, never real, at least not anymore. *It's mine, and I have work to do,* she reminded herself, still lost, frozen.

Hearing the front door bells jingle brought her back to the present. Her forehead creased. Either she wasn't moving as fast as she thought, or Jessica arrived here a lot sooner than she'd expected. Joy quickly wiped away the silent tears she had just noticed dripping down her cheek and dropped the bag back into the box. Not looking up, she took a deep breath and mustered up her best southern drawl. "Praise the Lordt, you're here! Hallelujah, Amen! I thought I was going to have to unpack all of this shit by myself." She hoped that covered any lingering emotion in her voice. "Now get your ass back

8

here and help me!"

"Ah, I'm sorry, hello?" a rather confused-sounding male voice asked.

"Fuck me," Joy exclaimed. That definitely did not sound like Jessica, and Benny was not supposed to be in till the afternoon. "Um, Jessica?" she asked, slowly making her way toward the front door. "Are you OK? You sound a, uh, a little different."

She heard a single, "Ha." While short it sounded rich and genuine, she wondered what his full-bodied laugh would sound like. She could just see the top of his tall head covered in thick dark hair. Something about it seemed so familiar. Like she had run her fingers through that hair before. Obviously, Mr. Good Hair hadn't seen the giant closed sign on the door.

"I'm sorry we're not—Shiii-take mushrooms!" She grabbed onto the corner of the wooden bookshelf she had just stubbed her toe on. "What is it with my toe today and all the things gravitating towards it? If I still have a nail left after all the stupid things I've hit it on, I'm going to be surprised. Shit, I just said all that out loud. Ugh," she groaned, closing her eyes. Her coffee helped her filter. She did not have her coffee, so she had no filter. She *had* to replace the broken pot in the back room ASAP. *Jessica, this is all your fault.* Taking a deep breath, and eyes glued to the floor, she stopped when she saw his shoes. Rubbing her forehead, but trying to sound sweet and professional, she said, "I apologize greatly, we aren't open yet, could you possibly come back later?"

"I am incredibly sorry miss," the disembodied voice responded. It sounded ever so rich, and warm, like honey in a hot cup of tea all wrapped up in her favorite soft blanket that she saved to comfort her during the stormy days. She couldn't bring herself to look. She didn't want to ruin it. She was sure she'd heard this voice before. It wasn't—*what's his name again?*—the delivery guy who was just here. Surely it wasn't one of her regular customers. Maybe she was just too nostalgic this morning and pulling at memories subconsciously. But if this was who she thought it was, she'd already made a fool of herself in front of him. "But I would be incredibly gracious if you would allow me to seek refuge for a few minutes? My *ass* could even help you move your *shit*?"

Her head snapped up at that and she stared at the gorgeous man in front of her, confirming what she'd already feared. *Shit.* Her heart fluttered, staring back into the abyss of his familiar but mysterious ocean depth-blue eyes. This must either be a dream or a joke. The one person alive she never thought in her wildest dreams she would ever see again, the only person who ever gave her second thoughts about agreeing to marry her college sweetheart, was standing right there in front of her. He also wasn't supposed to be here, ever. To add insult to injury as she stood there staring, the playlist switched to "Take a Chance on Me" by ABBA.

Of. Fucking. Course.

2. second comes Lucas

Chapter 2

Lucas Worthington. The. Lucas. E. Worthington. *Nope, absolutely not. There's no way in hallelujah high-diving hell this could be him.* He was standing right in front of Joy, not even five feet away, and asking for help. The man who starred in almost every one of Joy's favorite movies as of the last decade or so, since his big break right after she graduated college; from romcoms to action to sci-fi, he had a fantastic range and gave dimension to his characters. On top of it all, he was a humanitarian, feminist, and philanthropist. This amazing human was there by *her* door. Standing in front of her.

Nope, not him. Can't be. This man is even more attractive. Is that even possible? The way his silky hair shone was too bright, the blue of his eyes too deep, the bulk of his biceps too ripply. *He has to be some sort of very lucky, very handsome Luke-alike. Ha, I need to remember to tell Jessica and Benny that one. Dear Lordt, what if Jess paid some actor to pretend to be him?*

Those blue eyes bore into her as Joy's gaze drifted back to his face. She felt her face and underarms heat. She took a deep breath, raised an eyebrow, and asked, "Refuge?" He nodded, his face hopeful, pleading. Dare she say, nervous? She glanced outside at the clear sky. Her heart was racing. She crossed her arms and started chewing on her thumbnail, staring at him in awkward silence. *Come on, Joy. Put your customer service mask on, get your dirty nail out of your mouth and come up with a way to get rid of him. Think, woman!*

She smiled and wiped her hand on the back of her pants. "Why?" she finally asked. "You don't really seem like the kind of person who would need saving." Her voice was sing-songy, then darkened, eyes narrowing, suspicious. "It's not storming. You don't seem to be selling something." She tilted her head and muttered, "Although, someone that good-looking must be selling something."

"Good-looking?" He asked quietly.

Shiitake mushrooms, I let the inside thought out. Inside thoughts are IN for a reason.

"Thank you for noticing," the very attractive man who was sent to deceive her by her bestie said, "but eh, no, I'm not."

"Are you hiding from an overly enthusiastic salesperson?" she asked, ignoring what he said. She stepped closer to the window and peered over the display to try and get a better view of the street, and continued to ramble on. "Are you running from the police? Are you armed and dangerous?" She took a step back to look him over. "Did you rob a bank?

Did someone rob you? Oh, are you a really bad spy? " Her eyebrows raised, sizing him up, daring him to answer. *It's quite possible I'm overdoing the sarcasm.* She turned her gaze back to the window. "I could take you out easily, so don't try anything." She looked over her shoulder at him, scowling to see him smiling all innocent and cute and looking back at her. *So annoying.*

"I mean you no harm," he started. "I promise, I come in peace." His eyes widened and his smile dropped right before he did. His large frame was crunched low against the solid portion of the antique farm door. He placed one finger in front of his rather appealing lips and softened his voice, "I'm only truly terrified of one thing," he whispered.

"What?" she asked, still standing but slightly hunching her back, ready for action.

"Teenagers." He leaned his head back against the door right as several young women ran down her street. "Specifically larger packs of unhinged teenage girls chasing me."

They looked cute and harmless, just excited—until she heard one of them yell at someone she couldn't see. "Did you find him?" the girl screamed. Her face turned into a feral scowl as she gave instructions to the others to track down the person they were looking for. It was very disconcerting. Most people in the area respected celebrities. Sure, they asked for autographs and photos, but they left them alone for the most part. They certainly didn't follow or chase after them. One of the good things about the greater Nashville area—most

13

people around here understood that celebrities are just people like everyone else. These girls looked like they were out for blood.

And this man only was an unfortunate soul that happens to look like one, they forgot about innocence until proven guilty. She shook her head. *Not enough proof, yet.* She could feel her inner eyes roll as her heart skipped a beat. *Shit, just shitty shit shit.* She chewed the inside of her cheek, trying to remain grounded.

"That's fair, herd mentality is a bitch sometimes," Joy teased, wide-eyed at the realization that this was most likely the exact person she thought he was. *Play it cool, you got this boo.* She most certainly did not have this as her thoughts raced.

"But what about large packs of teenage boys? Is it just packs? How about random single women?" She winked, then quickly leaned over his hunched figure and loudly latched the door. She was close to him now, close enough to tell he smelled of coffee and that earthy evergreen manly musk that reminded her of campfires, and long hugs while overlooking a sunset. Her pulse quickened as she realized she was thinking about what it would be like to be wrapped in his arms. *What is happening? Why do I feel like I'm 16 with my hormones raging but no one to use them with? I can never leave my house without having my coffee first ever again.*

"Oh, I'm terrified of random single women, and lots of situations, but mainly herds when they're stampeding towards me. Have they not gone?" He smiled up at her, seemingly more at

14

ease. "Did you just lock me in?"

Omiword, did he just wink? Omiword, JOY, what are you twelve? "I'm not sure, stay down. And I'm giving your ass refuge," Joy replied. *Shit, did I just say ass? I wonder if—no. Stop it, Joysephine. What would Jessica say? You are a grown-ass woman, calm your tits. You're allowed to say whatever you want.* Joy still peered over him under the pretense of watching the girls long gone by now, trying to ignore his gaze. *Jolly holiday rancher. Tits? Ass? Not what I need to be thinking about right now. What would my mother say if she could hear my thoughts? What if I say it out loud? Again! Shit. Double shit.* "Why are they looking for you anyway? Did you take someone's coffee order, say a terrible pun, or 'your mom' the wrong person? I've done that, some people just don't appreciate a good pun or get 'your mom' jokes." *Now I'm rambling, great. Still an awkward teenager in a 34-year-old woman's body.*

"Well, it could have been that or they could know me from my movies. I tend to get a few fans following me occasionally." He mumbled his response softly at first, then louder and clearer. "But it was probably a pun."

Good Lord in heaven. I love puns.

"I make terrible puns."

Even better.

"Especially before my morning coffee." His eyes sparkled. "They'll bean better later."

15

That's amazing. "That's so bad," she deadpanned her response.

"I told you," he chuckled and stood up carefully. "Terrible."

She followed him with her eyes as he stood. "So bad it left an aftertaste." She smirked. *Wait, did he just say he was in movies? So is this really Lucas?* He was tall, just like she imagined, with those deep eyes drilling into her soul, and she was so much closer to him than she realized.

"Also, to answer you earlier, I wouldn't mind if you took me out." He smirked.

How dare he? And that was most definitely a wink. Wait, what just happened? Is he seriously flirting with me? Am I flirting? Why are we standing so close? Why does he smell so good? Seriously, I could just drink him in this morning instead of coffee. I'm missing something, did I ask him out? Is he asking me out? Is he joking? What I want to say is, 'Yes,' and many other things that would make my mother blush and then attempt to wash my mouth out with soap. Heck, they might even make Jessica blush, but only because she'd probably thought them too. He is apparently, after all, a movie star.

I can't be alone in thinking these things. That's what happens when you are famous and beautiful. Random people fantasize about you because you're not a real possibility. You're safe. You're never going to meet them and if you do it's not supposed to be in a real conversation. Locked in with you alone at your store. Did I mention, alone? Holy shit, it's been forever since I've flirted. Is the

AC not working? She could feel her sweat stick to her wrinkled brow.

"I... have work to do." Joy finally found a reply, still maintaining eye contact. "You are welcome to stay for as long as you like, until closing if you want to. I will be opening at 10. However, the public, including those girls, will be welcome in my store as long as they've brought their manners with them. So, you may want to head out when you feel safe." She swallowed hard, trying to keep her breathing calm and steady. She hadn't been this nervous around a man since, well... was it over a decade already? Wow. Joy's thoughts drifted down towards another rabbit trail.

"Thank you, I'd very much like to stay awhile longer," he answered, still smiling that sexy little smirk. "Is there anything I can do to help you? Or may I take a look at your books while I try to stay out of your way?"

"Of course! They're all local authors. So many interesting characters themselves. Knowing the writer puts a whole new perspective on the story... as does the writing introduce a new side to the author," Joy spouted off, managing to break the spell and step away from him. This was one of her passions. Reading, writing, the intrigue of figuring someone else out. All of it distracted her from... well, it served as a distraction and as a topic of conversation. She loved when customers asked about the various novels, ranging from kids' stories to murder mysteries and even sonnets. It was easy to slip into her spiel. She walked him to the book section, then pointed towards her luxe couches. "Make yourself comfortable while I finish opening. I'd offer you coffee but my maker's broken."

"Thank you, this looks fantastic, and don't worry about me, you've been an extremely gracious hostess," he replied, eyeing the shelves and cozy but fun surroundings. Returning his gaze to her, he continued, "Excuse my manners, but I've yet to ask the name of my heroine."

"I'm flattered, but no, I am no heroine. Benevolent overlord maybe, but either way you can call me Joy. And you are?" She wanted to hear him say it... maybe he was just a doppelganger or stunt double after all...

"Oh! I'm Lucas."

Dammit.

He reached to shake her hand. "Lucas E. Worthington. It has truly been a pleasure to make your acquaintance. My dearest overlord Joy, I will never forget the sanctuary you bestowed today, and forevermore be your grateful liege." He finished with a kiss on her knuckles and an exaggerated formal bow.

"Now if only I could get my employees to submit so nicely," Joy winked. "It's nice to meet you, too. Especially if you buy something." She framed the display shelf next to her with a grand arm gesture to make Vanna White proud. Seeing him start to browse, she began to walk back to her boxes. Almost there she remembered something. "Just one hopefully quick thing... *did* someone, anyone tell you or highly recommend you to come here? See an ad? Out of all the places you could've gone into, why did you choose this one?"

"No, I haven't talked to many people since I arrived. I happened to see someone leaving and assumed you were open, or at the very least hoped the door was unlocked. It was my first morning to explore after settling in my temporary home."

"Oh, OK... um, thanks..." Joy paused. "Temporary home? Meaning longer than a vacation? Why?"

"Yes, I signed on to shoot a season of a new show that is based here," he replied, looking up from the book he had just pulled. "Unfortunately I can't say much more about that, although I'd love to tell you more when I can." He winked at her, smiled then continued his inspection of the hardcover.

"Oh, OK, sounds fun... the shooting thing, I mean, the doing of the filming thing." Joy turned, flustered. "Thank you!"

Turning again to the task at hand, Joy shook her head, trying to focus and not really believing what had just happened. She kept finding herself looking over at him, first browsing, picking up a book, thoroughly inspecting the ins and outs of each cover, and finally a selection. *I wonder which one he chose. Now of course, he's sitting on my sofa, in my store, looking amazing and saying amazing things. Deep breaths, he's still just a person trying to hide out for a bit. If Jessica had anything to do with this, then I'll fire her. I'll fire her butt and make her buy me one of those flaming shots! Well, maybe not fire from the store, I need her after all but I will definitely yell at her. I mean, seriously how is he in MY store? Before it's even open? I'm alone with him, of all people?*

19

She hid behind the registers under the pretense of opening one of them but was actually texting Jessica.

Is there anything you want to tell me? Did you talk to anyone interesting or new recently?

Sent. No reply. Joy managed to finish opening the registers despite the added distractions. Normally she was focused, easily ignoring her phone as she counted the drawers, but today she had to recount the stack of ones three times.

Still. No. Reply. He was still sitting on her couch, legs crossed, engrossed in his find. *Why was she not answering? Surely she should be close now, or able to reply. She always replied, almost instantly, especially if it was during work hours. She was ignoring her. Or worse, something happened to her. No... I can't go there. Maybe the reception is just funky. Am I really going to have to talk to the extremely attractive, charming, intelligent, seemingly sweet, and somewhat flirtatious man just blatantly sitting across the room looking adorable before I consult my person? I am a grown-ass woman. I should be able to handle this. For heaven's sake, I can do harder things than this. Talking to another human being shouldn't be hard. I do this all the time. Then why does my chest feel tight and why are my palms sweaty? So what if it's been over a decade since I've flirted with another man besides Ryan...*

She spun the simple band still on the fourth finger of her left hand. Not that it meant anything anymore. She just felt naked without it on, but she wore rings on most of her fingers to confuse and distract from any questions about something so simple. At least that's what she hoped.

Her thoughts drifted to a recent conversation with Jessica. "You know he has a crush on you," Jessica stated as soon as the bells jingled to signal the delivery man had gone.

"Um... what?" Joy tilted her head and raised an eyebrow at her friend. "Where is this even coming from? And who are we talking about?"

"Chuck"

"Who?"

"Are you really this oblivious? Chuck! The guy who brings you the boxes! The one who is always lingering, wanting you to say more but is obviously too nervous to say anything extra to you!" Jessica exclaimed, waving her arms around to indicate carrying a heavy box. "I think he's scared since you're still wearing your ring. He thinks you're available but he's not sure."

"The delivery guy? He's sweet but I think you're reading too much into this. Seriously, no." Joy faced Jessica and took a deep breath, "Jessica, you know I am in a much better place but I am still not ready to even talk about this kind of thing; and besides, he's a baby. A cute baby, but still a baby. He's probably not even legally able to drink."

"You know I'm just trying to look out for you here. I don't want you to miss something that could be good and you know, maybe even healthy for you. Even if it's just a chance to practice your flirting skills or increase your confidence,

21

something... I don't know... you know?" Not getting the reaction she was hoping for Jessica switched tactics. "Okay... so you're not ready to talk but you're ready to think about the possibility of maybe what?"

"The only men I've been thinking about lately are either fictional or that guy from that ridiculous movie I love but you make fun of me for so I'm not going to mention it," Joy teased, continuing to shelve the new inventory.

"OK, not the fictional guys because while super fun, they don't count. Lucas Worthington, however, is dreamy," agreed Jessica. "And a good start."

"Yes, yes, he is quite dreamy." Joy started thinking about how in every movie he was in or every publicity picture she'd seen, it always appeared that his shirts were tailored quite snugly around his arms.

How odd that must be to fit? They don't seem to be overly large biceps. Who requests that? The wardrobe department? The director? Does he have a thing for tight-fitting sleeves? With the wrong material, that must be annoying. It didn't matter the length or color he dyed his wavy locks or stubble or clean-shaven he had embodied every version of what her prince charming would look like. But man, oh man, those dreamy deep eyes that seemed to beckon her from the screen... *and those biceps, ugh.*

"You're thinking about him now, aren't you?" pried Jessica. "What part are you thinking about, eh, eh?" She gave Joy her most awkward wink.

"Biceps." Joy sighed. "I know, I know, completely superficial but that's what I was thinking about. But, you know, I hear he has an affinity for good literature, both modern and Shakespearean, so I'm attracted to his potential smarts as well."

"Bwahaha," Jessica laughed, wiping a happy tear from her eye. "But seriously, maybe he'll read your book one day and come hunt you down."

"That would just be strange." Joy retorted.

"But what if he did?" asked Jessica. "Didn't you meet him once upon a time?"

"Once upon a time, yes, briefly," Joy replied. "Did what? Read my book? I am all for one more book sale." *Dear Lordt, no. Please don't.*

"No, hunt you down." Jessica wiggled one of her eyebrows suggestively.

"Ugh." She sighed out of annoyance, then replied honestly, "Oh, I'd totally unintentionally seduce him with my awkwardness because I wouldn't have any self-control. Then, ah, once I realized what I was doing, I'd turn and run away in embarrassment. Then hide. Sell the business. Sell my home. Hitchhike to Chattanooga. Go hike the Appalachian Trail. Never return to civilization. Hide forever. Get eaten

23

by a black bear or some cryptid which will absolve me of my humiliation at attempting to flirt. The end. That would be the end of me."

"First of all, no. You are absolutely not allowed to sell this place or run away without my permission, because you obviously have no idea where you're going. The Appalachian Trail is over 60 miles east of Chattanooga," Jessica said, one hand on her hip, the other wagging her finger in front of Joy's face, with her mom 'I'm not taking this shit' tone of voice. "You could at least go through Knoxville to Gatlinburg, there's an actual fucking trailhead in Gatlinburg."

"Ugh, Knoxville. You know that place irritates me." Joy rolled her eyes and groaned. "Besides—"

"Knoxville smoxville. Besides, you'd never actually ride in a car that long anyhow so we both know it's a moot point," Jessica interrupted. She continued her lecture, poking Joy in the shoulder. "So what if somehow he did find you? So what if he asked you out? You're an amazingly talented, smart, strong, gorgeous, absolutely stunning, cunning, resourceful, devilishly handsome, trash panda! You deserve all the opportunities for happiness in all the forms. If he ever shows up, or anyone else who strikes your fancy, get out of your head and go for it. You are worthy. And also, if he actually reads your book and then seeks you out then: ne, it means he wants to know you; wo: brush up on your vocab because if you actually seduce him then it means it worked, awkward or not. He probably has some awkward fetish himself so you'll be great together. Three, the two of you are probably destined to be together anyway so you just need to get used to it. And my fourth and final point: there is plenty of time to get eaten by a cryptid after your honeymoon," Jessica concluded, returning her other hand so both were resting on her hips. Her stare dared Joy to cross her.

"Like you said, this whole scenario is never going to happen, so why are we even arguing about this?" asked Joy, who smiled meekly. "And thank you for the compliment. I love trash pandas, they're adorable."

"I know you love them, they're crafty adorable little demons," started Jessica, an intense stare still plastered on her face, "And if you're so sure this will never happen, that lightning won't strike twice, then make me a promise."

"What kind of promise?"

"The kind where, if by some holy miracle, that man ever asks you out, you have to say yes." Jessica's eyes sparkled while her mouth twisted into a mischievous grin. "I need to know you'd be capable of saying yes to your heart's desires, even if the chances of anything happening are super unlikely. I love you; I'm not asking you to spend your life with him, although that is exactly where this is headed. I'm asking you to agree to say yes to something unlikely, so you will be prepared when something you really want, whether that be a person, or driving again, you'll do it. Please, pretty please, promise me you'll say yes." Jessica finished by grabbing Joy's hands, pouting her lower lip, and giving her puppy dog eyes.

Taking a deep slow breath, knowing her friend had won her

over with those adorable eyes, but not wanting to give her the satisfaction of a quick win, Joy took her time before answering. Swinging their hands back and forth, pursing her lips, and squinting her eyes, she finally began to speak. "Well, since you are so wonderful and love me so much, and this would make you so happy, and since the likelihood of anything actually happening is slim to none, *fine.* I will tell Lucas yes on a snowball's chance in hell of him ever asking me out. But only Lucas." She pointed her finger in Jessica's face and bonked her nose.

"You mean when, but OK, I'll take it!" Jessica hugged her friend, and whispered, "OK, but what about Chuck?"

"Who?"

"Oh. My. Word. You are terrible. The delivery guy who has a crush on you!"

"Don't even go there." Joy pushed her off. Customers had started coming in so that helped change the topic.

Man, I have some sort of mental block when it comes to the delivery guy. Her thoughts drifted back to the present. *More like a delivery boy. Nothing like the man who was on her mother-forking couch. Holy snickerdoodle. What is happening? Jessica must have known something. There was no other way. This was way too strange to be a coincidence. Someone must have given her a heads-up. Divine intervention maybe? Better be some divine intervention on Jessica's behalf if I find out she was somehow involved.* Her hands gripped the counter, holding on to keep

26

her steady. *Holy jamoly, I am weak in the knees, literally and I'm just looking at him. I've been staring at him for who knows how long. Oh, to be that book in his hand. Wait, what is it he's reading?*

"Ah." She let out a short gasp. realizing it was her first novel in his hands. He turned to look at her.

"Everything OK?" Lucas asked.

"Hmm, me? No, yes, I, ah, it's nothing..." Joy replied. Her phone buzzed, interrupting her. A text flashed on the screen.

OMW. Remember to unlock the door for me!

Great, so she'll be here soon... but still no explanation... maybe there isn't any. Maybe it's all in my head... Joy looked up from the screen to see Lucas still looking at her. "Sorry about that, my employee needs me to unlock the door, there were car issues and she left her keys somewhere, you know, all the drama. But, um, what about your face? I mean, did you see anybody... Any*thing* that looks good to you? "

"Yes," Lucas said, eyes still locked on hers. "I think I'll buy this and go. It should be safe now. I don't want to be a distraction."

"Oh, you can distract me anytime," Joy replied slowly nodding her head. *Shit, was that out loud?* "I mean, you look great, I mean you've *been* great. I mean you do look great but you probably know that already. What I'm trying to say is that

27

you haven't bothered me. You've been very polite and look tempting on my sofa. I mean, I know how comfortable my sofas are and I wouldn't mind sitting on you, oh God, I mean on the sofa with you. Wow, well, I obviously am not turned on, I mean my brain isn't, shit... Caffeine, I need coffee... to make the words go in the right order. Excuse me, I have to do the thing." Joy turned, hoping he didn't see her face turn completely red, and hurried to the front of the store to unlock the door. She heard him chuckle behind her.

Shit. Shit. Shit.

3. finally, coffee

hit. Shit. Shit. Shit. Shit.

Joy slowly meandered her way back to the resisters after unlocking the door for Jessica, internally chanting her newest mantra. *He* was still standing there, fiddling with some of the point-of-sale merchandise. From this angle it appeared that he was comparing some key chains; she had several local vendors who made key chains and they were all either adorable, hilarious or both. Her favorites were the leather-pressed ones with Tennessee-related jokes on them; jokes like, ' *Are you from Tennessee?*' on one side and '*Because you're the only 10 I see*' on the opposite. A perfect combination of classy and corny. She paused to straighten some books that were not perfect.

Determined to focus on anything other than the manly presence in her store. Barely 15 feet away from her. Nope, she determined that the candle display was not to her liking anymore and completely changed it, remembering Benny would just be mad if she touched his favorite display and put everything back the way it was two minutes prior.

Not even turning at all intentionally so she could see Lucas out of the corner of her eye as she shifted to the bath and body products. *Smirking. Dear holy mother of nature, he was smirking.* He found something that made him smile and he looked comfortable. She let out a sigh. And he looked up. She averted her gaze immediately. Joy bit her lip, hoping he had not noticed her gawking. *I am just as bad as a hormonal teenager at their favorite star's meet and greet.* She shook her head and focused on making sure all the testers were open and ready to use. Perhaps a little too aggressively as the rosemary mint lotion top fell off and left a glob of creamy goo in her hands. *Yum.*

Speaking of yum... Joy's gaze drifted back to Lucas while rubbing the lotion carefully on her hands, taking her time lathering up each finger avoiding getting any on her rings. Her heart started to beat erratically. She glanced around, searching to make sure there was nothing else blatantly out of place. Unfortunately, there wasn't anything except what was back at the register... her boxes and Lucas, who was most certainly watching her gawk.

Joy put on her best customer service smile, trying to hide the blush that was creeping back up as she walked back but instead of going directly behind the register, she hesitated. *If he was just a customer I would go up to him before going back there, be friendly, ask if he needed help, and show him things. I'd like to show him a lot of things. Joyanna, STAHP.* She walked up closer to him, despite the knot growing in her stomach the closer she got to him, her train of thought not helping, and pointed to the key chains. "What do you think of those? Any of them strike your fancy?"

"Actually, they're all quite funny." He smiled.

"Quite? Only quite?" she leaned in as he spun the display and pulled one off.

"These are cheeky perfection," He raised his eyebrows and handed the one in his hand to Joy. "But I think this one is my favorite."

" 'Country music lyrics are my love language', " she smiled, and reached over to see if her other favorites were still on the display. "Did you see both sides of this one?" as she pointed to one with a raccoon on it.

He shook his no, reaching to turn it over. He brushed her still-pointed finger as he did, making the knot in her stomach harden.

She then closed her eyes and recited, "'Trash Panda: TN state wild animal since '71' I think they're adorable creatures," she added. "Or any of these '10 I see' variations are popular. This one is like "we rate dogs," '12 out of Tenn.' Oh, oh, or this one, 'my mom is Reba, my dad is a guitar.'" She laughed, relieving some of her butterflies,' 'Oh, man, these still get me, they're so terrible, I love them." He joined in on the laughter as they went through more of the key chains.

The bell rang, interrupting. Lucas grabbed her wrist and whispered wide-eyed, "Don't let them get me!"

He crouched behind her, in what she assumed was an attempt to hide in case the herd entered. She attempted to move and his grip on her arm tightened slightly, she looked over her shoulder at him with a quizzical look on her face. His puppy dog eyes were wide with fear, practically pleading with her to protect him. Her stomach flipped, and patted his hand, giving him a reassuring look. He eased his grip as she turned to see who entered.

"Joy Elizabeth Moore!" a strong musical voice rang out. Joy stiffened and crouched next to Lucas, turning so she couldn't see his face as she felt hers heat. "Joy-bear! Have you seen? Oh. My. GOOD-NESS. You will never guess who is moving here!"

Jessica bounded in, her beautiful long brown bouncy curls just made her appear all the more bubbly while she continued, talking a mile a minute not waiting for her friend to respond. "I know you're in here, I saw your bike! Where are you? Ah! This is just perfect! Stop me if you've heard. But there's a new show that is filming here and HE's THE STAR! So, you have to say yes if you get the chance. You promised!" She practically sang, clapping and starting to maniacally chuckle, stopping only when she realized she couldn't see her friend. "But seriously, I have your coffee! It's from Bubbly Banana!"

Joy could feel Lucas's smirking gaze bore into the back of her head. There's no way he couldn't put together that her friend was referring to him. She popped up with a sudden determination to minimize the damage. She could feel him stand up behind her. She shook off his magnetic hold and waved at him to stay put while she intercepted her friend before she could see around the display shelf. "Uh, hey Jess!" Her eyes wide, she bore her gaze into Jessica's, begging her to change the subject. "We have company!" She smiled and rubbed the spot where his hand had just been, not sure if she was trying to calm the leftover prickle of electricity from the momentary contact or grind the feeling into her memory. *What is happening? Am I dreaming? This is all surreal. She dug her nails into her arm. Ow. No. This is real.* She peeled her fingers from her skin and took the coffee from Jessica's outstretched hand.

"Company?" Jess asked. Her eyes narrowed and she tilted her head. "Who?"

"Oh, I think you're going to be pretty surprised," Joy replied before adding in a whisper, "and if you're not, I'll have your head." She took a sip. "Oh, my goodness, what is this? It's amazing!"

"You couldn't handle my head, it's too big for you and that is their hummingbird express– espresso, steamed cashew milk, and banana syrup, then topped with a dash of cinnamon, a dried orange, and ginger garnish. I thought it sounded beautiful, hyper, and a little extra, just like you." Jess winked then lowered her voice. "Now, seriously, who is here? Cough once if I need to run and get help," Jess stood on her tiptoes attempting to see over Joy's shoulder. Joy rolled her eyes and

33

leaned to one side so she could see.

"Bwahahahahahahaha," she threw her head back and cackled. "No way. This isn't real." She said between guffaws. Wiping away a tear she looked back over at Lucas who was leaning against the key chain display, arms crossed. "You, you're real?"

"Last I checked." He replied with a sweet yet cheeky smile.

His face looked more relaxed, in fact, and amused at how tickled Jessica was. Good, maybe he's not noticing how red my face must be, Joy thought as she observed the two of them.

Jessica took a deep breath, stifling her laughter and collecting herself, then marched over to Lucas. "Hi! So glad that you're real and that you're really here. I'm assuming you're also really Lucas?" He nodded and he shook her outstretched hand. "Excellent," she continued. "Well, I'm Jessica, Joy's second in command and best friend. What brings you in this morning?" She asked, not pausing long enough for anyone to respond. Her eyes squinted as she sized him up, noticing the book still in his hand. The book he'd been reading earlier that she'd completely forgotten about.

"Oh! You're reading Joy's book? Did you come to hunt her down?" She turned to Joy and gave her the most awkward and obvious wink. Her entire body was smiling. Joy felt like an armadillo in headlights. "I told you he would! Well, I guess God answered that prayer! Ah, hahaha," She chuckled until Joy elbowed her in the ribs.

34

"That was quite the introduction," Lucas spoke as soon as Jess's laughter died down slightly. "Where do I start? Er, I was not hunting but was being hunted and dodged in here to escape. Joy graciously saved me from a bloody terrifying situation."

"Let me guess, a mob of teenagers?" Jess asked.

"Exactly."

"Figures, I have a preteen, and I have never been so terrified in my life," Jess replied. "Go on."

"Er, I did not realize this was Joy's book." He flipped to the back insert where the author's head shot was. Joy smiled back at him from the page. He looked up at Joy, "I would absolutely love your autograph if you don't mind that is."

"She would love to," Jess responded before Joy could process what he'd just asked.

"Uh, sure." Joy was not sure how red her face was but she could feel the awkwardness and panic setting in. She had played it as cool as possible, which honestly wasn't that cool, up until then because she thought this was all a ploy. But she had caught the last thing Jessica had said. An answer to a prayer. Jessica hadn't done this. What if this was an answer to her prayer... or more likely Jessica's prayers. "I can sign you when you're ready. I mean sign the book." Shit.

Lucas grinned, "I think I'm ready."

Joy noticed Jess slinking away to put her things in the back room. The phone rang. "I'll get it back here!" she threw Joy two thumbs up as she walked backwards through the door.

Joy grabbed a pen from the cup she kept out for guests to use. She flipped to the page she preferred to sign. He leaned in close to her, watching the process.

"Would you mind personalizing it?" he asked her. "Something like, 'to Lucas, Even though you appear to be strong and dashing, I know your weakness now. I vow to always be here to be your fortress from rampaging teenagers. Always yours.' Or something else similar like, 'Lucas, you're an answer to my prayers'." He teased, raising one of his eyebrows as she looked up at him. "What kind of prayers were those about anyway?"

"Not *my* prayers," Joy replied simply, "Jessica's." It was the truth, she never once mentioned him in any of her prayers... She didn't actually pray much anymore. Most of the time she was too exhausted and angry to say anything. Well, she yelled, cried out, her heart hammering, fists clenched, and body quaking, but she wouldn't necessarily call those prayers. More releasing of something deep within her being. Now her heart was beating erratically for a different reason.

Returning back to focusing on her breath, she continued to sign his book. She blocked his view with her left hand. Which was difficult to do with him being so close to her. Half of her wanted to push him away, and the other half wanted to lean into him. Was he like this with all the ladies? Was he really an ass, too? Or was he better? Was he genuine?

"Oh really? Why hers and not yours?" he pried, leaning even closer, trying to see what she was writing. Quickly she scrawled,

Dear Lucas,
I'll be happy to save you if the herds stampede again.
Forever your knight in shining armor,
Joy E Moore

Finished, she shut the book before he could catch a glimpse. "I don't know you well enough to answer that." She said abruptly but smiled, softening her tone. She didn't like discussing those kinds of whys with people she knew well, let alone complete strangers. She held the book on to him, then pulled it back, "No looking until you leave. Promise?"

"Scout's honor, no peeking." He promised, holding up his three middle fingers on his left hand, his right hand resting on his heart. Then he held out his hand for the book. She pursed her lips and squinted at him, not sure if she should trust him or not. She placed the book gingerly in his waiting hand, ready to snap it back if he started to open it. "I promise," he added sincerely, gently.

Time stopped for Joy only a few times in her life. That moment between heartbeats, that pause, and stillness, when all the world seems small, and nothing else matters at all. When Ryan had proposed, watching Jessica walk down the aisle at her wedding, the first time she held Peter, and the last... And

37

now, as they both stood there, that split second when both their hands were holding her book, she could swear that it lasted hours. Or did they stand there, locked in each other's gaze for hours and it felt like only a second? If it wasn't for Jessica's returning giggles in the background bringing Joy back to reality. There was something in his voice, in his look, in her heart that was calming, that was hopeful, it was beautiful, it was peaceful. A feeling of familiarity, like her soul was saying, 'Oh it's you.' Life was meant for these moments, these connections. *Well, shit.*

"Is it just me, or are you having deja vu too? Have we met before?" Lucas asked. They were both still holding the book.

"Oh, ah," Joy dropped her hand, as time began again. *Yes, we had, how could I forget? But never in my wildest dreams did I think he'd ever remember me. Maybe he's confusing me for someone else.* "Um, I *think* so... For like a split second, once upon a time, a very long time ago, back when I was in college, there was a press junket for the release of a movie that was filmed in the area, and I think we met in passing."

Joy pulled on a distant memory of a young actor at a press junket at her school she had been lucky enough to attend. She was interning in the PR and media relations department. Her boss had invited her to help take notes and pictures. The more pictures the better. He had been a relatively unknown actor at the time but there were other more famous people there. It was all very exciting for a girl who had never actually experienced anything like that before. She had run into him while they were waiting to start. She had gone to grab a cup of coffee and had nearly spilled it on him. "Are you alright?" He'd asked. He had locked onto her gaze and for the first time since she started dating Ryan, she had completely forgotten his existence, despite the heaviness of the ring on her finger. She wanted to stay there, in that moment as if he was reading her soul, and she, his. This gentle, beautiful man. This man, who was standing in front of her again.

"I think I remember now," stated Lucas. "But it was more than a split second. You tripped, and I caught you. We talked, I asked you out, and you... you turned me down, isn't that right?"

So he did remember. This could be a bad thing, or a good thing, or a terrible disaster for what's left of my emotional stability.

Joy nodded her head and managed to squeak out, "Yes." She cleared her throat before continuing, "Something like that."

"It wasn't because you didn't want to though, you had something else going on?"

"I think that there was a party I had to go to or something."

Jessica chose that moment to interrupt. "It was her engagement party, but don't worry Lucas. Despite all those rings on her fingers, while some may still be sentimental, she's as single as a slice of Kraft cheese."

Joy stared daggers at her former best friend. "I thought you were on the phone?"

39

She sighed. "It was just Mrs. Crustybutt Complainy Mcgee. You've input these right?" She indicated to the stack of the newly printed tote bags that Joy had barely begun to unpack. Joy just stared at Jess. "Cool, I'll put these out then." She turned and took the stack and Joy's breath with her.

Lucas just grinned and nodded his head. The bell rang indicating a possible customer. He checked his watch. "Unfortunately, I think that's my cue to go. May I pay?"

Joy didn't realize she was still holding her breath until she tried to speak. "You know what, don't worry about it, why don't you just keep it? It'll be your welcome to the neighborhood gift."

"Oh, no, I insist." He said while digging out his wallet.

"No, really, I want you to have it."

"Can I have one of these too?" He picked up one of the business cards displayed on the counter.

Joy shook her head, yes, the knot in her stomach was so tight she was sure it would explode.

"Well, Joy, it was a pleasure being saved by you today. I hope we can do this again soon."

"Uh-huh, sure." Joy's voice was barely audible.

"Excuse me, miss, can you help me?" Said an older woman

in a purple shirt and a red straw hat who had wandered up behind Lucas.

"I'll let you get back to your work then. Thank you." He turned to leave, nodding to the woman but turned back around and said, "Oh, and Joy, I'll be seeing you." Then he winked and walked out.

That happened. Her breathing quickened, her stomach churned, and she just wanted to sink to the floor and hide until she had time to process all that had just occurred. The heat electrocuting her nervous system, spreading from her skin up her arm, radiating throughout her torso all the way to every extremity.

"Well honey, do you have any fans?" Said the lady in the red hat, "Because I need to cool down after that. Whew, that man was hot!"

"Heckin' yes, he is," chimed in Jess. "Whew, I need water first after that, then I would love to help you!" Jessica replied, fanning herself with one hand and reaching for her reusable hot pink water bottle from under the counter with the other. Giving Joy her 'you can't be mad at me in front of people' satisfactory smile and she put it back. "And did you see how he was totes flirting with her!?"

"She better tap that."

"Yall." Joy replied disbelievingly, "Jess, are you sure you didn't have anything to do with him coming here today?"

"I promise I had nothing to do with this holy experience. I did have an idea he might be coming to Fortlin, but I didn't get the confirmation until today. You obviously beat me to the knowledge," she turned back to the customer, "she 'saved' him from something. So. Precious." She turned back to Joy, "So, I can honestly say no this time. Although I did pray some massive prayers. I almost sacrificed one of my kids, but Terry objected *THIS* time." She rolled her eyes. "Kids, amiright?"

"Jessica Leigh!" Joy scolded, smacking Jess's arm lightly.

"Oh, now, honey, I don't think we're supposed to take the Bible stories that literally dear." Joy wasn't sure if she was being sarcastic or not. Although she did have a good point.

"Ladies, goodness, I was just joking!" Jessica insisted, smacking her friend's arm in rebuttal, "*Future Mrs. Worthington...*" The look Jessica received from her friend was scalding enough to boil a thousand lobsters before they even reached the pot. "Now, how may I assist you today?" She asked as the lady took her to where she needed help reaching something.

Thankfully that was the last they talked of it until closing time. A steady stream of visitors had drifted in and out all day. Somewhat surprising for a Thursday, until one of the customers had shown her what Lucas had shared on his social media accounts; an artsy shot of the top half of her book in front of her store. She noticed the time stamp, he must have taken it and posted it just after he'd left. All you could see of him was his thumb. He had captioned it something about picking up a good read, then how charming the store was and

42

how captivating the employees were.

Charming, captivating, what is that supposed to mean? Anything? He was probably trying to repay her kindness this morning and that was it. *It was just a polite gesture. Nothing more. Although the increase in sales was very much appreciated. Everything else though, everything that happened this morning was just because I hadn't had my coffee, and didn't have much sleep. I was stressed and rushed. I was just reading into things.* Joy kept telling herself throughout the day. It was the only acceptable explanation. She just got swept up in her hormones for a few moments. That moment with the book couldn't have been as magical as it had felt.

"We haven't had a chance to discuss! How are you feeling about things? You were so red, but he was checking you out like crazy, please tell me you noticed that! Did you give him your number when you signed his book?" Jessica inquired as they finished their closing routine and gathered their personal belongings.

"Oh, you mean after you practically threw me at his feet?" Joy exclaimed! Still a little hurt by how forceful her friend was with the whole situation.

"I was just being honest!" Jessica replied. "It was your engagement party that night, I know because I was there, remember? You told me you were thinking about calling off your entire wedding after that chance meeting with Lucas. And now a second chance meeting? You have got to believe that there has been some divine intervention going on."

43

"There was definitely some Jess intervention going on for sure." Joy crossed her arms over her chest.

"And you are single now, just because you still wear your wedding band doesn't mean you're still taken. You don't even want people to think you're still married, if you did you wouldn't try to camouflage it with so many other non-marital-looking rings."

"Well, as true as that is," Joy replied, placing one hand on her hip, the other pointing for emphasis at her friend, "you could've at least been more accurate and say I'm as single as... as a white rhino!"

"Ooo, that's harsh." Jessica was taken aback. "Too soon Joy, too soon." Tears swelled in the corner of her eyes.

"Well, it's too soon for me!" Joy tried to emphasize her point, but she knew she had crossed a line. Jessica was an avid environmental conservationist, who especially loved African plains animals. The recent death of the last male white rhino had hit her hard. She had been following his story since he was re-homed from a zoo in the Czech Republic to the conservatory in Kenya. "At least there's always artificial insemination..." She tried to comfort her friend, patting Jessica's back.

"For you or the remaining female white rhinos?" Jessica sniffled, still holding back tears.

"For the rhino! They're still trying! I saw an article recently."

She pulled Jessica into a hug. While her friend had a large personality, she was actually quite small. Joy usually forgot how short she was unless she was having a rare emotional moment. Jessica was not a fan of feeling deep emotions, but sometimes they were just too big for her body. "See there's still hope." Tears were now forming in Joy's eyes.

Jessica sniffled and whispered into Joy's hair, "There's hope for you too, you know."

Joy rolled her eyes while still squeezing Jessica. A single tear rolled down her cheek.

4. bikes bring breaking points

She unfolded her wings, her favorite feature, feeling the release of them stretching before taking off. It was better this way, to fly, preferring to blur fantasy and reality... to feel the warm sun and brisk wind in her face instead of being cut off from nature driving. Joy was riding her old-fashioned pastel teal bicycle; complete with oversize wicker-style baskets, and a silver bell. She enjoyed feeling the flex of her thighs working. The burning sensation when going uphill especially reminded Joy that she was strong, and alive, though bitterly so. Her legs were her wings; although she never stopped wishing she could grow massive strong feathered black ones. Imagining she's soaring through the clouds as opposed to merely riding a bike fed her soul. That this world was bigger than the mundane. Plus it was nice to cut through stalled traffic and move around and through cars like she was the knight or queen of the chessboard and vehicles were mere checkers.

The fog suddenly whirled around her, engulfing her senses, and blurring her vision. Tires squealed, glass shattered, guttural screams of pain then the silence...

Shaking her head to try and rid the intrusion from her thoughts; she pedaled on, faster, heart racing. It was spring and there was no fog this morning. It was chilly compared to yesterday but by mid-morning it would be warm and blistering hot by the afternoon. Welcome to life in the South where the seasons are pretty much soggy bone-chilling cold or thick sticky heat. Thankfully this morning was a rare break being somewhere in between. No chicken noodle soup now. It was beautiful, practically perfect. There was no reason for the road to be this blurry.

Joy slowly recognized the dampness on her cheeks was from the tears flooding her narrowing vision. She pulled off as far as she safely could and tried to breathe. She stayed in her seat, setting her feet down on either side but folded over her handlebars, resting her head on her crossed arms. *Use your diaphragm, count to ten, one... two...* she coached herself. Forcing herself to take in a deep breath despite the tightness in her chest.

She tried to remember the other tools in her healthy coping mechanism tool belt, beyond breathing techniques, but she was rusty at this, it'd been so long. *Senses! Something I can see!* She looked down at her right foot. *Grass. Green, so much green. OK, what can I smell...* She inhaled through her nose. The salty-sweet stench of her sweat mixed with tears. *Gross. That works though. OK, what can I hear?* She closed her eyes for a brief moment and tried to focus on her hearing. The wind rushed past her ears, in the distance barely audible sirens, nearer there was repetitive hammering at a nearby construction site and closer still, birds. She focused on the birds. Twittering, chirping, fighting, and calling out to one another. A mix of a cacophony and a masterpiece orchestration; another masterpiece by Mother Nature.

Her tears and breathing slowed. Her heart fell back into place after being lodged in her throat. *Find the beauty, seek the joy,* she chanted to herself. Lifting her head, she took a sip of water from her bottle stashed in the front basket before pedaling back onto the road. *Almost there anyway. Focus on something else... Where was I? Oh, that's right, I was flying like a bird or an angel...*

She sang to herself the hook of "I Have a Dream" and pedaled on. *I can always count on ABBA to help me through it.* "Take a Chance On Me" *played* next on her internal playlist. Thoughts drifted to conversations with Jessica, to that fateful morning two days ago. *Take a chance on him maybe... maybe I won't have to. Maybe it was just that chance meeting. Although, being wrapped in those beautiful strong arms and being hugged right about now would feel really nice.* She thought about him sitting on her couch, remembering the line from his ear to his fingertips gingerly holding a book. She sighed. *Wait, he was holding my book!*

She knew he had it. She'd signed it after all. But this was her first published attempt at expressing herself. Sure she knew she'd be vulnerable, in expressing herself and sharing her thoughts with the world... well, whoever chose to read her words but it was also like it was a falsehood. She was no longer the person who wrote that. She had experienced pain when she wrote that. She had every intention of spreading hope and the happiness that she'd had during that time of her life. But that was before the accident, before she was completely, utterly shattered, and gutted. She knew that it was no longer an accurate representation of herself. Why did it matter?

She remembered his eyes, how their gazes locked. There was a sense of familiarity and strangeness. Like she wanted to tell him everything about why she wrote the book, all the pain she'd experienced but also the joy and the hope although she was scared of this. She had only had that one encounter, well, one of any substance, yet she felt connected. How could someone feel these connections so quickly? Yes, her connection with Jessica was instantaneous, as it was with a handful of others in her life, but how did this work? Like Anne of Green Gables, was it just a recognition of kindred spirits? Maybe it was just that she'd seen his face so many times on her TV... Maybe it was that she'd made a promise. Maybe it was nothing. Maybe this was all one-sided and she was reading way too much into this. Just a lingering fantasy. Nothing was real. Yet. No, just because she had promised Jessica doesn't mean it would happen. Just because she felt like he'd been flirting with her too... Well, was it flirting? She would just have to be grateful for the experience and confirmation that she is in no place to be open to being in a relationship. She was a hot mess. Obviously. She had so much more work to do on herself. Self-excavation, introspection. It had been a while since she'd seen her therapist. Maybe she should give her a call... maybe next week and set up a check-in appointment. Maybe it was time to write again. Even if just for herself. Maybe.

She pulled into the parking lot, an old water tower indicating a bygone era. A beacon to those seeking antiquities, excellent dining experiences, and local trinkets. It also pointed to the tents lined around the back of The Warehouse, home to the weekly farmer's market. Where the best produce in town was usually to be found.

Joy breathed in the tantalizing sweet crisp scent of the fresh strawberries she'd just purchased, bringing her back to simpler times in her college days, early morning rides with friends, laughter, and peace. Then carefully settled them in her sack. It's why she comes so early to the Saturday morning farmer's market, to get the best before it's too picked over, the warm nostalgia was just a bonus. Especially after her ride this morning. She thanked the farmer for her purchase and started to head to the flower stall down the next row. Jessica and Benny opened on Saturdays so Joy was in no rush. She wanted to get out of her head, and be present yet lost in her senses. To stop and smell the roses but first the basil and the rosemary and whatever else caught her eye or her nose...

She perused the stalls, making various purchases and strategically filling her reusable tote bags. They were the new ones that had just come in, her store logo printed on one side. She felt the vague prickle on the back of her neck that someone was watching her. She brushed her long dark hair back behind her ear, glancing quickly over her left shoulder as she did so, but all she saw was that the crowd had thickened and that her mermaid highlights Jessica had insisted that she try at their last girls' night were faded. Good, they were fun but took too much effort... too much for her. She sucked in a breath, stopping in front of the elaborate floral booth. They had a vast array of potted plants and cut flowers in large clear jars, elegantly lining the booth in a U shape. As she leaned over to smell the coral-colored roses she heard a voice that was becoming all too familiar.

"Well, if it isn't my knight in shining athletic wear! Good morning! How do they smell? Is their flavor as good as they look?" Lucas spouted off in his warm, bubbly voice. The kind only an extreme morning person had. He paused only to take a sip of the green drink in his hand. "Mmm, that is delightfully cucumbery. Extremely refreshing. Do you like cucumbers? Would you like some?"

Startled, Joy turned to find Lucas standing right next to her. Not too close to be invading her personal space, but definitely close enough for her to notice how close they were. She stared at him, taking a moment to confirm it was him. He was wearing a dark baseball cap and sunglasses that covered most of his face, but she could see enough of his eyes to tell that it was indeed him. She opened her mouth to reply but closed it when she realized she had no clue as to how to respond to anything he just said. He barely knew her and here he was offering a sip of his beverage? She squinted her eyes as she studied his face trying to determine if he was being friendly or facetious. She shifted her bags from one arm to another, both because she was weighed down at this point and to drag out the moment before she responded. Rebalanced, but still not understanding what the meaning was behind his words, she looked back at him. "Are you incognito or something?" She finally asked, completely ignoring his questions.

"Ha, well, yes actually." He grinned at her, then suggestively said, "You've caught me."

"Well, technically, you spied me, first," she replied. "Stalker much?" Giving him a side eye and just a hint of a grin before attempting to turn her attention back to the flowers. She leaned over to smell some peonies. "Mmm," she moaned at their sweet fragrance.

"That good, eh?"

Joy could feel the heat rising to her cheeks, and the snark slipping off her tongue before she could stop herself. "Eh, I've had better," she said, pausing only a moment before, "Is what she said," came tumbling out of her mouth. Not daring to face him she studied his reaction out of the corner of her eye the best that she could. He stopped mid-sip to laugh. Her thoughts raced. *Shit. He either thinks I'm wildly inappropriate or hilarious. Neither are good options for me. Neutral, I'd like to stay in the neutral zone. I might just need to skip the flowers today, and just go. Go before I say something worse. Although, I am hilarious.*

"So," he leaned in towards her, grinning with a wild gleam in his eye she could just barely see through his sunglasses, "Which flowers *do* you like?"

"Why," she turned to face him again, "do you want to know? Why does it matter?" Why was he interrupting her focus? She needed her calm and her focus today.

"I'm just curious," was his response. He shrugged and took yet another sip.

"What *are* you drinking?"

"Some refreshing cucumber juice blend." He slurped, shutting his eyes, and moaned his own "Mmm mmm mmm. So tasty. Fancy some?"

"So many mmms. Hmm? Would I like some of a practical stranger's cucumber juice?" She asked him back incredulously, raising her left eyebrow. "Sorry, I only swap spit with people I know, and actually like. *And* only if it's gluten-free. I have celiacs so I'm very cautious."

"Noted. You'll just have to get to know me better then, as you already like me," he had the audacity to wink at her. "At least enough to tolerate me. But, I was actually trying to ask if I could buy you a drink. After you saved me the other day, it's the least I could do."

Oh, he felt indebted to her. That makes sense. Then the memory of Jessica's voice reminded her to say yes... not that this was a date by any means, it was juice. The least date-worthy of beverages. "Okay," she said while nodding her head, and adjusting her tote bags again. "But I can't stay long, this was my last stop. I need to eventually get to the store today."

"Any amount of time with you would be fantastic," he smiled, holding out his arm. "May I help you with your bags?"

53

"No, it's really ok," she replied flustered as one kept slipping down her arm. "I'm strong, I've got this. I'm fine." She wasn't sure if she was speaking to herself or Lucas. *Ugh, maybe I went overboard on the sweet potatoes, but they're so good.* She sat the potato bag down to better attempt to shift the lighter bags.

"I never said you weren't, and I insist," said as he gently grabbed the bag she was struggling with and slung it over his shoulder, "See? Sometimes, it's just easier to share your load. Besides, I've got a free hand."

"Fine," Joy conceded as they began walking towards the juice stand. She chose a citrusy drink, he paid, then gestured towards a recently vacated picnic table. She gently set her remaining bags down and thinking he'd sit opposite her, took the seat on the end. Instead, he plopped down next to her, leaning back onto his elbows that he had set on the table behind him. He crossed one of his ankles over his knee. She turned slightly, angling her body to better see him, once again confused at his proximity, and now at his body positioning. It was strange to see him so casual when he usually had such an air of formality. Maybe it was just his accent. Their eyes met so she raised her cup to him, "Thank you."

"It's my pleasure," he replied, angling his body a little ever so slightly more towards Ann. Then raised his eyebrows and pointed out, "Now I know that you like citrus and dislike gluten, in addition to owning a store and being an incredible author."

"Well, it's not that I dislike gluten so much as my body rejects it. I get so sick if the smallest particle gets cross-contaminated with my food. Ugh, one time a woman tried so hard to sell me sourdough bread made with wheat flour since 'the yeast eats the gluten so it should be safe.' Um, no, that's not how it works with celiac disease. Maybe gluten sensitivity but please don't try to sell me something that is poison to my system...," Hot damn. She was rambling. *"Barley effing malt!"* She muttered to herself.

"I'm sorry, barley what?" he questioned leaning ever so slightly closer to her.

"Sorry, um, barley is also gluten. Gluten is death. Not everyone knows that, it's kinda a touchy subject with me and some other celiacs I know... so, uh, what are you doing here? I mean, what are you up to? Like, what brings you to the Fortlin Farmer's Market? Just checking it out or do you have a mission?"

"Duly noted about the gluten, I promise to do my best to never poison you," he replied earnestly. "I just wanted to get to know the area, I needed to kill some time before I meet up with my assistant, Liam, this afternoon to go over my new schedule. I also heard that this is also a fantastic place to pick up the ladies." He winked.

"I hate to break it to you," Joy looked around, truly taking in all the other people for the first time that morning. She was so focused on all the vendors and their produce she hadn't really seen all the young families wrangling small children, the typical suburban moms with their fancy athletic wear, perfectly highlighted hair, and very obvious wedding bands that glittered even in the shade. The teenagers dragged here by their parents were hanging around in scattered clumps. The older white-haired couples sweetly were holding hands and meandering through the crowds. "But at least 80% of the women here are taken." She heard a child's familiar laughter behind her. She turned to look but couldn't place it.

"I found you, didn't I?" He winked, again.

Shit. No, he didn't. Joy felt her chest clench as her heart began to race. She tried to take a sip of her juice without choking but it was hard to swallow. *Not now. Not now.* She felt her whole upper body start to clench, the soreness starting to settle in from her attack earlier. The memory started to creep up again. All these families. She needed to move.

"Yes,, but I, ah, I have to go." She stood up and started to collect her bag but her hands were shaking and she couldn't quite grip them.

"Are you ok? Did I say something?"

Do I tell him that I was triggered and now I'm at risk of having another episode? Or do I make something up? She just shook her head. "No, no, not at all." Tears started swelling in her eyes so she looked up and took a breath trying to calm down. "Um, not you. I just need to, ah, I need to not be here anymore. Sorry, I'm not normally like this." She gripped the table and closed her eyes as she heard a young child's laughter lingering behind her.

"Let me help you, where are you parked?" He asked as he picked up all of her bags and easily slung them over one arm. He gently grabbed one of her hands that were still clinging to the table, her knuckles white from gripping so tightly. "Can you show me?"

Joy shook her head, yes, opening her eyes to see him looking back at her. She focused on his calming gaze. She closed her eyes again, took another deep breath, and let go of the table with her other hand. She grabbed her cup, then took a small step. "I'm over there." She gestured slightly towards one of the light posts in the parking lot. Joy felt like her heart was going to leap out of her chest but her feet were lead. She grabbed his hand tighter and shut her eyes again, lightly leaning into his arm, letting him lead. As they approached the light post they slowed, she opened her eyes. She looked down and saw their hands entwined. She slipped her hand out of his grip and pushed her hair back behind her ear. "Um, thank you. I think I'm good now." She reached for her bags in his other hand.

"Which vehicle is yours? I'll help you load these."

Joy let out a light laugh as she leaned over and patted the ridiculously oversized basket on the back of her bike.

"Are you serious?"

"Indubitably," she said, raising an eyebrow and hoping her

face didn't show how terrible she felt inside.

5. friends and flowers

J oy checked the time on her phone and saw she had a dozen missed text messages from Jessica and Benny. *Shitake subway, why can't yall not freak out if I don't text you back immediately.* She rolled her eyes and proceeded to quickly change out of her sweaty black cropped yoga pants and oversized wide-necked shirt from this morning. Not that it mattered much, she'd just get sweaty again, but she needed to remove as many potential triggers as possible and get her ass to work.

She threw on clean black bike shorts and a matching athletic top, double-checked to make sure she had shaved her legs recently enough -and perhaps more importantly, making sure her big toe was also presentable... she hated when she had shaved legs and missed her toe. Not that she cared if someone saw her legs if they were hairy, she just preferred to not have to deal with that scratchy sensation on her thighs when they rubbed when the stubble was at a certain length. Not long enough to be soft, but not short enough to be smooth. Thankfully she was fine today. She could wear her favorite things- something black, comfortable, with pockets, and also looked stylish... enough.

She paused in front of her closet, searching for something light and flowy. Nothing confining, nothing that mattered if it got wrinkled or not. She closed her eyes, not worrying about mismatching as her wardrobe only consisted of black, black with white accents, or very very dark grey. Even her house was sterile, hospital white with black accents. A complete contrast to the store, where she had plenty to keep her mind occupied. No need to wear color anymore. Or be surrounded by color when home. Especially for how alone she was. Wearing certain clothes or colors brought back unbearable memories of finger-painted rainbows, simple conversations pointing out every color they could find, and listing all the shades of what she wore. Conversations that were no more. Black was neutral. A professional, quick, mourning uniform made for easy mornings. Her fingers quickly slid along the dresses until she felt the smooth airy texture of a cotton-linen blend. A simple tunic dress with pockets. She tossed that and her favorite black open-toe strappy sandals into her work bag.

Wiping yet another tear from her eye, she texted her team her apologies, that she was very much alive, and finally on her way in. She refilled her water bottle, grabbed a protein bar, locked up her home, and rode to work. Hopefully, her mind would remain clear enough that she would be ok. She thought back over how her strange morning ended. He had walked her home. He had offered to drive, but obviously and insistently, she refused. They walked in silence for part of the way, he didn't pry, and he was just there, pushing her bike for her as they walked together. Then he made her laugh. Random little stories.

I wonder if any of them were actually true. Or were they all exaggerations or improv?

Then he helped her carry her bags in, just inside the back door, made sure she was ok, and then left. He said he was meeting someone. Lee something. He was late, he didn't say so, but he had to have been. What normally took her only about 15 minutes on her bike, took them nearly an hour to walk. An hour. She had spent at least another hour in his company.

He smelled so good. Like Earl Grey tea, coconut, and his cucumber drink. Oh my goodness. He probably thinks I'm some sort of mental case for freaking out like that. Which, of course, he'd be correct as I very much am. What did my therapist say? Sounded like I was dealing with maxophobia and vehophobia just to name a couple... The only thing about cars I miss is air conditioning. Other than that, nope, nada, stay far away from me. Freaky fudge monkey machines.

"Where the frick frack apple jacks have you been?" Benny sassed Joy as she entered her store. "We are just now having a lull in customers. It's been busy all day. And Miss Stick Up Her Back End Drawers Mcgee called a few times as well."

Joy rolled her eyes, annoyed that he'd had to deal with that. "I'm so sorry. No one should have to handle her calls. Most of all you," she said, dramatically as she stared up at the large life black man in front of her, one hand on his hip, merchandise in the other. Benny had been her employee almost as long as

61

the store had been open. He was of epic proportions, both in personality and size, crowned with the most glorious dreaded man-bun she had ever seen. She loved him like family, and she had been so wrapped up in her own world she hadn't even thought to mention anything to him. "So incredibly sorry Benny," she said a little more sincerely, pouting her bottom lip out, and blinked the tears gathering at the corners of her eyes, away. "I'm here now! Let me go change then tell me what I've missed."

"What *you've* missed? Oh no, girl. What *I've* missed." He said, shaking his finger in front of her face. "So many people asking if we actually met Lucas E freaking Worthington! Do you know what I *have* to say to every single one of them? NO. Because someone did *not* inform me that he had been here. Girly girl, you know I would have dropped everything and been here in two minutes!"

"It was not intentional, and he was gone by the time the store opened, otherwise, I promise, I would have told you."

"Uh, huh, sure," he raised an eyebrow as he put the item on the shelf. "And that's why he posted this picture not even 30 minutes ago." He pulled out his phone and showed her his screen. It was a gorgeous Instapic photo, a close-up of her new reusable logo bags... with what looked like her bike... in her backyard with the back of her house barely visible in the background...

Wait, are those my legs? "What the hell?" She asked, grabbing Benny's phone. "When did he take this?"

"You tell me. Isn't that your beloved bike?" he asked, pursing his lips and raising his eyebrow. "And also looks like your cultivated calves."

"It looks like it, ugh, I think you're right, I think that's me in the picture. Shii...iitake mushrooms." Joy started but noticed a woman with a young child come around the corner. "Did he caption it?" Her voice was a horrified whisper now as he took his phone back before she could check.

"Everything. Later," He mouthed dramatically to Joy before turning to the woman and asking if she needed any assistance with all the charm and charisma of a customer service pro.

She scurried past Jessica, without even so much as a hello. Thankfully she was at the register helping someone. As she hurried to the back room to get ready she overheard a couple of ladies whispering loudly between giggles. "Look, Doris! I found the bags! Aren't they adorable? Now if only we could find *him* to go with them!" Their giggling intensified... as did Joy's discomfort level. Was everyone talking about Lucas?

She ducked through the door, dropped her bag on the counter, pulled out her dress then changed in the bathroom. For a full-size bath, it was still small. At least it had a simple walk-in shower now that gave her extra room to shimmy out of her sweaty clingy athletic wear. She hung her smelly clothes on the towel bar in the shower. She dressed and touched up her hair, moving it from the low ponytail that fit under her helmet to her more preferred loose high bun. Shutting the shower curtain to hide her drying clothes so as to not emotionally

63

scar the rare customer who used the employee bathroom. Most people had enough to deal with, they didn't need her skank on top of it. She tiptoed barefoot back to her bag. She fiddled with a few zippers, pulling out the final touches. She layered deodorant on, then spritzed a heavily orange-scented essential oil blend over her exposed skin, and swiped a barely tinted peachy pink gloss across her lips. She didn't even bother to check her handiwork in the mirror. Instead, she pulled her phone back out while meticulously shoving everything else back in their respective homes, pulling up his profile again in hopes to grab a better look at that picture before heading on out there. She put her work shoes on one-handed, scrolling with the other.

As soon as she found the picture, Jessica burst through the door. "Where have you been?" she said while frantically grabbing Joy's arm, and pulling her to her feet. "Come on! We need you in there, there is chaos, confusion, and delay!"

"Ow! Jess, what is going on?" Joy responded, trying to pull Jessica to a halt. "Wait just a sec, I need to finish putting on my shoe." She bent down to fix the heel of her left sandal, brushed her dress off, and shoved her phone in her glorious pocket. Jessica stood there, fiercely tapping her toe, arms crossed over her chest.

"Ready?" She asked with a huff, barely giving Joy the time to nod in response before grabbing her arm again and shoving her out of the back room. "We have a situation and you need to handle it."

"Already?" Joy sighed. "What kind of situation? I had kind of a rough morning, I'm not sure I'll be able to handle it appropriately." She tried to grab Jessica's vision to give her the 'please tell me what's going on so I can emotionally prepare myself' look. Jessica gave no indication of noticing Joy's puppy dog eyes or raised eyebrows as she kept maneuvering them around the customers and through the displays before reaching the register.

There on the counter was an elegant and enormous flower arrangement; a vast array of peach roses, coral peonies, and pink hydrangeas, filled out with eucalyptus stems. They were her favorites, just like the ones she had been looking at this morning when a certain person had interrupted her browsing. Her feet felt like lead all of a sudden but Jessica kept attempting to urge her forward. As she approached she could see that they were in a large wide-mouth vase that was practically the same color as her bike in the sun. It looked similar to a vintage green milk glass with its creamy but shiny tone, and intricate almost floral geometric raised design. Very art-deco. It was beautiful.

"That looks heavenly," Joy whispered, pulling Jessica to a stop again. "Will you tell me what the situation is now?"

"You're looking at it." Jessica nodded towards the bouquet. "He said he had *orders* to deliver *that* to you personally." Jessica's eyebrows were raised so far and her stare so fervent it sent shivers down Joy's spine that radiated out till her arms were covered in goosebumps.

"What do you mean?" Joy raised an eyebrow, "Who are they

for? Who are they from?"

"What, no, *who* do you think?" Jessica said sternly, lips pursed into a duckbill. She did that when she was trying to not lose it and laugh.

A quizzical look crept across Joy's face. She didn't know how to react to that. Slowly she turned and started walking again. Jessica didn't say anything else, she just stood behind Joy now, eyeballs practically burning holes into Joy's back pushing her forward with her special best friend powers. Joy tried to listen to the ongoing conversation she was about to interrupt.

A man she had never seen before stood with one hand still lightly attached to the giant colossal arrangement. He was dressed in white with a hip platinum comb-over so perfectly styled he could have come straight from the runway. The two ladies Joy had noticed earlier were standing near him, giggling like children. Benny was now behind the register doing a bad job at attempting to be subtle as he obviously checked the mystery man out. Joy smiled seeing Benny's eyes light up.

"At first I was like, what did you get me into? I mean, no offense," mystery man glanced over towards Benny at this and gave him the tiniest smile, "but this is actually totally one of those 'don't judge a book by its cover' type places. But seriously, omygollygeewhitakers, inside this place is absolutely adorable!"

"Or as Doris would say, adorrisable!" said the taller of the two ladies. More giggles ensued.

"Ooh, I like that," replied the mystery man. "Adorrisable. Consider it stolen."

"Oh, well, hey now yall, I don't know where you're from but we frown at stealing here, but I'm sure they wouldn't mind letting you borrow it." Joy teased and winked at the group with a sly smile as she approached the small gathering. She was slipping into her southern hospitality customer service mode. "Hi, I'm Joy. I believe you're looking for me?"

The mystery man narrowed his eyes at the mention of her name and slowly eyed her from head to toe and back again. Slowly he extended his right hand, "Hello there, I'm Liam. It's a pleasure." He drew out the last syllable that Joy couldn't tell if he was being sarcastic or not or just liked exaggerating his 'Rs'.

"Nice to meet you as well." Joy shook his hand gently at first then increased her grip as his gaze intensified. Smiling the best she could muster while continuing to return his unreadable stare. "Liam. Hmm, all the Liams I know are in the business. What about you? Music or show?'

"Ha." He quickly smiled. "Fair. Show." Their handshake paused for a moment before they released their grips during a brief silence before Liam continued, lowering his voice, "I am a personal assistant for an extremely well-known actor."

"Oh wow, really? Cool," Joy took a deep breath. *Shit. It's him. He probably works for him. Shit. He wasn't meeting Lee, he was meeting LIAM. Shitake. Whew.* "So, um, how can I help you or

67

this person? Er, who did you say you work for?"

"You don't know?" Liam asked as he tilted his head slightly to the side, and brought a hand to his face, cupping his chin like he was deep in thought. Joy's heart started fluttering during the unexpected pause in the conversation. The ladies covered their mouths and giggled.

Benny who had now wandered closer to Joy leaned in. He spoke in a whisper directed towards Joy but loud enough for everyone else to hear, "Girl, you are not this naïve. What well-known actor has twice appeared in your life this week?"

"She's still in denial." Piped in Jessica, beaming. She and Benny shared a low five that Joy barely caught out of the corner of her eye.

Wide-eyed, Joy gave a quick look to Benny and attempted to subtly elbow Jessica. Liam was still just standing there, blank-faced. "Oh, you work for Lucas?" She asked him in a meek voice.

"Mmhmm," he shook his head. "If you would, read this card. It will explain everything." With a knowing smirk, he produced what looked like a birthday card from behind the flowers.

"Oh, thank you," Joy accepted hesitantly. "Well, is there anything else I can help you with?" She asked, holding the card behind her back with both hands.

"Here's the dealio sweetheart," Liam replied, his hands clasping in steeple formation pointing in her direction. "I need you to read this and respond as that will dictate what my next task is."

"Oh, okay," Joy replied, bringing the card back in front of her, fumbling with the fold with her thumb, resisting the urge to ask him to open the doors so she could see all the people. "Um, why is that?"

"Read and respond," Liam said crisply, and cryptically, waving a hand grandly towards the envelope in her hand.

Did he just wink at Benny? "Oh... kay. On it." She glanced at Benny who winked at her as she walked over to the counter and grabbed a letter opener. She turned her body to block the view from the several sets of prying eyes she felt on her back. She slid out a simple card with a sepia-tone picture of a little boy helping a little girl ride a bike on the front. *Well, isn't that sweet?* Inside was a short handwritten note.

Dearest Joy,

I enjoyed running into you this morning. However, I believe I interrupted your flower shopping. I hope these suit your fancy and help lift your spirits. I would love to venture more into the local scene and would appreciate your expert advice. Would you please join me for dinner tomorrow evening? If that is inconvenient and you're willing, would you set something up with Liam as soon as your schedule allows?

Sincerely yours, Lucas

She closed the card and took a minute before turning around. Looking straight at Liam, avoiding all eye contact with everyone else. "If you'll excuse me just a moment, I just need to check something." Then she started to walk quickly back to the back room. She wasn't alone. Jessica was at her heels. She grabbed Joy's arm and brought her to a halt.

"What do you need to check?" Jessica hissed in Joy's ear.

"I need to look something up and I didn't want to do it in front of Liam." Replied Joy in a slightly louder whisper as they stood a few paces away from the group.

"What? Why?" Jessica questioned. "What did the note say? Did he ask you out?"

"He just asked for advice," she exasperatedly sighed, giving Jessica a look to indicate both how annoyed and overwhelmed she was. "It's not a big deal! He thinks since I'm a local business owner that I know all the cool hotspots or something. Which, you know perfectly well, I do not. I am here or I am home. Once a week I go to the farmer's market. Occasionally I go out to eat. With you." Jessica stood there, holding her gaze steady, her face stern and unreadable. "I don't know what's trendy or where the cool hipsters go. I don't even really know if hipsters are a thing anymore. Once in a blue moon, I'll take a Xanax so you can drive us to Rose Pepper. So, uh, yeah, case in point, I need to look something up so I can save face." Joy pulled out her phone, the card still in hand.

"Let me see that," Jessica said determinedly, then swiped the

70

note. "He did not just ask you for advice! He asked you out!"

"No," Joy said as she shot a look at Jessica and folded one of her arms across her chest.

"Sheesh, no need to throw your scary eye daggers at me," Jessica replied. "Anyways, it sounds more like he wants to spend time with *you*. So get back over there and tell Liam YES. I know you're free after closing tomorrow and Monday we're closed so it's perfect. It's not a 'school night' you can stay out late. So go, say 'yes, you would love to have dinner with Lucas... and possibly his babies.'" She said the latter in sing-song.

"You. Are. Such. An. Ass." Joy crisply emphasized each word. "More likely he just doesn't know anyone or anything in town, yet."

"Doesn't matter. You promised." Jessica replied with author-ity.

"I lied."

"That's one of your biggest faults," Jessica lowered her brow. "You hate lying. Gives you heartburn, too much of a guilty conscience."

"Well, I got over it." Jessica's glare burned into her and her stomach started to church. "Ugh, fine. I didn't lie." Joy rolled her eyes at Jessica. "Fine. Ok, I'll go." Joy put her phone back in her pocket and walked calmly back to Liam. Liam, who was leaning an elbow on the counter and talking to Benny. Benny was laughing at something. The ladies now had apparently finished checking out but were still hanging around. All of their eyes found her as she approached and the conversations lulled.

"I, uh, checked my schedule," Joy began, nodding her head, "and after closing tomorrow should work."

"Perfect. He'll be thrilled," Liam smiled and took out his phone. "I'll need your number to confirm the details." He held out his phone so she could type in her information. "If you don't mind, may I ask a little about what happened earlier? He would *not* fill me in other than he needed me to pick him up and take him back to his car which was parked at The Warehouse so he could get to his meeting on time. But not before he handpicked these and sent me on an impossible mission to find a minty blue vase big enough. Thankfully this kitschy little vintage shop inside had this. Have you been, Benny? "

"Oh yes," Benny piped in. "I love everything in the Warehouse. You should see it during the art crawl. It only happens on the first Friday of the month."

"Oh really? You should text me the details about the next one. Here's my card." Liam eyed Benny as he pulled out a business card from the back pocket of his white linen pants. Joy saw the sweet interaction out of the corner of her eye as she leaned in to smell the flowers and get a closer look at the vase. "Do you like them?" Liam turned his body back to her but kept his gaze towards Benny. "Lucas said they were your colors."

"Oh, yes, they're gorgeous," Joy nodded. "I love this vase. It's perfect. And, um, to answer your question, I just ran into him randomly this morning. I had a hard time with something so he offered to walk me home. He was extremely kind. And my colors? What is that supposed to mean?"

"He didn't tell me explicitly but," Liam held up one finger and closed his eyes, "from my recollection mint means tranquility. Peach roses specifically mean gratitude and pink hydrangeas are intense emotions."

"Oh, that's impressive. How do you know all that?" inquired Benny.

"I love symbolism and it's my job to make sure he doesn't send anything out that could lead to a misunderstanding. And I'm not finished. Hmm, peonies can mean compassion and the color coral harmony, but I don't believe there is any specific significance to a coral peony. So if we're going off of that he intensely wishes you peace and is grateful for you. Or it means he noticed you like those colors and wanted to get you something you liked." He crossed his arms over his chest and pursed his lips.

"I think it means you've a suitor, honey," said the shorter of the two ladies who up until this point hadn't addressed Joy directly.

"Oh Doris, we *know* that. We want to know why he thinks

those are her colors," corrected the taller lady.

"Does it matter?" She drawled in her thick-as-molasses accent. "What matters is, she's going out with him tomorrow, isn't that right honey?"

Joy's face warmed at this and her stomach clenched, yet she remained calm and professional as she responded, "Yes ma'am, I am going out with my new, ah, *friend* tomorrow. And what matters is that this was very thoughtful and I am very appreciative." She smiled as the knot in her stomach grew harder. She turned to Liam, "Do you need anything else from me?"

"Do you have any restaurant preferences?"

"Only that they have a gluten-free menu. Oh, and close to here."

"Perfect." Liam held out his hand, "It's been a real pleasure meeting you Joy." She took his hand and they shook again. She looked quizzically into his eyes as he stared back with a smirk. Like he knew more than what he was sharing. He dropped her hand after a longer moment than necessary and extended his hand out again but this time to Benny. "I look forward to hearing from you soon." He winked and turned, bowing his head slightly to the two women and Jessica, "Ladies." Then he sashayed out of the store. Benny sighed and went to the back room for his break. Joy quietly slipped away after he did, walking in the opposite direction to welcome some new customers who entered before Liam exited.

"Whew, well, I don't know what was more entertaining, Joy's denial or Benny's flirting," Jessica stated in a louder than normal and teasing tone of voice to the ladies after the break room door shut with Benny safely behind it. She knows I can hear her, thought Joy, she's trying to get a response. I'm not taking the bait.

"The flirting, definitely the flirting," The taller lady replied. "What do you think, Doris?"

"Oh Avery, you know a young woman's naiveté is a trope I can't get enough of." They giggled and talked for a few more minutes though Joy could no longer hear with clarity. They strolled by Joy, Doris smiled and nodded a knowing goodbye in her direction. Her eyes twinkled as the taller lady slid her hand into Doris's and pulled it to her mouth, placing a gentle kiss on her knuckles as they walked out.

6. Benny and the Jess

As soon as Benny returned from his break, the store was swarming with customers. HE stepped in to help those already not attended to by Joy or Jessica, with his charming smile, giving special attention to bag everything carefully so they wouldn't get broken, smushed, or terribly wrinkled. With as much sass as she got from him, Joy loved how considerate of a human he was, at least with her customers. Jessica passed on the people she was helping to Benny's capable hands to go on break. She left only after making Joy promise to spill all the remaining details about what happened at the farmer's market on her return. As Joy walked around the store, straightening shelves and trying to be available to help the small crowd that had been there dwindled and dissipated. As the store cleared, she wandered back to the register.

"Benny, can you please move these to the back room? I'm afraid they'll get knocked over out here." Joy asked, indicating towards the voluminous bouquet.

"What? You don't want the world to see you're being wooed by mister big time?" Benny responded putting his fists on his hips.

"Why is everyone reading into this?" Joy sighed, running her hands up to her hair, digging her fingers into her scalp. "He's new to town, probably just lonely. He knew I had to work, and where that was. He probably was just being nice, wanting to help me have a better day. Why are you making such a fuss?" She huffed and crossed her arms in defiance. She could feel her expression souring and a headache coming on so she closed her eyes for a moment, taking some deep breaths. Then raised her hand to her forehead, using her fingers to try and smooth out the frown line that held so much tension. She felt like her collarbones were trying to climb up into her vocal cords so she focused on rolling her shoulders back and down, trying to relax her neck muscles and relieve the tightness in her upper chest.

"Fuss? I'm not making a fuss. You, on the other hand, are being quite defensive, young lady." Benny pointed out. "Nice, he's *soooo nice*, that's what nice rich people do, right?'" He did a bad imitation of her voice, making dramatic hand movements and tossing his head from side to side every time emphasizing the word nice.

"I am not being defensive!" Joy huffed. " I was just shaken from my flashback and then the laughter..." She trailed off, bringing her hands down over her eyes. " It sounded so much like *his*." She placed a hand over her heart, leaving one on her forehead, trying to stop the pain from coming back. *No wonder he was so concerned, I probably looked like a hot mess.* She shook her head slightly then took a deep breath before continuing, "Anyways he's just nice and he's rich so he has the money to do things like this. It's not a big deal. That's what some really nice people do, right?" She pushed his giant bicep gently.

He stared down at her, studying her. "Oh, you so totally are being defensive, but I get it. It's 'cause you are still in DENIAL." Jessica popped around the corner back from her break. "And what was that about a flashback? You haven't had one of those in a long time." He placed a comforting hand on her shoulder and gave her a gentle squeeze then released his grip.

"It's nothing," she shrugged. "I just maybe had a small panic attack on the way to the farmer's market this morning, and then when Lucas and I were talking I, ah, heard this cute little geeky snort, it sounded so much like Peter's I just lost it," she stumbled over her words while speaking as fast as possible. She was digging her fingertips into the space between her shoulders and collarbones now, attempting to relieve even the slightest bit of tension to help release the steam before she boiled over. "Um, Benny, why don't you go ahead and take your lunch break? I know it's later than normal, you must be hungry."

"I can wait a bit. I'm fine," Benny walked over and enveloped Joy in a comforting hug. She leaned into his broad strong chest. "Unlike you. Why don't you go have a quick break before my shift is over?"

78

"Yeah, you should go have a breather." Jessica walked over and patted Joy's back.

"Y'all, thank you for your concern, but really, I'm ok," she slid out of his hug. She patted their shoulders then squeezed and shook them slightly trying to emphasize her point. "I promise, I'm much better now, just a little emotionally tender. I want to focus on work with my fabulous employee slash friends. Besides, I really need to finish getting ready for our big anniversary sale coming up."

"What is that again?" Jessica asked, tapping her finger on her chin. "I don't remember *anything* about your giant second-anniversary extravaganza." She said sarcastically as she placed her hands on her hips and stared intently at Joy.

"Haven't you had everything set up for ages now? And it's not even for another couple of weeks?" Asked Benny.

"I just want to confirm some things, y'all. And yes, it's not till the first week of June so we can coordinate with the art crawl, so not for another three weeks. I really want it to be fun for us, and I'd much rather stress about it now so even if there doesn't happen to be a huge turnout, we'll have fun. Aaand, I still haven't decided on what the bartender is going to be serving... a wine selection like most everywhere else, or do we want to serve sangria and margaritas? Or come up with our own cocktail?"

"Yes," Benny said, "to all of that."

"Agreed, You know, for former teetotalers, we sure do like our liquor," added Jessica, nodding her head. "Ooo, we should have something with gin."

"Jess, it's because we're *former* teetotalers," said Benny. "We're making up for the lost alcohol consumption of our youth. Responsibly of course. Which is why we need options. Sample size."

"See yall. I still have important things to figure out, like see if I can fit all of these fantastic ideas in the budget," Joy threw her arms out, "and see if they have gluten-free gin and ideas on fancy drinks." She stuck her tongue at Jessica who was rolling her eyes.

"I know what we should offer," offered Benn., "Margatinis- it's a classic marg with gin instead of tequila, and a summery watermelon sangria."

"That sounds ah-mazing, great work Benny," answered Joy. "Also, Jess, that reminds me, you still owe me a margarita."

"K," replied Jessica, now leaning on the counter. "How about Tito's Monday after dinner so you can tell me all of the details about your date tomorrow?"

"It is NOT a date." Joy gestured enthusiastically with her arms.

"It totally is a date," Benny said firmly, "AND speaking of details, you still owe me the entire story of all of your interactions, missy."

"Agreed," Jessica insisted. "Totally a date. It's easier to accept it." She smiled at Benny then they fist-bumped.

"Yall are relentlessly ridiculous." She punctuated by pointing her finger in their faces. "Ugh, sure FINE it's a date. I'll tell yall all the things, I promise. Later. Which won't take long because there's nothing to tell," Joy was loudly conceding at first until the front doorbell jingled indicating someone entering, so she whispered firmly, "After closing. Now, go move these," she pointed to the bouquet," And go take your break."

Joy walked to the front of the store. Benny and Jessica high-fived behind her back and shared a look before he picked up the flowers and set them on the gold rectangle coffee table in between the couches. "There, I moved them," Benny said as he walked to the back room to take his lunch.

The afternoon dragged on as more customers came in looking for the bags from Lucas's Instapic post. After the lull, during Jessica's break, there was a steady stream of people who kept the two then three of them busy. Joy kept catching Benny and Jessica sharing silly facial expressions every time someone asked anything about Lucas and pointed to her to answer the questions whenever she was on the floor. Even when they could have easily answered them. When she wasn't on the floor she was answering emails, getting orders ready to ship, and inquiring about their desired beverages for their special event. Her brain ached, and her stomach was starting to wake up, mewling for attention. Thankfully Benny was ringing up hopefully the last customer of the evening. Joy heard Jessica

81

say goodnight and lock the door.

"Y'all, thank you for all your hard work today," started Joy. "Y'all can go on home and I'll finish closing up tonight."

"You're not getting off the hook that easy missy," Benny replied. "Sit and spill."

"And don't leave out a single detail." Chimed in Jessica.

"Oh good grief, fine." Joy relented as Jessica and Benny settled into the blue velvet couch across from Joy to chat. She first filled in Benny on what happened when Lucas hid out in her store.

"That boy could NOT keep his eyes off of her!" Jessica interjected when she thought Joy wasn't giving enough detail.

"We were the only ones in the store!" said an exasperated Joy.

"Not when he left!" Jessica insisted.

"Whatever," Joy sighed, standing back up and brushing the wrinkles in her dress down. "Anyway, that's what happened the other day, and I already told you about this morning."

"Uh uh. No ma'am," said Jessica, still sitting.

"Sit your pretty little ass back down and give us the details about this morning," commanded Benny.

Joy rolled her eyes and sat back down. "Do you really think I have a pretty ass?"

"Of course," confirmed Benny, "I can appreciate the beauty of other people and not be sexually attracted to them. Now *spill* it before I beat it."

Joy filled them in on how he had started talking to her while she was at the flower stand, how he bought her a drink, she was triggered, and then he walked her home. "So see, he was just being polite. He told me he struggles with anxiety and panic attacks as well, so he knows how grounding it can be to have a hand to hold. What more do you want to know?"

"Hand to hold?" Asked Jessica. "I want to start there." Benny leaned forward and put his elbows on his knees and nodded his head in agreement. "Did that literally happen or is that one of your misleading poetic metaphors?"

"My metaphors are *not* misleading. And yeah, I mean he just held my hand when he helped walk me to my bike after I told him I had to leave."

"Sounds like he did not want you to get away and leave him behind."

"She can't read his mind, Jessica," stated Benny. "I want to know how his hand felt! Describe it. Was it firm and strong? Was it like a slimy, limp fish?"

"Ew, no," Joy replied, squishing up her nose and shaking her head. "Not like a slimy, limp fish at all. Ugh, I don't know, I was more focused on breathing and trying to stay calm." The two were silent, waiting for her to continue, staring at her like they were kids peering through the glass at an ice cream shop, just begging for something tasty with their puppy dog eyes and licking their lips. *Are they doing that on purpose? Why are they so cute and annoying?* Joy closed her eyes and tried to relive what happened, leaving the hard parts out. "He had all of my bags on one arm, and he took my hand and intertwined our fingers then led us out. His arm brushed mine almost the whole way across the parking lot, he did stand very close to me." She opened her eyes again, "There. Does that suffice?"

Jessica and Benny turned to each other and back to her. "No." They said in unison.

"What more do you want? That there were sparks? My whole body shivered when he touched me? That my hand slid perfectly into his grasp, and I felt hidden and small, protected during a very vulnerable moment when I just wanted to hide away? I don't know y'all. It did help me feel grounded, so firm I guess?"

"Acceptable. What happened next?" Jessica asked after getting a confirmation nod from Benny. "He got you to your bike and then *walked* you *all* the way home? Did he say why? What did you talk about? Did he hold your hand again?"

"Well, he seemed pretty adamant that he didn't want me to be by myself in that state so he insisted on joining me. He put my stuff in my basket then pushed my bike for me, and I walked alongside. When we got to my house, I unlocked the

84

back door, which is when he must have taken the picture, and he brought my bags in for me. Then he left."

"We asked for details," pointed out Benny, "not a summary. Go back to the walk, was there a discussion?"

Joy could feel her whole body participate in her rolling her eyes as being pestered for more information. "Well, not at first." She leaned down and took off her shoes so she could tuck her feet up next to her and get in a more comfortable position. "We just walked, him letting me lead since he didn't know where we were going. He didn't even ask where I lived, he just went. At some point, I stopped and let him know I was feeling a lot better and he could turn around if he wanted. He insisted that he wanted to make sure I got home safely, just in case I had another attack. That's when he told me a little about his anxiety. Then that led to him giving some silly examples of how he could channel that energy into his performances but how sometimes that backfired. He told me that once during a live theatre performance, he had so much anxiety that he didn't realize he was turning his mic off when going onstage and off when he was backstage. He had to crouch down to enter from a trap door during one scene, and he had to be in that small area by himself for a while until his entrance, and apparently, anxiety gives him gas so the entire audience heard him fart." Jessica started laughing and Joy giggled.

Benny just rolled his eyes and said, "Ew, oh, lawrd. Y'all are a gassy match made in heaven."

"I bet that *sounded* unfortunate," shrugged Jessica, "but hey,

85

gas happens to the best of us. Now continue."

"There really isn't much else. He told me some more stories about mischief he got into and mishaps in theatre. He told me he was meeting up with Liam today, whom we've all met."

"Pause," said Jessica. "We also need to talk about him. I saw someone doing a little *ass*-essing." She nodded her head towards Benny who was licking his lips.

"Mm-hmm," he nodded in agreement. "I am guilty as charged. That man was definitely a snack. Looking all LA fine in his tight open-front button-down white shirt, sleeves rolled to his elbow to show off his forearms. Don't get me started on his tight white pants and designer sandals. Whew." He was fanning himself.

"Whoa, whoa, whoa. While I agree Liam was extremely well dressed and attractive, what about Juli?" Joy asked. "Weren't y'all trying to work things out and get back together?"

"Julian gave me the ultimate ultimatum. He will only move back in if I remove Drake and Jake from my life." Drake and Jake were Benny's bonded cockatoos that he'd had for at least a decade already. "They have been with me through many Julis and will be with me through however many more. If someone can't handle my birds, they can't handle me."

"Good for you," Joy encouraged, "You deserve someone who appreciates you and your birds."

"You know what," mused Jessica, "now that I think about it, Liam kinda looked like a cockatoo in his outfit today. I wonder if that's his normal attire, 'cause that'd make some precious family photos."

"What is it with you and pairing people off the second they meet?" Joy asked.

"Only those who belong together. I have really good intuition," Jessica responded with a wink toward Joy and nudged Benny's arm. Benny smiled in return. "So, enough distraction, what happened after yall got to your house?"

"Ugh," groaned Joy who had hoped they were done dragging this topic out. "I insert the key into the lock. I opened the door to my kitchen. I take seven steps in and set my purse down on the table. I turned around and he was standing in the doorway holding my bags. He asked where they went. I told him anywhere was fine. He took two and a half steps over to the table and set them down next to my bag." Joy remembered how his arm muscles flexed in that simple movement, so close to her. She started to feel warm starting in her gut and radiating through her chest and up to her cheeks.

"And?" Benny asked, interrupting her thoughts.

"And what? He left. The end." *And I maybe checked out his end.*

"You're totally blushing!" Jessica pointed out, "What are you leaving out? He set the groceries down and then what?" She had stood up in her excitement, throwing her arms out wide.

Joy groaned, "Don't read into this." She sighed and stood up in front of Jessica. "May I use you as a physical stand-in? It's easier if I show you."

Jessica nodded in eager agreement. "What do I need to do?"

"Just stand there," Joy indicated to the side of the table as she walked up to meet her. "Ok, you're me, I'm him. K?" Jessica nodded. "So he did this." Joy took her left hand and gently tucked a loose strand of Jessica's hair behind her ear, then barely Jessica's right arm as she dropped her hand to Jessica's, and gave a little squeeze. Jessica's eyes grew wide as this was happening and her lips turned upward into a huge grin. "Then he asked if I was sure if I was ok. When I told him yes, and that I needed to get ready for work, he told me he needed to go but I'd be hearing from him soon. And he left." Joy finished as nonchalantly as possible despite the flutter in her stomach and the memory of his touch.

"How soon did he let go?" Asked Jessica. "Like it was just a quick squeeze, then he asked you? Or did he hold onto it until you finished talking?"

"And who let go first?" Added Benny.

Shitake mushrooms. "Um, I guess he let go first? After, uh... " Joy paused. Trying to remember she went through the motions again with Jessica standing in as her. This time mentally repeating what he'd said as she was holding Jessica's hand. "After he said I'd be hearing from him soon," she raised Jessica's hand slightly and bowed a little, "He let go then. See."

88

Joy dropped Jessica's hand and turned away from her, but still towards Benny. Her heart was beating faster.

"He bowed?" Asked Jessica.

"Not just bow, did he Joy?" Benny asked rhetorically, before stating, "He kissed her hand." He looked at her, lips pursed and eyebrows raised. Joy nodded her head once, the heat burning through her forehead now. "Thought so."

Jessica let out a high-pitched squeal, "He what? He kissed your fucking hand and you waited until now to tell us?!" She moved in front of Joy and was shaking her arms now. "Bwahahahha. I was right! I told you! He likes you!"

Joy rolled her eyes and attempted to move away from Jessica's tight grip. "This is why I didn't want to tell yall. I knew this was going to get blown out of proportion. He was just being polite."

"Pshh, believe what you will, honey," replied Benny while trying to pull Jessica off of Joy. "Come on Jess, we got our info, let's call it a night. Have a lovely night, Joy." He winked at her. They gathered their belongings and headed out while Joy finished the closing duties.

Joy looked around at the empty store and took a deep breath. Nothing else really needed attending to. She was tempted to just stay the night here, but she needed to go home, to her bed, and more importantly her shower. She turned off the lights and walked out into the setting sun.

7. rings of dreams

T houghts of the day and suppressed memories of his laughter kept chasing all the counting sheep away. Joy kicked off the sheets and her thin quilt. It was too hot and uncomfortable as she lay in bed, covered in a sticky layer of sweat to have the usual comforting weight on her. Despite having fallen asleep as soon as she laid down after her emotionally and physically exhausting day, her physical and emotional discomfort kept chasing all efforts of staying asleep away.

She sat up and turned her favorite pillow over again, searching for a cooler spot but finding none. She reached out and felt under the other pillows looking for any relief but everything felt hot. Exasperated, she turned over on her belly in a crumpled mass, then slid off the side of the bed feet first. Not wanting to move but needing to escape from the heat she waited as long as she could before slowly rising to her feet. She flipped the fan on and then thudded down her short hallway to the kitchen to get a glass of ice water. The clock on her oven said it was just after 3 a.m. "Ugh, asshole," she muttered out loud to the clock, "Stop taunting me."

Returning to her room, she walked over to her bedside table and set her glass down. All ideas of attempting to go back to sleep were gone. She sat on the edge of her bed and pulled the top drawer open. She reached in, fingers brushing the soft, wood interior. Dragging her fingers across the seemingly vast void bottom until finding the smooth cold round metal object she was looking for, not even needing to turn on a light. A plain thick gold band. No embellishments or stones. Simple, just like the man it once belonged to. Simple, strong, and stubborn as a mule with a stick up his ass. Joy fiddled with it, slipping it on over the only ring remaining on her fingers, the one she never removed- her wedding band, knowing it would be too large. She liked the reminder of how large his hands had been. Every thought she would never describe any of herself as small, his still dwarfed hers. She took it off her ring finger to hold and study the texture of it before sliding it over each finger in turn. Relishing the smooth comforting texture.

"Dammit, Ryan," Joy spoke out loud to the dark, "I... I... I don't know what to do," her voice breaking, crying without tears. "I've done so much without you that I never thought I could do and I never thought I'd ever want to." The words hung in the air. She looked over to the other side of the bed, what was once his side. She needed to do something. She couldn't just be in silence.

She stood up, ring in hand. She took a calming deep breath before walking over to her small writer's desk. As she sat in

91

her plush white chair, she turned on the little light. She gently placed Ryan's ring on the painted wood surface in front of her and pulled her dusty notebook and favorite pen out of the drawer. She blew the dust off the cover, flipped through the ancient notes until she found a blank page, and began to write. Dumping the words clogging her brain out into lines. Lines of randomness at first that slowly formed more cohesive prose, clearing her head of all the feelings that were bubbling and erupting from her soul. Then ramblings of her past life, of words she was never brave enough to say, to herself or Ryan.

Once upon a time, I chose you. To do life with you. To make choices with you. And once upon a time it was not at all what marriage is ever supposed to be. It most certainly was not what I signed up for when I chose you and you chose me. Not to have you dictate my life to me, taking all decisions from me aside from what we would have for dinner. I have talents and passions too. Just as important as yours. I am and was just as important as you were. I never expressed that in ways for you to understand. You should have known that already but I should have made that clear. Now you're naught but a voice in my head.

Join the factions. No, the legions are in there. I am a writer, no, an author. I hear and create worlds. I am a business owner. I make the decisions now. I tell others what to do, but not like you. No, I lead and I create. Reflections of myself, my life, creation itself. Is not everything just a mere reflection, repetitive, cyclical?

Everything pointing to that which was created first?

Art and life are simply mirrors. Mirrors made of glass are easily shattered. Shattered as my soul has been with and without you... without Peter.... Shards are strewn across my existence like the windows that imploded upon that impact dispersing crystal-like particles. There was no projecting of rainbows, only projecting heartache and grief instead. My love for you was true. I know you loved me badly too. Only now it is time for me to pick up what I can, to stop choosing this guilt that consumes me, and choose hope, choose me instead.

One question still remains. How? How do I let myself choose me?

Laying her pen down to crack her knuckles and her neck, pausing only for a moment longer before she picked up the pen again, turned to a new page, and continued. Layers of ink on paper. Outlines of a general story arc and scene ideas developed, characters, random thoughts and pieces of dialogue, settings, and even a few wistful lines of poetry flowed from her. Words and ideas buzzed in her brain, as if her very own muse had flown back to her shoulder to whisper delicately to her and started a fire in her cortex. Or maybe she was finally still and quiet enough to hear more than the birds gossiping outside her window every morning, who were now overshadowed by a lonely mourning dove's coo, surely attempting to woo a silent mate.

As the darkness of the night faded and turned to the early golden hue of a Tennessee spring dawn, she finally rested her pen in her dimple, tapping slowly. She smiled when she realized it was to the beat of the dove's call... woohoo woo woo woo... tap taap tap tap tap. Her hand was starting to cramp from being out of practice. But her thoughts still burned, she couldn't stop yet.

She pulled out her laptop from underneath a stack of papers. Shaking out her hands and popping her knuckles while she waited for the now ancient electronic beast to awaken from its lengthy snooze. She rarely used the thing anymore since she used her phone for almost everything. But now, she needed to feel the keys beneath her fingers. She needed to type and continue to organize her thoughts. She felt the weight dripping off her shoulders with each word written, each sentence typed. She needed to email Eryn. Eryn, her creative content editor, mentor, and friend, would want to know she was finally writing again. This was different than all the flimsy attempts she'd made after the accident. Her heart hadn't burned like it was now. This was a need, a need to work through this through to the end.

A quiet upbeat melody started, gradually increasing in volume, interrupting her thoughts. *Shitake fricking ice balls. What time is it? Time to get my ass ready, apparently.* She saved her progress before shutting her laptop and turning her phone alarm off. As she stood to get ready, fatigue and the desire to sleep hit her like a brick wall. *After everything that had happened over the last 24 hours, let alone week, that's fair, body, but unfortunately, I own this circus and if I don't show, this monkey makes no money. But first, coffee.* She yawned, stretching her arms overhead, and caught a slight whiff of her residual sweatiness. Then deodorant, she nodded to herself and plodded on her way.

Her Sundays were different than the ones she had growing up. She no longer felt the pressure to attend weekly services. Her faith had molded and changed so much since she'd left her parents' home, then the accident. She couldn't tolerate the intolerables as she described them to Jess. The ones who told her that everything happened for a reason, that God wouldn't give her more than she could handle. She knew that was crap. She knew she was good with God and she had suffered enough. She didn't needlessly have to endure any more emotional torture.

Now her Sundays were Mondays. Sundays were just another workday. One foot in front of the other. Gracious for the feet she still had, for where they could take her. Today they will take her to her store, then home, no, wait. *Shit. Shit. Shit.* She remembered what she had agreed to do today.

After completing her morning routine, she arrived at her store. Locking her bike in its normal place, she flung the door open and stormed to the back, sputtering nonsense on the way. All sense of calm she had found in the early hours before the sun rose had disappeared; anxiety stood in its place after it crept in like a weed. As the sun grew higher, it took stronger root.

"Good morning to you too, sunshine," Benny hummed from behind the register where he was working on inputting new items into the system.

"Benny, what am I going to do?" She asked desperately, dropping her bags on the floor as she crossed her arms on the counter in front of him, leaning over to rest her forehead.

"Give me a raise?" He asked sarcastically.

"If I could, I would, Benny." She answered sincerely, keeping her head down but raising one finger, "I am hoping to give yall raises in the fall if the summer keeps up like it has."

"Oh honey, you just gave us a raise! I was teasing." He set down what he was working on and walked around to her. He placed his hands on her shoulders in a comforting gesture. "Sheesh, you must be frazzled today if you can't tell when I'm being facetious."

"Oh, oh," Joy replied, raising her head. "That's right. Okay, well, that's good then."

"What is going on hon?" he asked, stepping back to allow her room to turn around. "Did you have another run-in with lover-boy?"

"No," she sighed, now leaning back on her elbows, facing him. "Wait, what? He is NOT my lover-boy. Ugh, but I will."

"Make him your lover?" Benny asked teasingly in a breathy voice.

"NO!" Joy yelled, reaching over to lightly push his arm. "Run into him, you know, later today!"

"That's what she said," winked Benny, putting his hand out in case she tried to smack him. "Run *into* him."

"That's what your mom said." Joy retorted as the bell jangled announcing Jessica's arrival.

She bounded up to them with a wide smile and an extra pep in her step. She looked from Benny to Joy and back to Benny before asking, "What did I miss? Is she having another existential crisis?"

"You know it." Benny nodded to Jessica, putting his hands on his hips.

Jessica turned to Joy and commanded, "Out with it, let's skip the denial part this morning," She continued as she checked the time on her phone, "We have approximately thirty-five minutes before we open so let's get this over with."

Joy made an incoherent groan at Jessica's demands and slapped her hand to her forehead.

"Be a big girl and use your words." Encouraged Jess, with the same soothing voice she used with her children. Benny sniggered and covered it quickly with a little cough.

Joy peeked out from behind her fingers as she dragged them across her face. "It's just, so many things! I haven't been alone with a man who wasn't my friend or family in ages and he wants info about our area and I'm so out of touch that I don't even know who my competition is anymore!" She started pacing back and forth in front of the register, dramatically waving her arms around, the volume and desperation of her voice steadily increasing.

"Okay," Jessica responded. "And?"

"And, I don't know. It's just, I don't want to appear incompetent, I just don't do the things anymore," Joy continued talking out loud but more to herself now and the other two stood there watching her pace, occasionally pausing to address them but not leaving room to answer. "I used to do the fun things, once upon a time in college before all the life and grown-up things consumed my soul? We went to Centennial Park a lot... poetry readings at the Parthenon, Shakespeare in the Park, and swing dancing... do they still do any of that? What about downtown? That dueling piano bar... it had an amusing name, what was it... the big banger? And the Frist and the Symphony... I never really did the country music scene or the other touristy stuff... but what if he is asking more about Fortlin? Shit, I don't know! What do we have? Coffee? Food? Civil War battlefields? The statue commemorating the fallen racist confederacy? Oh, oh, oh! We could go paintball the scary-looking statue off of 65! I've always wanted to do that. No, no, I'm a grown-up and a business owner, I shouldn't encourage vandalism... And that's not Fortlin. Ugh, we have like 5000 events a year and I can't remember anything except the art crawl because I am a terribly self-absorbed homebody who hasn't even been to an actual movie theatre in who knows how long because I just wait for it to come out on streaming!" Joy collapsed dramatically on a couch. "I miss Blockbuster."

"Well, first of all, it's the Big Bang. More importantly, I don't know if you know this but you're just old now," responded Jessica nonchalantly, sitting next to her and pulling Joy's feet in her lap. "It happens to the best of us. One second you're going out at 9 o'clock, hitting up all the cool new spots, then the next thing you know, you're going to work, going home, then to bed before 10, 11 on a weekend. But hey, it's just a frame of mind, this is your chance. Reclaim your youth!"

"So, I'm just old?" Jessica nodded yes in response to Joy's question. "That helps me feel a little better. But what am I going to tell him? What are we going to talk about?"

"Tell him about your very single, handsome, strong, humorous employee who would love to be taken advantage of by his personal assistant," replied Benny. "Then, take him on a walking tour of downtown Fortlin!"

"Or you could always suck it up and drive him to see the Parthenon!" suggested Jessica, while pushing Joy's legs onto the ground and pulling her up to a seated position. Joy glared at her. She put her hands up in defense. "Hey now, I'm just joking. Unless you feel like you're ready for that. But I think you shouldn't worry, you should just be you. He's obviously seen something he likes, and why wouldn't he? You're an enchanting force." She pulled Joy into a sidearm hug.

"That's so sweet," Joy returned the hug. "You're pretty

99

enchanting yourself."

"Yes, yes, you're both enchanting," said Benny, reaching for their hands and pulling them up. "Now that we have established you will be fine, we've got a lot to do ladies. Snap to it."

"Aw, you're enchanting too Benny!" Joy patted his back reassuringly. "And since when have you been the boss?"

"Since you hired me. Just wait till I own the place." Benny winked at her before turning back to finish the task she had interrupted.

8. texting trouble

D espite the steady stream of customers flowing through, which usually kept Joy's mind occupied, making the days fly, instead the day dredged on. She was flooded with constant inquiries about the photo and her relationship with him. By about the sixth person she had come up with a basic script. He was apparently a happy customer. That she was glad he had a good experience and grateful that such an influential person had shared his compliments. She had completely forgotten about that detail until the questions started.

"Ma'am, can you reach that for me?" Joy raised her arms and stood on her toes to help the substantially shorter woman pointing to the last lavender candle on the tallest shelf of that display. *Buzzzzzz.* Her phone vibrated incessantly in her back pocket.

"Here you go." Joy handed the candle to the customer. *Buzzzzz* "Is there anything else I can assist you with?"

"Not at the moment, thank you!"

"Anytime. Please let me know if you need anything else!" Joy replied with a smile. She walked to the back of the store near the small corner section where handmade sweaters and other winter items were located. No customers were near there so she could have some privacy but still be able to pay attention if someone needed her. She pulled her phone out to make sure it wasn't a business-related message. Instead of the expected vendor check-in or update about new products or ideas; she had seven text messages from Liam.

Instead of asking her in one long message, he had several one-liners, each asking a different question. *Great. Another reminder about tonight.* Joy took a deep breath to help steady her faster heartbeat. *It's just dinner. Why is this idea making me feel so nervous? Get your act together.* She tried to calm and encourage herself as she opened the message app.

> *Do you have any allergies besides gluten?*
> *Preferences?*
> *Vegan?*
> *Vegetarian?*
> *Paleo?*
> *Lucas said you can't drive?*
> *Would you like a car to pick you up?*

Joy yawned and brought the back of her free hand to her mouth and rubbed one of her eyes before replying. *Oh, good grief. I told him all these answers yesterday!* She groaned internally. *Joy, be nice. Give him the benefit of the doubt, he's probably just double-checking.*

No other allergies. No real preferences, except good coffee available. Absolutely no car needed. Bike or walking distance from my store only.

No, that sounds too demanding... She deleted it and started over.

Just gf! Somewhere close to the store with good coffee would be great. Thx!

There, that's better. Hmmm...

I prefer to stay within walking distance, if possible

She sent the second message. Perfect.

Liam responded almost instantaneously.
Roger that.
Would you like a fresh outfit for the evening?

What in the sam-hill does he even mean by that? Does he not think I know how to dress myself? Good grief. She responded with a bunch of question marks.

"What's up? Why are you on your phone so much today?" Jessica had walked over to re-shelve a few things that were left in the changing room. "Is something wrong? Is it your mom? Your face is doing that scowl thing it does when you talk to her." She said, attempting to mimic Joy's expression

103

and pointing to her furrowed brow.

"No, not my mom." Joy sighed, as she took the last couple of shirts Jessica was holding and put them on hangers. "Thank goodness, I don't think I could deal with my family today."

Being the youngest of five, and the only 'whoops' child, they had never been close. Joy had always felt loved, but never truly included. Since her father's death, she hardly heard from her mom, then the accident happened and her siblings faded out as well. Which was fine with her. Fewer people to drudge up her past, or to reassure her that she was 'fine' even when she wasn't.

They sent pictures and email updates occasionally when any of their children had any major accomplishments. Like, when Sampson had recently sent her Taylor's college graduation announcement... he had emailed a scanned copy of the physical announcement and some pictures of the ceremony. A week after it took place. Thankfully she already had set aside items for a care package so she threw in a gift card and voila, a graduation present.

She had tried to stay close with her nephews and nieces but you can only do so much. It's not like she babysat her oldest nephew and his younger brothers when they came along all throughout her high school career. He was born during her 8th-grade year. Ester and Mary weren't far behind after they got married. Both of them were pregnant during her sophomore year. Theo, although the second oldest, had waited the longest to have his first child. He and his wife had finished their PhDs her senior year and had Davey her freshman year of college. The only nephew she didn't watch consistently since she had moved a day's drive away. She had been the only one to leave the state for college and then to live away. It was like they forgot her then. Out of sight out of mind.

Joy rolled her eyes at the memories and hung up the shirts, Jessica following. *Buzzzzz.*

Just offering (shrug emoji)
Since you've refused the car, (eye roll emoji) he wants to walk
with you to the restaurant.
5:30?

"Then who?" Jessica asked as Joy could feel her scowl deepen trying to read into Liam's messages.

"Liam," Joy gave Jessica a glance over the top of her phone as she typed her response.

5:30 works, I assume meeting here?
Where?

"What does assistant to mister leaves you breathless have to say?" Jessica asked, standing back up after fixing the bottom shelf.

"He's just confirming the details," said Joy as she fiddled with the shirts, regrouping them by size and color. She held up a grey one in her size, a silk-screen print of the Nashville skyline emblazoned on the front.

"And?"

"He's meeting me here at 5:30," Joy responded nonchalantly as she replaced the shirt.

"Ooooo, where are you going?" she asked slowly, stepping away to go help Benny at the register.

"I don't know yet," Joy shrugged her shoulders. "I'm sure it'll be somewhere tasty. You can't really go wrong around here. I promise I will let you know if something noteworthy happens." *Buzz.*

Somewhere fabulous

For shit's sake, really? Whatever. Joy yawned as she slid her finally quiet phone into her back pocket. Not sleeping well last night was catching up with her. She looked longingly at her couches. Currently, a couple of dad types were relaxing opposite each other. Mirroring each other with their heads leaned back and eyes closed. Shopping bags and purses piled next to them. She giggled when one of them let out a rumbling snore.

"Ugh, Mom, go wake up Dad, he's embarrassing." She heard a teenage girl looking at the nearby clothing racks say to the woman standing next to her. The mom shook her head in reply before presumably, her dad made a loud guttural sound. "Puh-lease!"

"Shh, the longer he sleeps, the more we can buy," The mom replied.

Joy smiled at that. *Yes, please buy more. The more you buy, the more money that goes to support not just Jess and Benny, but the artisans who made these items... and the sooner I get to do some more repairs on my home... and pay off some business loans.* She took one last look around and saw that Jess and Benny had everything under control. She ducked into the backroom for her break.

She walked over to the fridge and got out her salad she brought from home. Fresh lettuce, strawberries, and goat cheese from the farmer's market, topped with leftover roasted chicken, cranberries, and sliced almonds. She also pulled out her bottle of her favorite poppy seed dressing that she kept stocked at work and home. She sat down, drizzled her salad, keeping the dressing on the table, just in case she needed more, grabbed her gold-colored fork, and stabbed away.

If only I could pierce through and demolish my emotions like my food. Staring at all the ingredients she was able to get on those little spears. Once a bite of every taste was loaded she munched away. *Delicious.* As her blood sugar began to stabilize, she remembered the mystery caption. She finally was able to pull it up without any more interruptions.

Discovered a lovely shop in Fortlin the other day. The charming setting and unique local finds were almost as enthralling as the enchanting force of the proprietor. #imenchanted #charming #Fortlintn #Fortlinmerch #supportsmallbusiness #bosswoman

107

#underherspell #impressive #wheninFortlin #shoplocal #loveth-elogo #lovethebags #ditchplastic #reusablebagsrock

There must have been a dozen more hashtags. *Oh. Well, that explains a lot.* She tried to swallow her bite of chicken but found her throat was dry. She pounded on her chest a couple of times trying to help while she grabbed her bottle of water out of the fridge. *It's not a big deal, he's just nice.* She took a slow sip. *It's not a big deal, Joy, it's not a big deal. He doesn't like you like that. Jess and Benny are just reading into things.* She continued to reassure herself as she packed everything up, and checked her reflection in the mirror to make sure there were no leftovers in her teeth. She checked the time on her phone, sliding it back into her pocket before heading back out onto the floor. *Three. Just two and a half hours until he'll show up on my doorstep... again.*

The next couple of hours passed too quickly, and yet not quite fast enough for Joy. Jessica closed the registers after the last customer left happy with several of those gosh darn bags.

"You're going to have to order some more!" Benny pointed out to Joy after he locked the front door and switched the open sign to closed. She nodded in agreement as she straightened up a few of the shelves.

"I can go work on that in a minute," Joy replied while she bent over to pull open the almost hidden bottom drawer. "I want to finish refilling this soap shelf." She looked over what was left and sighed, the drawer was practically empty. On her knees now, she started stacking what she could find on a shelf within arm's reach. "I guess I'll need to see if Amber has more in stock, hers have gone so fast."

"You can do it all tomorrow," said Jessica, pausing between counting bills, "now you need to go freshen up. Or at least reapply your deodorant. I can smell you from here."

"Hmm," Benny leaned over Joy's crouched mass and sniffed long and loudly twice. "You are a little ripe." He laughed.

"Ugh," Joy stood holding the last of the soaps. "Yall, it's not that bad, is it?" she asked with a slight pout.

Benny giggled, "You are so easy to troll, doll. It's not that bad. But you should let me finish this and you should do as Jess says before she unleashes her inner beast on you."

"You know it's true!" Jessica said in a sing-song tone.

"Fine, here," she said curtly then handed off what was in her hands. "Thank you," she added, "I mean it, thank you both! You know I wouldn't have such an amazing place without you!"

"We know, we're wonderful, now scoot!" Benny pointed towards the back.

Joy grabbed her toiletry bag she kept at the store from the middle drawer of the small bathroom vanity. After powdering her nose, so they say, she returned having changed, fixed her hair, and added extra layers of mascara and lip gloss. And deodorant. She must have put on four layers of deodorant, and vanilla mint lotion from the display dispenser of the week. She was wearing the same linen dress as the other day, only in white. She wore her favorite black open-toed Roman-inspired flat sandals and her small black purse hung over her shoulder. She wore the same simple gold hoop earrings she had on earlier, but she had added a couple more rings to the existing stacks on her fingers.

"Well, what do you think? Do I smell better?" Joy asked as she stepped out of the back room, looking down, checking to make sure she had her store keys in her handbag so she could retrieve her helmet and larger bag later.

"I think you look stunning," said a voice. "But I'd have to get closer to smell you."

Joy's head popped up and saw Lucas standing up from the couch facing her where he had been sitting with Jessica and Benny. He was wearing dark khakis and a coral pink button-up collared shirt, rolled up to elbows that simultaneously drew attention to his forearms and his biceps. *Dear Mother of Pearl.* Benny and Jessica quietly low-fived behind the back of their couch so only Joy could see it.

"Oh, um, thank you?" Joy asked as her voice rose. A knot formed immediately in her stomach and her throat went dry. She cleared her throat quietly then spoke, "You look nice yourself." Jessica gave her a thumbs-up behind the couch and threw her a wink. Joy threw her a quick wide-eyed and subtle shake of her head as if to say, '*What the absolute fuck are you doing? You couldn't have told me he was here? Shit.*' Jessica just

110

raised her eyebrows and smiled with silent maniacal laughter in her eyes. She switched her gaze to Benny. "So um, are yall good? Anything I need to do before yall leave?"

"No hon, we're good," Benny replied. "We'll lock up after we leave. Don't have her back before 9, you hear?" Joy's nostrils flared at that. *Et tu, Benny? Et tu?*

"Wouldn't dream of it," Lucas said, winking at Joy.

"Have fun you two!" Jessica added with a little wave.

"Thanks, Mom, thanks Dad," said Joy sarcastically as she walked up and patted them each on their upper backs. She turned her gaze back to Lucas, "Ready?"

"Whenever you are." He responded simply with a smile that reached his eyes, once of the crystals from the overhead chandelier threw light on his eyes, giving the appearance that his eyes twinkled. Joy started walking towards the exit.

"You have your keys, right?" asked Jessica.

"Right here," Joy triple-checked her bag as Lucas caught up to her. "And my wallet, my phone, and my favorite lip gloss."

"Don't forget to leave room for Jesus!" Benny added as Jessica let a cackle escape.

"Don't worry, he was a very skinny man," Jessica added. Lucas chuckled.

Joy threw an incredulous look over her shoulder and started walking faster towards the door. "Thanks yall. Really. Love you, byeee!" She shouted to them as Lucas held the door open for her. They paused for a moment on the front porch of her store. She could feel Lucas looking at her, fiddling with her purse then looking everywhere but him. The warm breeze rustled through her dress slightly rippling the light fabric, and sending cool shivers down her spine. It was that golden time of day, the spring sunset that lasted forever, throwing soft light on all it could caress. She met his gaze and broke the silence, "So, um, hi."

"Hello." He responded, breaking out his breathtaking smile again. "Your friends are quite entertaining."

"They keep me honest, that's for sure."

"Thank you for agreeing to join me."

"You're welcome," she answered, starting to walk down the short steps to the parking lot. "So, which way are we headed? I'm assuming you know where we're going? Liam wouldn't tell me. Which seems unfair, since I'm the local."

"It's off of Main Street. Something about the frog and smog?" He followed her, easily matching her pace.

Joy glanced over at him with one eyebrow raised, "The Hog and Pog?"

"That's it!" He exclaimed. "Silly name, but Liam said it was very nice."

"Yes, it's very swanky. That's quite the malapropism," Joy shook her head and rolled her eyes. "I'm impressed."

"I'm impressed you understood what I meant," Lucas flashed his brilliant toothy smile at her.

"Eh, I like puns and puzzles," Joy shrugged, letting the praise roll off her back. Trying to shake it off before it settled in her stomach like a bolder. Compliments were like popcorn that cooked just a couple seconds too long, not completely burned but singed enough to leave a disgruntled aftertaste.

They continued to make safe small talk as they meandered their way down and over the several blocks from her shop to Fortlin Main Street. Her store was tucked away among other small businesses in converted homes. Thankfully, Fortlin was indeed a small town and fairly easy to navigate on foot. The golden light spotlighted the charm of the older buildings. Making it almost seem like they were stepping back in time for a short moment.

He held the door for her as they entered the Hog and Pog. They walked up to the hostess and Lucas gave her the name Liam had reserved their table under. Joy looked around, taking in the oddly warm ambiance that the combination of hanging crystal chandeliers and butcherknife-lined walls produced. As her eyes turned back towards the waiting area, her eyes were drawn to the door as it opened. In walked a stunning young woman, wearing an elegant one-shoulder slightly ruffled cocktail dress stretched tight over her presumably pregnant belly, emphasized by the dress' detailing. The man who followed her caught Joy's eye. Their gazes locked, frozen. Her heart dropped. She reached out to get Lucas's attention and grabbed his hand without looking. "I'm sorry, I can't eat here." She whispered to him in a faint voice. "I'll be outside."

Joy stormed off back through the doors and walked a few feet before hearing footsteps behind her. She paused, hoping it was Lucas.

"Mrs. Moore?"

Joy closed her eyes. *Not Lucas. Seriously, shit.*

9. frozen layers

"Mrs. Moore," the man spoke again, "please, can we talk?"

"It's only been five years," Joy spoke quietly, the words barely audible over the quiet rumble of a passing truck. She opened her eyes, and clenched her fists, forcing herself to face him. Slowly, as if she were pushing against a fierce wind she turned. She couldn't focus on his face, she looked over his shoulder instead. She could see Lucas walking up behind him, slowly. "I thought you wouldn't be out for another 3! How?" She asked, louder, but still, her voice cracked.

"Um, I'm out on parole Mrs. Moore." He reached behind his head and gave it a scratch. Lucas stopped hesitating and went to stand by Joy's side as the man continued to speak, the words tumbling out like a waterfall. "I've been out for almost two years now. I, ah, just wanted to say that I'm sorry. I am so incredibly sorry. I'll be sorry every day for the rest of my life. I, ah, I have to serve community service as part of my parole, and I'm speaking to groups, lots of high schools, and some colleges about the dangers of distracted driving. I know it's not enough, but I'll try the rest of my life."

Joy blinked the tears away forming in the corners of her eyes and nodded.

"I know it won't bring them back, but uh," he continued awkwardly, "maybe it'll help someone else make a better decision."

"Congratulations," Joy replied with a slight smile.

"What?"

"On your family. I'm assuming that was your partner and future child?"

"Yes ma'am. We've been married almost two years," He stumbled over his words, "Thank you, ma'am."

"Um," she chewed on her bottom lip before continuing, "Thank you for your words, I know it was a terrible mistake. Don't take this the wrong way but please don't talk to me again." Joy replied, her voice cracking again. "It's too painful."

"Yes ma'am." He shook his head, then reached into his back pocket and pulled out a card from his wallet. "I understand, I promise, I won't bother you ever again. But if you ever need something I can help you with, please reach out to me." He held out the business card in his right hand as he returned his wallet with his left.

She stared at it for a minute before walking towards him. She took the card with her left hand and placed her right firmly on his shoulder. She looked up into his desperately pained eyes, the fine wrinkles showing his face rested in a mournful position. "I don't wish ill of you, I just wasn't prepared to see you." Then she pulled him down into a gentle embrace. He resisted at first, then returned the gesture and gave her a tight squeeze. She softly whispered in his ear. "It'sOKto find happiness again. Don't let three lives be taken by that accident. I give you permission to live and find joy, understood?" She took a step back and wiped a tear away from her eye.

"Yes ma'am, understood," he sniffed, shaking his head, his eyes were red and wet, the dam holding steady, waiting to release a flood if ever given the opportunity. "Thank you."

"Good night," said Joy, turning her body towards Lucas who was standing quietly to the side, watching, waiting for her. He turned to meet her and offered his elbow, she slid her arm through it, giving his arm a grateful squeeze, as they started walking away.

"Good night Mrs. Moore." The man said behind them.

"Do you want to talk about that?" Lucas gently asked her.

"Nope." Joy responded, popping the 'p' and leaning into him ever so slightly more.

117

After walking a short block in silence, Lucas leaned down and asked her gently, "Do you mind if I ask where we're headed? Or if we're just walking?"

"Hm?" Joy looked up at him. "Oh, um, I'm sorry, did I not say out loud that I need Sweet Bee's?"

"If you did, I missed it." He smiled at her, "What is a Sweet Bee exactly?"

"The best-frozen yogurt and toppings bar. They have several options, and the flavors change by day or week. They'll give you free samples of whatever flavor so you make sure you pick out the best one for you. No regrets." Joy moaned a little thinking about all the wonderfully tasty options. She pulled her arm out of his and started to mime the correct procedure.

"The trick is, you fill your bowl with toppings first, so they don't fall out, then add the frozen yogurt, then the whipped cream is added last. Then they weigh it and you pay by the ounce... and the best part is that most of their options are gluten-free and safe for me." She said, swinging her arms freely. For a moment her heart was light and all pain and nervousness were gone.

"So dessert?" He asked, catching her hand with his as it brushed by, his fingers slipping easily between hers.

"Life is short," she said. Her voice had a tinge of ice then lightened. "Sometimes you need a little dessert first."

"Sounds delightful," he squeezed her hand gently.

Joy felt warm and comforted. She was aware that he was holding her hand, but it felt so natural she didn't think much of it. They walked that way until they entered the cheerful little frozen yogurt shop off of Main Street. Joy loved the colors, the pink and green walls, and the turquoise counter. So much pink. Pink and green were relatively safe colors.

She showed Lucas how everything worked and then left him to create her masterpiece. Heath crumbles, Reese's Pieces, mini marshmallows, strawberries, blueberries, and blackberries. Then onto the main event, the yogurt. Joy always read the options first then started on the left layering in her chosen flavors- espresso, strawberry sensations, watermelon sorbet, and white chocolate mousse. Not fully satisfied with the amount of yogurt filling her cup, she went to the basic chocolate and topped it off. "Perfect," she said out loud. Looking around for Lucas, she saw him at the toppings bar, gently shaking some chocolate sprinkles on what appeared to be vanilla and strawberry yogurt. She walked around him and grabbed the whipped cream, topping off the already overflowing cup. She hurried to the register so they could weigh it before something fell off.

"I've got that man behind me too." Joy pointed to Lucas still at the toppings bar and handed over her loyalty and credit cards.

"Yours makes nine, so his is free," said the teenager behind the register. "So yall are good to go!"

Lucas walked over as Joy was gathering extra napkins and handed him a spoon. "We're good, let's go!"

"Don't we need to pay?"

"I already did," Joy responded, heading to the door, and pushing it open with her back. "Come on, it's nice outside, let's go see if we can find a seat."

"Let me pay you back for mine, at least. After all, I'm the one who asked you," Lucas insisted, taking a bite of his froyo. "Mmm. This is delectable."

"Isn't it tho? And nope. I can pay for dessert," insisted Joy. "Besides, you can pay for dinner, which we will eat after this, eventually somewhere." She took a small bite before continuing, "As much as I got, I will need some sort of veggies to chase this." She motioned to the small park across the street. "I see a free bench over there if you don't mind staring at the racist memorial statue to commemorate the confederacy."

"Um, sure?" He said hesitantly.

Joy looked both ways and seeing it was clear went ahead and hurried across the street. Lucas followed. They ran across the grass and around the cannon and claimed the bench. "It's getting too crowded here," Joy said somewhat sarcastically. "Benches and real estate go quickly." She winked and settled into her seat, licking the yogurt sliding off the side before it could fall.

Lucas took another bite then asked, "So, why is this statue racist?"

"I didn't even realize the history of it until I hired Benny," Joy started, "Thankfully he had the energy to point me towards some better resources and point out how deeply systemic racism runs in our quaint little town. I am terrible at dates and details but essentially it was put up to remind Black people of 'their place' by essentially the female version of the triple K. Instead of physical, they inflicted emotional and systemic fear and pain. They wrote school history books, twisting the reasons behind the Civil War. They put up statues to remind us of white supremacy. They did so much more and it's woven into our society. It's utterly ridiculous. I hate it."

"That's terrible. So why is it still here?" He asked.

"Good question." She answered. "I don't understand it. So many petitions have come and gone to take it down, and yet, it stays. Although, one in a neighboring town was taken down in the last year or two. Hopefully, this one gets taken down in my lifetime."

"Hmm," he responded, seemingly pondering the situation.

"Hmm, indeed," Joy agreed. "As much as I love the South and I love it here, I hate that there's this and so many other giant blatant reminders of centuries of oppression. I just wonder what it will take to wake up the majority." She sighed, digging back into her yogurt when a renewed interest.

"I find it's good to be critical of what you care for. How else can you appreciate when something has grown." He took a bite of his yogurt.

"Like your favorite characters, the best have flaws but their arc lets them grow and still maintain that they're imperfect. Like us. I just hope we don't turn into a dystopian urban fantasy."

Despite the heavy topic, they sat there, her shoulder brushing his bicep, in comfortable silence, gazing upon uncomfortable reminders of history. Joy mostly looked up at the brightly lit soldier, missing that Lucas kept stealing glances of her. She did take notice that they were both nearing the end of their bowls and asked, "Are you immediately hungry for dinner, or do you want to walk around a bit?"

"We can walk," Lucas responded, standing and holding out a hand to help her to her feet. "Why don't you show me something else that you *do* like?"

As she took his hand, she noticed the way he was looking at her. Her heart started to flutter again. The warmth in her chest was returning. *He is just being nice, she repeated to herself. He wanted a tour, he wanted to get to know the area.* A little tiny voice in the back of her mind poked her. *But wouldn't it be nice if maybe, just maybe like you too?* "That'd be nice," she responded, not knowing which question she was answering. "But I do love discussing what I don't like."

They resumed holding hands after finding a trash can to toss their rubbish. Joy wasn't sure how it happened. She didn't realize he grabbed her hand or did she grab his subconsciously? "So this is Point Five. We'll go back up along Main Street which is also Fortlin Road, which is also State Highway 431. This was the main highway before 465. This road will take you all the way through the heart of Nashville, where it becomes, do you want to guess?"

"Erm, I don't know," Lucas shrugged. "31st Street? Main Street?"

"18th Avenue. Which then becomes Old Brickory."

"Ah, well," Lucas looked over at her, furrowing his eyebrows and pursing his lips, "that makes perfect sense." She showed him some of her favorite stores and talked about some of her favorite festivals. The conversation continued to be light-hearted as they walked up to and around the roundabout and then down a side street. Wandering nowhere in particular.

"The art crawl is my favorite day of the month!" Joy gestured with her free hand dramatically to emphasize her words, "I used to love just walking around and getting lost, absorbed in all the artwork, and swept away by all the bursting creative energy. Although, now that I think about it, that could also be all the free wine. But we started hosting this year so I haven't been since December. But next month is our big second anniversary so we're having a big sale, and hopefully, we'll have a big turnout for our party during the art crawl. You should come! Check it out! I heard from the bartender today that they can do watermelon sangria and margatinis!"

"I would love to come check you, er, it out." Lucas cleared his throat, bringing his fist to his mouth momentarily. "When is it? I'll have Liam see if we can make that happen."

"First Friday of every month," Joy replied. She heard a low soft grumbling noise, "Is that you? Are you hungry? I'm so sorry, I've been jabbering away, I haven't even noticed what time it is. Southern-style fish or meat and three?"

"I'm not sure."

"Barbeque?"

"I love barbeque." Lucas smiled.

Joy nodded her head then took off south, back towards Point Five from a side street. They turned again and walked through a parking garage. "Sorry, this isn't part of the scenic tour." They came out the other side and there was a small strip of restaurants, which looked to be closed. "Brickette's," Joy started smiling. Stopping momentarily to make sure the way was clear before continuing to drag Lucas across the road. She opened the door before he could grab the handle and then stumbled in. Joy glanced around, taking in the small, homey environment and seeing no painful memories. Perfect.

"Table for two?" the host loudly asked as they approached, as a small two-person band had just started another song Joy didn't recognize. Probably singer-songwriters. Perfect. She nodded to the host and continued to pull Lucas behind her as they followed meandering through the seats to where the host sat them. Near the bar, but they could still see the band play.

"My hands are sticky, I'll be right back," Lucas said after they got to their table.

Joy took the opportunity to look around and see how everything was still the same. The same barn wood paneling. The same posters over the bar. The same string lighting was woven through the metal piping lining the high ceilings, softening the industrial feel. Her gaze landed on the stage where the lead singer was strumming her acoustic guitar. Joy let the melody wash over her and reset her thoughts.

"Did you know you have to walk practically through the kitchen to get to the toilets?" Lucas asked in surprise upon returning to the table.

Joy shook her yes and passed him one of the waters that the waiter had brought while he was gone. They continued their lighthearted conversation as they read their menus.

"I think I'm going to get the briskette barbeque platter," Joy said as she set down her special gluten-sensitive menu down. "I love their sweet potato fries. Do you see anything you like?"

"Several actually," said Lucas, his eyes popping over the menu. "Do you mind if I look at yours?"

"Um, sure," Joy handed him the simply laminated paper gluten-sensitive menu. "All of this should be on there."

"Just wanted to check something," he replied as he quickly looked over both sides. "I was just checking to see if what I wanted was on here, and it is. Well, they both are. The ribs and the ribeye look excellent. Do you have a preference?"

"Oh? Um," she thought for a moment before answering. "The ribs, you can get a good steak in a lot of places, but southern ribs are the best. I thought you didn't have food issues?"

"Ribs it is then. And you're right, I don't, but you do," he stated. "I want you to, eh, feel safe with me while we're eating."

Joy went to say thank you but the server walked up to them before she could find the words. They placed their order, and Lucas emphasized that both wanted the gluten-sensitive option. The small band continued to play, filling the room with a cross between jazz, country, and a hint of bluegrass. They mostly listened to the music as they ate their food. Despite having their dessert first, both of them were still ravishing. Occasionally they'd catch each other's eye.

"Do you want to try a bite?" Joy asked when she was about halfway finished. "If I don't offer any now, I won't." She smiled at him.

"Yes, that would be lovely." He smiled back a little bit of barbeque sauce dripping from his lip.

"You got a little something right here," Joy indicated to the drip. "Mmm, I bet that's tasty." She meant to think but instead said, thinking of how it would be to lick his lip for him.

"What was that?" Lucas asked, attempting to wipe his mouth.

Joy's heart skipped a beat. "Um, your ribs," Joy recovered. "They look tasty."

"Would you like to try?"

"Mmhmm," Joy nodded yes. *I'd like to try more than the ribs. Shit. Joysephine, not this again.* She pressed her lips together to make sure she didn't betray herself again as Lucas held his plate out to her so she could choose one. "Thank you." She let herself mutter before dipping it in her own sauce and taking a slow bite. She let out a little moan as she closed her eyes, sinking into the satisfying fall-off-the-bone melting sensation. "Mmmm, delicious." She opened her eyes and saw Lucas looking intensely at her from across the table. His eyebrows were slightly raised and his mouth hung open ever so slightly. Despite the dim light, she could swear his cheeks looked a little pink. It was probably just the reflection from his shirt. "Something wrong?" she asked. "Do I have sauce all over my face or something?"

He cleared his throat and shook his head slowly a couple of times before answering, "Nope." He emphasized popping the 'P'. They maintained eye contact a moment longer before he dug back into his food. They finished their meal with relatively little conversation.

Lucas paid while Joy excused herself to the bathroom, where she discovered she had managed to eat barbeque sauce in a white dress and not get anything on herself. "Huh, I must really be a grown-up now." She said to her reflection as she washed her hands. She smudged the little bit of mascara that had started dripping and checked her teeth before returning to the table. Lucas stood at her arrival, and they headed out.

The spring night air welcomed them into a nice warm hug as they stepped outside. Joy let out a yawn. "Excuse me," she said as brought her hand to cover her mouth. "I should've ordered coffee."

"We can go get some, somewhere if you'd like." Lucas offered.

Joy pulled her phone out to check the time, it was after 9, on a Sunday. "That sounds lovely, but Bubbly Banana is already closed." She shook her head as she yawned again. "I should probably get on home anyway, I didn't sleep much last night." She started walking back in the direction of her store.

"Perhaps another time then?" Lucas asked hopefully, following.

"Sure," Joy replied. "Have you been to the one at the Warehouse? You should experience as many local places as possible, at least that's what I used to do when I traveled."

"I agree, nothing like getting a taste of the local people by trying out the small businesses in the area."

"Well, this small business owner appreciates the sentiment." Joy looked up at him and winked. They continued walking slowly, their full bellies slowing their progress. The night songs of the local fauna filling in the gaps in their conversation. As they turned on the street her store was on, Lucas reached out and grabbed her hand again. This time, it sent a shock into Joy's system. Lucas E. Worthington was holding her hand. Had been holding her hand off and on all night. She felt like a teenager being walked to her door by her first date. Unsure of what to do, or what comes next. So, with her heart beating erratically, she just let him hold her hand as they walked along.

"Joy," Lucas began, "do you mind if I ask you a question or two about what happened earlier this evening?"

She took a deep breath. *Was that only just a few hours ago? It felt like a lifetime.* "Um, sure, but no guarantee I'll answer it." She replied, trying to sound as calm and nonchalant as possible.

He came to a stop, coming to face her and grabbing her other hand with his free one. "First, I'd like to make it clear that even though I don't understand what happened, I have enjoyed every minute of this evening. I think you're an incredibly fascinating and wonderful person, who is obviously extremely caring," Lucas started, "I would love to continue to get to know you and I don't want to overstep here, I am however curious as to who that was and if you're ok? Whatever that was about sounded, er, incredibly serious. I don't want to pressure you, but I am here if you want to talk. I hear that I'm a pretty good listener."

129

Joy looked deeply into Lucas's concerned eyes. *Of course, he'd want to know who that was. How could I even begin to explain?* She closed her eyes to steady herself. She squeezed his hands, both to reassure herself of her reality and hopefully silently communicate that she needed a minute. He didn't say anything, just stood there, holding her hands. She slowly opened her eyes and took back her right hand to wipe away a few of the escaped tears from her cheeks, then returned them to his steady grasp.

"I am asOKas I can possibly be," Joy eventually spoke, trying to keep her voice even. "I can't go into the details right now, but maybe one day. But ah, um, that man, that was Jack Glan, the man that killed my family."

She took a deep before continuing. "My husband, and my, uh, my son." Her voice cracked as she shut her eyes and nodded her head. Silent tears started uncontrollably escaping. Lucas let go of her hands as she felt his strong arms envelop her in a hug. Her forehead rested on his chest and it was as if every emotion she had been trying to suppress over the last few years liquidated, falling from her eyes and soaking his shirt.

10. enchanter enchiladas

The cool breeze whipped Joy's hair into her face as she took off her helmet. Spitting hair out of her mouth as she stowed her helmet in her basket. She untucked the black and white midi sundress from her shorts, dancing a little to help it fall into place. She grabbed her purse and double-checked all her locks before turning toward the restaurant. Tito's was located in a newer subdivision further south of downtown Fortlin where its sister location was, but this was closer to Jessica's house. This meant a little extra chat time before she would have to leave to meet her kids at the bus stop. Although Joy was not necessarily in the mood to chat long enough to delve into all that transpired the night before.

Joy had barely walked past Fantastic Lambs when she heard a high-pitched 'eek' from the mostly vacant patio section.

"Joybelle!" Jessica yelled from one of the tables raising a very large margarita in the air. "Hey, Joysephine Leigh! Over here!"

Joy rolled her eyes and waved at her friend, trying to hush her up. "Hi!" Jessica stood and opened the gate behind her to let her in. "I don't think I'm supposed to do that," Joy whispered, reading the exit-only sign.

"It's really fine, I asked," Jessica winked dramatically, which meant she didn't actually ask. "It's just so people won't cut in line. I already have a table." Joy sighed audibly and walked in quickly to minimize any attention drawn to her breaking a rule. Jessica giggled while giving Joy a quick bear hug then indicated to the table she had been sitting at, "Have a seat and tell me everything!"

"Can I at least look at the menu first?" Joy responded. "Sheesh, woman."

"Um, it's not like you're going to order something different today," she taunted, "mixed fajitas, corn tortillas, and a margarita on the rocks, right?"

"Mmm," she groaned thinking about how perfectly tasty that sounded. "I at least want to read the enchilada options."

"Mmm kay. That's totally fair." Jessica nodded. "I'm getting tacos."

"Ooo, their Asada tacos are amazing." Joy practically drooled. 'You know what? I think I'm going to change it up. I'm getting chicken enchiladas and an Asada taco on the side."

"Wow, color me impressed," Jessica replied as she folded her menu again and took a sip of her margarita. "What's up with you being all adventurous?'

"Adventurous? Because enchiladas are so thrilling," Joy replied. She was looking wistfully out over the empty field between the parking lot and Brewisburg Pike. The blue sky was dotted with puffy clouds which delicately kissed the tops of the brilliant green landscaped trees of the mature neighborhood across the street as the wind gently blew them along. She leaned forward and rested her elbows on the table, gently touching her pointer fingers to her chin.

"Actually, one day I still want to go on a road trip to the southwest US and sample all the enchiladas. Hit up San Antonio, Santa Fe, Phoenix, San Diego, and then maybe even down to Ensenada." Joy closed her eyes and moaned a little thinking of all the journey her taste buds could go on, the dry heat instead of the tortuous humidity.

Jessica spit out a little of her margarita. Wiping her mouth she replied, "Road trip? You? Really? Shit, I'd give you gas money to go on this trip if you would get in a car again. No, I'd do better than that, I'd come with you and film it."

"Um, of course, you'd come with me. You promised me in college you'd come!"

"Well, I've slept and had two kids since then," Jessica responded matter of factly, "so forgive me if I forgot."

Joy raised an eyebrow, "Last I checked you had three kids."

"I do," Jessica said, more like it was a question than a statement. "Ah, yes, yes, I do, isn't that what I said?" Joy shook her head no. "Oh, well, case in point," she shrugged.

"Well, if you're up for it, I also want to go skiing in the Rockies and see the giant sequoias, maybe go on a backpacking trip and hunt for BigFoot. Maybe even win the lottery. A girl can dream, right?" Joy set her menu down and took a sip of the water in front of her before continuing, "So, tell me about you? How are you doing? How's work? Is your boss still a bitch?" She winked as she placed her cup back in its original place.

"Oh, she is such a hard ass," Jessica replied with dramatic flair. She leaned forward, whispering loudly, "Keep it on the D-L but my coworker and I are planning a mutiny to take over running the joint. We're recruiting pirates and treasure. It's going to be epic. But, um, yah, after that I will totally go with you if you're ready. Other than that it's just life. Just trying to balance all the things.

"Cool, cool. Sounds good. I'll keep you updated." Joy said, nodding her head and pursing her lips. "So, what about Terry? WorksOKfor him? School goingOKfor the kids?"

"Eh, they're all fine." Jessica shrugged and replied nonchalantly. "Same old same old. Terry goes to work, the kids go to school, they come home, they eat all of the food in the house, do their homework, and then they go to bed. We juggle chores, and schedules, sometimes we work out. Most importantly we try to find time to teach the kids how to take over the world-they have yet to decide if they're going to be supervillains or heroes... yet. Once they decide we'll be able to move on to the next phase of their training. Occasionally we make sure they shower and brush their teeth. See, same old same old."

"Man, I forget that your life is so boring." Joy shook her head in mock pity, trying to suppress a smile as she noticed the server approaching their table. The two friends cheerfully handed over their menus after placing their orders, making sure to be extra polite. Having both done their time in food service during college, they both knew the stress and chaos well. As the server walked away, Joy continued to keep the focus of the conversation on her friend. Both because she didn't want to tell her everything about last night yet, although it was inevitable that she would, and she felt like they never talked about Jessica's life much anymore. Somehow the conversations tended to steer back to Joy's life or lack thereof. "So, did you decide if you're doing another marathon this year?"

"No, I don't really have the time to do all the long runs," Jessica answered. "But Zach wants to run the fireworks 5k with me this year!"

"That's so awesome," Joy replied. "I can't believe he's old enough to do that kind of thing. How big is he now? You don't bring your kids by enough, they're always a foot taller every time I see them."

"Ha, uh, thankfully no. Although Zach is almost taller than me already." Jessica said, dramatically setting down her margarita glass and emphatically waving her hand to emphasize her point. "It's not fair. Nothing can emotionally prepare you for your kids to surpass you in height."

"Oh man, that's hard but that's still awesome," Joy commented with a halfhearted smile. "I still can't get over that next year he'll be in middle school."

"Right? How are we old enough? It seems like yesterday we were pregnant together." Jessica said wistfully. A quiet awkwardness hung in the air before she reached across the table and squeezed Joy's forearm. Joy smiled and reciprocated the gesture then they slid into a gentle handhold.

"We're not, we were babies having babies. "Joy mused as her smile grew slightly. She drifted back to warm memories of the two of them trying to figure out how nursing bras worked, discussions about all the things they were never going to do as moms, how both of them called each other out on how they did half of those things before their babies even turned one. One of the most beautiful things in life was the mystery and creation of life. And nothing more terrifying than being in charge of a life that was not your own. To make so many decisions with so much conflicting knowledge and knowing you will make so many mistakes. There's nothing new under the sun and yet each child presents their own unique challenges to his or her own family unit. Joy brought herself back to the present and gave Jessica's hand a reassuring squeeze. "What about the other two?"

Jessica reciprocated the squeeze. "3rd grade is rough man,

poor Erin usually has a ton of homework most nights. She's keeping up with it mostly. Thankfully Nick is just in the read to me 20 minutes a day phase. Now that we've caught up on me, tell me..." She started to demand as the server brought out their food.

Joy quickly unwrapped her silverware as the server walked away, and took a giant bite of her still-steaming enchilada. "Mmm, so good, hot, hot, hot, but good." She mumbled, trying to keep the food in her slightly open mouth as she reached for her water.

"Where were we?" Jessica asked, slowly and determinedly unwrapping her silverware. "Oh, that's right." She took her time, gently smoothing her napkin in her lap. Raising her head, simultaneously cocking an eyebrow, locking her narrowed eyes with Joy's. "You were going to tell me everything that happened last night, starting from when you left the store and Benny and I couldn't see you anymore." She picked up her fork to take a bite of rice, then gestured at Joy to begin. Joy swallowed her hot bite and continued to sip her water. Trying to escape Jessica's burning gaze. "Joy Elizabeth." Joy shrugged and waved her free hand in front of her face as if fanning away the heat, the other still holding the water to her lips. "This is the whole reason we're here. Why are you avoiding telling me? Do you want me to assume he declared his undying love for you? Tell me, Mrs. Moore."

Joy slammed her water cup down and visibly cringed, her shoulders immediately raising to her ears, her eyebrows practically becoming one as she scrunched up her nose and shut her eyes. For some reason whenever anyone called her Mrs., it made her feel as if nails were clawing a chalkboard in the back of her head. "Holy crap. That was unnecessary." She took a deep breath. "No, Not anything like that. And I wasn't avoiding it. My mouth was literally on fire, I was becoming a dragon! Did you not see me practically breathing smoke?"

Jessica held Joy's gaze as she took a bite of her crunchy taco. Her nostrils flared slightly as she chewed. Her stern gaze softened as her eyes shut and unintelligible soft murmurs of pleasure escaped her pursed lips. "So amazing," she muttered, opening her eyes and finding her point again. "But anyway, if he didn't confess his undying love, why are you so shifty?" her eyes darkened, "That bastard didn't hurt you, did he?" She grabbed her knife subtly, her fist tightening its grip.

"Calm down there, Stabby McStabster," Joy shook her head as she continued to cut her enchiladas into more appropriate bite-size pieces. "He did not hurt me." She picked up a small piece with her fork and blew gently on it before continuing. "Mostly I just took him on a walking tour of downtown, and we ate."

"Where did he take you?"

"Um, well, he tried to take me to the Hog and Pog."

"Oh, fancy," interjected Jessica.

"But we, ah, ran into a problem," Joy continued. "So we

grabbed some fro-yo, I showed him around, then we finally ate at Brickette's."

"Uh, huh," said Jessica slowly, nodding her head slowly as she absorbed the limited details her friend gave her. "So, did he kiss your hand again?"

"No," began Joy as she felt the now-familiar heat rise from her chest to her cheeks. "He, ah," she cleared her throat, "did not. At least I don't remember him doing anything like that."

"What does that mean? Did he kiss you?"

"Ohmyword, no." Joy rolled her eyes, taking a deep breath before groaning quietly. She brought her left hand to her forehead and gently massaged her temples. "It doesn't mean anything, ugh, it means he didn't do anything, or if he did, I didn't notice it. And no real kissing. Really, there isn't much to say."

Joy thought back to the previous evening, trying to bring back the details she wanted to keep. His strong arms supporting her crumpling form. He had expressed concern for her safety so he insisted on walking her home again. She had insisted she was fine. So they compromised. She rode her bike home, and he followed behind in his rental car. Unnecessary though it was, it was comforting knowing she wasn't alone. She had expected him to continue on his way home as she waved to him when she arrived at her home. She hadn't noticed that he had parked when she put her bike in her minuscule detached carport for the evening. When she had turned around to head

139

towards the back door, she could see his car on the street, just on the other side of the short deteriorating white picket fence that lined her side yard. He was waiting, presumably for her just inside the dilapidated gate perpetually open to her gravel driveway. He was looking up toward the stars. Running a hand through his hair then crossed his arms over his chest. The shadows dancing on his face made his expression hard to read.

Had he been annoyed with her that she had so many issues? That she practically took over the evening then had a breakdown? Or was he nervous? Probably nervous that she was going to break out into tears again and leave more mascara stains on his shirt. Shit. But then why did he insist on making sure I got home safely? Because he's a kind person. And my story tends to demand pity and concern any time I tell anyone what happened. Even people who had a hard time with empathy attempted to console me. Even when I'm not a bawling disaster.

"Real kissing?" Jessica's question brought her back to the present. "Ok, wait, wait, wait. Let's start at the end of the night and backtrack."

Joy sighed deeply, still envisioning the comfort that his presence gave her. Not sure how to express that to her friend without giving her or herself unnecessary hope. "He made sure I got home safely. He walked me to my door after I put my bike up. I thanked him for being so understanding and considerate. He thanked me for showing him around. Then we hugged, and he kissed my forehead." Her voice trailed off. The heat solidified in her face and she couldn't help the slight smile forming as she opened her mouth for another bite.

"I'm sorry, what?" Jessica had stopped moving. The salsa dripped from the taco she held in midair. "OH EM GEE. One more time, more elaboration and detail please." She set her taco back down and wiped her hands on her napkin. Before bringing her hands up to her face then waving a finger in Joy's face. "Remember I'm living vicariously through you, too. Where were his hands? Where were your hands? How did you feel? What was the tone of his voice?" She was practically jumping out of her chair she was so animated by the time she finished rambling off all of her questions.

Joy giggled at her friend's reaction. "Oh, my word. Sit down before you knock your drink over."

"That would be tragic." Jessica pointed with one finger. She collected herself, adjusted her seat then calmly gestured one to Joy like Vanna White indicating the next correct letter. "Please, continue. Details. More, please." She picked up her taco and took another bite.

"I don't know," Joy began, "it was weird, the whole night, not because of him. He was great, such a gentleman, extremely nice. I don't know how to describe it." Joy paused for a moment, unaware of the smile pasted on her face. "Safe? Respected? Like my whole world was collapsing around me and he pointed out we were still on solid ground. He didn't try to fix anything, it was like he got it."

"Got what, exactly?"

"All of it," said Joy. She started over to the beginning of the night. Filling her friend on the missing details of running into Jack, and his pregnant wife. The change of the evening's plans. The random discussions. How Lucas was supportive, inquisitive, but not in an overstepping way, in an' I'm here for you' way. "Despite not being the best way to start an evening, it ended way better than I could have expected."

"Wow," Jessica responded, shaking her head slightly. "That was an epic one-act play of a night just by itself. But it sounds like Lucas treated you well and you still obviously like him. You haven't stopped smiling since you said he kissed your forehead. Even when you were talking about that other jackass."

Joy brought her fingers to her brow and shut her eyes, leaning forward slightly and groaned, "Ugh, of course, I like him!" She sat back up, holding up a finger for each positive aspect she listed. "He's kind, funny, and respectful, and I get intense butterflies every time I see him, but he also makes me feel like I'm the only one in the room, although that could be my narcissism. And that's just his personality. He's even more attractive in person than in his movies. I don't even understand how that's possible but I just want to lick him sometimes and then I feel dirty. This is terrible. I'm terrible." She crossed her arms on the table and collapsed her head into them. "Fuck me."

"Maybe he will," Jessica giggled a little, Joy looked up just enough to glare at her. "Why is this terrible? It's completely normal to have feelings of wanting to devour someone as attractive as he is, even if you don't like them." She patted the top of Joy's head. "And of course, he's more attractive in person! He's real, slightly asymmetrical, with flaws, and a good personality, not just some unattainable airbrushed fantasy. Real is hot." She fanned herself dramatically. "And it sounds like he likes you too! So, just go with it!"

"I highly doubt that," said Joy, looking up from her arms, head still resting on the table. "Even if he was remotely interested before last night, I probably scared him away. Who wants to date someone with so much tragic and heavy baggage?"

"Someone who has rippling biceps and an interest in drama?"

Joy's expression dropped and she gave Jessica a cold, annoyed glare from underneath the fallen strands of hair blowing in her face. She rolled her eyes and ran her hand through her hair in an attempt to put the rebellious strands back in their place.

"What?" Jessica asked with a shocked expression. "I'm just saying, it takes a special kind of person to handle all of this," she pointed at Joy, circling her finger in the air around her face. "Like me." She added with a giant smile. "And maybe Mr. Worthington will actually be worthy." She winked.

11. bless your snart

A steady influx of customers kept Joy on her toes over the next few days. Not as dramatic as the weekend had been, but definitely more than the average spring week usually brought. Not that she was complaining, more bemoaning that she needed an extra set of hands and a pair of eyes when normally she was enough when Jessica or Benny wasn't there.

Thankfully she had a few people coming in for interviews for seasonal and temporary part-time positions on Friday when Jessica could handle it. Hopefully, they could hire a couple of people in time to train in time for the big anniversary sale and stay on through the summer so she wouldn't have to keep finding more people. Benny would also be able to work during the week more often this summer.

Possible vendor interviews were also on the books for the week. As everything was as local as possible, and a lot were people working the side business or selling the products of their intense hobby, like Miss Sally who made a lot of key chains she showed Lucas the first time he was in her store. She had been a part-time stay-at-home mom to two kids with special needs, a part-time elementary school teacher's aide, and she happened to be heavily into leather working. Thankfully Joy had a surplus since they were selling so quickly and summer was approaching. Miss Sally didn't work over the summer, and she was also short of the help she normally received during the school year. It was also important for her to always have backup vendors in case she ran out of stock of someone else's. Since most items were sold on commission, it was also helpful to the budget to be able to try out new items for a while, if they didn't sell, she could always send things back. Everything except the bath and personal hygiene products. Joy bought most bath products wholesale since they were one of her best sellers, and she figured if she went bankrupt she would at least be able to bathe.

And with all the flowers Lucas was sending her, she could just dry all the petals and have luxurious relaxing bubble baths for the rest of her life, and maybe have some leftovers for potpourri. Sometimes they would be delivered to her store, but much to Benny's chagrin, not by Liam. Instead a rotation of local florists. Sometimes they would be delivered to her home. The bouquets started in a similar color to the original but morphed into a variety of bright cheery colors as the week dragged on. However, they were all smaller and easier to manage in size. Joy appreciated the consideration. She did not appreciate how Benny or Jessica managed to grab the note that accompanied each delivery to the store before she did.

The first came Monday evening to her home. The note was a

simple thank you for showing him around. She had texted him a picture of the flowers and thanked him. He responded that he was glad she liked them and asked how she was holding up. While she had thought about insisting that she was fine, like she told everyone, she was honest about how she was actually feeling. Still shaken, and emotionally sore, but ok, and thankful for the busy week ahead. He had a busy week as well. His schedule was packed it seemed, over the next few weeks, but Liam had also texted to confirm the anniversary sale and art crawl date. The flowers kept coming. The notes were short and sweet. Always along the lines of wanting to bring a smile to her face. Not too much fuel to add to Benny and Jessica's teasing fire, though they tried.

"What sort of person sends you flowers every day for almost a week?" Jessica asked Friday afternoon while refolding a stack of shirts as Joy found an empty space for the newest flower arrangement. "Except for someone very interested in you."

"Stalkers," Benny chimed in quietly as he walked by helping a customer to the register with an armload full of goods.

Joy rolled her eyes at him then bit her tongue while forcing a smile as they passed so she wouldn't say anything inappropriate in front of her guests. She rubbed the tip of her nose with the back of her knuckle trying to calm an itch before continuing. "How many times do I have to tell- ah-ah-ah choo," she sneezed into her arm. "Ugh. Tell you!? He has given me no indication that he likes me. If anything," she brought her hand back to her nose, attempting to stifle the reforming tickle before sneezing several times in a row.

146

"Bless you!" Jessica said in addition to several of the nearby customers. "Are you okay?"

"I'm fine. I just need to take more allergy meds," she added, rubbing the corner of one of her eyes with the back of her knuckle. "Anyway, what was I saying?"

"You were explaining your utterly ridiculous denial of this man's obvious obsession with you," Jessica paused in her tidying. She stood up straight and put one of her hands on her hips, the other was rubbing the crease in her brow. "Do you really not see how most people when sending flowers send simple bouquets to friends and coworkers. Not these designer floral pieces of art usually reserved for weddings and shit!" She stopped rubbing her head to indicate not just the arrangement Joy was still fussing with, but the others placed around the store. "Didn't he send you one to your home, too?"

"Two, yes. And this is not a de dennnn choo," she sneezed again, "Denial." Jessica groaned and went back to her chore. "Honestly," Joy insisted, "if he liked me, don't you think I'd pick up on it?" She paused to sneeze several more times. The choral of Bless Yous echoed around the room. She lowered her voice, "He probably thinks I'm on the verge of a mental breakdown or something. Which is totally fair, since I pretty much did and I was. Praise Jesus for antidepressants and therapy, amiright?"

"Heck yes! Hit it!" Jessica held one of her hands up for a high five.

147

Joy reciprocated the gesture before continuing, "It also makes me think I must have made a-ah-ah-achoo, bi-bi-bi choo bigger, whew," she paused pulling the front of her dress up over her nose and breathing in some un-pollinated air, face still slightly covered she continued, "a more distressing scene that I originally thought. This just reinforces how wonderful of a person he is to be so concerned about this complete disaster of a human being." She pulled her head out of her dress, letting it fall back into place while she tugged some of the greenery out of the vase a little. Fixing the balance back to its original glory. She attempted to quiet her next three sneezes again, which must have worked as instead of a chorus, she heard only a quartet of bless yous before backing up a step to get a better view of the elaborate arrangement.

"See! He does care!" Jessica said smoothing the shirt she just finished folding.

Joy raised her left eyebrow and leaned her head to the side slightly. "You're infuriating," she stated and turned.

She had barely taken a step when Jessica called, "That's why you love me!" Joy looked over her shoulder and stuck her tongue out playfully at Jessica in response. "Oh, go take your meds!" Jessica said before returning the gesture. The two of them shared a quick smile.

Joy restarted her attempt to go on to her next task, reloading the key chain display. She went to the back to get one of the recently arrived replacements. Finding it among the meticulously organized but chaotic-looking boxes stored on a baker's rack in the corner. She placed the small cardboard box on the break table, opening it to double-check it was the one she was looking for. Satisfied she grabbed her bag and dug around until she found an older but not yet expired bottle of a generic non-drowsy allergy pill. "Yes! I thought I had some with me." She said to herself out loud in triumph of her find. She swallowed a pill, taking a sip from her water bottle, though she didn't need it to swallow the pill. Sometimes it's harder than necessary to stay hydrated when you're working retail so she gladly took advantage of the opportunity to rehydrate. She put her things back and then grabbed the box from the table.

She walked out to see Benny still at the register and Jessica showing someone how to close the changing room curtain. There were a few other customers towards the front of the store, but no one appeared to need help at the moment. As she started to walk to the key chain display, her phone vibrated in her pocket. She stopped in her tracks, stepping to the side to not block the aisle. She shifted the weight of the box to access her pocket easier.

While Joy was pulling her phone out, she didn't see Jessica sneaking up behind her. Peering over Joy's shoulder Jessica whispered loudly in Joy's ear, "Who's that?"

Joy jumped and muffled a scream in one hand, pulling the phone to her chest with the other, and dropping the box. Key chains spilled all over the floor. "Jessica! Fudge monkeys! For someone so small you are so scary." She squatted down on her heels to clean the mess, brushing her hair over one shoulder so it wouldn't obscure her view.

"Nah, you're just easy to troll," Jessica smirked, patting her on the shoulder as she leaned down in front of her to help gather the key chains. "So, who was that? Monsieur Fleur?" she asked in a terrible French accent.

"Maybe, maybe not, I don't know. I was interrupted." Joy shrugged before coming back to a standing position. She smoothed the simple black dress she was wearing again out. "Oh, look that customer waaay over there looks like she needs help, go do your job." She stuck her thumb out and indicated to the other side of the store where a teenager was trying to reach something on a high shelf.

Jessica put her last handful of key chains back in the now upright box Joy was holding again. "First of all, what is this?" Jessica mocked Joy's hand movements, "Are we doing the hand jive? Are we a musical now? If so, I want a solo." She first pointed to Joy, "Secondly, you know I can't reach that!" then pointed towards the shelf in question.

"Then grab a step ladder," Joy said dryly, "Or, a Benny. He's twice as tall and twice as helpful as you anyway. And yes, if we all burst into song, you can have a solo." Jessica rolled her eyes and went to go see if she could be helpful. Joy watched as she grabbed Benny from behind the register and made sure they were both occupied and glanced one more time around to make sure she didn't see anyone in need of help before looking at her phone again. Hoping it was one of the applicants confirming their interview. As she pulled up her notifications, she saw she had only a new text, no recent missed calls message, and that she was still about 5,000 emails behind. Not too bad, down from 12,000. She opened the text, a smile spreading across her lips as she read the name. That all too familiar heat returned to her entire body. Four simple words. *I didn't know how four simple words can make my heart flutter. Maybe he cares? Maybe a little?*

Do you like them?

Yes. Thank you.

She typed immediately and then hesitated before adding and sending:

you know you really don't have to keep sending me flowers, right?

She went to put her phone back in her pocket, but the moment it slid in, it vibrated again. She felt the heat creep up into her face. She glanced at the register to make sure no one needed help before looking at her phone again.

Did they make you smile?

Joy could feel the dimple on her right cheek growing deeper reading his text.

Maybe...

Ugh, no, that's too juvenile and flirty... She deleted it then typed again, paused for a moment, chewing on her bottom lip, doing a poor job of trying to real in the expression on her face.

Yes... but just a little.

She hit send. *Ugh, what if he thinks that, nope,* she interrupted the thought. *No what-ifs, too late. What did her therapist always say? Most what-ifs only distract from the here and now, unless it's a, what if I did the thing that I really desire... as long as it's not harmful to myself or others... What if I just chose to live a little and maybe even thrive instead of barely existing?* She took a deep breath, then walked over to her goal, the display at the counter. *Key chains. Focus.*

She heard a loud sneeze from the front of the store where she had placed another one of the bouquets. "Bless you!" She said to discombobulated sound, joining the chorus of bless you from around the store. *Ah, yes, southern politeness and hospitality. Never miss a chance to bless you or your heart depending on how much you were liked... Maybe I should ask him to... NO, just stop.* She looked around the room. Several people were rubbing their eyes and wiping their noses. She looked down at his response as it flashed on her screen.

Then I have to keep doing it... Your smile is worth it.
She pocketed her phone, not knowing how to respond anymore. Maybe it was worth the extra allergy meds. She pulled one of the engraved leather pieces of miniature artwork out of the now slightly dented box. Fingering the soft edging, before finding its home. As she slowly and precisely organized the display, her thoughts drifted to the last time she lingered at

this very spot, with him. Skin touching skin in that brief moment they brushed hands, electric shocks radiated throughout her body the longer she dwelled on the memory. "Mmm", she moaned a little louder than she realized, thinking of how he had smiled at her, how he seemed to really want to get to know her, then on their outing together- to hold her... *He is such a delicious man.*

"Ah, ah, AH-CHOO!" A woman sneezed loudly as she placed several items on the counter, signaling she was ready to check out.

Joy's head snapped up, she smiled the shock off her face and managed another, "Bless you." She walked around to the register, placing the box of key chains on a shelf under the counter on her way. She rang up the customer's items, delicately placing them into a paper shopping bag.

While the woman waited for the total, she leaned into a peony in the bouquet on the counter, taking in an audible whiff. Almost immediately she sneezed into the hand holding her money. "I'm so sorry, I love the smell of peonies, but I'm so allergic," she said, handing the small bundles over to Joy, she could see the dampness of the droplets ever so delicately spread over the bills.

Joy bit her tongue to suppress a gag. Instead, she kept her customer service smile plastered on her face and responded, "I understand, it's no problem, really," as she fished out the customer's change from the cash drawer. As soon as the woman turned around Joy pumped hand sanitizer into her palm, hopefully cleansing her enough. *No, nope, never mind. Not worth it.* She dug up her phone and started typing away before she lost her nerve.

I really appreciate it, but I think you might need to change tactics... You don't have to handle the money people are sneezing on (winky face emoji) You know, if I matter to you so much.

What am I implying? Ugh, no. That's not right. She started to delete the last line. Out of the corner of her eye, she could see a figure approaching. She raised her head to see who it was, just a couple of browsing nearby, obviously in conversation and not wanting to be interrupted. She looked back down to fix her message. There was no longer a draft text. She had hit send. She had only managed to delete *so much.* And there was a typo. Instead of "it", there was an "I". She quickly added,

you know, my smile ...

Oh, shit. Wasn't that even more flirty? Or does that make me sound like I'm an idiot? She bent down to dig the box of key chains back out. She used the opportunity to shut her eyes and calm her erratically beating heart.

Understood...
I'll just have to figure out how else to make you smile...
How about lunch?

Joy slid to the floor to respond. Why is this so difficult?

Sure... after next week sometime after the anniversary party? I'll

154

text Liam my availability?

She rested her head on her knee, then added;

Are you coming? To the party
Fantastic. Looking forward to it. Xx
...Wouldn't miss it.

Wouldn't miss it! He wouldn't miss it! She leaned her head back against the shelf behind her, closing her eyes and letting the excitement and anticipation of seeing him wash over her.

Joy felt someone poke her arm and they shouted, "Boo!" loudly into her ear.

"Ah! Shit!" she jumped slightly, looking up at who surprised her. "Benny! What the heck?"

"You were in my way. Some people actually do work around here," he responded playfully as he grabbed a bag from the shelf her head had just been resting on. "Please excuse the wait, ma'am." He said to the customer who was waiting to check out, as he continued to tease Joy, "My boss was laying down on the job again. Can't find any good employers these days." He said slightly sarcastically, shaking his head and pursing his lips.

"He's right, you know, I'm not a *good* employer," Joy said nonchalantly. Pausing to brush herself off as she stood, grabbing the box of key chains along the way. "I'm fantastic," She said with a straight face then gave the customer a wink, and nudged Benny with her elbow. "But seriously, how has Benny been treating you? Do you feel taken care of?"

"Oh, yes," said the woman genially, "he was extremely helpful, polite, and so funny!"

"I am so pleased to hear that, and I don't expect anything less from him. He really is going to take over this place one day if he has his way." Joy replied, nodding her head towards Benny.

"If you think this store is fabulous now," he replied dramatically, "just wait till I get my hands officially on it."

Joy helped Benny bag the woman's items as they continued their witty but friendly conversation. As the woman walked away, Joy turned to Benny and asked him, "Do you really want to take over one day? You've hinted at it a lot more recently."

"Oh? I thought I was being subtle about it," He replied airily. She crossed her arms across her chest, rolling her eyes and arching her eyebrow in reply. "OK, fine. I'd love to be a business owner one day, to be my own boss, but I love it here, and I love you, so I'm torn. Plus, I don't have enough experience yet."

"Benny, I love you and appreciate you so much. Don't let me, or imposter syndrome, or whatever it is, ever hold you back from your dreams, OK?" she asked. "You are such an intelligent, talented, and creative young man. I hope you know that I think you are a fabulous employee and are very capable of running your own place, but if you're wanting more hands-on experience and to really learn more about how I run things, we can make that happen."

"Really?"

"Yes, really," Joy replied reassuringly. "Besides, I want you to stay here as long as possible, you make working with Jessica so much more bearable."

"Well, that's obvious," he replied sarcastically as Jessica walked up to the counter.

"Did one of you say my name?" Jessica asked, tapping her fingers on the counter. "Do you need something?"

Benny and Joy both suppressed tiny giggles. "Oh, what? Oh, you must have heard me telling Benny how annoying you've been lately," Joy replied matter-of-factually, then gave her a wink and blew her a kiss.

"Ah, how dare you!" Jessica mocked being offended, "I'm not annoying, I'm exasperating. Now, I'm off to take a break, whether you like it or not."

"Glory-be, hallelujah, honey," Benny replied, placing a hand over his heart, the other raised towards the heavens. "Good riddance, I mean have a good break," he winked at Jessica as she rolled her eyes at them, then turned around to walk toward the back room. Before she had taken a step he added a perfect "Bless her heart." They could see her shake her head in annoyance as she continued on her way.

"Whatevers," she replied without turning around, "I'm out! Byeee."

"Aw, I love you!" Joy yelled. Jessica cupped her hands into a heart over her head, then smiling, shot a peace sign at them as she disappeared into the break room. Joy turned towards Benny, clapping, "Oh, oh, I know how you can start getting more experience!"

"Oh? How?" He gasped, smiling. and clapping his hands in return.

Joy gave him a toothy, cheesy grin, "You can start meeting the morning deliveries!"

"Oh." His smile dropped slightly.

"Next week. There's one on Tuesday and another Thursday. Are you available?" Joy wiggled her eyebrows at him. She knew he hated early mornings. He was fine coming in by 9, sometimes 8, but earlier? He always had an excuse, and deliveries arrived before 7 a.m.

"I have a dentist appointment Tuesday."

"Thursday?"

"I'll be there." He said begrudgingly. Muttering "shit" under his breath.

12. Merry Joy

The day dragged on like the last few drops of molasses meandering their way out of a jar on a cold day. Joy was glad she had decided to open later than normal. She didn't think she could handle the quiet much longer as the three of them were oddly not their chatty selves, and she had over-prepared. There was nothing left to do but wait until the next person needed something.

Eryan and Aaron came in around four to man the store and let the 'A' team, according to Benny, take a dinner break, get changed if needed, and for Joy to be able to focus on making sure everyone was all set. The caterers and bartenders arrived to set up around five. She had them set up a small station inside and a larger station outside on the tiny grassy lawn on the side of the store.

Satisfied everyone had what they needed to set up, Joy walked out the front door, crossing the small parking lot, towards the road. Stepping onto the sidewalk, she closed her eyes, turning slowly around. Her breath caught in anticipation, and she opened her eyes. Her gaze drifted over the small banner announcing her anniversary sale, draped over the front porch's railing. Fairy and café lights strung in elegant chaos from the porch to the food, connected to the only two trees on the property. The sun was setting slowly now, but not lingering as long as it would in a week. The lights should be stunning for most of the evening. She smiled, happy with all their effort.

She crossed back to stand under the lights hung from the front porch to the crepe myrtle, on the other side from where the food was. Joy paused for a moment, looking up at the triangle-shaped strands, then up to the bright orange sky above. Few clouds painted the sky, like ellipsis following the dark grey poufs that had threatened slightly earlier in the afternoon. They seemed to promise to abate any storms tonight. The sun cast its final goldenrod beams; softly caressing all it could reach through the dense air. Leaving all tinged thick yellow, making it appear as though sweet tea had been poured on everything.

Taking in the natural beauty accentuated by the aesthetically pleasing fairy lights, she began to twirl slowly, slow-dancing with herself. She swayed to a song flitting around in the corners of her mind. A swallow singing advice about following your heart and you can do impossible incredible things no matter how small or unimportant you feel. Closing her eyes, she drank in the pink warmth of nostalgia, her success. She wanted to linger in that rare feeling of inner peace and satisfaction, of love and pride for herself, for her employees, for her friends, and for her community. Knowing all too well how quickly those moments fade like the sugar in boiling water.

"Thinking of someone special?" chimed a familiar honeyed voice from behind her.

"None more special than myself," Joy said breathily and a slight hint of exasperation. She smiled and rolled her eyes as she turned to face the woman who addressed her. "Isn't that what you're always preaching, Miss Sally?" she asked, raising her hands, forming a 'W' with her arms.

"Sounds like you almost believe it, too," said the older woman, giving Joy a little wink. "Now, come give this old woman a hug, and maybe a hand." She gestured for Joy to come closer.

"Why else do you think my arms are open?" Joy asked as she approached her friend and occasional mentor. They embraced tightly. "It's been too long! You need to come see me more often."

After a long sturdy hug, the women continued to catch up as Joy helped Sally set up her table full of small handmade leather goods. Bookmarks, key chains, earrings, bracelets, and a small slender rod with one end dripping in intricately knotted minuscule ropes that resembled a miniature cat of nine tails.

"This is new," Joy said, holding up the intriguing yet slightly disturbing item, dangling it in front of her like a cat toy. "What is this?"

"That is whatever you need it to be," replied Miss Sally raising her perfectly coiffed eyebrows reminiscent of Groucho Marx. "Cat toy, bookmark, pocket-sized entertainment for the diehard 'Scarlet Letter' cosplayers for behind-closed-doors usage, if you catch my drift." She winked and blew Joy a sultry kiss. "I find that miniatures are fun of all kinds of things."

"Mmmm-k," Joy nodded and sucked in her lip. She could feel a little heat rising in her chest, not knowing if it was because she was shocked or that she thought it sounded fun. Gifts. Yes. "How much?"

"Ooo, got someone in mind?"

"Two in fact," said Joy, a smile spreading over her face. "But don't show these to Jess or Benny!" She added in a whisper.

"I got you," said Miss Sally, getting a small paper bag out. "And it's buy-two-get-one free for you, so find a special someone to use it with."

"None more special than," Joy started.

"I am not talking about yourself here," Miss Sally interrupted. "You need to have some fun! Live! Enjoy life!"

"I am living!" scoffed Joy. "And I'm having fun tonight!"

"And what do you do almost every day after work?" Joy pursed her lips and didn't respond. "And what do you do on your time off? Besides going to the farmers market or grocery store?"

"I mean, I usually use Instashipt so I don't even have to go to the store..." trailed Joy, tapping her thumb to the tips of her fingers, attempting to remember the last few times she had been anywhere besides her store and home. "Sometimes I meet a friend for a meal," she added defiantly. She paused to see if that would fulfill Miss Sally's curiosity. The older woman just waited, saying nothing verbally, yet saying everything with her eyes to draw the story out of Joy. All of her attention, laser-focused and sharp after years of practicing her listening skills. The fading sunlight gleamed behind her, giving her the added appearance of being an ethereal being or possessing some hypnotic power. "You know, you've really perfected your 'tell me all now mom-glare', sheesh woman."

"How many times in the last month?" Miss Sally asked, crossing her arms.

"Twice," Joy answered proudly.

"How many times in the three months before that?"

Joy scrunched up her nose and let out a forceful sigh, "Gah, I don't know, another two or three times?" Her voice rose higher towards the end of the question. Miss Sally glared at her from underneath her furrowed brow. "Ok, fine. Once. I went out once during that time."

Miss Sally gave a satisfied "mmhmm" then pointed her finger

at Joy. "There is more to life than work and home."

"I'm not going back to church," Joy said gently.

"That's not what I'm saying! Church is supposed to help. It isn't meant to hurt. So if it is hurting you, if you don't feel safe there, don't go. And definitely don't give two pickles about anyone else's juice." Miss Sally said while coming to stand next to Joy and throwing an arm around her shoulders, leading her gently back outside to the front porch. "I'm saying you are still so young, you have so much life to live! Find a new hobby- take advantage of your good knees and go dancing or mountain climbing. Take yourself out to dinner. Do something crazy- wear a dress without underwear."

"Miss Sally!" Joy gasped, turning to face her. "I don't need to talk to anyone about my undergarments or potential lack thereof!"

"My dear child, that is not the point. You don't have to tell anyone unless you need an accountability partner." Miss Sally placed both of her hands on Joy's shoulders, turning her slowly to face the parking lot. "Look at all these people, look at what you've planned. I know you've accomplished one of your greatest desires, but that doesn't mean you have to stop here. There are so many things you used to tell me you wanted to do, back before... back when we had our long conversations working in the nursery. Don't let all your dreams die with them." She squeezed Joy's shoulders, then slid her hands down Joy's arms, grabbing her hands tightly. "You are loved, honey, and you are worthy."

164

Joy nodded, blinking tears out of the corners of her eyes. Squeezing her hands.

Miss Sally smiled and let out a little chortle. "Remember honey, sometimes you have to tear the broken things completely down before you can build them back up so they're safe and beautiful."

Joy half smiled, taking a breath through her nose, and as she opened her mouth to respond, a seemingly friendly large group of people all laughing together poured up the stairs. A few of them stepped close to where they were standing on the porch, squishing Joy back against the wooden railing. Someone from in the store called for Miss Sally, she reentered the store before Joy could weave her way out of the small crowd forming.

As Joy stepped through the doorway, Jessica grabbed her elbow and swung her back outside.

"Whew, I need a quick breather while I can!" Jessica exclaimed, squeezing Joy into a tight hug. "I wanna grab a sangria too!" She led them down the stairs and over to the exterior drink table where a young woman in a white button-down uniform shirt handed them each a plastic cup full of the fruity summery beverage. "Cheers!" she held up her cup to Joy's. They clinked their cups and took a sip. They moved to the side to chat and watched the crowd ripple along the sidewalk, some branching off to stop and linger at this place or that. Everything from athletic wear to cocktail dresses were dispersed among the various groups of people mingling and meandering along the way. Some people were on dates, some having casual friend nights draped in comfortable maxi dresses or leggings, then there were the young families pushing strollers, trying to contain the flying sippy cups and fruit snacks.

And there, down the street, amongst the designer yoga pants and jean shorts was Mister tall, beautiful, and brilliant himself.

Lucas stood out from the crowd, an air of dignity and mystery, his presence parting the way like Mr. Darcy sauntering out of the fog. No one stopped him, somewhat surprisingly, but this was the greater Nashville area and most people were used to seeing celebrities occasionally and respecting their space. As one should. That was usually the norm, unless they were tourists.

Joy remembered back in college when she found herself standing in line behind a certain country singer to get food from Bread and Co., which sadly no longer exists, nor could she eat there now anyhow, stupid celiacs. She knew her face had taken a journey through her realization of who he was. Yet these people are walking by him like he's in camo! It had taken all of her to not whisper how much she was a fan of his actress wife. It was thrilling to be so close to the spouse of someone you admire. But she had done nothing because this was *Nashville.* He was just getting food. Let the man be. He's just another human. If he hadn't been on the phone then maybe she would have mentioned something.

Hmm, maybe that encounter could be slipped into my new novel somehow, just vague enough that if on some off chance, they read it, they'd think, hmm, that sounds like that could've been me. Perhaps he'd write to her saying something like, 'Thank you for not interrupting my day, but I appreciate that you were and are a fan of my wife'. You're welcome, country star. You're welcome. She shook her head, clearing the memory and ensuing fantasy from her thoughts.

This wasn't just someone she was a fan of or even their spouse. This was the man she'd had a crush on since college, even when she was madly and deeply in love with her husband, her thoughts drifted to that first meeting for so long every so often. It didn't help when he had gone from virtually unknown to making appearances in random films to having his face be on everything she wanted to see or was it that she wanted to see him so he was everywhere? It didn't matter because there he was. In all his glory. And he was real and he was rapidly approaching her direction.

Surely he hadn't seen me. Why do I hear my heartbeat? Why do I feel like I could fly and freeze time when this is a man I've been having conversations with via text and a couple of short phone calls over the last two weeks. I feel like I'm 17 again, just a hormonal lust-filled mess. Maybe this was what Mr. Sparkly Vampire dude felt like when he was away from MS. wanna be sparkly for too long? Like his senses were so overwhelmed and all he wanted to do was... oh goodness.

"Earth to Joy!" Jessica nudged her. "Look who came!"

"I'm looking at-," Joy began but stopped when she tore her

eyes away from Lucas and realized Jessica was pointing to someone standing in front of her. A man in an extremely fitted light blue checked shirt that showed off his eye-level bulging biceps and khakis was smiling at her. "Oh, hi!" Joy said, trying to place the familiar-looking face, plastering her customer service smile on her face, and praying her expression didn't give her away. "Sorry, I was, I thought I saw someone I was waiting for."

"Oh? A boyfriend, maybe?" He asked, his voice getting the tiniest bit higher.

"Oh, ah, oh no," Joy replied.

"What she means, Chuck, is they've been on a date," Jessica interjected, then emphasized, "But they're not official, yet. So she's still technically single."

That's Chuck? The delivery man? Goodness, his lack of a hat combined with wearing actual pants, and he's gorgeous. Joy took a sip of her drink, hearing her talk, but not taking in what Jessica was saying.

"I didn't know you were open to dating again," said Chuck leaning in. "If I did, I would've asked you out," he added playfully "a lot sooner. So, what are you doing after your shindig? Would you like to join me for coffee?"

Joy was taking a sip of her drink while he was talking. She gasped at his words, inhaling a small amount of liquid causing her to cough uncontrollably.

"Are you ok?" Chuck asked as Jessica started patting her back.

Joy held up her pointer finger to them as she turned away, Jessica still rubbing her back. She closed her eyes, taking slow steady breaths between coughs until she could clear her throat. She took another sip to wash away the feeling of grit. She heard Jessica make a pointed ahem sound behind her and opened her eyes to find her favorite deep eyes peering into hers. "Oh," she softly moaned.

"Are you alright?" Lucas asked, concern drawn all over his face.

Joy cleared her throat again and nodded her head fervently. "Oh, um, yes! I'm fine, my drink just went down the wrong tube is all. Are you? You look," She reached her hand out and patted his upper arm gently to comfort him, then lingering, drinking in the juxtaposition of the softness of his cotton shirt over his solid musculature. "Stressed," she finished her sentence after fumbling for a word to describe his beautiful concerned features. As she felt her insides melt, the worry on his face dropped away. As her insides were replaced with fire and butterflies, she dropped her hand quickly and returned it to her side. She fiercely clamped her other wrist on top of her forearm, restraining the urge to reach out and touch him again.

"Now that I know you're ok, I'm perfect," Lucas replied with a soft half-smile.

The electricity of his words ran all the way from her fingertips up her arms, and she froze. She wanted to move, to look away from his gaze, but for this moment she was stuck. Her heart fluttered while her stomach clenched. She could feel the others' eyes on her lack of movement. Or did time stand still again and maybe only a breath had passed. Time warps happened more frequently with him around.

"Good to see you again Lucas," Jessica's voice broke the silence, reaching over to grab his hand and shaking it vigorously. Jessica's left hand was still on Joy's back, the only thing grounding her at the moment as she still couldn't look away from his face. Letting go of Lucas's hand, Jessica gestured towards Chuck, "Chuck meet Lucas, Lucas this is our friend Chuck."

"Chuck!" A deep loud voice boomed. "My man, you made it!" Joy heard the familiar voice say, but still couldn't find the willpower to stop staring. "It's good to see you out of uniform." She blinked and forced her head to turn slowly but kept her gaze on Lucas until the last possible moment.

"Hey, man! Good to see you not in handcuffs," Chuck replied to Benny in a teasing tone. Joy was pulled out of her daze and she turned to watch the two shake hands and half hug.

"No, no handcuffs," Liam interjected as he walked up a half step behind Benny. He slipped his arm seductively through Benny's available arm, trailing his fingers down Benny's forearm. Benny's face beamed into a broad smile as he grasped Liam's wandering hand. "Later is another story. If he's lucky that is," added Liam.

"Don't you mean if you're lucky?" Benny gave Liam a side-eye wink and blew him a little air kiss. He turned his attention back to the group, while still gingerly drawing circles on the back of Liam's hand.

Joy turned to Jessica. They locked eyes and her eyebrows were raised. "Wait, what?" Joy said quietly.

"I'm sorry, Joy," Benny said at the same time not hearing her, "but there's an issue with one of the registers that I have not seen before."

"Ok, I'll go check it out," Joy said, feeling some of the tension leave her at the opportunity to escape.

"No, Joy, I'm on it!" Jessica said, grabbing Joy's wrist with one hand stopping her from leaving and raising her other one like a student volunteering to give their presentation first. "I installed half the software on those things anyway. If I can't fix it, which is doubtful, I'll call you so turn your ringer on!" She pointedly said to Joy as she started walking away backward from the group. Joy gave her a thumbs up, the tension creeping back up her spine but she managed to force a small smile. With a satisfied yet mischievous grin on her face, Jessica turned to face where she was going. Joy swore she heard her cackling as she walked away.

"So you know what we're up to later now,' Liam said, raising his eyebrows suggestively. "But what about you lovebirds?" He continued pointing his finger back and forth between Lucas and Joy a few times then stopped on Lucas. "He wouldn't let me plan anything and I am dying to know what you have in store for your after-party date."

"I'm sorry, wha-hmm?" Joy stumbled over her response stringing barely audible confused noises as the phrases love-birds and date echoed in her head. *Date, date, that's not what this was... but maybe? Lovebirds? Love? We barely know each other. He's probably just teasing, he thinks of me as just a friend.* "Hmmph," she said as she brought her arms up. One laid across her lower chest, her hand grasping the side of her ribcage, desperate for comfort and supporting the elbow of her opposite arm. She first tipped that hand out, à la the emoji, if the emoji was holding a drink, then slowly brought it to her face, covering her gaping mouth. Making sure to hold her breath this time, she took a sip. Her heart pounded at the awkwardness. She snuck a glance out of the corner of her eye to see how the others were reacting. Chuck had his eyes on her. *Oh, that's right, he said something about a date too...* Benny had a huge grin on his face and seemed to be enjoying his boss being tongue-tied. Joy narrowed her eyes in his direction, hoping he'd say something to his obvious date.

"I thought..." Liam trailed off as he looked from Joy to Lucas, to Chuck, gave Benny a side-eye then back to Joy. Out of her periphery, Joy thought she saw Lucas give a subtly shake his head. Liam paused, then cocked his head to the side and smushed his face together in a confused and questioning expression. "Maybe I overheard wrong." Liam was obvi-ously squinting at Lucas like he was trying to read his mind. "Anywho, is anyone going to introduce me to this strapping young man you were manhandling just a few minutes ago?

Maybe he'd like to join us later?" Liam gave Benny a little elbow nudge in his side and raised his eyebrows up and down a couple of times.

"I want you all to myself," replied Benny in a light teasing tone and gave Liam a sultry wink. "At least for tonight." His tan cheeks turned a rosy shade. Still teasing he continued, "But this, this is Chuck. He is our regular delivery man. He keeps us well stocked with big packages. " He winked at Joy.

Attempting to take another sip and finding her cup empty, Joy asked if anyone needed anything then used the opportunity to slip away and get a refill. She found her way to the caterers and checked to make sure everything was ok. She grabbed another drink then decided she should go in to check on Jessica and the newbies.

Before she could get very far, she was stopped by a long-time customer who thanked her for hosting another site for the art crawl. Joy continued her meandering through the crowd towards her store but kept getting stopped by people she knew, or who knew her. They were either expressing gratitude or congratulations. She finally made it to the bottom of the ramp, as the steps were too crowded when someone tapped her on the shoulder. She turned around to see Chuck.

"Hey, what's up?" Joy asked, hoping against hope he'd forgotten that she hadn't given him a response yet to his bold request.

"Wanna dance?" he asked, holding out a hand, and giving her an expectant smile.

"Um, I, ah," Joy started to answer, looking over her shoulder at the store then back to him. She wasn't sure how she felt about dancing with anyone at the moment. *Sure, I could dance, that doesn't mean I'm giving him a chance. What's the harm in getting to know someone better?* But she needed to check on her store first. Before she could think of what to say another guy she didn't recognize took Chuck's hand and enveloped him in a giant bear hug. She giggled at Chuck's surprised expression as another couple of guys joined in.

"Hey guys," Chuck started, but one of them placed a finger on his lips.

"Shh, just enjoy the love, man," said the one wearing a backward baseball cap and a light blue polo shirt with the collar popped.

"Maybe another time Chuck," Joy said, "I've got to go check on Jess, and looks like you're needed too." She turned and walked up the ramp giggling at their silliness before he could respond.

She walked in. The entire place was crowded. People were

interacting with the artists who came, especially Miss Sally who could always capture a crowd with her storytelling and radiant smile. The newbies looked like they owned the place already. Before she could go in further, Jessica showed up and dragged her back out.

"We're fine," Jessica said. "Go away, I got the register fixed, it just needed new tape in the receipt dispenser. We've got this, go have fun."

"Oh, that reminds me!" Joy stuck her hand in her pocket and pulled out one of the trinkets she had bought earlier. "This is for you, for you and Terry to have fun with too."

"L-O-L!" Jessica exclaimed, dangling the miniature whip in front of her face before giving it a few practice cracks. Her eyes grew wide as a smirk crossed her face, "It's so cute! It'll go great with our random miniature collection! Terry is going to love this!"

"I'm sure he will," said Joy. "Have you seen Benny recently? I have one for him too."

"I think he was giving Liam a tour of the backroom," Jessica winked.

"I'm sure he was," Joy rolled her eyes then returned Jessica's wink. "I'll go make sure he's being thorough enough."

She left Jessica and started making her way through the crowd of people. She made sure to check on Miss Sally and the other two artisans' display tables. It looked like everyone was doing well, not running low on merchandise, but everyone had sold enough to make the night worth it. As she passed the books, she sighed, pausing long enough to drag her finger over a few of the spines. She should have more time to write starting tomorrow, she consoled herself. Nodding to herself, she continued her journey to the backroom, helping a few customers along the way. When she finally arrived, she knocked lightly on the door before opening it slowly. It looked like Benny was showing Liam a few of his famous dance moves. She didn't think they heard her knock since neither one acknowledged her as she hesitated in the doorway. It was nice to see such a giant smile plastered on Benny's face, and from the quick glance, she got as Benny led him through a simple swing dance spin.

Joy fake coughed as she let the door shut behind her. "I'm sorry to interrupt the moment, but can I borrow Benny for a minute?"

The smile on Benny's face immediately dropped into a suspicious furrow as he walked over. "No, no problem," he said loud enough for them both to hear. As he crossed the small room he dropped his voice and whispered emphatically, trying not to use his hand to talk. "What's going on? Is there an emergency? I'm trying to woo him," he hissed.

"Here," Joy smiled and held out a fisted hand. "I thought this might help. It's one of Miss Sally's creations. I thought they were fun." She gave Benny a wink as he stared at her with a confused expression. "I'll leave you two to it then, I hope you have a magical night!" Joy heard Liam saying bye as she turned and walked out before Benny could say anything. He was hardly ever speechless and she enjoyed the satisfaction of making so.

Going was easier than coming. She saw Jessica was now behind the registers with Eryn. She flitted her hand in Joy's direction to leave. Joy took the hint and went with the flow out of the store, down the stairs, and back to the drink table. Grabbing another cup, she continued her journey to make sure everything was ok, pausing only to dance with herself a few times.

As she swayed to the music, she stumbled over her own foot. She giggled at her clumsiness and went to take another sip of her drink. *Ugh, the last drop.* She took a step towards the drink table for a refill but saw the crowd around it, her head felt lighter than it had in well... a long while. *Probably best to switch to water for now.* She walked over to a nearby trash can and tossed her cup. She looked up toward the entrance to her store and smiled at seeing more people entering. Reaching into her pocket, she pulled out her phone. No missed messages from Benny or Jessica. *Everything should be fine.* She slipped it back into her pocket.

For once in the last two years, she wasn't needed at that moment. She smiled at the thought of a break, relieved but fought back the shadow hovering on the edges of her heart. Shaking it off, she took a swaying step away from the trash can, still looking at the people on the porch, staggered and relaxed poetically like a Renoir party painting. She stumbled, colliding with a solid, warm body, and staggered back. A firm but gentle hand gently grab her upper arm, steadying her before she could fall.

"Sorry! I wasn't," her gaze drifting over the long fingers still supporting her and followed the line up to rest on his charming features. "Looking," she trailed off as her heart skipped a beat.

"Well, lucky for us both, I was," Lucas responded, raising both eyebrows and giving her a sly smile. His hand slid slowly down her arm and took her hand in his. He leaned in and whispered something she couldn't quite make out over the loud laughter that had erupted from a group of people near them.

"What?" She asked, furrowing her eyebrows and cocked her head a little too fast as she felt the ground begin to sway.

Lucas squeezed her hand and looked around before responding, "Come over here," he said as led her away from the growing crowd and into the shadow of the neighbor's magnolia tree. "Can you hear me now?" he asked her.

"Much better, thank you." She smiled at him. "So, what's up?"

"I asked if you would like to sneak away with me,' he gave her a sheepish grin, then ran his fingers through his hair.

Oh lordt, those lips, help me sweet baby Jesus. "Looks like you got your wish." Joy bit her bottom lip just for a moment as she imagined tracing those lips with her tongue. *Maybe I need some water.* The now all too familiar burning sensation crept from her core to her cheeks. *I am one of Pavlov's dogs, and he is my bell. only instead of salivating it's blushing, and being awkward.* Her internal self rolled her eyes. *OK fine, maybe a little bit of drool. I definitely don't need to drink this much without a chaperone. Thanks for abandoning me, Jess. Sheesh.*

"Not quite. I would love it if you joined me in viewing some of the other artists. Maybe even getting some frozen yogurt," he paused, then winked and added, "If you're lucky."

Joy placed her free hand on her hip, furrowed her brow, and pursed her lips. "Hmm, tempting," she pulled her hand gently out of his to dig her phone out of her pocket for the thirteenth time in the last fifteen minutes, "No 911s from the crew." She looked over her shoulder and saw all the happy people milling around. People going in, some coming out, even a few with bags, couples holding hands, friends standing in

179

circles laughing, some dancing, a couple kissing passionately under the streetlamp. Her heartbeat fluttered as she turned quickly back to Lucas. "Looks like there aren't any fires at the moment," Joy double-checked her phone again, seeing no new messages she slid it back into her pocket. She gave him a cheeky smile. "Let's go," she said, raising her eyebrows up and down quickly.

"Fantastic!" Lucas exclaimed as he grabbed her hand again. "Let's cross to the darker side of the street, if you don't mind, less chance of being noticed." He started with a little hop step towards another venue closer to the square. Joy followed a little extra hop in her step as well as trying to match his gait then abruptly stopped, pulling him to a stop with her.

"Oh!" she exclaimed, pulling her hand free and patting her pockets. Not finding what she was looking for, smacked her forehead, a little harder than she had intended. "Ow," she muttered, "Ugh, hold on, I forgot my wallet."

"Not to worry," said Lucas, "I've got mine."

"What if there's an emergency or I want fro-yo or emergency fro-yo!?" She looked forlornly over her shoulder towards her store, pouting her lip. Sneaking back in and back out without being seen or pulled aside to help someone would be challenging. She turned back to him and shoved her finger into his shoulder. " And you're being a little sus. The dark side of the street. No ID. What are you trying to do, kidnap me? Keep me away from fro-yo?"

"I swear," Lucas smiled, placing his right hand over his heart. "I have no felonious nor ill intent towards you." He started backing up slowly, pulling her gently with him. "I promise if there's an emergency or an emergency frozen yogurt situation I've got you covered."

"Promise?" she looked back over her shoulder.

"On my honor," he responded.

"Ok," she shrugged and gave him a cheeky smile. He took her arm and threaded it through his. Leading them down the dimly lit street to the next venue. Stars in each other's eyes. Not seeing the delivery man with disappointment painted across his face from across the way.

As the couple explored the various exhibits they discussed everything from the art on the walls to grilling each other about their friends.

"I trust him with handling my life so I think he's a fantastic catch, what about Benny? Do you think he will take care of my Liam?" He asked as they left the church near Point Five.

"He is one of the most caring individuals I have ever met. That's probably his biggest flaw, he stays loyal long past a lot of people's healthy breaking points," Joy responded as they crossed the Point Five intersection to get to Sweet Bee's. After Lucas paid for their treats they walked back out to find the same bench from their first outing together. Joy sat near one end, Lucas waited till she was settled before sitting in the middle. She took her time, embracing every spoonful like it could be her last. This night was too perfect to end.

Lucas scraped his spoon on the bottom of his cup, then licked the last drop off his spoon. He fiddled with his cup for a minute then he took the arm closest to Joy and stretched it on the back of the bench behind her. An older man in khakis nearly pulled up to his rib cage took the seat next to Lucas without a word. Wordlessly they both scooted closer to Joy's end of the bench, Lucas scooting more than she did so his leg was touching hers.

Vibrations sent shock waves through her body at the touch. She felt incredibly sober in that split second and was suddenly very conscious of him. *Why is it when I'm in actual conversation with him, that it feels like he is the most regular person that I've ever connected with? Then tsunami waves of feelings hit and I'm no better than a middle school girl talking to her first major crush. Why is it happening in these moments of silence? Not that they're awkward, but they're quite comfortable, actually. But there aren't that many people I can be in comfortable silence with... Why is that?* She looked down and saw that her dress had slid up a little when she scooted over. *Great.* She gave it a slight tug and saw Lucas raise his eyebrows ever so slightly out of the corner of her eye.

"I think this might be my favorite night here, yet," Lucas said, breaking her silent introspective monologue. "I hope you're enjoying yourself as well."

She raised her head quickly and turned towards him. Her pulse increased rapidly, she hadn't realized how close he had gotten.

All I have to do is lean forward slightly and I could taste his lips.
She blinked and forced herself to look him in the eyes. She
could only pause there for a moment as that sent her off the
deep end maybe even worse than his sultry lips. The drops of
sweat were glistening on his forehead. *Ryan sweated so easily,
he hardly ever glistened, he went straight to dripping. Not that
that matters.*

"I am," she managed to finally say, finding his eyes again. *It
feels like he's peering into my soul. Great. He is probably reading
all my confusion and desire right at this second, but what does
his expression mean? Is he just being nice? Wanting to be with
someone else?*

"Ohmigawd!" a loud voice interrupted her thoughts. "He
schlooks like Lucassss Worthington, who's he with?" Out of
the corner of her eye, Joy could see a small group of women
standing by the street lamp staring- at them. She squeezed
her eyes shut, hoping they'd leave.

Lucas brushed a hair behind her ear and whispered, "Come
on, let's move on."

*What did Miss Sally use to say? 'You don't ever move on- you just
find a way to move forward, eventually, and you take them - their
memories with you.'* She opened her eyes to find him looking
at her with an intense but warm, steady, supportive gaze. The
gaze of someone who knew life wasn't always easy, who knew
they'd never fully understand but they could spend the rest of
their life trying. Or maybe it was just the sangria whispering

hope in her ears and spinning the stars in his eyes.

"I know a less crowded route," Joy answered in an equally quiet voice. She led him into the crowd of people across the street, hoping to blend in so they could lose them if they followed. They turned down a side street going the opposite direction from their destination before looping around a few streets up.

He teased her about not knowing where she was going as they made their way down the darker side streets.

"I know exactly what I am doing," Joy smugly responded despite speaking slower than her normal. "I will fade into the darkness and leave you right here if you continue to mock me. You'll never find your way." She poked his chest with her pointer finger.

"I think I'll be OK. It's not that big of a town and I can just have Liam come pick me up," he winked then stuck out his luscious bottom lip in a sultry pout. "Besides, I would mind you leaving me more." He grabbed the hand that poked him and wove his fingers through them.

"Well, I wouldn't mind kissing you more," Joy sighed, still staring at his mouth.

"Is that so?" The light from the street lamp reflected off his toothy grin.

"Is what so?" She asked airily, slurring her words slightly. All the sobriety she felt earlier had left. Now she was so tired and her head was spinning.

Lucas leaned down close to her ear. With a smile, he softly whispered, "I think you're a bit merry."

She gasped at his words slightly and shut her eyes. His warm breath on her ear sent shivers down her spine. Her knees felt weak. She felt the heat creep up from her core, but it was different, it was fire. Her entire body ignited from the electricity forming in the slight space left for the Holy Spirit in middle school dances. She wasn't in middle school anymore though. She reacted on instinct. No second guesses. No other faces flitted in front of her eyes. Slowly she opened hers. He was starting to unfreeze as well. Before he could move much further she turned her head and closed the distance between their lips. Fast, and light. Just for a moment, she had relief from the burning sensation. She pulled back ever so slightly and whispered, "Well, Merry Christmas."

13. Disgruntled Joy

"Looks like Lucas had a hot and steamy date last night," Jessica said while thumbing through her phone, apparently catching up on the latest gossip news of Mr. Tall Dark and Worthy. "Too bad, I thought he was single and really into you. He couldn't keep his eyes off you at the party."

Joy stopped rubbing her temples and peeled her upper body away from the other side of the counter, her eyes wide. The evening was fuzzy and it was hard to string coherent thoughts together. *Who was his date? Surely, I would've seen him with someone, he hung around me most of the evening... Maybe after he walked me home? Ugh, I should've just crashed on one of my velvet couches, but he insisted.* That memory was extremely clear.

"What are you talking about? And can you please shh just a little? " She held a finger to lips with one hand as the other one held up her pointer and thumb close together, then returned to rubbing her temples.

Jessica rolled her eyes and shoved Joy's water bottle in her face. "Drink more water."

"Thanks, mom," Joy moaned. "I don't think I've ever felt like this after drinking before." She forced herself to take a sip.

"It's because you never went through the crazy party stage. Chug all the water today, it'll help, I promise," Jessica said quietly. "And I'm talking about, 'Lucas Worthington Spotted on Night Out in TN with Mysterious Brunette,' duh duh duhhhh. 'Is she worthy of Worthington?'" She balked at the headlines with sarcastic dramatis. "Oh, look! There're pictures. Hmmm, I wonder if we know her." Her sarcastic tone intensified then morphed into a moan of frustration as her phone took its sweet time loading the images.

"Oh.My.GAAWD," Jessica jumped in place, squealing like the twelve-year-old in all of us. The earsplitting excitement made Joy flinch and cover her ears. Jessica looked up from her phone and sized up Joy, back to her phone, back to Joy, mouth agape.

"What? What is it?" Joy questioned, trying not to sound as disappointed as she felt. Maybe she had misread and misremembered the entire night.

"You kissed him and you didn't tell me?" Her voice rose in pitch as she held out her phone for Joy to see. "That is totally you in what looks to be some serious lip-lock."

"No," Joy squinted and took the phone from her. "No, no, nooooo! Oh, no!" *I'm not mysterious. I'm plain. Plain Jane.*

187

I'm smart, odd, and a little nerdy... maybe a little awkward but I am so far from mysterious. Anything but mysterious. She barely glanced at the picture before shoving the phone away from her. "Nope, must have been someone else that looks like me."

"DENIAL DENIED! She's wearing exactly what you wore last night, her hair is in a twisty bun in this picture like how you always do your hair, and oh my word, it's actually down in this one. Look at you, you're flirting! Ahh!" Jessica started jumping up and down again. Joy took the phone from her again and scrolled through the images. "What happened?"

"It's me." Joy gasped. *That is definitely me. That is definitely him.* The memory hit her like a ton of bricks. *Shit. I did. I kissed him. Shit. Shit. Shit. But, he kissed me back. After I said, 'Merry Christmas' he murmured something about how mistletoe was underrated then brushed his sultry lips against mine, so divine. Softly at first. Barely tasting the sweetness still on our tongues. Then he walked me home and kissed me. Again. And that's when—oh lordt, I practically devoured him then.*

Joy had pulled him down into her, intertwining her fingers of one hand in his luscious hair, holding him to her. The other hand had roamed over his shoulders, his strong solid arms. *Oh Gawd those arms!* She internally facepalmed at her thirstiness.

She touched her lips, remembering how good it felt. Her heart stopped and her head took over the beating. "Who took these? Why are they online?" These were from the first kiss, not of them at her door. She swallowed dryly. "Is this it? Are there more? Gah! There was no one around!" *This is creepy. Far creepier than anything I've ever done. Maybe not thought of—I AM human—but actually done? NO.*

188

"I'll use my magic power of internet research to see if I can figure it out, later. Much later. Ahh!" Jessica squealed again. "I thought you were here the entire time!" She grabbed Joy's arm, shaking it like a small child begging their grownup for a treat. "Tell me! Tell me everything! What did he say? Where did you go? How did it happen? Did you sneak off and I missed it?"

"I mean, maybe we walked over to a couple of the other venues." Joy took a sip of her water. She set the bottle back down then pulled bobby pins out of her hair, shaking it free and making it easier to rub her tense scalp, trying to stimulate her memory. "He asked me to join him and I wanted to make sure he saw the haunted gallery just around the corner, then I wanted to show him the church so he could make some comment about how new it was compared to everything where he's from. Then we got fro-yo. We headed back here after that. I wanted to make sure you closed alright. Before we got here, I kissed him, we grabbed my bike, and then he walked me home. I maybe got a drink almost everywhere we went to help with my nerves and he didn't trust me to get home by myself. I think I overdid it." She crossed her arms on the counter and tried to bury her head in her elbows.

"Like I couldn't tell," Jessica said facetiously. "Come on, keep talking. What led you to this epic moment?" She continued to plead, pushing her bottom lip out as far as it would go.

"Ugh, not now," Joy mumbled as the front door bells jingled. "Customers."

A steady stream of people filed in, flowing into the corners of the store. Jessica flitted around, her laugh filling out the room. Joy forced herself to drain her water bottle before stashing it under the counter. She brushed out her clothes and took a deep breath. This day will eventually end.

Benny came in to give the ladies their lunch breaks. Jessica filled him in on everything Joy had told her thus far, with her begrudging permission of course. Although, she was extremely thankful that she did not have to rehash the story of last night's events and for the giant mug of Benny's famous homemade hangover-cure tea he had brought her after Jess had texted him upon seeing her physical state that morning.

Joy thanked the customer visiting from Mississippi as she handed her the carefully wrapped hand-carved bowl set and a few other trinkets she had just purchased. She tidied up the counter, straightening the crisp recycled packing paper and grabbing the box of extra key chains to refill the display, yet again. *Miss Sally must have sold a couple dozen of these last night alone.*

"Oh my god, Denise, look it's her." Joy overheard a loud whisper. From the corner of her eye, Joy could see two young women, probably still teenagers perusing some rings.

"What do you mean, it's her?" asked the second girl, presumably Denise, with a disinterested sigh.

"I thought the cashier looked familiar, it's the mysterious brunette from the photos. Look, she's the owner of the store. It's the same person." The girl continued holding her phone up to Denise.

Joy was trying to not eavesdrop but she *knew* they were talking about her. She tried to keep her focus on hanging more and straightening the key chains. When she ran out she moved back behind the counter to work on something else, hoping the girls would move away, but they continued to discuss her in their loud whispers while still trying on rings.

"I wonder what he sees in her." Denise seemed intrigued now. Joy's heart began to race in a completely different way than when Lucas was around. "Did you find anything else about her? Like why her? He hasn't been photographed with a woman on a date in months, maybe even a year."

"Oh, Ohemgee, Denise! Look!" the first girl exclaimed, no longer attempting to whisper. She was holding her phone in front of Denise's face again. "Oh, my god, she killed her family! Look at this article, she killed her husband and her child in a car accident! She was driving!"

"Talk about *scandalous*," said Denise. "Do you think they were having a secret affair and that's why she offed them?"

Joy's head snapped up and she could feel the blood drain, pooling somewhere between the soles of her feet and the depths of hell. She looked over to the two of them, huddled over the unnamed girl's phone. Fury flooded her body from her heart to her fingertips. Her vision became clouded by boiling crimson rage tinged with the translucent painful searing white of grief. Her bottom lip quivered in a futile attempt to keep her mouth shut.

"Excuse me?" Joy interrupted, harshly, unable to control anything but the volume of her words. "I suggest you turn off whatever you're reading and leave it alone."

"You were the one driving, right?" the girl persisted, unfazed by Joy's interruption. "So you killed them?"

Her vision turned a murky orange as the rage burned the grief temporarily away. "Do you really think I would be living out here? Free, owning and managing this store right here in front of you, if I had really killed my family?" Her voice cracked as it elevated in pitch. Her face was so hot, she was surprised she wasn't producing steam as her tears dripped down her cheeks, falling on her rapidly rising and falling chest. Her lungs felt like they were in a vice grip. She wished she were a dragon so she could breathe fire at them.

"What kind of monster do you think I am?' Joy continued, not realizing everyone was staring at her. Jessica hurried over to her from across the store. Everyone else was motionless. "How dare you come onto my property and throw the worst part of my existence in my face! You have no idea what I've been through. You have no idea how much pain I have suffered, what the loss of losing the most important people in my life has done to me, one of which is my own child. No, you have no empathy. I won't tolerate it, this, you!" she stammered while gesturing stiffly towards the girls, reminiscent of placing a hex on them. "You! You need to learn grace and compassion and you need to leave. Now!" Joy pointed a firm but trembling finger to the door as she started to close the gap between them. They stared back at her as if she had grown two heads, not moving.

Jessica silently reached out to pull Joy's shivering arm back. Joy attempted to shrug her off, but Jess's small hand held her in place. "Go!" Joy spat to them, then turned to Jessica, ignoring all the other customer's eyes on her. "They need to go, now. They need to go away and never come back." Then she tore her arm out of Jessica's grip and stormed off to the back room.

Jessica quickly ushered the girls out, took their names, and warned them not to return unless it was to apologize, pro- fusely. The few customers in the store began to trickle out. Benny slunk to the counter and helped the few who had wandered up to the counter complete their purchases while shaking their heads. They murmured to each other to see who had any more information. Benny could hear various 'poor dears', plenty of 'bless her poor heart having gone through so much', and 'bless their hearts, they didn't know any better'. Most who witnessed the heated exchange just put the things they were holding on the nearest surface and snuck out before Joy reappeared. A few conveniently "forgot" they were still holding merchandise, but thankfully Jessica had stationed herself at the door to help jog people's memories after returning. A few more trickled in, not knowing the reason behind the tension in the air.

As the number of people in the store dwindled, Jessica took advantage of the break to check on Joy.

"I don't want to talk, Jess," Joy said when she heard the break room door squeak. She was pacing the room, but her tears had temporarily halted and she felt like could breathe properly again.

"You don't have to, I was just going to say, Benny and I talked, we can both stay late, why don't you just go on?" she suggested. "It doesn't have to be home. Maybe a long ride? It's cooler than it was this morning. I think the rain is supposed to hold off until this evening."

Joy started to shake her head no, then saw the sincerity in Jessica's gaze and switched to shaking it yes in return, the movement making her feel a little woozy. She already felt dehydrated—again.

She washed her face in cold water, refilled her water bottle, took another acetaminophen, then left. Without another word she grabbed her bag, not even bothering to change back into her bike shorts that were still hanging out to dry in the shower; she had plenty of spares at home. She just needed to get away from here. *My ass could handle it,* she thought as she hopped on her bike.

People liked those girls; they had no real experience with life. Maybe today they'd learn an inkling of compassion... maybe. Maybe they'd learn that everyone wasn't a robot who thought like them, that people had differing lives, emotions, feelings, opinions—that words mattered. Maybe it would turn out to be a good day. It was a nice, warm spring afternoon but the clouds were filling in thickly, blocking the usual afternoon heat, but still dancing swiftly across the sky.

Weather like this reminded her of playing outside with Peter. He loved to draw with sidewalk chalk, mostly simple lines and rainbows. His favorite was telling her how to draw when he lacked the skill. He loved her shapes and trains. So many trains. It was fun, annoying at times but what wouldn't she give to have one of those fleeting moments back.

That long ride before heading home to clear my head was probably a good idea...

Remembering one of her coping mechanisms, she started to sing to herself, about dreams and thanking ABBA silently as she took in the Victorian homes around her.

She loved to ride past the old stately homes south of town. They stood tall and strong, beautiful remnants of a tormented history. She wondered how many of these were built before the Civil War or if they were all after... She was in awe of how beauty can come from so much pain. She imagined what it would be like to be in another era, walking these streets. Were the trees even there then? Were these massive magnolias but saplings in these elegantly landscaped gardens or had they already grown tall enough to create shade? The sun peeked through the clouds; she closed her eyes for a moment, enjoying the warmth on her tear-stained cheeks. She opened them again to turn at the approaching intersection. Almost too late—she hadn't seen the man just entering the crosswalk right after she shut her eyes. She slammed on her brakes, managing to stop mere inches away from him, almost falling off her bike.

"Oh shit! Are you okay?" she asked, attempting to get off her bike, then wrestled with the kickstand. *Of course today would be the day I almost maim someone right after being accused falsely of manslaughter.* "I didn't hit you, did I? I am so so so so sorry, I didn't see you!" Finally getting it set back up, she looked up at the man she'd almost run over. He was laughing. Even though the sun was glaring through a break in the clouds right into her eyes, blocking most of his face, she could recognize that mouth anywhere.

"Lucas?" He shifted his gaze and the glare off his sunglasses left. He was wearing a runner's hat. *Maybe his way to try not to blend in? Although his tight-fitting pale gray athletic t-shirt and darker grey running shorts would still be attention-grabbing on him enough as it was.*

"It's okay, I'm fine," Lucas replied reassuringly, looking much better than fine, now that she could take him in, even with his face all flushed. "You know, you don't have to run me over if you want my attention, you've only to ask." He leaned in, putting his hands on her handlebars next to hers, his pinkies barely grazing the outside of her index fingers. The hot, velvety sensation was like warm sea air to ailing lungs. She chewed on her lip, not sure what to say.

"So, what brings you out this way today? I can't help but hope you were looking for me"—he winked as a sweat bead rolled down the side of his face—"but your flabbergasted expression tells me a different story."

"I'm sorry," she blurted out, finding her voice again. "I was... ah, there was a... and I, um, Jessica said it was fine." She

196

stumbled, paused, closed her eyes, and inhaled deeply. *Quick, what can I smell?* A hint of sweet evergreen and eucalyptus, the delicate floral of the peonies... She'd spied them along the white picket fence lining the sidewalk nearest them. Fainter, the sour stench of Bradford pear mingling with sweat.

She moaned softly as she exhaled, shook her head, and tried to explain again. "I went on a ride to clear my head. But now I'm thinking maybe I should walk for a bit," she said, more to herself. "Are you sure you're alright?" Joy asked, not realizing the emotion she put behind those words or that her face was wet from tears.

"I promise, I'm okay. But are you?" Lucas asked, gently wiping away some of her tears with his thumb, "Are you injured? You look like you're in pain." The concern lacing his dreamy features wove a magic spell of comfort and distraction.

"No, oh, fuck no. I'm fine, I'm fine, ah..." She started as he dropped his hand to her bike again. Seeing she was OK to stand, he took it from her gently and propped it up on the side of the road and out of the way of oncoming traffic. Joy's helmet strap suddenly felt like it was a small python constricting its prey. She ripped it off her head and followed him. She felt unsure about what to tell him if anything but she couldn't stop herself either. "There was a teenager at the store who was being a jackass and accused me of murdering my family and now I'm pissed," *and I can't get the image of Peter's mangled body out of my head either.* She hugged her helmet tightly and closed her eyes, trying to slow the angry tears.

Lucas pulled her into a slightly awkward and very sweaty hug. Slowly she dropped her arms and let herself be comforted.

She had been numb for so long and now—wrapped in this man's arms, again, on the side of the road no less—she felt safe, safe enough to let everything all out for the first time in a very long time, no holding back. She told him every pain that she carried in her heart. She filled in the gruesome and heart-wrenching details of the crash, about her life since then, trying to hold on to her sanity, about how badly she had wanted to join them. How she sat in the shower one afternoon for hours letting the lukewarm water run over her as she stared at a razor debating. How difficult it was to get out and call her doctor to try something different. How much counseling had helped but she still couldn't get in a vehicle without taking Klonopin (even then, it was still hard). How the girl today had voiced things that she had thought herself. She felt guilty for so long, even though she knew logically it wasn't her fault. It didn't change the fact that they were gone. He just held her, not shushing, not saying anything, just listening. He was there, steadfast, calm, and caring.

A few minutes passed after she stopped telling her story; they breathed each other in, her tears slowed. He pulled her in even closer and laid a swift but sweet comforting kiss on the top of her hair. Though she couldn't feel the kiss exactly, she felt something shift in her, a feeling. Maybe she could move forward and not have to leave them behind.

"Thank you—oh, I'm sorry," Joy said, pulling away, wiping her cheeks with her hands, "Oh, I got your shirt wet."

"It was already quite, eh, moist," he chuckled. "I'm not worried about your tears if you're not worried that I got my sweat all over you."

"I was sweaty already too," she said while shaking her head and rolled her eyes at him. "So no, not worried at all."

He pulled her back into a hug, only this time it was lighter, more playful. "Is there anything else I can do for you?" he asked, rocking her side to side. He stopped and grasped her biceps, bending down to look her in the eyes and asked her with all seriousness, "Would you please join me for a walk?"

"Actually yes, that'd be nice."

Lucas pointed to a house just down the street. "That's where I'm staying, let's drop your bike off there."

Joy's gaze drifted to where he was pointing. *You've got to be kidding me. Am I in a dream?* It was one of her favorite homes in this area of town. She loved to ride down this street just to look at this life-size dollhouse. It wasn't one of the biggest or grandest homes, but it was more than enough, with so much charming architectural detail and that was just the exterior. They entered through the little gate and she followed him around to the carriage porch where he parked her bike next to his car. Then they set on their way.

They walked along the sidewalk in peaceful silence for several minutes until Lucas slipped his hand in hers. "Would you tell me more about your son?" he asked. "But only if you feel up to it."

"Um, sure. I think I told you that his name is Peter." Joy began, "He has blonde curly hair and baby blue eyes. He is such a bundle of energy, like Tigger on crack, bouncing off the walls kind of energy, but just as ferociously sweet. He had the sweetest little voice, like honey."

She paused trying to recall the sweet sound, and smiled thinking of how often he'd climb into bed with her in the middle of the night saying something sweet like, "I want my mommy spot" or just "I need you, mommy, I need you."

"He is—" she paused, realizing for the first time what tense she had been using. "Sorry, he *was* definitely a mama's boy."

"He sounds adorable." Lucas pondered for a moment. "I wish I could have had the chance to meet him. I can't imagine how difficult everything has been for you. That loss is huge. No matter your privileges, the pain of losing someone you love so much is daunting."

"It was. It is. But the living live on, you know?" Joy sighed the script she'd repeated so many times she hoped that one day she'd believe it to be true.

"I think so. I know it's not the same," he answered. "I do think I minutely understand. My grandmother was very present in my upbringing, and she was an avid cyclist. She died in an accident while riding on her way home from watching my siblings and me one evening when I was eight. It was too dark..." Lucas trailed off.

Joy stopped walking and turned to face him. "Oh, I am so sorry for your loss." She grabbed his other hand and squeezed tightly while finding his gaze. "I want you to know, in my opinion, everyone is worthy of being able to grieve over their lost loved ones. We should all be allowed to grieve in our own way, as long as we're not harming ourselves or others, and it's okay to miss them forever." He nodded his head in understanding and they continued walking. "Wait, is this why you don't like me riding my bike alone at night? Why you've walked me home?"

"Not just that, but in a nutshell," he answered while eyeing her slowly. "I care about you. I hope I've made that clear."

"Oh, um, thanks." She felt her face flush. Looking down, she swept a loose hair behind her ear. She dropped his other hand and slowly turned to walk again. "That's good to know. So, ah, what else is going on with you? How is your show going? Didn't you say you were leading up to a big action scene?"

"I am, but not yet," he answered, wringing his hands out, keeping pace with her. "My character is creating some serious intrigue this week that will lead to next week's big action sequence. So far it seems like there's a good balance between the action and plot. I like that. I like it here. It's a different change of pace."

They walked on, transitioning to more lighthearted and somewhat superficial topics like the weather, which color shutters they prefer with which brick color, and what the proper color paint for fences should be. She described the importance of southern colloquialisms like "Y'all" and how they were actually beneficial to the English language. He spouted Shakespearean sonnets.

Somewhere along the way, their hands found each other again. Their walk slowed as they entered a park and meandered along the green way. They ambled down to look over the river; small as it was, it was still enchanting. As their conversation paused again, she found herself resting her head on his arm and closing her eyes. They both smelled of sweat and the outdoor, grassy musk that the humidity bathed them in—a very human smell. She couldn't remember the last time she felt this comfortable, this safe with someone else. Even with Jessica, she felt like she had to put on a show to some extent, not wanting her to worry too much.

The rumble of thunder in the distance interrupted her thoughts. She looked up at him as he looked down at her, giving her a half-smile. She noticed how the clouds were much darker now as thunder cracked and rolled in louder.

"We better turn back," Joy suggested, pulling away, acutely aware of how physically close she'd let herself get to him. He didn't seem to mind though. Walking quickly and as directly as possible back in the direction of his house, he still held her hand with no indication that he wanted to let go. She smiled to herself.

How could any of this be real? No, this all must be a dream. I rode my bike home and went to bed. I'll wake up tomorrow morning, alone, all of this washed away by the sun's rising rays. A few small drops of rain on her arms woke up her sensibilities, a little too late as lightning struck something near them and the thunder crackled almost instantly. They were barely halfway there.

Joy paused, turning her face upwards, and embraced the ensuing downpour. *Perfect. Would this all be washed away before I even have a chance to finish my dream? What is this really, a leak over my bed?*

He pulled her along as they ran back the rest of the way. They didn't stop until they got to the top step of his covered front porch, laughing at the sight of each other. They made it but not before getting drenched.

"I am so sorry. I thought it wasn't supposed to storm until later. Otherwise... well, I would've suggested heading back sooner." She noticed his slick hair was curling in the rainwater as he searched his pockets for his keys.

"Well, it is later." Lucas chuckled as he dug his key out of the tiny zippered pocket in his running shorts as another loud boom rang out.

"Well, I had fun, but I better get home," she said, lingering as his wet hands fumbled with unlocking the door.

"No!" Lucas exclaimed. "I mean, please come in and let me at least get you a towel. You're welcome to stay until the rain stops."

"That would be nice, but I'm okay, but I should go before it gets any worse. It'll be dark in a bit anyway."

He opened his door. "Then let me drive you at the very least."

"No, thank you, but really, it's okay. Besides, I don't have any meds on me," she replied. "By the way, you kind of remind me of a wet golden retriever."

"Hehe, surprisingly that's not the first time I've heard that." His smile grew.

"It's really not that far from here, I'll be fine."

Lucas sighed, his smile turning into a pout. "I think it's only supposed to be a short storm. Please don't add to my anxiety. Come in and wait it out. Have a cup of tea with me, please, I insist. I have a variety of hot teas, sweet tea in the fridge..."

Joy pulled her hair out of her fallen low bun while she contemplated his offer. "Earl Grey?" she asked.

He nodded.

Wringing out her hair the best she could, she watched the water ricochet onto the porch floor. The rain picked up harder and sent a shiver up her spine.

"Okay," she agreed, "I'll stay but only until it's safe to go."

He nodded and held the door open for her.

14. dancing joy

Normally Joy didn't mind being wet from a renewing warm spring rain. This, however, was torrential. She followed Lucas inside and stood just in front of the door and watched him switch on some lights. They flickered a little with the next lightning flash. Her shoulders tensed and her heartbeat sped up to keep in time with the erratic thunder rolls. .

"I'll be right with you, make yourself comfortable, please," he said before walking down a striped wallpapered hall to her left.

Joy loved to watch him walk away. *Ugh, this is so unfair.* Her head tilted slightly as she watched him walk through a doorway then forced herself to shift her attention to the room in front of her. Someone had paid attention to keeping a lot of the house's original charming features with the crown molding, glass tile fireplace surround, and hardwood floors but the furniture wasn't stiff or formal... it was soft, giving off a warm and cozy academia vibe. Very inviting. Her gaze was drawn to what was left laying out on the coffee table: a used teacup... *classy*; a Sudoku puzzle book and pen... *pen not pencil, interesting*; a newspaper... *Wow, I didn't know people still read those anymore*; a short stack of books but she couldn't see the titles, and on top rested what looked like a worn leather-bound journal. If she wasn't concerned about dripping on the carpet, she'd have loved to investigate that room more.

"Here you are," Lucas stood behind her holding out a fluffy white towel.

Their fingers grazed as she took it, sending sparks up her spine. Her gaze drifted from his hand to his person. He had replaced his wet shorts with a pair of navy blue sweatpants, and he was shirtless. *Is he trying to make me swoon?* Another towel hung haphazardly around his neck, framing his broad chest. As Joy took the towel he offered, he tugged at one of the ends and rubbed his damp hair. The motion drawing her gaze down his ribs to his abs. *Sweet mother of mercy.*

"Now, would you like that cup of tea?" he asked, pulling her attention away from ogling his sculpted body.

"I'd like to drink *you* up," she muttered under her breath as the vague memory of last night's kiss fluttered into her thoughts.

"I'm sorry, what was that?" he asked, leaning in. He took the towel back and wrapped it around her shoulders, then squeezed the ends of her hair to help the drying process..

"Hmm? Oh, um. Yes, I said, I'd like to drink a cup. Please."

Joy dropped her head and noticed her soaked clothes were creating a puddle on the floor. "If you don't mind, I'd like to wring myself out first. Where's the bathroom?"

He dropped the towel over her shoulder and trailed his fingers down her arm and found her hand. *He sure has a knack for just slipping his fingers into mine.* She let out a soft sigh and bit her lower lip.

He gave her hand a little squeeze and said, "This way." He pulled her slowly down the hallway he'd just come from. "Here you go," he said, stopping in front of a different door. He held up one index finger, and said, "One moment," then went in the door he had just come from. He quickly returned, holding onto something dark grey and fuzzy. "Here, why don't you take my robe, if you'd like? Then I can run your clothes in the dryer."

Joy nodded in response. Their fingers grazed again as she accepted it, this time making her toes curl. *This is getting ridiculous Joysepher,* she scolded herself and then was suddenly aware of how close they were to his bedroom. *Maybe we can go there later...* Her stomach flipped at the thought. *Who am I? Am I still drunk?* "Thank you," she said, smiling back and trying to control the blush she could feel spreading across from her chest to her face at her indecent thoughts. She tore her eyes away from his and stroked the robe—it was even softer than it looked. *Of course it would be.*

"I'll leave you alone and go make that tea," he said, but out of the corner of her eye, the look on his face said he wanted to stay with her.

Or, is that what I want him to want? Are the walls closing in? I need to breathe. And a spray bottle so I can squirt myself in the face every time I have these thoughts. She was still confused by him: what his presence did to her senses, what he wanted, why he was amusing her. *Is he confused? Or maybe it really is all in my head and I'm the only utterly confused one?* She chewed on her lip as her gaze continued to drift over his form.

"Sounds perfect," she said, inhaling deeply to try and control her speeding heart as she entered the bathroom. She turned and said, "I'll see you soon." Joy hoped her eyes didn't convey too much of what she was thinking as his gaze held her captive as she shut the door ever so slowly.

Joy turned to see her soggy reflection staring back at her from the ornate framed mirror. While Lucas looked like a damp ancient god of muscles and thoughtfulness, she looked like a worn-out scraggly stuffed animal that the dog chewed on then dragged through a muddy yard. *Not fair. Nope, don't go there.* She shook off the negative thoughts as she peeled the sogging scrap masses of fabric that were her clothes and ferociously rubbed herself dry. While she was active, strong, and mostly healthy, she still had the extra loose skin around her middle from pregnancy, stretch marks, and scars. She had never been and would never be Hollywood skinny. She scrunched her nose up as she ran her fingers over her belly. *Nope, would never be the same, but worth every mark.* She pushed her fingers gently across her skin, watching it move like elegant gentle waves sparkling in the evening sun. *Definitely worth it.* She

209

took a deep breath and looked at herself in the mirror again. She smiled. "Well, that's one way for him to get my clothes off," she chuckled, slipping on the robe.

The robe. *Ugh, the robe.* It was more luxurious than any robe she had ever felt. It was a heavy plush and Sherpa lined. It slid against her dampened and now chilled skin like velvet. She wrapped it tightly around her, rubbed the soft collar on her cheek and inhaled. It smelled of him, Earl Grey with a hint of spices and citrus. She knew Lucas was a tall man, towering over her 5'6 ¾" frame (5'7" after a visit to the chiropractor), but the robe dragged the floor. Not much made her feel small; she was usually the taller friend, especially compared to Jessica, and except for Benny. Ryan hadn't been much taller than her. Not that it mattered; height, like anything, was just a number, a measure of matter, not the content of one's character. She knew this, just like she knew the size of her love handles really didn't matter. Still, she wasn't sure of Lucas's character—not yet anyway—though she felt comfortable with him, so much more comfortable than she expected to be around another person. Regardless, it was nice to have the extra fabric, especially now that she was shivering after stripping off her drenched clothes and drying off the best she could. She tied it as tightly as she could, looked in the mirror, and locked eyes with herself. *Okay, Joy. You got this.* She meant to shake her head yes, but found herself shaking it no. She took a deep breath and leaned closer to her reflection. *You're right, you don't.* She looked up at the ceiling. *Dear creator, higher power and all good spirits, oh and grandma*—she smirked—*please forgive my obsessive ogling. Give me strength and will power, to... well, not ogle... as much. And*

*to not break down again, today and... and for guidance with... well,
everything. A woman.*

Checking again in the mirror to make sure she was still decent
after wrapping her clothes in the towel he gave her, she
ventured out to find her host. She tiptoed her way back to
the living room she was in before and heard humming coming
from what she expected was the kitchen. Following the peppy
sound through the dining room, she found him boiling some
water on a gas stove and gathering things for tea.

"Is that an ABBA song you're humming?" Joy inquired as she
observed his still shirtless arms pour the water in a pot. "I
didn't think you'd be a fan."

"I'm a fan of good music that fits my mood, which is extensive," he replied. "How do you take your tea? Sugar? MIlk?"

"Just a splash of milk, please," she responded, wondering
which was more extensive, his music taste or his moods. If he
was anything like herself, it was both.

"Fantastic, that is a fantastic way to drink proper tea," Lucas
said enthusiastically, smiling from ear to ear as he poured the
tea and handed her a cup. "Here, let me take care of that."

"Oh, okay, of course." Joy handed off her wet things to Lucas,
gasping a little as her hand brushed his arm. He was so very
close. "Thank you."

"I'll be back in just a moment." And for the second time that evening, she immensely enjoyed the view while watching him walk away. Shivers ran up her spine as he walked by the kitchen table. Joy puffed her cheeks and let out the breath she was holding slowly like an engine letting out steam.

Her eyes danced over the table. *That looks sturdy.* She chewed her lip as Lucas came back. Wordlessly, he walked directly to her. He tucked a wet strand of hair behind her ear, his eyes searching hers as if in silent question. She nodded her head and stood on her tiptoes, closing the gap between their mouths. He pulled her to him, simultaneously pushing her back against the table. He broke away from their kiss only to leave a trail of kisses along her neck. She tilted her head, exposing her neck. With one hand she braced herself on the table; she explored his chest and stomach with the other one. He picked her up and... her thighs wrapped around him. Joy could feel the heat rise in her chest.

JOY, what were you just asking for in the bathroom? I wasn't ogling... I was imagining. I KNOW, I'M YOU. She blew out an exasperated breath and looked up at the ceiling. *Although, I do have a point.* She rolled her eyes at herself. Quietly, she pleaded, "Good Lord in heaven, help me! It's been so long," not really knowing whether she was asking for help to make her dreams come true or for better self-control.

Hoping she wasn't blushing too heavily, she fanned herself then tried to wash away the sultry images her mind had conjured with a still-scalding sip of tea. She tried to focus on the heat of the cup in her hands, and stop looking at the tempting table. Instead, she attempted to divert her thoughts to discovering the design details of other parts of the elegant yet homey kitchen.

White countertops, antiqued black cabinets, black and white angled checkerboard tile floor, the fixtures, and finishes were all dark... either oil-rubbed bronze or black, she couldn't tell without all the lights on, except for the giant white farmhouse sink... her eyes drifted over the cabinetry to the simple colonial chandelier that hung over that dangerously tempting pale green farmhouse kitchen table with thick, sturdy legs. *Sturdy enough for... food. For lots of food.* She shook her head and closed her eyes, bringing images of charcuterie and fruit trays. Of him lounging in a toga, opening his mouth for the next bite of... *Grapes, I'd love to feed him grapes, He'd pull me close then, pepper my neck and collarbone with kisses... maybe even nibble a little. Mmm...*

"How do you like it?" Lucas interrupted her thoughts.

"Mmm, delightful," she replied dreamily. Opening her eyes, she smiled up at him before blinking rapidly. *He's always doing that... interrupting during the most inopportune and/or embarrassing thoughts... At least he has on a shirt now. That's a little better, at least a little less distracting.* "I love Earl Grey, it's my favorite."

"Something we have in common then," he grinned, picking up his cup off the counter.

"Well, that's at least two things then," she replied. "I also enjoy a good ABBA tune when the mood is right. I wonder what else there is?"

"Do you play cards?"

"I have played in the past, it's been a while since I've had the opportunity."

"Poker?"

"Oh, no. Well, I mean I know how to play," she explained, "I learned how to play with my Girl Scout troop. We used to play all the time but I still have a horrible poker face and I go all in too early. Really, I'm terrible, really," she emphasized as he gave her an inquisitive look. *Oh Good Lord those lips.*

"Me, too," he smirked. "We should have a game of something and be terrible together."

"Hah, okay then, but you'll have to help jog my memory. I'm assuming you have cards?" she asked, somewhat hesitantly. She was fantastic at solitaire but it had been years since she had played with another person. Maybe a lifetime ago, she might have been halfway decent at spades or speed or something. She couldn't even remember what she was good at.

"Always carry a deck with me. I believe there's a stash of board games in the front room, too."

"Ha, Fantastic, allons-y." *Oh, Joy... you're letting your dorky nerd side show. He's not ready for that yet...* "Well, lead the way,

214

and show me what you got!" *Games or otherwise... Joy, stop it,* she internally scolded and bit down on her tongue.

He giggled and appeared to be thrilled with this arrangement. *Maybe he just really likes games? Or he's just lonely? But, games with friends are always fun.*

He led them to the dining area which opened to the living room they had first entered. Lucas found the cards in a drawer of a cabinet and pulled out a stack of board games.

"Is that Scrabble? Do you know how to play? Let's start with that!"

"Words with Friends, the original, right?" he quipped.

"Ha ha, yes."

"I must warn you, I have an extensive vocabulary," Lucas said, raising his eyebrows in concern as he brought the stack of games to the coffee table.

"And I must warn you, I play dirty. Do you like dirt?" *Joy, I told you to stop it!* She bit her tongue harder this time and pursed her lips together so as not to fall apart.

"Oh, I dig it," he replied, turning to face her, and nodded towards the sofa across from where he was pulling up a chair.

"Ha! Love it. Let's play," she said, pulling the robe tighter around her as she walked towards the sofa. *Stop it, Joy. 'Love it.' But that was a pun. Ugh. Puns are amazing.* Despite her conflicting thoughts, she just couldn't help herself from flashing him her dorkiest smile. She sat, making sure she was decent before reaching for the bag of tiles.

The late afternoon turned to evening. The storm worsened, yet they played and flirted on. Lucas was not lying: although she may not have had as extenuating a vocabulary as he, she played strategically. In the middle of playing a triple word score, laughing about another pun, the windows rattled and the lights flickered as thunder clapped loudly.

"I think you were wrong about the storm being short," she commented.

"I will agree with you on that," replied Lucas as the lights flickered again then it went dark.

"'I've got a bad feeling about—'" Joy started to quote. "The dryer! Oh, shitake fudge muffins, my clothes, do you think they're dry?"

"They're probably fine," he reassured her. "I'll light some candles and see if I can find a torch, then we'll go check. If you're not comfortable, I might have something you can borrow if you'd like."

Lucas silently rummaged around a couple of drawers in the side tables, finding a lighter and some pillar candles. He placed them around the room, lighting them as he went, stealing glances at Joy who was sitting with her elbow propped on the arm of the sofa, fiddling with her many rings and shaking her crossed legs. She occasionally let out a long sigh.

We've been having a lovely time up till now so why is my chest tightening? I should have been home already, I need to head home, but why? There was nothing there. I have no plans, not really, to wash my hair maybe, no not in this storm... maybe it was just the storm. My succulents aren't going to wither away overnight. This is just unplanned. I don't like unplanned spontaneity. I don't have my phone charger with me and the battery was low, last I checked... not that it matters if the power is out. The store was closed. There really shouldn't be an emergency. Maybe the tea went to my head? Too much caffeine late in the day. Pfft, yeah right.

Right then her stomach growled softly. She patted it gently. *Maybe it was low blood sugar making me feel anxious?* She was very aware of her food anxiety. —rightly so, when one contaminated bite could throw her system off for weeks. She wasn't at home in her safe gluten-free kitchen. Normally, she kept snacks in her bag. *Maybe I still have a protein bar with me? I'll check my bag after I check out Lucas—I mean check ON Lucas—I mean, check on my CLOTHES. Where did I put my bag? Was it still in my bike's basket?* The thunder grumbled loudly, gathering volume and intensity.

Lucas took a candle to the kitchen and came back holding something else. He flicked it on, illuminating the warmly lit room with a sharp beacon.

"Oh, you found the flashlight, that's great!" She jumped up, flashing more of her leg than she probably realized. "Show

217

me the laundry room, now, please?" she demanded more than questioned.

"This way, my lady," he retorted cheekily, bowing.

"Crap," she muttered as she felt around in the dryer. "They're still damp. Damper than I expected." Joy frowned and stood up quickly from her crouching position. "Oh," she gasped as she bumped into Lucas who had been standing over her. "Sorry," she said quietly as she turned around with her back against the dryer. She was practically wrapped in his arms as he was leaning his elbow on the door frame of the surprisingly tiny laundry room while the other hand had been shining the flashlight at the dryer.

He leaned forward, shifting his weight, and shined the light to a dark corner, illuminating a drying rack. "We can hang them up until the power turns back on," he said in a helpful, cheery tone.

"Perfect, thank you." Joy turned and crouched again, pulling out her clothes then hanging them as neatly as possible with her shaking hands. *He is so close to me, again. That's a good sign, right? What next? What could possibly happen next?*

"How about I make us something to eat and see if I can find something else for you to wear if that would help you feel more comfortable? Sandwich?" Lucas asked.

He wants me to be comfortable here, with him. That's a good sign, right? "Clothes would be great but actually, no," she said sadly as her stomach growled. "Did I tell you I have celiac disease? So, I can't eat bread unless it's actually gluten-free."

"Yes, yes, I do believe you've mentioned that once or twice," he said with a wink, leading her back to the kitchen. "More importantly, I actually remembered, and I stocked up. Well I had Liam stock up for me, just in case. I know I saw some gluten-free treats here yesterday," he said, opening the pantry door.

"You bought me treats?" she asked incredulously, leaning back against the counter next to the pantry, and crossed her arms over her chest. *He bought me treats. Gluten-free treats. That's random and wonderful. And good. So sweet. Food. Nourishment would be good right about now. Food would help me focus right about now and not get distracted by how warm it's getting with him towering over me.* It took all her willpower to not trail her fingers down his chest. *Mmm, I bet he would be tasty.*

"Yes, well, ah, here they are," he said, pulling a couple of boxes of cookies down from the top shelf. "I meant to offer earlier," he continued, "but I was distracted by a ravishing woman in my bathrobe and her sopping wet clothing."

"Ah, I didn't know you had someone else stashed here," she teased, partly a jab at her insecurities, partly flirting and hoping he'd reassure her, partly hoping he was just teasing. "You should just tell her to leave you alone next time, cookies are too important to forget," she added as she took the boxes he offered her.

"Can't be helped," he said, closing the pantry door. Crossing his arms, he leaned against it so he was facing her as she opened one of the boxes. "I think she'll always bewitch me," he added in almost a whisper.

Joy coughed a little on the whole chocolate chip cookie she had just shoved in her mouth as he spoke. She finished chewing and swallowing completely before she responded. "Water?" she asked, realizing how dry her throat was. He immediately fixed her a glass which she downed before saying anything else. While she was drinking he was pulling out a couple of plates and appeared to be searching for other safe food items, like bananas. *Why is a man getting me safe food so sexy? Not fair.* "Can I ask you something?" Joy asked, clearing her throat. "And get a completely serious and honest response? No worries about hurting my feelings or anything."

"Anything," he turned around to face her again and shrugged. "For you, I'm an open book."

"What do you want from me?" she blurted before she could chicken out.

"What do you mean? In what way?" he asked, tilting his head slightly.

"I mean," she paused, thinking carefully how else to phrase what she wanted to know. "What are you wanting to happen"—she took her index finger and pointed it to him, and back to herself—"with me? With us?" Lucas walked slowly towards her and she looked down at her feet. "You know, what do you want from this? Where is this going in your mind? Am I reading this wrong, that you might want more than friendship?"

He stopped right in front of her, tucking one of her still wet loose locks behind her ear. He trailed his thumb along her jaw, from her ear to her lips. She was sure there was more electricity striking in that touch than in the storm raging outside. He brushed her lip gently before lifting her jaw slightly so her head was raised. She met his gaze. Her heart was pounding.

"I want to know you," he started answering, licking his lips. "All of you. I want to hear your hopes and dreams. I want to listen to you, to talk with you about everything, to hear your opinions." His fingertips drifted down the side of her neck, down her arm to find her hand. "I want to have fun with you, to hold your hand. I want you to hold me." His voice lowered. He leaned in further and continued, "I possibly want to fall hopelessly and madly in love with you. But right now, what I want more than anything is to kiss you again."

"Oh, oh,OKthat sounds nice," she muttered, not able to tear her eyes away from his, just inches away. Joy's heart pounded and she wanted to scream. *OMG! Me too! I do! I want those things too! I've been daydreaming about kissing you since the first time we met!* A pang of sorrow and guilt twisted her in her gut. She bit her lip trying to stay focused on what was happening right now and not daydreaming about what could be or what has been, "It's just...um, I don't think I'm... I'm not ready yet."

"What part are you not ready for?" He held her gaze, trying to read her.

"I, uh, it's been a long time since I've done the dating thing, and um, I'm not sure I could date casually. I've never really done the dating around thing and after what I've been through..." She trailed off, licking her lips. *I don't trust myself. I'm scared. I really don't want to lose anyone else I love, and I am a completely muddled mess of emotional baggage.* "I just don't know if I could give my heart away after that. Not so soon, anyway."

"What are you comfortable with, then?" he asked, still holding her hand, sending that blissed electrical current up her arm through to her heart. "As I know I don't want to stay away from you unless that's what you truly wish from me. I wasn't looking for romance when I stumbled into your store. I was..."

"I'm not sure," she interrupted. "Casual friends? Acquaintances? Two adults who keep randomly meeting and like holding hands?" She smiled as she held up their intertwined hands. "I don't want you to go away, yet. I do know that." *I know I want you in my life. I feel safe with you.* But she couldn't bring herself to say those thoughts.

"Ok, then let's not decide anything yet. Let's just eat and finish playing our game, for now..." he replied ominously. "But if something changes, promise me you'll let me know." He quirked an eyebrow.

She barely nodded her head and let out a breathy, "Promise."

He smiled and pulled out a couple of glasses and a bottle of wine on the counter behind her. "I can live with that."

They returned to the candlelit room with lots of snacks and the wine in tow. They continued to attempt to play. Despite the difficulty of seeing in the dark, they were still neck and neck in Scrabble points.

"Guess we'll just have to play another round," he mumbled through a yawn. He rested his chin in his hand and started humming a familiar tune, stopping to finish the wine in his glass. As he set the glass down on the table, she felt more than saw his gaze drift over her body. She raised an eyebrow questioning his intensity. "Would you change your mind," he questioned wistfully, "and Take a chance?"

"Hmm?" Her brows furrowed.

"On me?" Before she could process the movement, he was leaning forward on one knee in front of her and taking one of her hands in his. "Take a chance on me? I know you've been through some horrible things that I have yet to barely grasp but you are absolutely fantastic; you're funny, you're intelligent, you are breathtakingly beautiful and I am completely captivated. We can take things slow, whatever you're comfortable with. I just want to be around you... more intentionally."

"Oh. I-I, ah..." Joy stammered, not sure how to respond. "I don't know, maybe?" She still couldn't believe this was actually happening, that she was here, stuck at his house, having a wonderful time... She thought back to her conversation with Jessica, her bargain, Jessica's prayers, her prayers, her promise. *Maybe, just maybe it will be better this time. Maybe the wine has just gone to my head. But maybe, just maybe not everything had to end in tragedy. Right? I'm not some cursed princess in a fantasy novel, right?*

He sat next to her, their knees touching and held her hands, "Please, just one chance?"

Those eyes, those damned puppy dog eyes. "Hmm, okay. But only if you ask me in song and you get bonus points if there is dancing," she deadpanned with the tiniest tinge of sarcasm, despite her actually wishing he would. If she was going to open her heart to this kind of... opportunity again, she wanted all of it. Like the romance in old movies, and the smuttiest of romance novels. The smooth-talking, the banter, the dancing, the wooing, all of it. She knew it was ridiculous, that falling in love and staying in love were so much more than gooey feelings and grand gestures, but she wanted a taste of that fantasy. Ryan was hardly romantic and she had been through so much; that's part of why she had chosen Lucas when Jessica had pressed her. She'd read his interviews expressing remorse at the passing of true romance in today's modern society. He said he wanted to... at least in his interviews. It was so far-fetched. She thought it would never happen, that she would ever find someone who wanted the same things she did out of a relationship. Yet here he was. However, that was an interview and may have been taken out of context. You can't really get to know someone without taking the time and effort...

"Song and dance?

"Woo me," she demanded, slightly raising her eyebrows.

"As you wish." He grinned and stood up dramatically and began to belt out ABBA's "Take a Chance on Me". He paused momentarily to hold his hand out to Joy, motioning her to join him, and continued singing to her. She accepted and they danced their best like a bouncy ABBA video. For the finale, he spun her and pulled her in for a nice, long dip.

"How could I say no to that?" Joy laughed. He was still holding her close. It felt nice; she was giddy for the first time in a long time. She'd had good moments, peace-filled moments, but this was the first time joy was sparked in her in so long. He brought her hands to his lips and placed a delicate lingering kiss on the back of each hand. Joy gazed back into his sumptuous stare, her heart pounding, her body eager for more, head spinning at taking in every detail that she could. She traced his lips with her thumb, reciprocating his movements from earlier—only this time, instead of tucking his hair behind his ear, she gently pulled his face closer to hers. Standing on her tiptoes to meet him, she pressed her lips against his. This time she would not forget.

"So, does this mean you'll take a chance?" he asked as they gently pulled away. "Will you be mine?"

"I'm not property," she pursued her lips and cocked her head slightly.

"I know that," he chuckled, leaning forward and rested his forehead on hers. "But, I am already yours. If you want me, that is." Joy smiled and wove her fingers in his hair. She pulled him closer to her, raising her mouth back towards his. Lucas pulled back just enough that their lips were barely apart. "Is this a yes?" he asked, his breath soft and hot.

Joy rolled her eyes and nodded her head once. "Ok, fine, yes! I'll take a chance on you." She kissed him again with slow and sweet fiery passion. *You better be worth it,* she contemplated as he enveloped her in his strong arms. As the lights flickered back on, he put on ABBA's greatest hits and they danced into the night.

15. dust and debris

J oy was flitting around the store, making mental notes about what needed to be done before she left. It had been two weeks since she'd been stormed-in at Lucas's house. Two weeks since she had woken to the sun filtering through the unfamiliar blinds, feeling confused yet safe as she took in the living room around her. Two weeks since the slight shock of the discovery that the weight of what she thought had been her weighted blanket was one beautiful arm wrapped around her waist—his arm. The previous evening had come flooding back to her. She felt refreshed, surprisingly so despite being in a somewhat awkward position. It hadn't been a dream, and she hadn't had any nightmares either. In fact, her sleep had been more restful, and the nightmares woke her less frequently.

Other than that morning, they hadn't seen each other in person much as his work schedule had picked up, and their schedules were crossed. He was pursuing her relentlessly though: he texted several times throughout the day on his breaks, he called her in the evenings after he knew she'd be home safe. He had even sent her flowers again—just one bouquet, much smaller than his original attempts. Tonight was different though. Tonight would be their first official date—well, in her opinion, since she agreed to take a chance on him. She smiled and tried her best to stay focused. Thankfully there weren't many customers lagging around. Benny was set to close, as Jessica was off that day.

Benny had always been a hard worker, but there was a new spark in him. Joy wasn't sure what had inspired this change. Was it because he was in training to be a manager? Was it pure pettiness in response to the police incident? Or was it a certain personal assistant putting a little extra pep in his step?

Staring intently at the shelf of hand cream samples in front of her and tapping the top of her favorite pen on her chin, Joy was oblivious to the bell ringing. *What was I supposed to be figuring out? Oh, what we are out of or almost out of, right, hence the clipboard.* She paused her tapping as she noticed a change in the atmosphere around her, almost electric. She made a couple of quick notes then commenced tapping again, drifting back into the rabbit trails of her mind.

"Eek!" she gasped as she was suddenly lifted a couple of inches off the ground as she was enveloped in a giant sneak hug. She turned her head and saw it was Lucas. "Oh, it's just you," she rolled her eyes and let out a sigh.

He loosened his grip and let her turn to face him, still holding her in his arms. "Hi," he said, smiling and planting a kiss on her forehead.

"Hi," she said, squeezing him back. She released her grip, leaning back, and gently patted his chest. She bit her lip while slowly checking him out. The familiar heat that came with his presence was flaring, but it was comfortable now, like she was getting used to being internally scorched. She wasn't sure if this was good like an intensely hot bubble bath that made her feel like a delicious boiled lobster or if she was indeed an actual boiling lobster and enjoying the burn on the way to her demise. "I'll be with you in a moment," she said, tapping her index finger on his chest. He smelled so good, his body heat giving her shivers. "I've just got to finish up a few things here." She chewed on her bottom lip.

"Take however long you need, I'm yours all night." He winked at her and kissed her cheek before letting her go.

Oh good Lord in heaven help me, that was a sexy reminder. Too sexy. She went to finish up so she could get out the door as quickly as possible when she noticed Benny sighing and pouting while he was unpacking a box of merchandise. Tall, dark and handsome hipster Benny, who was always in a good mood, was droopy and mopey.

Joy stopped in her tracks. Something was not right. "Hey, what's up?"

Benny looked up at her with a confused look. "Huh? Oh, I'm just working."

"What's going on? Is something wrong?" Joy pressed, trying to be delicate but also make sure she didn't need to postpone her date.

"It's fine," Benny sighed dramatically. "I just think I'm falling in love with a man who will be gone in less than three months."

"Oh," Joy paused, not sure how to proceed. "Wow, you're already feeling those deep feelings, huh?" Benny nodded. She lowered her voice and stepped closer to him, "How do you know?"

"I don't really know how to describe it, it just feels right. I want to be better with him. Like, he challenges me, but in a good way," he replied shrugging. "When did you know you wanted to be with Ryan?"

"I, um..." Joy furrowed her brow. *How did I know? It was the logical next step in our relationship. We'd been together for years when he'd proposed—in front of everyone—how could I have said no? I didn't dislike him. I loved him, or at least I thought I did. I chose him. He chose me. We were comfortable together. We had so much potential to grow into at that point... I thought we'd have the rest of our lives to get better, to grow together... I didn't think anyone better would've come along. Nobody as wonderful as Lucas...* She chewed on her lip and shook her head slowly, her heart skipping a beat. "No, I don't think there was a specific time, not exactly. But I was so much younger then. I didn't know myself as well as you know yourself." She paused before asking, "So, what do you want to happen with Liam?"

"I want him to stay," he replied, no hesitation.

"Have you asked him?" Joy caught a glimpse of Lucas across the way.

"Heavens no!" Benny followed her gaze. "Have you asked him?" he asked, nodding his head in Lucas's direction.

She watched as Lucas browsed one of the shelves. He stood focused but relaxed. *Golly gee whittakers, that man. It's so unfair. Ugh, yum. Mmm.* "Hmm?" Joy asked, refocusing her attention on her friend. "Well, sounds like that's your first step," she said as she patted Benny on the shoulder.

"Mhmm," Benny replied sarcastically, rolling his eyes. "That's so helpful."

"Well, you'll never know unless you ask," she responded enthusiastically.

"Well, you should take a dose of your own medicine," he retorted, crossing his arms across his chest.

Her gaze found Lucas again. "Maybe I will," she replied with a smile. "Maybe I won't. Maybe I need more time, and I definitely need to get going," she winked. "Maybe you need more time too."

Benny shook his head at her, smiling. She finished her chores then left the store in Benny's capable yet disgruntled hands.

Joy found that Lucas had wandered back to the section he had found her in, smelling candles. "I'm ready," she announced, juggling her things that she hadn't taken the time to shove in her bag.

"Are you sure?" he replied with a smile, following her to the door.

"Yep, let's get out of here," she said, fumbling for her bike keys and dropping her water bottle. They both bent over to pick it up, their hands brushing. They looked at each other, both smiling. "It's ok, I got it." She noticed a used paper coffee cup and napkin on the shelf behind him. "But, if you want to help me, you could grab that and toss it on the way out for me?" she asked, indicating with her water bottle as she stood up.

"My pleasure," he responded.

She watched as he bent over to pick up a larger piece of trash, expanding her view of his backside. *That was nice. He takes orders well... I wonder what other orders he'd follow. Joy, omiword, where is this coming from?* She shook her head and blinked a few times. *Stop it. Stop thinking like that. Deep breaths, whew.*

"I'm so sorry I took longer than expected," she said as they walked down the front steps after successfully fitting everything in her oversized purse. "But thank you so much for getting that, and for waiting for me so patiently, I really appreciate it. I owe you one."

232

"I'm happy to help, it was truly my pleasure." He took her free hand in his. "And you don't owe me anything but if you don't mind, before we do anything else..." He pulled her in close, leaned in and whispered in her ear, "I would love to taste your lips, to kiss you just enough now, that it leaves you breathless and wanting more." He stood up straight, shrugged his shoulders, and casually said, "You know, just in case we get interrupted again."

"I'm sorry, you, um, want what?" Joy stammered a little, biting her lip, shaking her head a little in agreement. She glanced around and didn't see anyone around, her heart beating rapidly "I mean, um sure! Yes, absolutely, that ah, actually, that would be nice."

Still holding her hand, he leaned down ever so slowly and kissed her ever so gently. Joy let out a small moan. She couldn't remember the last time her lips had been caressed like that—perhaps never. Lucas pulled away but she followed, not willing to let go. She wanted to drink him in. She dropped her bag and let her now-free hand roam up his arm to his neck and pulled him back into her, not nearly as gently as he had been. Just when Lucas started to wrap his arms around her waist a series of bright lights went off. The couple pulled apart, staring at each other questioningly.

"Shit!" they heard a muffled voice shout from outside, "I forgot to turn the flash off. Sorry! You can go back to what you were doing! We're just fans and wanted to prove to our friends at home we actually saw you!"

They turned to see a handful of people standing on the store's porch, watching and apparently taking photos of them.

"Well, that's um, awkward," stated Joy, her insides burning with internalized secondhand embarrassment, while Lucas was waving at them. With his 'I am so dashing and totally not at all anxious or irritated' photo-op smile. *He should teach a class on how to do that.* The porch people wished them a good night and left, laughing about the adventures that had already occurred on an evening that had barely begun.

The evening was enchanting, dragging into the early hours of the morning. The days grew longer, the nights shorter. Springs melted into summer as the heat sweltered, and with it her feelings for Lucas. At some point, it was speculated amongst his fans that she was his girlfriend, although she still refused to put a label on anything. It was both a blessing and a curse for the store. An increase in business was fantastic, but she could hardly get through her day without being pestered by people attempting to get a glimpse of him.

Gratefully, with Benny taking over more responsibility at the store, he and Jessica were an unstoppable management team over their new recruits. Joy was able to work from home more, allowing her more time to write, and was also able to avoid the awkward situation that was Chuck. Every time she was there to meet his deliveries, he made it known what his intentions were, that he was ready and waiting for her to give him a chance. Whenever she was ready, of course. All her attempts to dissuade him were futile. He wasn't creepy exactly; he was actually very sweet. It was just exhausting. Perhaps if

Lucas had never entered her store... But he had, and despite her best efforts, she had fallen hard—harder than she thought possible.

Joy's routine was to now show up in time to give breaks, well after any regular deliveries and opening. She would pick up paperwork and the deposits, then leave before closing. She found fewer people attempted to follow her route home that way. Today she showed up earlier than normal so they could have their monthly team—now management—meeting.

"Ah, sweet unity," Joy sighed, wrapping her hands around her cup of hot tea and sitting across from Benny and Jessica on the green sofa.

"First of all, how can you stand to drink that in this weather?" asked Benny as he fanned himself. "Secondly, what is sweet unity?"

"Uni-Tea," Joy replied, indicating the narwhal tea ball. "Narwhals are unicorns of the sea and this is my unicorn of my tea. My sweet Uni-Tea." She motioned her free hand dramatically framing her mug. "You could say that's a whal-ity pun? Eh? Nod nod wink wink," she said, winking and nodding as awkwardly as possible.

"L-O-L," Jessica chimed in as she took her seat next to Benny. "Did you really just say nod nod, wink wink out loud? And that pun was absolutely terrible."

"You mean terribly brilliant," she sassed back. "Besides, all

235

puns are horrendous which is what makes them wonderful."
She muttered, "Well, Lucas liked it."

"Oh, well maybe you've been spending too much time with him," Jessica teased.

"Well, that is all your fault," Joy replied, rolling her eyes and taking a sip.

"Fine, fine, that's fair," said Jessica. "I accept full responsibility. Hey, is that a new shirt? Wait a minute, that's green! You're wearing an actual color!"

"What? Oh," Joy said looking down at her new shirt. "I think it's grey."

"No girl, that's green," said Benny. "Like a hazy clary sage, but definitely in the green family. This is probably the first time I've seen you wear color the entire time I've known you," he commented with a puzzled look on his face.

"I can't remember the last time I saw you wear a color. Wait," said Jessica, her eyes growing wide. "Are you ok? Was this intentional?"

"What? Oh, huh, I guess it is kinda green. I just liked this shirt and I—" she paused. "Well, when we went out last week, I spilled my iced coffee all over my shirt so Lucas went and bought this one for me from a store we passed on the way there while I got cleaned up in the bathroom. I didn't think anything of it."

"Does this mean that you two have, ah…" Jessica asked in a sultry tone, sliding her left fist over her right pointer finger, "connected?" Benny leaned forward, resting his chin on his hand, eyes wide, intrigued.

Joy rolled her eyes and huffed. "Ohemgee, No," she insisted. "I mean, we've connected, but not like *that* anyway. We're taking things slow." Jess and Benny looked like they didn't believe her. "Seriously guys, do you really think I wouldn't tell you? You know everything! Just like we know Benny still hasn't asked Liam to stay even though they are inseparable besides work hours."

Benny reclined, spreading his arms on the back of the couch, and crossed an ankle over his knee. "You know it," he said with a grin. "And don't worry, I'm planting seeds to warm him up and working on the perfect way to ask him to stay."

"Ooo, what are you thinking about doing?" Joy asked.

"Are you going to elaborate on how you and Lucas have connected?" asked Benny, raising an eyebrow. "And I mean explicit details of every base." He exaggeratedly licked his upper lip and gave her a wink.

Joy threw her hand to her forehead and dramatically fell back against the couch. Quietly she said, "Can't talk if you've swooned."

Jessica grabbed a pillow and bopped both of her friends. "Guys, y'all, come on now, we have work to do, although I expect a full report later from you, boss lady," she said, her tone light but her features showing concern.

Joy was still thinking about the concern in Jessica's eyes as she asked if her color choice was intentional when she got home that afternoon. She dropped everything on her kitchen table and lifted the hem of her shirt so she could see the color better in the light. It hadn't triggered anything when she put it on this morning. A little rainbow started to dance across her shirt as the few clouds parted, letting the sun radiate through the window, bouncing through the etched glass on her original kitchen window. Her fingers outlined the highlighted spot.

She let out a frustrated groan and ripped her shirt off, tossing towards the laundry closet before going to change. Walking down the hall, she dragged her fingers along the wall. She paused and felt around the hole she had punched one night after a brutal nightmare and neglected to do anything about. That wall needed to come down anyway. Eventually. She shook her head, entering her bedroom and looking around the room then went back out to the hallway and the hole in the wall. Her gaze meandered to the bathroom as she debated her next steps. Sure, she had plenty of paperwork to do, and a bath sounded nice, but that could wait.

She put on the oldest t-shirt she could find. Black. Black was safe. She walked over to her desk and huffed as she collapsed in her desk chair. She turned her computer on and attempted to write, but thoughts of rainbows and all the colors Peter loved so much, of Ryan who could be such a jerk. Of him getting so angry because of stupid things.

She pulled up a new document and started typing a letter. Of all the feelings she had been struggling with. Of things they never worked out. *It's wrong to speak ill of the dead. Pssh. Even when the dead weren't perfect? I'm so tired of it. That thought process is so wrong. I'm done censoring even my thoughts.* It was time to let it out.

My dearest Ryan,

For so long I have desired to talk with you again. I write now, knowing you will never answer, though I wish you would. I am writing because I realize I have so much left to say, so much I've realized, that I wish I'd said sooner... We cause each other so much pain. Or we did. It's still strange for you to physically not be in the present. All my tenses have jumbled, please forgive me for not editing myself. I feel that if I stop to figure out which one to use I will lose the nerve to say these things. Even now, after so long, and you've been gone for all this time to never return. It's not fair. You were ripped from me, right when I wanted to leave. Now, all of that's left is this utterly consuming guilt and grief. If I had been brave enough to tell you how I felt earlier, we would have never gone out that day.

We never learned how to support each other. I think that was the root of it. I wanted you to be the you I thought I knew, the one I thought would always be there, the you I thought you would become.

I wanted to be a good wife to you, even if it meant I wasn't me anymore. I wanted that until I ... I just wanted it to be easier. I was exhausted emotionally then Peter came unexpectedly and brought us life again. After the newness faded and the sleep deprivation overtook us, I didn't know how I could be a single parent. It was hard enough taking care of him with you. You were there, demanding attention, throwing your dirty socks on the floor, complaining when dinner was later than you desired, and let your dirty dishes pile up. These little things kept piling on. We fought. We yelled. Peter cried. I cried.

It was this. All those little things were just symptoms. I thought it was me, but it was us. You never treated me as an equal. You didn't respect me or my desires or even needs when they conflicted with your whims.

Through the years my desire to help, support and respect you dwindled drastically. But I think we could have gotten help. I think it could have gotten better if we had tried, actually tried. If we had found a counselor, or worked through some program together. Instead, you did nothing but constantly complain about my unacceptance of your constant belittlement of me. Of you not doing anything to show that you cared about me. I tried to take notes to keep track of every way you said or showed me that you cared for me, and not just when I had the house like you expected it to be. That journal is still empty.

We could have been beautiful. Together we could have touched the moon. But you, I don't know if you stopped loving me, or if you never truly did, if you never truly loved who I was, or just the idea of me. I still don't know how to process this realization. I'm not even mad at you. I'm furious with me because even with all of that I feel like a piece of me is still missing since you are not here with me.

Even with all of that pain you cause me, I still love you. I never stopped loving you. Although I think at first, maybe I didn't even know what love was and now... Now, I can't stop loving you even though you're gone for eternity. I miss you. I still want to hear your hello again as you walk in the room, even though its icy tone used to slice me through. I never will again. I know this. I tried to leave everything behind, I moved, I stored away what I dared to keep and gave away the rest. I removed all that triggered the worst of my pain. Why can't I move on? Why am I still stuck?

I know I wasn't perfect. I have my faults. I know it wasn't just you...

In life, my words froze and I bit my tongue. In death, the guilt stays. I beg you, let me go. Take this hold off me. Why can't my life begin again? I won't ever forget you. You will be a part of me for the rest of time, as will Peter. I hope the two of you are together and happier than you ever were with me...

I'm seeing someone now. The things I feel for him are so vastly different than what I felt for you. I feel alive again and it terrifies me.

I know I need to keep living. How I wish you could come with me.

Love always,

Your Joy

Joy saved the document and shut her laptop. She sat staring at nothing for exactly five deep breaths then, without much further thought, she instinctively stood up and walked down the hall. Her fingers traced the outline of the hole again. *This plaster wall needs to come down. Now.*

She dug out her small sledgehammer from her toolbox hidden

in the back corner of her laundry room. Returning to the offending erection, she carefully made the hole big enough to make sure she wasn't going to knock into wiring or plumbing then swung as hard as could. It was as if all the pent up anger she had been hiding for so long took over, bulldozing whatever she could. She grew frustrated with the sledgehammer and began kicking and pulling at the wall, grateful for her strong legs. At least biking helped something. Silently screaming, using her sheer will, the wall fell piece by piece. Dust flew everywhere, coating everything in sight including her hair and eyelashes.

The doorbell echoed loudly through the quiet house.

Great. I'm in the middle of this. I have a 'no soliciting' sign for a reason and I'm not expecting any packages. She hated being interrupted during a home project. Unless prior arrangements had been made, she never wanted to be disturbed while at home. Home was solitude., her fortress. Hardly anyone had ever been inside, other than Jessica. Lucas had only ever walked her to her kitchen that one time. All the other times he'd walked her home, she hadn't let him inside... *Phone calls, texting, emails. Please use those methods of contacting me to set up a time to come over.*

She shook out some of the dust from her hair. The plaster fell to the floor, reminding her of a bad case of untreated dandruff during the winter. "Oh well," she muttered to herself as she watched the dust fall, "maybe it'll scare whoever it is off faster."

Attempting to muster up her best bitch face to intimidate the intruder away, she swung her front door open. The air movement shook some more dust from her hair and into her eyes. "If you're selling something I'm not interested," she said, brushing the dust away before it further blinded her. Blinking rapidly, she could barely make out who was in front of her.

"Hi," Lucas greeted, one hand leaning on her front door frame. "Are you alright?"

Well, shit. Joy shook her head causing more dust to fall and chuckling to herself. "Of course it's you."

16. first comes demo

"Of course! It had to be you," Joy couldn't help chuckling at the juxtaposition between his immaculate outfit and dazzling smile, and the mess that was her, her house, and well, her life in general. "What're you doing here? Come on in," she stepped back and held the door open for him. "I thought you had to work late tonight?"

"Sorry for the intrusion. There were some technical difficulties so we wrapped early," Lucas said. He stood in the middle of her front room, eyeing her space as she closed the door behind him.

The room was a stark contrast from her store filled with bold colors. The television stationed at the end of the small rectangular living area stood out brashly against its pale surroundings. Everything was layered in white, like a sanitized southern home magazine farmhouse spread. From the white entertainment center- if you could call it that, to the cotton white coffee table standing on the cream rug to the parallel ivory sofas where various shades of complementing off-white blanket of varying textures were strewn about.

Nothing adorned the paneled walls painted a smokey white which almost passed as pale grey. In what used to be the formal dining room was a solitary oversized linen white chair facing the white bookshelf which held some of the only other source of contrast in the space in the spines of the books overflowing their shelves. Even the hardwoods were bleached. It was crisp, clean yet surprisingly cozy.

"I didn't have anything I absolutely had to do," he continued. "So I thought I'd surprise you and see if you were available for dinner."

"Well, that was very nice of—of-of—" she attempted to say until she sneezed. "Ah-achoo. Excuse me—you." She rubbed the back of her hand on her nose. "Um, hold on," she said as she backed out of the room. She shook the plaster from her hair again and attempted to brush it off her arms as she walked toward the kitchen, leaving dusty footprints in her wake.

"It's nice to finally see beyond the kitchen," he said, following several steps behind to avoid the cloud of the unknown substance trailing off her, lingering just past the doorway that led to the rest of home. Joy grabbed a towel hanging from the cabinet below the sink and held it under the faucet. "So what's all this?" he asked as she finished her attempt to scrub her face clean and turned to face him. He nodded his head, indicating towards the pile of rubbish and scattered tools all over the hallway as she blinked and opened her eyes.

"Oh... that." She leaned back against the sink. "I started writing again," she said nonchalantly and shrugged her shoulders.

He raised his eyebrows at her. "Ah, yes. That perfectly explains why you answered the door while holding a sledge-hammer, covered in what I hope is dust, and looking like you were ready to pounce like a cougar."

She looked down to see the tool laying on the counter beside her; it felt so second nature to her, she had forgotten she was holding it. She shrugged.

Lucas tilted his head and said, "I must say, the dusty look works for you."

"Gee, thanks." She looked down at her feet. "It's a compli-cated process, you see," she said coyly and smirked. "I was trying to get back into writing mode. It helps clear my head but sometimes I have to clean something else up in my life so that my head has enough room to clear itself out. I tried to brain dump but it didn't help today. So I decided to take down a wall. Does that make any sense?"

"Actually, absolutely." He plucked a piece of debris out of her hair then continued. Joy's heart fluttered as she leaned into his hand for just a moment. "When I'm preparing for a new role, I have to research the character and try to get in his head. When it's time to perform, I tap into that but I feel like I act my best when I first clear my thoughts of myself," Lucas explained.

"Right, exactly." She nodded her head up and down, then side to side. "No, I have no idea what you're talking about but wait... hmmm." She started stroking her chin in thoughtful agreement. "Hmm, yes... I think I get it." *Clearing the thoughts of myself, hmm.* She continued stroking her chin, trying to see if she could clear her mind. Her thumb ran across a random chin hair that she had obviously missed for a long time as it felt at least two inches long. *I wonder what it would look like if I grew it all out instead of plucking almost daily. Would I have enough hair to pull off a goatee?* While she had a full head of thick hair, and a face covering of peach fuzz, she also had not-so-peachy fuzz over the majority of her body, which she routinely rid herself of ever since her middle school friends caught on that she hadn't actually started shaving despite her best deflections. She had begged her mom for her own razor that very evening and thus started the whole now-loathsome routine. *Would it even bother me to stop shaving? There is nothing like the satisfaction of the feeling of freshly shaved legs slipping into smooth clean sheets. If I slipped into bed a full-on woolly mammoth and rubbed my legs on his, would Lucas mind if my legs were furrier than his? Well, if we were entwining other things then maybe not so much, if we ever get to that point... maybe I can look into laser-hair removal.* She let out a soft sigh and smiled to herself, biting her lower lip.

Lucas cleared his throat. "That's quite a thought journey you've been on, if your facial expressions are any indication."

"Oh!" She jumped. *It's so easy to get lost in my thoughts whenever he's near. Or maybe it was just kitchens?* She eyed her small round table. *Damn, that kitchen table would just not work like his would.* Her gaze drifted back to find him looking at her expectantly with his eyebrows raised. *Shit, I still haven't answered him.* "Wouldn't you like to know?" she asked playfully, raising an eyebrow.

"I am intrigued." He pursed his lips and shrugged his shoulders.

"If you're lucky, maybe I'll show you later," she said with more confidence than she felt. "But I need to finish this first." She winked.

"Oh really? Then by all means, please continue... eh..." He gestured to the mess. "What exactly is your plan?"

"Um, I'm knocking a wall down," she said like it should be blatantly obvious. She strutted over to the wall that framed in the breakfast nook of the kitchen. "Well, a hole in the wall. I need to see if this is load-bearing, which I think it's not. I think that one is load-bearing." She pointed to the wall creating the hallway between the living room and the kitchen. "So, if it's safe, then I'm going to knock this one down." She gestured back to the wall with the hole. "And eventually, I'll at least make that doorway larger if not take the whole thing down. This place is so small that just this tiny change will open up the whole house." She held her arms out wide then shrugged. "Then maybe one day I'll flip it, but it works for now." *Since it's just me.* She envisioned the finished space, sipping coffee at her table, looking out on the living room. The empty living room. *Le sigh.* Her smile slipped into a frown.

248

"It sounds like you've got it all figured out then," he said as if he had all the confidence in the world in her. She looked up at him to meet his gaze and flashed him a smile.

She was almost numb to the scorching of her insides that getting lost in his gaze produced. "So, you wanted to hang out? What would you like to do? Wanna watch or help? Or have a cup of tea or something?" She bit her lip as the image of pushing him up against the shower wall flashed across her mind... the dust turning to mud as it mingled with the water rolling down her skin to escape down the drain. Maybe she didn't *have* to finish this project tonight...

"Why not both?" He shrugged, then started rolling up sleeves, revealing his luscious forearms. "It'll be fun."

Joy inhaled sharply as he leaned over to pick up her other, even smaller sledgehammer. "Mm," she grunted, "so fun."

The two of them worked together to tear out the rest of the small wall. He kept teasing her, finding ways to reach around her, touch her, tickle her. The first couple of times, she wasn't bothered. The look she gave him the next time warned him off. —*this is demolition time, not flirty flirt time*, she thought as she smirked. Lucas raised his hands as he backed off and gave her plenty of room. She was able to finish tearing down the lath and push through the plaster on the other side. While doing a small celebratory 'I'm a bad ass' dance, she noticed he was just standing there, looking at her and giggling. Her smile dropped.

"What?" she asked.

"Nothing," he grinned. She squinted at him, staying silent, waiting for more. "You're fantastic," Lucas added. "You just kicked a wall down, barefoot. It's very... "

"Very what?"

"Let's just say, I might have discovered a new kink."

"Oh, OK." She couldn't help smiling at his reply. "Good. I guess I am kind of a bad ass, aren't I?" She flexed her bicep and patted it. "Good job, girls," she whispered.

"A breathtakingly beautiful bad ass." He walked over to her and leaned his forehead against hers. "A beautiful, disgusting bad ass that I would like to properly kiss if you weren't completely covered in debris."

"Um, gee, thanks," she replied, heavily lacing in the sarcasm. "You're pretty nice, but gross yourself, you know."

"Oh, I know." He pulled her into a tight hug. "How about we clean up and have that cup of tea?"

"Sounds tea-riffic." She smirked as he let out an amused grunt.

She pulled out a couple of trash bags and her dustpan and broom from the laundry closet in the corner of the kitchen. After they filled one bag with debris, she took it out then scrubbed her hands enough to start boiling some water in her white electric kettle. She found her white ceramic teapot and her favorite Earl Grey loose leaf tea. She prepped the tea ball and set out two white mugs while he continued to sweep up the smaller bits and dust meticulously.

He makes even the mundane look appetizing. She licked her lips, eyeing him up and down. She immediately regretted it as the gritty sour dust coated her tongue. *Eww, gag. This must be why people wear protective gear like masks, to prevent disgusting mistakes like that. Next wall I pledge to at least wear a bandana.* She grabbed a towel to wipe her face on, then set out a clean hand towel for Lucas. The back of her hand was stained; she glanced at him, then down at herself and back to him. She shook her head—he was going to need a bigger towel and another trash bag. While he had escaped most of the calamity that she had fully fronted, he was still covered in clumps and dust. *Still drool-worthy, tho. Not fair.*

They finished tidying up what they could without getting a mop out as the tea steeped then sat at her small round white kitchen table.

"Thank you," Joy said as she poured. "That was so much easier with an extra pair of hands."

"I'm happy to be of service," he replied. "How is your head? Did it work? Any clearer?"

"Well, to be honest, it's cleared of my earlier clutter, but it's filled back up with this new dusty distraction of an incredibly delicious man in my kitchen," she teased.

"Oh, is that so?" he said, setting down his cup. He pointed to the door and acted like he was going to stand up. "Do you want him to leave? I'm sure he wouldn't mind if that was what you actually wanted."

"No!" Joy exclaimed, boisterously as she grabbed the arm he was pointing with, preventing him from leaving. "I mean, I'm not in the mood to write anymore," she attempted to recover. "I like him—you. I like you. I like you here, with me. I know you're just being silly, but—" She stumbled over her words and interlaced her fingers with his. Giving him a coy smile, she locked eyes with him, her heart beating faster than a hummingbird's. "Stay?"

"Well, if you insist," he sighed sarcastically.

"I do, in fact," she said, pulling him closer to her and wrapping his entwined hand around to the small of her back. "Why don't you finish your tea, while I shower then I will make us dinner? And maybe watch a movie or something?"

"I think that sounds marvelous," he said, wrapping his other arm around her and she raised hers to his shoulders.

"You know what?" she asked, brushing some of the debris off his shoulder. "I think I even have something you can wear if you'd like to shower too."

"I'd love to shower too," he raised his eyebrows a couple of times quickly. "With you, if that's an option," he added, biting his bottom lip, hiding a cheeky grin.

Joy's breath hitched and her fire within competed with itself where it should turn, her cheeks or her gut. *This man was sent to torment me. Not fair, not fair, not yet, yes but not yet... maybe... No, not yet.* "After me," she squeezed out, eyes wide, her breath returning. "Maybe... sometime in the future," she mumbled and immediately felt the fire of discomfiture and desire making its decision to dominate and claim her entire internal anatomy.

"Is that right? So, you're telling me that in the future, there's a chance?" he asked, squeezing her tightly against his chiseled chest and glancing down at his watch. "Five minutes far enough?"

She immediately leaned back as far as she could against his grip and squinted at him. She pursed her lips then rolled her eyes as she patted his upper pec. "Hold your horses, mister, you weren't supposed to hear that."

"I'll hold them for you, waiting for your word that you need their service."

"Well... I'll just have to hold on to that piece of information," she said, flustered. "Now, let me go or we'll never eat."

He gave her one more squeeze and slowly released his grip on her, trailing his fingers down her back. Joy left him drinking his tea at her table. *Not in the shower, not the first time, especially not when I have no idea if any of this grossness has seeped to any unsightly places.* She reassured herself as she locked the bathroom door, more for her lack of trust in herself as a visible reminder to not call him to join her. She turned the water on and undressed.

While waiting for the water to warm up she wiped the counter down and double-checked to make sure it seemed to be a presentable bathroom. Not immaculate like a hotel, but clean enough for guests to come over and use without them fearing for their safety or your hygiene. She stepped into the stream of perfect lobster boiling-temperature water, soaking her long hair and applying conditioner first to help the paste slide off. *That's what we did after food fights at camp, so that should work... Right?* She scrubbed off as much of the white grimy powder that was now a cakey mess that she could with her washcloth. After shampooing and conditioning several times, her hair eventually became more manageable. *Should I shave? Just in case?* She picked up her razor and stared at it. *No, I shouldn't. But I want to... but do I need to?* She felt behind her knee. *Definitely, I should.* She rinsed the shower out after she finished, then tidied her bath products, making sure everything that he might need was out and easy to see.

Wrapped in one of her fluffy white bath sheets, she took a deep breath before opening the door and walked determinedly to her room. Even though it was only about three quick steps before she was in her sanctuary, it felt like a mile tonight. Making it there without incident, she reached for her favorite grey sweatpants and a black tank top with a built-in bra—comfortable, supportive enough, and coverage all in one. She debated choosing something a little racier while digging around in her drawers; her hand grazed a black satin PJ tank and shorts set with the lacy trim. She loved to wear this with her vintage black and white floral silk robe when she was feeling dramatically nostalgic and inspired to write, or just when she wanted that smooth sensation caressing her skin. She wrinkled her nose as she fingered the lace. *Nah, definitely prefer the call of cottony comfort. The sweatpants go better with tea anyway, the silkiness goes better with coffee.*

After dressing, she scrunched her hair in her towel to make sure she wasn't completely dripping, then gently laid it over the back of her desk chair. S picked up the men's sweatpants and oversize t-shirt she had also laid out while searching for her clothes. They had been her grandfather's; she had worn them mostly when she was pregnant but kept them because of the sentimental value. It was probably the only thing she had left clothing-wise that she could tie to Peter. She smiled at the warm memory as she set them on the bathroom counter next to the clean towel she had already placed there for Lucas.

She walked back, tiptoeing around the messy corner but Lucas wasn't there... but his shoes, socks, and something else were in a crumpled pile by the back door. She peeked through the opening to the front rooms and saw him standing near her TV, looking at one of her movies. He was in his white undershirt and had rolled up the bottoms of his pants. *So that's why ankles were all the rage back in Benjamin Franklin's day...*

"Hey," she said, shifting her focus on the TV behind him before she lost all the cool she had just gathered while getting dressed. "Just wanted to let you know the shower's open."

"Fantastic, thank you," said Lucas, putting the movie down on the coffee table where it had rested with her stacks of recently watched favorites. The rest were somewhat hidden in the TV cabinet, one of her few unkempt habits about her home. "You have quite the collection. Most don't bother."

"Huh, I guess. Never thought about it much," Joy answered. *Dear Lord, please let him not have noticed I have every single one of his movies.* She cleared her throat and blundered on, "I'm too cheap for cable or internet at home, so I buy used copies or rent. The library is so close, it's easy."

"It's a very eclectic collection. Some of my favorites actually." He held up one of his superhero movies and gave her a wink before setting it back down and picking up a couple of her sci-fi space movies. "But I love these. The cinematography is gorgeous, the practical special effects and the nostalgia of it all are just utterly enchanting."

"Oh, mhmm." Joy chewed on her bottom lip. "I like all that too, but the pew-pews and the swishes are what really brings me, uh, joy."

He raised an eyebrow and cocked his head to the side. "The sound effects in general or specifically the pew-pews?" Lucas chuckled. "Why do you think that is?"

She shrugged. "I don't know. I haven't really thought about it... it's soothing or something...but I do like to imagine what someone is doing to make all the extra sounds. You know, the not-natural ones picked up during filming. You probably know all about this—" Joy paused a moment, then took a big step into the room. Her words sped up as rambled on, waving her hands around enthusiastically emphasizing what she was saying, "Like, I know there's a lot of computer-engineered sound but you can't do that for everything. For instance, the art of making all the sounds in an animated film per se, it's pretty cool how they start from scratch. I like to wonder about how the sound effects people just lock themselves in a sound room with so many microphones and a whole world of objects at their disposal to just *play* with and *create*." She dragged out the words 'play' and 'create' like she could stroke them and make them purr. "How do they make the specific sound they're going for, like for the swish, did they use some fabric and hold it like a cape and swish their arms around, or were they jumping around the room trying to get the fabric to brush up against different objects and a fan, or was it made by using some sort of brush stroking a makeshift drum? I just think that has to be one of the most fun jobs ever... playing and getting paid. Who wouldn't want to just play all day? So cool."

Joy's gaze drifted back to Lucas. He was just staring at her, a goofy smile on his face. Joy realized her hands were still in the air, so she immediately brought them down to her sides before grabbing one of her elbows, her free hand swinging slightly. She hadn't realized she was making such a dramatic scene; she only talked with her hands when she was really enthusiastic about something, which was rare now for her to let her guard down. She was normally careful and in control of herself. *Oh great, there I go infodumping again.* She sucked in

257

her lips. *What was it about this man that befuddles me so much?* "Sorry," she apologized.

"Whatever for?" He chuckled, flashing her his adorable grin.

Oh my goodness, he's cuter than a puppy dog. "Word vomit?" She shrugged and brought her hands together, fiddling with her rings that she still hadn't taken off.

"I have never given that much thought about sound production before. That was beautiful. I have always loved acting; to take on a different role, the psychology behind each character, to explore someone else's psyche. I never thought any other part of it sounded as fun, until now... listening to you describe it. What else do you like?" Lucas asked, grinning again.

"Your smile." Joy sighed. "Oh, shit." *I said that out loud. I said shit out loud too. Shit.* He giggled and flashed her a cheesy grin. "Oh, don't go inflating your ego too much, it's just... I'm still not used to seeing you in person. You're supposed to be virtual... like your movies and on Pinterest but now you're here in my living room... and you're just *so* nice. Nice to talk to *and* nice to look at and I'd be lying if I said otherwise." She hoped her cool tone was good enough to convince him that she, in fact, was still as bad as any other fangirl of his.

"So, what you're saying is, you've pinned me?" he said, grinning harder and eyeing her mischievously, that mischievous smile she loved, that smile she'd seen a thousand times before, especially when he played a villain, stepping towards her. "And that you like me, here, in your home? How many boards am I on?"

Oh dear God, help me dead sweet Lord Baby Jesus, she prayed silently, bobbing her head up and down. "Mmm-hmm... um, shower. You should shower... and I'll forage for food."

"You have, haven't you?" His eyes twinkled.

Did his teeth just sparkle in the light? This is so incredibly unfair.

"And if it's any consolation, I've pinned you too. Well, your book."

"Oh, OK." She cocked her head slightly to the side and shrugged. "So I guess we're even then." She turned around, eyes wide and mouthed *"omigawd"* to herself.

"So you're admitting it," Lucas pressed, moving right in front of her.

"Yes. Fine, I admit it. I have pinned you. I have pinned you in everything from when you were the villain to the crazy doctor to just you. I think you're a beautiful man and you seem sweet and fascinating and I just like to look at you. You give me hope that fantasies can come alive," Joy responded more boldly than she intended. *Shit, I just meant to say yes. Oh well, bandaid's off now.* She continued stoically, "While we're confessing all the stanning, I've also listened to you read Shakespeare."

"Hehehe, really?" Lucas chuckled, blushing slightly. "Did

you like it?"

"Did I like it? Pssh. Of course I did. It's the voice. If you didn't notice, I like it. I kinda have a thing for it and think it's adorably sexy and incredibly unfair since you're already freaking fantastic without that or this." She gestured from his face to his feet and back up again, eyeing him the whole time.

"That's nice to know."

"I'm glad you're flattered. But now I really need to find food for me at least." She puckered out her bottom lip, pouting and rubbed her stomach. "Poor thing is saying she's being neglected." Joy turned on her heels and walked to the kitchen. She mouthed 'holy shit, what was that?' to the floor in front of her before adding, "You're not sitting on my couch without a shower. Clothes and towels are on the counter. Chicken or fish?" she yelled over her shoulder while eyeing the practically empty freezer save for two items, a half-eaten container of ice cream and a frozen bag of spinach.

"Either would be wonderful," he said, barely audible as he made his way down the hall to where she had disappeared earlier.

She crossed herself before opening the fridge and pantry, praying that she had something else edible and enough of whatever to serve both of them. After digging through all the drawers of her fridge and pulling half the contents of her pantry out, she managed to create a simple cranberry and walnut salad while she roasted salmon drizzled with olive oil and topped with fresh basil and garlic. Thankfully she still had a gluten-free baguette hiding in the back of her freezer behind the ice cream carton as she had discovered her kitchen was seriously lacking in carbs due to her having already eaten all of them in their divine deliciousness.

After he returned, looking divine himself in those borrowed sweats, they devoured their dinner, sharing flirty glances across the table. Without being asked to, he helped her clear the table and rinse the dishes before they chose a movie. After she put on a classic parody, he reached for her hands and pulled her to sit next to him, still holding her hand, delicately, gentlemanly, comfortable.

As the movie stretched on, they stretched out, collapsing into each other the more they laughed. When the movie ended, they froze, Joy suddenly aware of how unguarded she had become.

"I'm thirsty, do you want something? I have iced tea and water," Joy asked, standing up, avoiding looking at his face in the dimmed light.

"Water would be lovely," he responded sweetly.

"I'll be right back," she said, walking to the kitchen.

She pulled two clean glasses down, her shaking hands clanking them together. She felt like she had been electrocuted, like she'd grabbed onto the wrong wire of an electric horse fence., enough to feel the uncomfortable heat but not enough to cause major damage—yet. The feeling of his chest under her head, his arms holding her, more comforting than a weighted blanket... *That night we got caught in the rain was a fluke, right? Other than holding hands and a few not-so-chaste kisses, we haven't touched... much. He was so respectful of my desire to take things slow. But that was the logical side of your brain and fear,* her internal monologue analyzed. *Your heart says go deeper, you fell a long time ago. Doesn't your body instinctually keep leading you to him? You're like magnets.* She took a deep, clarifying breath. *What if I stopped letting fear win?* She put the filtered pitcher back in the fridge then turned to go back to the living room.

"Oh!" she gasped. Lucas had followed her and he was leaning against the door frame. He looked like he walked straight out of a magazine. She handed him his glass. *Maybe I should spill it just to see if he'd take his shirt off. No... don't be creepy, but I do wonder what it would feel like to trail my fingers down his bare chest. Get it together Joysephine! Well, it has been years since Ryan... since the last time I touched any man, not just holding hands and sweet kisses, really intimately touched someone.*

"Thank you. Do you want to watch another movie?" Lucas asked, taking the glass she offered him and drinking a sip.

Joy shook her head slowly no.

"It is getting late. I can go if you want," he pointed out, his bottom lip pouted slightly.

Joy chewed on her bottom lip and shook her head no again. His piercing eyes locked onto hers as she reached for his free hand. She backed up the short hallway, pulling him with her. She stopped just outside her bedroom door. "I want to do something else... if you're OK with it," she finally spoke, her tone insinuating so much more. Her heart was pounding. Lucas raised an eyebrow, his turn to answer silently.

He took a step closer to her. "Are you sure?" he whispered.

"Yes," she breathed, closing the last of the gap between them.

Joy pulled away from the passionate kiss briefly, shaking her head yes. "Extremely sure." Lucas followed her into her bedroom. She took both of their water glasses and set them down on her desk. How they had managed to not spill them already, she had no clue, but she did not want broken glass tearing up her fun. Goosebumps ran down her spine as she felt his warm breath on the back of her neck. "Mmm," she moaned, leaning back into him for a short moment before turning around to face him. She found the bottom of his shirt and pulled it up. He got the hint and helped her take it off. She trailed a finger down his chest, then playfully pushed him back against her bed. Sitting, he pulled her to him.

"Joy, I think I—" he started saying before she interrupted by kissing him. She was ready for this; she wasn't ready to say or hear what she thought he was going to say.

"Shhh," she put her finger to his lips, then pushed him all the way down to her mattress. Leaning over him she panted,

"Words, later, unless you want to stop." He shook his head no. They recommenced their embrace, taking it deeper. Slowly, he touched every inch of her, awakening parts she had long since thought dead, and some she never knew she had. She returned with a fervor she had never experienced before.

When all had been exhausted, they collapsed into each other once again—this time, instead of freezing and panicking, she felt like she was floating, drifting on a cloud down a tropical resort lazy river. She nestled into him and let out a contented sigh as she drifted down her river to dreamland.

Lucas returned her contented sigh, delicately combing his fingers through her hair, pulling loose strands out of her face.

"When I came into your store that first day," Lucas whispered to her, assuming she was already asleep, "once my panic settled and I really saw you, I thought I was imagining things. I never forgot our first meeting. I've tried, but I've never felt so connected to anyone, even after months of trying. When I knew it was you, I never believed in a higher power more than in that moment. I just wanted to get to know you, to see if there was any place in your life for me. To see if that connection was just in my head." He paused, listening to her inhale and exhale deeply. He leaned down to kiss the crown of her head. Lowering his soft voice even more, he said, "I think I've known ever since I met you, and every moment since I've been falling deeper. I love you."

17. second comes termites

"Really?" Joy asked, her free hand pressed to her temple, closing her eyes and wincing, the other hand holding her phone to her ear. "Are you absolutely sure?" she paused, chewing on her bottom lip while waiting for an answer. "OK, OK, I understand... Yes, it has to be fixed, I get that, but how long will it take? Uh, huh... Can I come back and pack a bag or should I just, oh, OK, good. So, how much do you think this will all end up being? Uh huh... I know you need to see if there is more damage, but as it is now? Oh... wow... um mhmm... OK. More if the joists need to be replaced completely versus reinforcing. Understood... Well, I'll see you later if you're still there when I swing by... No, I don't think there's anything else I need at the moment. Thank you... Uh huh, OK... OK, sure... bye." Joy's head fell to the table, groaning as she hung up.

"Well, that sure sucked the pep out of your step," Benny commented as he reorganized and unpacked a box of Christmas ornaments in the backroom storage area in preparation for the Christmas in July blowout. "What was that all about?"

"Money burning in the wind is what that was," Joy whined, head still glued to the table. "I have termites, and they damaged all the things, and because of where they're going to have to tear up after they kill the bugs, then they have to test for lead and asbestos and arsenic and old lace before they can do anything. They recommend I not stay there until after they get it all resolved 'cause of all the risk of exposure since they'll be stirring up dust or whatever."

Benny brought a hand to his mouth in shock. "Lead, asbestos, and arsenic. Oh my!" he gasped. "That sounds exciting. Terrible, but exciting. How long will it take, do you think? What are you going to do?"

"So today..." She raised her head and rested it on her fist, tapping the table with her other hand. "Let's see... They said it would probably be just for a couple of days but to pack for at least a week and to remove all my indoor plants. They should be fine if I put them by my shed. And then I wait until the all-clear and pray it's the lower estimate." She shrugged and sat back.

"Where are you going to stay?"

"You know what? It's only a couple of nights." She shook her head and inhaled sharply. "I'll just stay here. I'll be fine. I have a sleeping bag, and that shower works—it's gross but it works. It'll be fine. It's just an annoyance." Joy stood up with a determined look, clenched her fists, and shook her head. It would work.

"What about staying with Jessica? You know she'd let you stay in a heartbeat."

"She's too far away." She slowly moved her calculating gaze to lock in to Benny's. "Do you mind just keeping this between us? I don't want her to worry." She squinted, trying to sear her desire into his brain.

"I don't know what you're talking about," he replied, turning back to his job.

"Ms. Joy?" Eryan popped her head in the break room door. "Um, or Mr. Benny, could umm, one of you help me with something?"

"I'll be there in a second, Eryan," Joy responded. "Benny, finish what you're doing. I can't wait to Christmas the shit out of this place. Woo! Go, team!" She mustered up as much enthusiasm as she could, shaking off her worries. She followed Eryan, humming "It's Beginning to Look a Lot Like Christmas" loudly and off-key.

Joy snuck home as soon as she could after helping Eryan with her register issue. She threw a week's worth of clothes and her toiletries in her black and white striped duffle bag, thankful that it was warmer out so she didn't need as many layers. She pulled her now-ancient sleeping bag out of the back of her closet. She'd had the flannel-lined, now faded navy blue bag since she was in Girl Scouts. It was one of the few things she had held onto and something she hadn't used since she first moved in when she slept on the floor until her new mattress was delivered. She had sold all of her old furniture before she moved. The couple of smaller family heirloom pieces they had been given, she had returned to her mom or to Ryan's parents. Everything she had currently was new or at least new to her: pieces she had collected that were beautiful and simple, things that had meanings but that she could let go of in a heartbeat if need be.

She shoved everything into her giant bike basket after safely storing her plants then headed back to work. It was nearing closing time and she wanted to make sure to get there before they locked her out—not that she couldn't get back in, she just didn't want to have to deal with the alarm. Thankfully Jessica was not working today so hopefully, Benny would actually keep his mouth shut so she wouldn't find out till after she was back snug in her home.

When she arrived, the first thing she noticed was that Lucas was chatting with what looked like a small family group. *What's he doing here?* She parked and locked her bike up, then watched him very graciously take a few photos with them and bade them farewell. She watched him saunter over to her and she was applesauce.

"Hi," he said, coming to a stop in front of her.

"How do you do that?" she asked.

"What?"

"Stop time, and make me mush," she said smiling. "You

must be magic." She took a step towards him, closing the gap between them.

He pulled her into a tight embrace and gave her a sweet kiss. "Hmm, the way I see it is, you're the one with the magic."

She sighed, leaning more into him and wrapping her arms around his neck. "Well, you're a nice surprise at least. What are you doing here? I thought you were booked most of this week?"

"This evening's plans were canceled so I thought I'd surprise you." He booped her nose. "Are you free for dinner? I'd love to cook for you and then maybe we could, ahem—" he wiggled his eyebrows and smirked "—watch a film or play a game or anything you're up for. I just thought having a nice relaxing evening with you would be delightful, and if you stayed the night, even more so." He shrugged and gave her his best innocent expression.

She squinted her eyes at him. "Who told you? Benny or Liam?"

"I—" he began to reply but Joy's phone started ringing loudly.

"I better check that," Joy said, slipping out of his arms to grab her phone. Of course, it was Jessica. Rolling her eyes, she answered as sweetly as possible, "Hey, Jess. What's up?"

"I just got off the phone with Eryan. She said she was concerned about you because she overheard that you're going to be moving into the store because of termites?" Jessica was practically shouting. "What exactly is going on? Are you OK? Why didn't you call me?"

"First of all, I am fine, thank you for your concern. I just haven't had time to call you yet," Joy answered calmly, then turned and walked a few steps away from Lucas, lowering her voice. "I am not moving into the store, I'm just planning on staying here a couple of nights while they fix some things so I'm not exposed to terrible things like asbestos and heavy-duty pesticides."

"Ugh, well you can't stay at the store! That's gross. I would offer a couch for you but my Erin is having a couple of friends sleep over tonight," Jessica grunted. "What about staying with Mr. Wonderful? Maybe you two can, *you know*, finally..."

"Well, part of why I haven't called you is because I need enough time to properly update you about *that* situation," Joy replied, glancing back over her shoulder at Lucas who was watching her intently.

"You didn't?" Jessica gasped.

"Yep," Joy popped the p and felt her face flush. "That situation was handled, ah... appropriately."

"Eek!" Jessica squealed. "Was it magical? Tell me every-thing!"

"Mm-hmm." Joy subconsciously shook her head yes and bit

her tongue so she wouldn't squeal herself. "I can't give you all the details as to the exact solution at the moment." She took a few more steps away from Lucas and lowered her voice. "But it was the most intense, exquisite feeling I have ever experienced." She covered her mouth with her hand under the pretense of scratching her nose and scream-whispered, "And I don't know if I dreamed this or not, but I think I heard him say that he's been in LOVE with me ever since we first met!"

"OMG, OMG! At the store?" Jessica's voice raised an octave and Joy had to pull the phone away from her ear.

"No, my college," Joy whispered.

"Oh! Oh! Oh! OMG, you're the one who got away!" Jessica burst out. "Doesn't he always allude to some mystery woman he's been pining for? You're the fan Easter egg! That's so perfect!"

"Yep, mm-hmm, not sure about that but it would be if that's the case." Joy couldn't keep the smile off her face anymore but still managed to keep her voice calm and low despite the butterflies in her stomach. "But, um, hey, can we talk about this situation later? I need to go check on the status of a couple of other things before closing."

"Wait, is he there? Is that why you've been so cryptic? I thought you were just avoiding customers," Jessica giggled maliciously. "Wait, I thought you said he was busy this week!"

Joy stifled a groan and rolled her eyes but plastered a smile on

271

her face. "It's highly possible to the first one, and as to the second, that's the information I was given."

"Can I talk to him?"

"Why?" Joy's head jerked to Lucas, who was looking around casually, hands in his pockets. "What do you want to say?"

"Um, hello, how are you? Pretty please?" Jessica pleaded.

"Somehow I don't believe you, but I'll ask if he's available.—if and only if you promise to behave," Joy replied sternly, turning her back to Lucas again. Out of the corner of her eye, she could have sworn she saw him smirk.

"Of course! I always behave, scout's honor," Jessica said, her tone dripping with saccharinity.

Joy turned back to Lucas who seemed much closer than she remembered. She held the phone to her chest and asked, "Jess wants to say hi, do you mind?"

"Not at all," he replied with an amused grin and holding his hand out for her phone. Joy hesitantly gave it over. "Hello, Jess? It's Lucas... Mm-hmm... understood... would be a pleasure... sounds delightful...absolutely... fantastic... Looking forward to it... Always a pleasure. Lovely chatting with you as well." He smiled and gave Joy back her phone.

"Are we good?" Joy asked Jessica, raising an eyebrow as she studied Lucas's expression. Damn actor acting like her best friend hadn't asked anything shady of him.

"Yep, I'll talk to you later and I need details!" Jessica said as fast as a hummingbird's wings. "Love you! Byeee!"

"Bye friend, love you too," Joy could barely get out before Jessica hung up. Shaking her head, she slid her phone in her pocket. "Sorry about that, it sounds like Benny found a loophole."

"About not telling Jess about the termites?" Lucas asked.

Joy furrowed her brow at him. "Hey now, I haven't even told you about the termites yet!" Joy poked his muscular chest. Her annoyance at the entire situation barely kept that spark from utterly consuming her at the contact. "So, you never answered, who told you?"

Lucas shrugged. "Jessica..." Joy poked harder. He only smiled and continued nonchalantly, "confirmed what someone else may have mentioned about how you would probably be appreciative of the offer to spend the night in my guest room for a couple of nights." He slipped his arms around her waist and leaned down to whisper in her ear, "I wouldn't mind sharing *my* room with you though, only if you wereOKwith that arrangement." He kissed her neck lightly and Joy shivered despite the summer heat. "Either way, I cannot let you stay here with a barely working washroom when I have an insanely comfortable bed at my house. And if that makes you uncomfortable, then let me get you a hotel room."

She shook her head at that. *Ahh, this could be good. This could be bad. I should just stay here. But ew, public germs. And it's him.*

273

"No, I don't need a hotel room. Did you hear the part that it might be a week?" She scrunched her nose as she spoke. He nodded and she cocked her head to the side, "Are you sure I wouldn't be a burden?"

"I did and no, not at all." He took her hand that had been poking him in his chest and brought it to his lips, placing a delicate kiss on her knuckles. The sensation burned through the last of her resolve. "You'd never be a burden to me."

She inhaled deeply. "OK, fine. All y'all win." Joy said as she nodded, sighing at her concession.

"So what else were you talking to Jessica about?" Lucas asked, leaning in closer, raising an enchanting eyebrow.
   Good lord, even his eyebrows are better managed than mine. Joy pursed her lips, not wanting to answer both because she didn't want to tell him and because she didn't trust herself not to make some embarrassing comment about even being attracted to his facial hair.

"Ahem." Benny cleared his throat announcing his presence and impeccable timing. Joy rolled her eyes and took a step away from Lucas, feeling like a guilty teenager caught flirting in the stairway during class time. "So, Prince Charming, did you talk her out of her ridiculous scheme?"

"I believe so," Lucas replied, looking down at Joy by his side and sliding his arm around her waist, pulling her closer to him.

"Good, my work here is done then," Benny said, handing Joy's forgotten bag to her then brushing his hands together as if he were washing them clean of her. "Here are your belongings. I have taken care of closing so you do not need to come in again and reignite the fire of derangement in your soul."

"Thank you—" Joy paused "—Bennett." Her chagrin oozed from her pores, reminded of his scheming to circumvent her request. *I have to hand it to him, he is creative and on top of things. He's a better manager than I am by far. That doesn't make him any less annoying at the moment, however.*

Benny was having none of her attitude. "I wouldn't have said anything if your idea had included a real residence. I would have even accepted that you wanted to go camping, but no, you wanted to sleep on those gorgeous but nasty couches. Do you know how many random butts a day sit on those things? Just think about how many farts have soaked in!"

"Hey now! First of all—" Joy held up a finger for each of her points as she listed them. "Ew, gross. I did not need that imagery. Secondly, I wasn't going to rub my face on those things! I brought my sleeping bag! Third of all, I didn't even think about camping, that's genius. Why didn't you mention it to me earlier?"

"Mm-hmm." Benny pursed his lips and placed his hand on his hip. "One, it's hilarious and you know it. You love a good fart joke, you twisted queen of beans. Two, still not enough layers between face and public farts. Three, it is too hot to even think about that. You'd never sleep and come in extra grumpy. Joy, it isOKto rest and relax so you can deal with whatever happens. Now, you two have fun... and be safe." He spoke with all seriousness until the last three words in which a smirk appeared and he gave Lucas a wink that Joy missed.

Joy closed her eyes, pressing her thumb and finger to her forehead, and took a long inhale before responding. "Ugh, I hear you and I appreciate you. You're awesome and you're a good friend and manager Benny. I should've promoted you sooner."

"I'm thankful you realize my greatness, and you can make it up to me by letting me be completely in charge one day." Benny winked at Joy. "Well, my dears, have a blessed evening."

"Good night, Benny. Love you," Joy said as he walked away.

"Shall we?" Lucas asked, sweeping his arm in the direction of his residence.

"We shall," Joy responded, shaking her head slightly and shutting her eyes for a brief moment. *Oh, we most certainly shall.*

The next several days passed rapidly. Joy enjoyed them so surprisingly more than she anticipated, even with the added stress of her home repairs. At first, things were moving along rapidly at the house, just like the hare. The contractor was hopeful they could get the work done quickly, and it seemed she'd be able to be back home after two, maybe three nights. Then the hare took a nap and lost the race.

A couple of nights turned into a couple of weeks, possibly a month. Black mold was discovered under the bathroom caused by leaky pipes that were only noticed when they were under the house installing the extra support beams. Not only did they need to remediate the termite damage, now they had to re-pipe her entire house. Never was she more thankful to only have one bathroom. Before they could get in to do that though, they needed the mold treated. If that damage was as extensive as they guessed, she'd have to redo the bathroom. It was on her list to eventually update it, but she loved the original black and white fifties tile.

Lucas was a tad too excited when she told him about the extension, but he did his best to hide it, and comfort her. He always did everything to make her feel warm and welcome. In the mornings, he would leave extremely early to make his call times. Before leaving, though, he always brought her a cup of coffee with just the right amount of creamer in an ever-hot travel mug so it would be hot whenever she was ready for it.

Each morning, he would leave it on the bedside table and kiss her forehead, even if she was still asleep. If she happened to be awake then she would try to show him her appreciation and anticipation of his return. Warm-hearted giddiness would overtake her every time she relived the memory of him bringing her beloved creamy brown hot stone fruit juice of the gods. *I honestly didn't know what is sexier, the hot coffee in bed, or him... in bed.*

As happy as it made her, once she started moving around when he was gone, the anxiety of being in someone else's home

277

by herself would take over. In an attempt to compensate, she tried to be at the store more frequently than she had been recently. Lucas's house was slightly closer to her store which made commutes more tolerable, especially in the heat. Benny and Jessica, however, would shoo her away frequently, knowing she needed to write. With Eryn and Aaron's help, they had everything almost under control except the paperwork that only she could take care of. There was always more paperwork.

"Dammit, I trained them too well," Joy muttered to herself in the quiet of the breakroom on the morning of the third day as she pulled her laptop out, prepping to work through a stack of financials. As she had a mix of products she sold on commission and products she purchased wholesale, it made billing a little more complicated and keeping track of sold inventory that much more important. As she made her way through the yellow and white slips, Benny entered and sat down across from her at the table. Looking over the top of her computer, she saw he was staring at her intently.

Raising an eyebrow, her heart leapt. She stopped typing and placed her hands on the edge of the table, poised and ready for action. "Does someone need help?" she asked enthusiastically.

He laughed and shook his head. "No."

She let out a sigh and relaxed her posture, leaning back in the chair and crossing her arms over her chest. "What's up?"

"I have an idea for the business if you have a moment," Benny stated in a professional tone.

"Sure! Would love to hear it," she responded, leaning in and placing her elbows on the table. She rested her chin on her knuckles. "Shoot, I'm all ears."

"What do you think about possibly expanding our vendors? It would still all be made in Tennessee." He paused to see her response.

"Expand how?"

He took a deep breath as his hands started talking before he did. "I was thinking that we could contact some of the prisons and see if they would be interested in making some products for us to sell. I know they have rehabilitative and educational classes like woodworking, so we could work with the teachers and the prison to provide another opportunity for inmates to have a creative and hopefully productive outlet."

Joy nodded her head, taking a quiet moment to process everything. She stuck out her bottom lip slightly and shrugged. "This could be a really good thing. You be in charge of creating a plan and making it happen and I'll sign the dotted line."

"Are you sure?"

"Yeah, why not?" she said, nodding her head enthusiastically. "You have an excellent head on your shoulders, your idea seems well-thought-out and, at least right now, there doesn't seem to be much risk on our end."

"Oh. My. Gosh. Thank you!" Benny got up and hurried over to her, arms wide. He paused in front of her, silently inviting her in for a hug. She stood up to reciprocate and he enveloped her in a bone-popping embrace.

"No thanks needed, just keep me updated." She patted his back, trying to squeeze him with as much intensity but failing. "Speaking of updates, how are you and Liam?"

He relaxed his grip, holding onto her biceps as he looked at the door and over his shoulder. "I am planning a surprise for him actually, can you keep it hush? No one is doing anything dumb, gross, or dangerous."

"Haha, well if that's the case, of course I can keep a secret" She rolled her eyes. "I'm not you or Jessica."

"Ouch, you wound me, sis. But true." He nodded his head in short jerky motions. He leaned down and whispered in her ear, "I found the perfect ring, wanna see?"

"EEK!" Joy gasped, clasping her hands over her mouth. She held a finger up to her mouth, reminding herself to be quiet so as to not attract attention. "Eek! Yes," she whisper-yelled, quietly clapped, and did a little happy jig.

"Girl, you are so white," he chuckled. He reached into his pocket, pulled out a small emerald velvet box, and opened it slowly. Inside lay a thick banded Art Deco white gold and solitaire diamond ring.

Joy started tearing up as she took the box to get a closer look. "Oh, oh, it's so beautiful! He's going to love it!"

"Oh, he does," Benny replied in a singsong voice.

"Have you already asked him?" she asked.

"Oh, no. No, no, no, no, no," he said, shaking his head and eyes wide. "No, I just went with him to that cute little antique and heirloom jewelry store down the street to pick up something his boss saw online. While we were there, we had a little hypothetical conversation and enjoyed a little look-see. His eyes lit up brighter than the sun when he saw this one. It was just under my budget so I went back the next day to get it."

"Aww, I love that place!" She knew it well. Located not far from her store, she loved walking past and looking longingly at all the beautiful sparkly things she wanted but never thought she could afford. Her jewelry was mostly all costume—nice enough not to turn her fingers green, but not anything nice enough to be sold there. "You little sneak, that's so sweet!" Joy handed the box back then clasped her hands together, and held them to her mouth to block the sound from her squeals. She unconsciously traced the various rings she always layered on. When she brushed her old wedding band, she paused. Her smile fell and her eyes grew wide. "Wait, what? What did you say Liam had to pick up for Lucas?"

"Hmm, what?" Benny asked, storing the box back safely in his pocket.

"Benny," Joy whispered, all of a sudden frozen. "Benny, it's not too fast for you, but it's too fast for me." Her heart thundered in her chest.

"Breathe," Benny put his hand on her shoulder. "It's not what you think. They have so many other pieces of beautiful jewelry, not strictly for engagements and weddings, and besides, the man does have other women in his life."

Joy exhaled, "Oh. Okay. Whew. Wait, what?"

"His mother, his sister."

"Right, I knew that," she laughed at herself. "Silly ole me, being a little self-centered is all. Oh, the in-*vanity*. Sorry about that. Well, future congratulations to you both! Let me know if I can help with anything and keep me posted about this idea of yours!"

"Thank you, and no worries, we're all a little conceited. Especially when we look as good as we do." He framed his face and winked at her. "I better get back out there and you better get back to the grind, missy."

"Roger that." She saluted him and sat down in front of her laptop as he left.

Another week passed with similar results, more delays on her home, Benny dropped more details here and there about his proposal plans and made headway with the prison product project—and she spent more time with Lucas.

He had a short week so they made plans to spend the entire day together. Nothing special, just a day at home. No work, just being with each other—reading, relaxing, playing games, whatever the mood struck them.

Joy was curled on one end of the couch with her toes under Lucas's thigh, his free hand resting on her knees. They sat in cozy silence reading after a busy morning of eating, walking, playing an intense game of speed, and eating again.

Lucas put his book down and turned his head towards her. "I'm going to make iced tea, would you like a glass?"

"Mmm." She looked at him as he stood. "You read my mind." She moved to stand and go to the kitchen with him.

"No, you stay here and stay comfortable," he said, leaning over her and planting a sweet kiss on her lips. "I'll be back in a jiffy."

"If you insist," she responded, melting into the couch and sighing.

He returned a few minutes later carrying a tea tray and set it on the coffee table.

"Well, aren't you fancy? Thank you." Joy commented as she sat up, criss-crossing her legs and admiring the tray of goodies. "You've got everything here, tea, cookies, but what's that?" she pointed to a little wrapped box. *This is it. This IS it. BENNY you better be right.* "A sugar box?" Her voice went higher as she asked, her heart pounding in her chest. She looked up at him as he picked it up. "You know, you're not supposed to add dry sugar after the tea has cooled..." she trailed off.

"This is something that when I saw it, I knew instantly that only one person could do this piece justice." He sat on the couch and held it out to her.

"You really don't have to get to me anything." She hesitantly took the gift, tilting her head and sucking in her lips. Much like compliments, she enjoyed receiving presents; she just didn't know how to respond when they were unexpected, and even more so when this could mean so many things. "What's the occasion?" Joy inspected the exterior of the square box.

"Does there have to be an occasion other than I wanted you to have it?"

"For most yes... but no, I suppose not." Joy smiled her thanks and carefully undid the bow, pulling one strand and letting it unravel; the tension released and it easily slid off. She slid one of her short but sharp fingernails under the tape, one fold at a time to reveal a simple cardboard gift box. She inhaled as she lifted the lid and pulled out a little green velvet box—the same size and color as the one Benny had to hold Liam's engagement ring.

She held her breath for a moment then remembered that Benny said it wasn't what she thought. Her heart thudding against her rib cage was the only thing she could hear as she tried to take a deep breath. She popped it open and gasped. Inside lay a large black opal ring, surrounded by emeralds and diamonds in a gold filigree setting. She'd never seen anything quite its equal. "Oh, wow," she exclaimed.

"Don't worry, it's for this hand," Lucas said as he took her right hand then teased, "I didn't spend nearly enough if it was for the other one."

"Ha, ha." She rolled her eyes and gave him a cheeky smile. She took the ring out and slid it onto her naked fourth finger on her right hand; she hadn't put on any of her collection of rings since they weren't planning on going anywhere. "It fits perfectly." She held up her hand to better inspect it. "I love it, thank you." She wrapped her arms around him and pulled him into a deep kiss. Her head was reeling with emotion. No one had ever gotten her anything so perfect before, and the last time someone tried, things ended badly. Maybe this will be different. A tear escaped the corner of her eye as they pulled away.

"What's wrong?" he asked, his eyes searching hers as he gently wiped away her tear with his thumb.

"You, you're too... "she responded breathlessly, returning his gaze. She was so easily lost and found again in his eyes. "Too easy."

"Don't tell my mother," he chuckled.

285

"Not what I mean," she laughed, then sighed while gently shaking his shoulders. "I mean you're wonderful, so wonderfully amazing and kind, and thoughtful, and I love being with you, but this..." She pointed back and forth between them. "This is too easy. In the past, I've always had to fight or work so hard together or it didn't happen. Everything worthwhile takes effort and I'm—" She paused. "I'm afraid I'm going to wake up one day and this will all have been a dream or we'll finally fight about something and that will be it, everything will unravel."

"Well, I think we just haven't found what we need to work on yet." He gently swept a loose hair away from her forehead. "So we'll just have to do more research."

"Sounds like a plan." Joy leaned into him and let this moment with him sweep her away.

18. panic time

A couple of weeks later, Benny, Jessica, and Joy gathered for their regular business meeting before the store opened for the day. Benny and Jessica took their regular seats next to each other on one of the lush velvet couches, chit-chatting as they waited on Joy to join them. "Thanks again Chuck!" they heard Joy call out before the door slammed behind her, jangling the bells. She joined them shortly thereafter with an amused expression on her face and a bounce in her step.

"So, get this guys," Joy said enthusiastically as she settled in across from them, placing her cup of hot coffee and a notebook on the table in front of her. She held her hands out in front of her, almost like she was commanding the orchestra of their reactions. "You know how I was able to get back in my house the other day?"

"Yes, I remember you said something about that," replied Jessica after taking a sip of her vanilla caramel iced latte. "Any updates on how that's all going?"

Joy shut her eyes and shuddered. "No real updates other than everything is costing double what it was projected to be." She let out a long sigh and shook her head. "Anyway, what I wanted to tell you is that I decided it was a good time to sell my old wedding dress, and I already have an offer!"

"Really? Good for you," said Benny.

"That's not even the best part!" Joy squealed. "It's just the backstory. So this guy responds to my ad, asking me all sorts of questions about it—not just the size and for extra pictures or like is it crisp white or creamy white, but strange things that could just be considered eccentric, like was the marriage successful that the dress was first worn in and were there any numbers anywhere on the dress."

"Ooo, a number fetish? That's kinky," purred Benny.

"Or, maybe he or the bride are math teachers or accountants?" suggested Jessica.

"I'm not so sure about either of those." Joy shook her head side to side, tapping her chin, then continued. "What was I saying? Oh yeah, he specifically asked if there was anything that resembled the number six in the design and if it did, how many were there. So, when I replied, I told him that my husband had passed but that we had a pretty decent relationship, but nothing that resembled numbers that I could tell. He replied saying he'd buy it for the full amount I had asked for!"

"That's awesome!" said Jessica.

"But that's not all." Joy paused dramatically, holding out her hands again for emphasis. "He then asked if my dress was hexed, jinxed, or cursed and if it wasn't, he would pay me an extra hundred dollars to put a hex on it of my choosing!"

"Wait, what? Why?" asked Jessica, a confused expression on her face. "Is this dress for his fiance? Why would he want it hexed?"

"I don't know!" answered Joy. "I have so many questions!"

"I could see how someone would want that," stated Benny nonchalantly, stirring his tea. The women looked at him but he didn't say anything else.

"So, did you sell it to him?" asked Jessica after a pregnant pause, turning back to look at Joy. "Did you hex it?"

"Oh, heck yes I did! He paid me after I sent him a few selfies I took of the process, and Chuck just picked up the package!"

"That boy is still sad that you aren't picking up his package," said Benny under his breath. Jessica elbowed him and Joy glared. "What? It's the truth, he told me. Anyway, was it a real hex?"

"No. Well, yes. But not in a bad way. Apparently, you can hex good vibes onto something. I did NOT tell the buyer that, but basically I lit a candle and essentially prayed over it. I asked that it brought truth, healing, and love to whoever wore it."

"Well, the truth can certainly feel like a hex to some people," commented Jessica.

"Mm-hmm, that is quite profound Jessica," Benny said while shifting into a position reminiscent of The Thinker.

"Well, I just emailed him the tracking information and asked out of curiosity why he wanted it hexed, so maybe we'll get some answers!"

"Speaking of answers, what made you want to sell your dress now?" Jessica asked, leaning back and crossing her arms over her chest, still holding on to her iced latte. "You sold so many things before you moved into that house, why didn't you sell it then? You never really explained."

Joy scrunched up her nose as she picked up her coffee and leaned back, mirroring Jessica's position. "I wasn't emotionally ready to before?"

"Are you asking us?" asked Benny.

Joy rolled her eyes. "No, it's just I wasn't able to get rid of everything that I didn't have much emotional attachment to, but the truth is, I am now. I still have boxes of mementos in the attic that I'm not ready to go through. But, I have no reason to keep my dress and every reason to get rid of it now."

"But why now?" prodded Jessica lightly.

"Because..." Joy dragged out the word while looking towards the ceiling, her fingers fidgeting, interlocking and releasing their grip as they passed by each other like the waves rolling to and fro, reaching out only to recede again.

"Because why?" Jessica crossed her arms over her chest and glared at Joy with one eyebrow raised.

"I might have to sell more than that to help pay to fix my house, if you know what I mean," Joy said as she wiggled her eyebrows and gave a little shimmy, leaning towards Jessica. Jessica's eyebrows knitted together as her glare intensified to the point Joy was sure laser beams would shoot from her eyeballs and slice through her skull to cut the answers out. Benny sat there, sipping his drink as his gaze drifted between the two women. As a connoisseur of drama, he knew when to tease and instigate, and when to sit back and enjoy the show. "I might have to decide between selling the house or the store if they keep finding things wrong with it at this rate."

"Are you seriously considering selling the store?" Benny asked. Joy couldn't tell if his tone was excited, intrigue or scared.

'Not seriously, but if my fairy godmother said she wanted to buy the place, I'd entertain the idea."

"That's any small business owner though," interjected Jessica. "It's good business to always look at all your options on the table, but I want to know more about why the dress, why now?" She leaned forward and placed her chin on her hands, setting her empty cup on the table between them.

"I have pictures of it; it doesn't need to sit rotting, never to be used again. I have no one to pass it on to, and if I ever get remarried, I'll want to wear something new," Joy rattled off the many reasons.

"Oh, and are you planning on getting remarried any time soon?" Jessica asked in a sing-song tone.

"I think Benny would be the better one to ask that." Joy nodded in his direction.

"What's that supposed to mean?" asked Jessica, looking back at Benny who was frowning at Joy.

"It means that Liam knows more about what Lucas is thinking than Lucas does and Benny's intuition knows more about me. So, by default Benny knows more about our relationship than I ever will," Joy said teasingly.

Benny rolled his eyes, "I think you're just trying to dig for information about my relationship status with Liam."

"Are there any updates you'd like to share with the class?" Joy asked, hesitantly getting excited.

"I don't know if I'd want to share with the entire class but with you two..." He paused, looking the two of them over. "I think you can handle it."

"Handle what?" Jessica shouted, her eyes wide.

"He said yes!" Benny exclaimed tears in his eyes.

"What?! When?" Jessica shouted as Joy shouted her congratulations simultaneously. The two women converged and attacked Benny with hugs and shouted questions, wanting to know all the details.

"We'll have to throw you a bachelor party!" Jessica declared.

"Do you know about when? I want to make sure I line up extra help so you can take a long honeymoon and—" Joy was interrupted by the loud ringer of her phone. She pulled it out of her pocket to silence it. "Sorry, oh. Speak of the devil—it's Liam." Joy was confused; he hardly ever called her anymore unless it was to confirm something that she and Lucas had already planned. Maybe it was about their plan to meet up for frozen yogurt this afternoon, but they didn't need reservations for that. If Lucas needed to cancel, he'd text or call her on his next break. "Why is he calling me?" Joy looked up at Benny.

"I have no idea." Benny threw his palms up and shrugged. "Why don't you just answer it?"

"Right." Joy hit the green icon and held the phone to her ear. "Hello?"

"Hello, Joy? This is Liam," he said. He sounded distracted like he was having two conversations at once. Knowing Liam, this was highly possible.

293

"Yes, I have your number saved Liam." She looked at Benny and tilted her head to the side.

"I'm calling to let you know that Lucas needs to reschedule."

"Oh, ok," Joy replied, rolling her eyes. "Does he need to move the time back or cancel altogether?"

"Mm-hmm, OK," Liam said but sounded distant. "Hey Joy, sorry about that. Listen, hon, there was an accident on set today…" He paused again, and she could hear someone in the background talking but couldn't tell who was talking or decipher what they were saying. Accident? "Can you come to the hospital?"

Joy's vision darkened around the edges and she felt nauseated. "Of course, yes! Where is he? Is he OK?"

Liam gave her the pertinent details but wouldn't divulge what happened or what condition Lucas was in, only that Lucas had told him to call her and apologize for messing up their date. Jessica and Benny must have heard something as they quietly stared at her, concern painted on their expressions.

"Thank you so much for calling, Liam. Let him know I'll be there as soon as I can," she said before hanging up. Joy turned toward her friends. "One of you needs to drive me to Nashville, NOW. The other can just put a sign out and open late since Erin isn't coming till later."

"Whoa, what happened?" Jessica inquired, wide-eyed. "Are

you sure? You haven't been in a car in over a year."

"I'm sure." Joy picked up her notebook and coffee cup. She locked eyes with Jessica. "Lucas is in the hospital, I'm going to him."

"I drove my truck today," Benny volunteered, looking over at Jessica who nodded her agreement. "I can take you."

"Don't worry about the store, it'll be okay." Jessica hugged her friend. "Call me as soon as you can and deep breaths on the way there. You can do this." Joy nodded and accepted the hug but didn't reciprocate. When Jessica released her, she went to the back room to grab her things.

Jessica watched the door shut then turned to Benny and grabbed his arm. "Call me when you get there and do not leave her alone until we talk or until I can get there." She spoke in a low but insistent voice.

"Roger that," he replied.

"Thank you for driving her," Jessica said sincerely. "I'm in the focus today."

"Even if you were in the van today, I'd have still volunteered. I can carry her easier if she passes out." Benny winked at her.

Joy walked out of the back room, her bag on her hip. "You ready? Let's go."

Joy buckled herself in Benny's large white truck. She gripped the seat on either side of her thighs. Benny revved the engine and backed out of his parking space. She glanced out the window and saw how she towered over her bicycle as they passed the front of her shop to exit the small parking lot. Her heart jumped into her throat as they pulled onto the empty road. There wasn't a cloud in the sky and the hot sun bounced off the pavement making it appear as though it were wet. She closed her eyes, concentrating on her breathing. *Breathe in peace, exhale love. Breathe in peace, exhale love.*

Benny drove in near silence, the only sounds the purr of his loud engine, Joy's rhythmic breathing, and his phone, narrating the quickest route according to the current traffic issues.

Joy lunged forward in her seat as Benny had to come to a quick stop. Joy opened her eyes. She failed to see the luxury vehicle enter the highway near the shopping mall, swerving and cutting off every vehicle on its path to the far left lane. All she could focus on was the owl on the bumper sticker of the dark grey minivan in front of her until she was no longer seeing what was actually in front of her.

"Oh, no! Oh No! Mommy!" Peter had called her desperately, "The owl! The owl is broken, mommy!"

"Let me see." Joy had looked over the garden owl that Peter loved so dearly. "No, he's OK. He just fell down is all. We can fix it."

"Oh, OK mommy. Owl, owl are you OK?" He gave the plastic bird a big kiss on the forehead. "Are you better now, owl?"

Peter handed the owl to his mother to put back on its post.

I hope Lucas could be fixed just as easily... and not like him... not like them.

They were on their way home, the three of them. Joy was driving because she liked to be in control. She thought she was the better driver. Ryan was better at knowing the ins and outs of the back roads but drove like a mad man. It was like he had an internal GPS. She knew how to use her turn signals at least. Ryan hardly ever used them and when he did, it was only long enough to hear the click twice. If it was longer than that, Joy knew Ryan would just be frustrated. Driving was in general frustrating to him—heaven help him if any other driver did anything remotely wrong.

While it had been a nice outing, warm and mostly sunny during their family hike and picnic lunch at one of their favorite parks, the weather quickly changed. A lonely crow had flown in on that last ray of sun to a branch just out of reach of the tree under which they laid. It watched their little group a little too intently until the wind picked up, and off it flew. The boys hadn't noticed. It was long gone before they looked.

The wind brought the clouds and cold; they had hurried to pack the car once it had started misting. The fog whirled in, slow enough at first that you could barely notice it until Joy was wondering if it was actually after three in the afternoon or if they had possibly entered some time warp. The misting turned to a solid sheet of rain. Joy turned on the headlights

297

as she flipped the wipers on and slowed down in the ever-increasingly eerie fog. Thank goodness they were almost home now. The one thing they both agreed on was that most drivers in the middle Tennessee area didn't know how to drive safely in any sort of weather unless it was partly cloudy and dry.

Flipping on the left blinker, she merged into the turn lane. No oncoming headlights could be seen coming down the hill through the thick fog. Joy hesitated, just to make sure. She hated that hill. The speed limit dropped on the other side, just before the incline but no one ever heeded it. Despite the residential area, people were constantly speeding. No one seemed to care about the kids running and playing along the sidewalks. Not seeing anyone through the fog at the entrance, she glanced again up the hill, looking for the lights of any potential oncoming vehicle. Seeing no one, she made her turn slowly, cautiously eager to get to their picturesque home at the end of their quaint little cul-de-sac. She never saw any headlights because the oversized grey SUV barreling down the hill had never turned on his.

Months later, she would know his account of things. He saw her headlights but not the blinker. He recalled vividly that he had looked down at his phone to switch to check an incoming text message. He never saw the car turn in front of him. If he had only been going slower, had his headlights on, or not looked down at his phone, he would have seen.

Joy would have seen. They were both in a hurry, one to get her family home safe, one to get to an emergency at work. In the end, neither mattered.

Joy heard the screeching of the tires first. Ryan had turned to check on Peter in the back seat. He had dropped his book. Ryan never saw what was charging at them. Peter was screaming in frustration already because he wanted his favorite book, then it altered to a scream of terror of the great grey beast. Joy realized she was no longer in control of the car. She felt like she was watching everything happen but couldn't feel any of it. A loud crunch and grinding metal overtook Peter's screams. The car kept moving in the wrong direction despite her turning the wheel and applying the brake. Glass shattered as she heard Peter's scream turn to gurgling. She knew later from the autopsy report that the gurgling was him drowning in his own blood. It was a painful way to die. 'Drowning burns,' someone from her church had told her off-handedly only weeks after their funerals. It wasn't her first time back, but it had been the last straw. Why would someone tell a mother that?

The car lunged again and settled. Joy tried to turn her body but was pinned. She could only see Ryan's hair. "Ryan!" she cried out, trying desperately to reach him, to check on him, to get him to check on Peter. "Ryan! Can you see Peter?"

Nothing. He answered with silence. Nothing was coming from the back seat.

"Baby! Peter? Can you hear ommy?" Her voice startled to tremble. "Baby? Mommy loves you. We're going to be ok, we'll get out of here, ok?"

More nothing. The nothing called out to her like the drums of war.

"I love you, baby. Mommy's here baby. I love you," Joy repeated over and over until she caught a quick glimpse of sun shining through a window even though she could still hear what she thought was the rain bouncing off the car roof. Blood trickled down her forehead into her right eye, distorting her vision. "I love you. Mommy loves you. Daddy loves you. Ryan, please, please answer me."

Joy didn't feel any physical pain but tears welled in her eyes. It was too quiet. No one was answering her. The two people she loved most in the world were so close to her but she couldn't reach them. She couldn't save them. She could barely move. She began to sing the song she had sung to Peter so many nights before bed and so many times when he was sad to cheer him up, and just because she wanted him to know how special he was to her. "You are my sunshine," she sang, reaching as best as she could until she was able to snake her arm through debris to feel her child's eerily still-warm hand. Her voice choked on her tears, but she kept singing.

The driver of the SUV was the one who called 911. It took the fire department less than six minutes to arrive on scene and get to work. Joy heard more crunching and metal popping as they plied the car apart. As they worked to free the woman pinned in the driver's seat, the emergency workers could hear her small voice singing in the stillness of the wreck, begging in song for her child to not be taken away from her.

Other than seatbelt bruises and airbag burns, the other driver was fine. Joy survived with a mild concussion, small contusion and lacerations to her head, and a broken arm. The police waited until she had been treated before breaking the news to her, that her family had perished in the accident.

Ryan and Peter were dead on arrival. They then had her identify the broken bodies of her husband and four-year-old child. Cruel but necessary.

That morning, she'd been wife and mother in her little imperfect family trio; by evening, she was a widow, and... and...and...empty, empty and nothingness.

19. hospital snuggles

Joy centered on her breathing again, trying to bring her mind back to the present. She hoped Benny was too busy driving to notice that she had been lost in another vivid flashback. She kept her eyes focused on the clouds for the rest of the drive, trying to calm her aching heart.

Despite being on the verge of a panic attack, she calmly insisted that it was better if Benny dropped her off at the entrance, then he could join her after he parked.

"Are you sure you'll be OK?" Benny asked, glancing at her over his shoulder..

"Call Liam and tell him to look for me and report back to you, if that makes you feel better." Joy offered a weak smile. " Surely he's close since I'm pretty sure he was Lucas's emergency contact." *Liam is pretty much Lucas's everything. I wonder how he'll handle it when Liam and Benny get married. Won't Liam stay here with Benny? Or will Benny leave her to go obe with and travel with Liam? This train of thought is doing nothing to calm my nerves. Shite on a stick. I can't process the thought of one of my best friends moving away right now. Besides, it's his life, and I will be happy for him whatever he choses, no matter how sad it makes me.* Joy wiped at a tear forming the corner of her eye. Hoping she got it before Benny noticed. *Dammit. I love my people too deeply. Must it always hurt this much when they leave in whatever capacity? Ugh. And Benny hasn't even left—yet.*

"Go straight there," said Benny. Joy shook her head, trying to clear her thoughts and pay attention to what Benny was saying. Something about meeting her somewhere. "Promise you'll call me if you need me."

"It's OK, Benny, really. If you're that worried, how about you just go hang out in the cafeteria and I'll text you as soon as I find out what's going on. I'm sure Liam would love to grab a coffee with you, even if it's a quickie."

Benny smirked, but the smiled didn't reach his eyes. "Are you sure?" he pressed her again, pulling up to the visitor entrance.

"I'm sure," she said, trying to hide her shaking hands by grabbing her bag with one hand and waving her phone in front of his face with the other. "See? I have my phone and my charger. You will definitely be able to get a hold of me."

"OK," he replied solemnly, placing a hand on her shoulder and squeezing gently. "I love you."

"I love you, too, Benny." She slid out of the truck, mustering all her strength to appear confident so Benny didn't jump

303

out and demand she get medical attention. Shoulders back, head held high, she walked through the main entrance to the elevators. Stopping, she looked around, her shoulders slumped slightly. *How am I already here?* She looked back over her shoulder—no Benny. She pulled up the text that Liam had sent her about where to go. *He had to be in somewhat serious condition if they were keeping him. He's fine.* Her stomach clenched. *He's going to be just fine.* She ground her teeth together as the elevator jerked to a stop.

The doors opened, and she saw Liam on his phone. He stood by an eerily quiet nurses' station at the fork of two long hallways. He saw her, smiled, and pointed to the longer hallway behind him.

He doesn't look frazzled; he's calm, laid back like this was just another routine, monotonous day at work. Then again, it is Liam. He's the epitome of cool as a cucumber.

Joy walked rapidly, her comfy soft-soled sandals barely making a sound on the tiled floor. She paused at the door under the pretense of taking a squirt of hand sanitizer from the wall. She could hear Liam follow behind her at a less rushed pace. Not knowing what to expect was clawing at her. She inhaled deeply and turned her ear towards Liam to see if anything could be gleaned from his conversation.

"Hold on, please," she heard Liam say behind her. She glanced over her shoulder and he stepped towards her. "Hey hon," he said, giving her a quick side hug. He then whispered, "Go on in. He doesn't know you're coming, but he'll love that you're here." He gave her an encouraging nod towards the door.

She nodded and mouthed thank you. Closing her eyes, she knocked quietly, then turned the heavy handle and pushed the door open. Taking a quick breath before the smell over- whelmed her, she whispered, "Lucas?"

She tiptoed to the foot of his bed. He appeared to be asleep, his left arm propped up and in a cast. She walked over to his right side and laid a hand on the bed rail. His eyes fluttered open.

"Hey, there. What are you doing here?" He smiled at her, always that devilishly handsome grin, and reached for her with his good arm. "Did Liam tell you to? I didn't mean for you to have to come here, I only wanted you to know where I was."

"Of course I'd come, I'm here!" Joy choked out, holding back tears. Slipping her hand in his, she leaned forward and placed a gentle kiss on his forehead. "What happened? Are you going to be okay?"

"Oh, I'm completely fine. They're being over cautious, is all. There was a small issue with a stunt. I was rigged for falling but wires broke or something like that, details are a bit fuzzy and they're investigating. Basically, I made an ass of myself and fell. I'm really OK." He smiled reassuringly. " Just peachy, a bruised peach, but peachy nonetheless." He tried to pull her hand to his mouth.

Before he could kiss it, she had pulled away, stepping back and waving her arms. "You most certainly are NOT peachy!" Joy yelled, ending with her voice cracking in an incomprehensible sound. "You can NOT be completely fine. You're here!" Joy whisper-yelled. "What else is wrong?" She moved to poke his good arm but stopped herself. "They wouldn't have moved you to a room if it was just your arm."

He reached for her again and laced his fingers through hers. "Joy." He tugged on her, making her step closer to him. "I'm here mostly for observation. I was unconscious after the fall for a short amount of time, or so they tell me. Purely precautionary. But you're here and that's all that matters to me." He pulled her gently until she was half-sitting on the bed next to him.

"Are you sure?" Joy glared at him as she relaxed into a fully seated position. Her eyes wandered over his body, checking for any other signs of visible damage. While she studied, he pulled her hand to his lips, sending shivers down her spine. "Nothing else is wrong with you?" she sighed. "You're not bleeding internally? You don't need extensive surgery or anything?"

His hand wandered up her arm then slid down her shoulder to her back, finally resting on her waist. "The only thing I need extensively is your mouth on mine."

Oh, dear Lord. Death of me. Her toes curled as she thought of how many ways this man undid her.

He raised one eyebrow and stuck out his bottom lip into a pout. "Please?" he asked sweetly, pulling her closer to him.

Joy mustered up all her drama and sighed as loudly as she could and rolled her eyes. Not letting herself make eye contact, she then let them roam about the room. *Nope, not getting lost in his hypnotic gaze.* She felt his pout burning into the side of her skull. *Nope. If I look, the dam will break and my tears won't stop.* She rested her gaze on the square ceiling panels before falling to take in the sterile, cold white hospital room, and settling on the large tinted window. Through the slanted blinds, she could see the line of cars forming on the street below. She blinked away the tears that were starting to form. She forced a smile then turned back to him and mimicked his pout. "You want me to kiss your booboos to help you feel better?" she asked in parentese.

"Oh yes, all my booboos and owies need your expert help," he replied pitifully, his tone not matching the gleam in his eyes while wiggling his eyebrows.

"You're incorrigible," she giggled and rolled her eyes again, but she conceded and leaned in to kiss him while his grip around her waist tightened. Just as she was settling in to his mouth, she heard the door handle click. She gasped and jumped back like they were repressed teenagers getting caught innocently holding hands in the youth group room before service.

Lucas let out a soft disappointed moan at her lips' abrupt departure. Joy tried to stand up, but Lucas's arm held her by

307

his side like a child clutching his favorite teddy bear.

"Knock, knock," said a familiar voice. Liam entered the room, typing something on his phone, barely giving a glance in their direction. "I let Benny and Jessica know you arrived safely, Joy," he spouted, still staring at his screen. He paused and raised his head momentarily to ask Lucas what he preferred about some scheduling snafus.

As the two of them talked about business, Joy slowly relaxed back into Lucas' grip. Her exhausted mind started to wander. On another day, she would attempt to follow along. A lifelong learner, she was fascinated about most new things: in this instance, Lucas's work, as she hadn't known much about that business before, and his schedule. She gleaned information from not just their conversation but what was left unsaid and the dance between obviously two close friends and co-workers. While Lucas may be the boss, he treated Liam as an equal. He was such a good person. She melted into the spot between his strong, warm and comforting arm and soft but muscular chest, like a firm, heated body pillow. It was almost as if he knew she needed the extra support, even though he was the one who was injured.

Her thoughts were interrupted when Liam cleared his throat. Joy saw that he was typing on his phone again. "OK, just to be clear, you'reOKwith them continuing with a stunt double only until you're cleared for stunts again? And you're ready to return as soon as you're cleared—if they let you?"

"Yes, that's correct," Lucas confirmed. "I want to get right back on the horse again, presuming they've fixed the rigging."

"Alrighty, I think that's all for now, I'll let them know your wishes," Liam responded, shaking his head as he finished typing. He raised his head and looked at the pair of them. "OK, I'll be in touch to get your lunch order soon. Joy, I'm assuming you'll eat here then need a ride back to Fortlin? I'm going to meet up with Benny for coffee so I'll let him know if you want him to wait or to come back and pick you up later?"

Joy was still in a sleepy, overstimulated haze and slowly processing everything that she just heard. "Um, sure to lunch." She chewed on her lip; she had no desire to get into a vehicle again so soon. She hadn't thought this through when she asked for the ride here. "Let me think about when I want to go back. I'm sure someone else can give me a ride if Benny needs to go home." *Or, I can just walk. It'll take all night, but I can totally walk.* "Thanks, Liam."

"Sure thing," Liam replied with his eyes on his phone again. He walked towards the door but turned and tossed them a final goodbye warning before opening it. "Don't do anything without clearing it with your doctor first." He gave Lucas a knowing look and Joy a wink then was gone.

"No," said Lucas.

Joy looked at him quizzically.

"You're not walking or biking home from here."

"Don't worry about how I'll get back. I promise I'll be safe." She waited until the door was completely shut. She turned to face Lucas, worry creasing her brow. "Are you sure you're clear-headed enough to be making those kinds of decisions? You really want to get back on the stunt horse again? So soon?"

"Yes, it's my job, and I love it," he replied in a reassuring tone. "Besides, I can't do anything until the physicians clear me."

"I know it's your career and your life..." She paused, trying to think of how to express her feelings. "I just wish you would let the stunt people do more of your stunts or... or at least wait until you make sure you're better before making calls like this."

"I promise you, my thinking is crystal clear." His dreamy eyes peered into her soul. "This sort of thing happens occasionally. I was never in any real danger. This is all precautionary. I promise you, I'm fine."

"OK, I don't want to talk about it anymore right now," she responded softly. Closing her eyes and shaking her head slowly, her last attempt at damming the flood brimming behind her eyelids. "I just want to hold you," she managed to say finally, breaking the silence. Her voice cracked as the tears finally broke through.

"Oh, darling," he said compassionately, loosening his grip and scooting over so she could curl up next to him on the small hospital bed. "Of course, come here."

"OK," she muttered, her lips trembling and adjusted her position. Carefully, she laid on her side next to him, her head on his resting gently on his chest, and her free arm wrapping around his waist. "Is this OK? Does this hurt?"

"Not at all," he replied, wrapping his arms around her, resting his braced arm gently on her back. "That could be the painkillers though."

"Oh," she gasped, tensing and lifting her head and arm up so she was still touching him, but no longer had her full weight on him.

"I was teasing, you're fine," he chuckled, pulling her back into him. Joy squeezed her eyes shut and slowly relaxed into him again.

"I love you," she whispered into the damp spot on his hospital gown where her silent tears had collected. "Don't die on me, okay?"

"I love you, too," he replied, giving her a squeeze and kissing the top of her head. "I promise, if death comes knocking, I'll have Liam reschedule."

20. tears and giggles

Hours passed as they lay entwined in that fuzzy liminal space between sleep and fully awake. They were interrupted by a nurse to check his vitals every so often and again when Liam returned with a late lunch for the two of them.

After they ate, Lucas insisted she go home, that she would rest better there and that he should be released the next day. Reluctantly she agreed. They said their sweet goodbyes and Liam led Joy to where Benny was picking her up. Joy was numb the entire ride back to Fortlin. She leaned back in her seat, her arms crossing her chest while she watched the skyline. Her thoughts were eerily quiet as the clouds dabbled and the tree line danced against the brilliant blue of the evening sky. She didn't realize the dance had stopped until Benny opened the door to help her out. She was confused as she looked around, expecting to be back at work so she could ride her bike the rest of the way. As her thoughts cleared, it sunk in that they were in front of Lucas's empty house already, and she could see her bike was magically on the front porch.

"Did you get my bike?" she asked Benny, standing stock-still by the truck door. "I thought you were with Liam all day."

"I was," he confirmed, guiding her a few steps to the side so he could shut her door. "Jessica moved it for you."

"Oh." She nodded her head and slung her bag over her shoulder. "Thank you." She managed to force her head to look him in the eye. "Thanks for everything today. I'm sorry I ruined your announcement, if I'd have known it wasn't as serious as it sounded, I wouldn't have asked."

"That's what friends are for." He rolled his eyes and pulled her into a big hug. "Saving your ass, being there for each other."

She patted his back. "And for celebrating each other too."

"Oh, you'll celebrate me." He winked at her then opened the gate for her walkthrough.

"How about a shower?" she asked, stepping through. "Jessica throws excellent bridal showers."

"I could be convinced," he replied with a Cheshire grin. "If it comes with a stripper."

"Oh good lordt." Joy let out a raw hollow chuckle. "I'm sure Jessica can arrange that too. I'll go hide in the corner. Good night, friend."

"Night, boss lady," he replied sweetly. He stayed at the gate

313

until he saw her safely inside and the door shut. "Bless her traumatized little heart," he mumbled beseechingly as he climbed into the driver's seat and drove off.

Joy stood unseeing in the dim entryway. The only light was the bright golden glow of the evening summer sunlight filtered through the living room's plantation blinds. The shadows were eerily reminiscent of prison bars on the wall of the hallway looming in front of her. She leaned back, letting the back of her head hit hard on the door with a thud. She flipped the deadbolt to the locked position as she slid to the ground. Her head met her knees as her fingers wove through her hair, digging her nails into her scalp, clawing at the assaulting memories flooding through her mind's eye. She was transported backward through time, to every loss, every pain. Her bones ached, reliving past injuries. Her stomach was clenched and queasy, her chest felt ripped in two. Her silent sobs trickled into calm tears as the distant memories slowed and focused on the recent memory of Lucas on the hospital bed.

She dug the heels of her hands into her eyes, roughly wiping the remaining wetness away. *This is so stupid, Joy. Get a fucking grip. He's not...* Her breath caught. *He's alive.* She sniffed. *This time.* She rolled her eyes at the irritating voice narrating her thoughts. *I am my own worst enemy.*

Joy collected her crumpled self enough to walk herself to the shower. She let the heat burn her skin, bringing the feeling back to her limbs. She was cold despite the summer heat. The entire day she couldn't get warm. It was as if her bones were stuck in a wet windy winter day, the kind where no matter how many layers you wore, the freezing weather would cut through to your core. When her skin looked like she'd been sunbathing without sunscreen all day and the feeling in her toes returned, she turned the water off. *Praises for tankless water heaters and their everlasting heat.* She didn't bother toweling off and instead just dripped on the floor, and wrapped herself in the luxurious robe Lucas had been letting her use—the same one from that first night. She smiled at the memory.

Feeling more relaxed, she crawled into bed, physically and mentally exhausted from the day's emotional rollercoaster, and fell asleep.

Joy rolled over, searching to comfort her child who had climbed in beside her, begging for a midnight snack. Finding it empty, she shot up and turned on the bedside light. She wasn't in her old bed, or even her new bed. As her senses came to her, reminding her that she was alone in his house, her stomach gurgled and growled. The soreness of hunger must have been what infiltrated her vivid dreams and woke her up. Her heart ached and she wished she could return to the dream. *He was so real... my sweet Peter.* Her stomach rumbled again, demanding her attention.

"Ok, fine," she mumbled out loud to the quiet night air. "I hear you, I'll feed you."

She padded her way to the kitchen and rummaged around in the dark until she found something that looked appetizing enough to eat: chocolate hazelnut spread goodness, fruit, a slice of cheese, and a stack of gluten-free chocolate chip cookies. As she munched, the pain in her stomach eased but the longing in her heart grew. At her house during those nights when she couldn't sleep, she'd pull out Ryan's ring to bring her comfort, to remind her that she wasn't always this alone. But tonight, here in her lover's house without him, without his warm embrace, his soft lips, his piercing gaze, soothing voice and peaceful being, she felt abandoned.

I should never have said yes. She let that thought echo as she cleaned up after herself and shoved her plate in the dishwasher.

Feeling too awake to go back to sleep and not wanting to engage with the rabbit trails her thoughts kept drifting down, she decided to work on her book. Opening her notebook and holding her favorite kind of pen was like embracing a couple of dear old friends. If she couldn't engage with her thoughts, she could engage with her characters. Her editor had sent her some notes that she hadn't worked on yet; she could turn her laptop on and bring that up. Instead, she stared down at the blank lines in front of her.

How daunting is a blank page to a writer or an artist filled with dread? That their ugly thoughts could only impair the page and yet the only way for their ugly, their pain, or their grief to turn into something beautiful is to pour it out. The pressure crushes like the ocean waves above as a diver descends. One must just put pen to paper and try. But stories of love, of hope, of humor, escaped her.

All that was in her mind was Peter's sweet voice begging for chips as he tried to pull her out of a deep slumber.

Son of a chips. That crunch, that salty flavor, and a glass of water. Is all he wanted... oh, my sweet darling child. If only I could go back in time and get you that instead of forcing you to choose a fruit or vegetable that caused the ensuing meltdown. To just cuddle you one more time. To kiss your boo boos. To make it better.... One more time. She was too dazed or maybe too dehydrated for tears to form, but she felt as if her whole body was leaking. She tapped the paper with her pen, trying to direct her thoughts back to what she wanted to work on. But her mind needed her to do this instead.

The tapping slowly turned into script. A word turned into a line that developed into a letter. Another letter that would never be sent, never to be read by the intended.

My darling Peter,

I dreamt of you. A memory, it was as if you were here with me again.

If I had only known how little of how much it didn't truly matter it was to just get you the chips I would have. I would let you have five million bags of Cheetos with no wipes in my white house if I could have one more moment with you. You were, no, you ARE worth every stain, every spill, every rip, every hole in my wall, every drawing not on paper. None of it matters, none of that kind of stuff matters. What matters is you. You are so amazing. Your laughter, your humor, your feelings, your thoughts. You were such a little philosopher. I loved how you saw the world. You brought out the best in me by chipping away at my worst. My life is better because you were in it and I would give anything to have even one more moment.

For one more moment with you, I would do all my least favorite things about being a mom a hundred times over. Even if that moment was the worst of you, I would do almost anything.

And you had plenty of worst moments, being your mom was never easy. I don't know how much of that was me being unprepared or having too many unrealistic expectations but I know it wasn't because of you. Somehow you still thrived in your short life despite my screw-ups. You still loved and trusted me, even when I yelled too much or cried too often.

But loving you was the easiest thing I have ever done. You are and always will be precious to me. I am so grateful for the time we had together, I wish we could have so much more. Mommy misses you so much, my sweetheart. I love you, big. So big. Bigger than all my hugs, bigger than all my kisses. Bigger than the whole universe.

You are my sunshine, you are my stardust...

Aren't we all stardust in the beginning... and the end? She sniffed and laid her pen down on the table next to her. She carefully ripped the letter out of her notebook along the creased line. She folded it neatly in thirds as if to mail it. She brought the crisp paper to her lips and sealed it with a soft kiss, like the ones she would plant on his forehead when he would run to her for a hug.

Feeling the emotional weight bear down on her again, she walked back to the bed. She climbed under the sheets, firmly grasping the letter to her chest like a weighted blanket, and closed her eyes.

Joy lay staring at the dancing light bouncing off the chandelier on the ceiling. The late morning light caressing her cheek had been beckoning her to move for who knows how long. Her entire body was a lead balloon and stuck like an electromagnet to the bed and thus she couldn't look to check the time. Not that it mattered—Benny and Jessica had both insisted she not come in today. She heard a muted thud like the door shutting coming from the kitchen, the one off the carport that Lucas usually used. There was a detached carriage house-turned-garage at the back of the drive but he never parked in it. Her heart skipped a beat as she heard another thud and the skidding of a chair being pulled out at the table.

Lucas is back.

Helium replaced the lead in her balloon of a body as she sat up. The letter fell from her chest, no longer crisp, but still tri-folded. She glanced around until she saw her handbag on the floor by the door. She folded the letter into thirds again and quietly padded across the warm wood floor. She found her wallet and shoved the letter inside. She stood up and quickly put on shorts and a favorite tank top with a built-in bra, then threw the robe back over her, tying it tighter.

Joy poked her head into the kitchen and saw Lucas sitting at the table facing the counter with his legs propped up on the chair across from him. His broken arm rested on the table, the other supporting his head on the back of the chair. He

319

and Liam were having a quiet conversation as Liam unpacked what looked to be a brunch spread.

Liam turned around and saw Joy leaning against the door-frame. "Good morning, gorgeous!"

Lucas turned in his chair and gave her that look that could send her to her knees every time—thankfully the doorframe was doing an excellent job in supporting her. "Hey, you," he said, holding his good arm out to her.

"Hey, y'all." She smiled at both of them, her heart as light and fluttering as a hummingbird, and crossed to Lucas. She wove her fingers with his and he pulled her into his lap. "How are you feeling?" she asked, searching his face for any indications that he was in pain.

"Actually, I am feeling a little sore.

Her eyes grew wide. "Oh, where? What do you need? Ice?" She leaned forward, trying to stand, but his arm pulled her back gently, mustering all his strength into giving her his most charming pout.

Lucas held up his injured arm, showing her. "I think a kiss or two would work wonders. It's just a little sore, right here—" hee pointed to his cheek"—and here," pointing to his other cheek.

She pursed her lips and nodded. "Uh, huh, I think I know how I can help with that." She winked at him then looked over her shoulder. "Hey Liam, come here, Lucas needs some help," she called to him with a cheeky grin.

"Not in my job description, hon," Liam replied, not even turning to look at them as he fixed himself a plate.

Lucas giggled. "Not anymore at least." Joy turned back to face Lucas. "It's all yours." His voice lowered, fingers tracing the back of her neck and brought her closer to him.

"Oh, is it? I think I can fit that in my schedule today at two," she responded, checking her wrist as if she were wearing a watch.

"I'm going to need you to reschedule," Lucas demanded, leaning his forehead on hers, their lips inches apart.

"I think I can manage that," she whispered.

"Good," he breathed, closing the small distance and hungrily kissing her. Like a desert traveler searching for a palm tree, her mouth searched his like an oasis, quenching her thirst. Her body responded instinctually, her hands trailing down his shoulders, exploring his chest, squeezing him to her. "Mmgh," he grunted, breaking their kiss, "gentle please."

She immediately released her grip. "I'm so sorry."

"Me too, that shit was getting good," Liam commented before taking a bite of scrambled egg, then, in all seriousness, egged them on. "You can continue, I love a meal and a show."

321

"Oh, bless it," Joy murmured before the three of them broke out into giggles.

21. all better now

The next couple of weeks passed in a blur. Her house was still a disaster, but there was some rough progress. However, at this point, she still wasn't sure if she would be able to afford to finish it. The store was the only thing running smoothly in her life, and it wasn't because of anything she did. Benny was distracted planning their wedding with Liam. October. Three months. Three months together before deciding that they were it for each other. Then another three months to plan the ceremony to commemorate and celebrate that decision. Joy was in awe of their confidence, both in themselves and in their love. Despite her best efforts, she could feel herself sinking back behind the cage she built to enclose herself, safe from others affecting her emotions.

Joy and Lucas felt like they spent more time consecutively during those couple of recovery weeks than they had in their three months. And still, she felt it was all a dream, a fantasy.

Joy walked into Lucas's house after a hard day at work: not because anything happened, but because she was disappointed in herself that she couldn't be as free as Benny or as strong as Jessica. She heard Lucas talking, presumably on the phone since she couldn't hear anyone respond. She set her things down quietly on the table by the front door, then followed the sound of his voice like he was the pied piper. She paused at her supportive door frame, watching him pace elegantly, carrying himself with such grace you would never know he was still recovering.

His musical laugh carried as he turned again, finally noticing her presence. He flashed her a smile and held up a finger. "Uh-huh. Excellent... I hate to end this so soon, but I'm needed... I just wanted to make sure you received the clearance letter... Perfect. I'll see you on Monday. Bye... and hello to you," he said after he hung up and slid his phone into his pocket. He crossed the room and took her in his arms, his braced arm sneaking under the hem of her shirt, his gentle fingers delicately tracing her skin, an enticing contrast to the scratching of the stiff fabric.

She responded with a greedy kiss, her whole body desiring him. Lost in their embrace, it took her a moment to realize what his conversation was about. She pushed away gently, trying to catch her breath, and looked up into his hungry gaze and raised her eyebrow. "What was your phone call about?"

"Good news, I'm cleared for work," he replied wiggling his eyebrows, "and other more extensive exercises."

"Already?" she asked, ignoring the latter part of his statement.

"Are you really going back? Like all the way back? So soon?"

"I'm only doing a few smaller things, and they have several stuntmen in better health taking over until I'm completely healed." He tucked a loose hair behind her ear. "It'll be OK, I will be OK."

"What about when you've healed completely?" She pulled away so she could better look him in the eye. Her stomach flipped. "What about the next project?"

"I will only do stunts when I am cleared completely," he said softly, "and then, only if I think it's safe."

"I see." Her eyes and heart fell to the floor, her stomach now in icy knots.

"It'll be alright darling, really, I'm fine." He took her hands in his and kissed her knuckles.

She took a deep breath, trying to steady the swaying she felt in her heart and in her head. "Well, I'm not." She breathed firmly, shaking her head and taking a step back. "I'm not fine. I... I can't do that again. No, not can't... I don't *want* to go through that again. I don't want to lose another person I love." Her voice faltered only for a moment, then she started speaking faster to try and get everything out before she lost complete control. "And I can't watch you get hurt again like that, knowing that it was just for entertainment. Not that there's anything wrong with what you're doing, just, gah..." She pulled her hands free and covered her face. She started again, slower, shaking her head again, staring at the seam of his collar to avoid his gaze. "I don't know, I don't know how to say this. I just don't want to. I don't want to stand in your way either." She let out an exasperated sigh as she raised her eyes to his.

His expression was unreadable—concern perhaps, or confusion. Maybe he was actually frustrated with her for once. "Let's see if we can sort this out," he finally spoke, rubbing her shoulders.

"I... I don't know how we can, how I can." Her eyes searched his, her heart pounding, each beat a beckon, demanding she run: run to her bike, get on and go, go, fly, just get away. "It's not fair if I ask you to not do your job, it's your career. You deserve someone who will support you completely." She chewed on her bottom lip, waiting to see if he'd respond but he just stood there quietly, listening. Seeing he wasn't going to say anything, she continued. "And it's not fair to me to... to be in constant fear..."

He shook his head. "Let's make a cup of tea, sit down, and see if we can come up with something we both can live with."

The walls were starting to cave in around her. Her vision started to blur around the edges. If they talked, she would lose her nerve. *He's going to be the death of the rest of my sanity, the rest of me if I stay.* "No," she said softly. "I'm just going to bow out before we... before I fall any harder. I'm sorry, I'm just not strong enough."

"Joy, please." He rubbed her arms then slid his hands into hers, squeezing them reassuringly. She wasn't sure if he was reassuring her or himself. "It'll be alright. You're—"

"Don't," she interrupted, pulling her hands away. "Don't tell me I'm being unreasonable or that I'm overreacting. You know I barely survived after losing my family, I can't do that again." She took a couple of steps backward into the living room. She fiddled with the ring on her right hand. She looked at the only ring she had worn the last few weeks. Sliding it off, she held it out to him. "I don't think I can wear this right now."

"What do you mean?" he asked, his brow furrowing.

"I mean I can't do this." She gestured back and forth between the two of them. "Right now, I can't wear your ring or be yours. I know this seems out of nowhere. I am so sorry. Here, take it." She shoved the ring in his hand as she turned to walk away but he grabbed her wrist instead. Her hand balled into a fist at his touch. The ring jabbed into her skin. "I'm sorry, I should have never told you I'd give you, give us a chance. I wasn't ready."

"Joy, please," he begged her. "Let's just talk. You don't have to wear the ring, just don't walk away, not right now, not like this please, Joy, I..." She let him gently pull her into a hug.

She leaned into his firm embrace, her forehead resting on his chest. *How many times has he been there for me in the short time we've been together? And even now when I know I'm hurting*

327

him... She squished her eyes shut and stifled a silent sob before she pulled away. "I can't talk anymore right now. Maybe another day. Today, right now, I need to go. I need to be alone."

"Alone together?" he asked with a hint of hope. His voice turned gravely. "Or just alone?"

She paused. "Just alone."

"I see," he paused, then looked at her hopefully, "Will you still stay in my guest room? Or I can move in there. I promise to leave you alone."

"I don't think I can do that right now." The pounding in her ears was deafening. She wasn't sure if her vision was getting worse because she was tearing up or going to pass out. She knew one thing: if she stayed any longer, she wouldn't be able to stay away from him, and the ache in her heart whose jagged edges had finally smoothed would shatter and pierce her again. "I'll see if I can stay with Jessica, I'll get the rest of my stuff later."

"Can I call you tomorrow?"

"I don't know... I suppose you can. If I'm not ready, I won't answer..." She rubbed her forehead and shut her eyes, ignoring the damp feeling caressing her cheek.

"Before you go, I need you to know..." Lucas stood there, stoically, like in so many of his movies—but unlike the movies, the tears gathering in his eyes were real. "Joy Elizabeth Moore, I love you with my whole heart, more than anyone I have ever fallen for before. And I promise, I will wait for you until you tell me to stop waiting."

"And that's exactly why I have to go." And with that, she turned to walk out. She paused only long enough to gather the things she had left on the entry table just a few short minutes ago—or was it days ago?—and replace them with the ring he had refused to take back. *Should I go back and apologize? Am I being unreasonable? Am I even in the state of mind to talk things out?* She took a deep breath. *No, I'm not ready... yet.* She knew if she turned around she'd be lost in him and she couldn't afford that again. Her hand gripped the handle and yanked the door open. "I love you too, Lucas," then added an inaudible, "Please wait," as the door slammed behind her.

Lucas followed her steps to the door and grunted, "Dammit," as he rested his head on his forearm. Light glinted off the ring she'd left behind, catching his eye. He delicately picked it up; the tears welling in his eyes reflected the shine of the ring as he held it to his eye line. He stormed off to his room and yanked his top drawer in his bureau open. He reached between his carefully folded socks and pulled out the box. His fingers dug under a random rolled pair of socks in the middle. When they found the hidden object they were searching for and pulled it out, he opened the small velvet jewelry box containing the other art deco ring he had been saving for the next perfect moment to give to her—the one he had planned on giving her the day he was injured, at their bench when they went for frozen yogurt. He tossed the black opal ring in with the diamond and emerald piece and shut the box fiercely. He dropped it in his drawer, no longer needing to return it to its exact hiding place, and slammed the drawer. Plans had changed.

22. gettin' hitched

With her head held high and shoulders thrust back, Joy strutted across the pavement. *Got to hand it to Benny, he does know what he's doing. I feel exceptionally attractive from every angle. Even this neckline accentuates how amazing my boobs are. I guess that's important on a day like today.* A day when cameras would be aplenty and pictures would be posted everywhere, aesthetically pleasing or not.

Her hair looked great; her makeup, pearl necklace, and little white dress that Benny personally picked out were classic yet on point. Her neck was long and strong as she was focused on maintaining her good posture. Her low heels clicked with determination on each step, demanding attention.

She was a tomato.

Outside, she was shiny, confident, bright, and ripe in appearance but inside? Inside, she was just a squishy mess of fruit wondering if she should have been a vegetable.

What am I doing? It's not my day. It's theirs. She sucked in her breath and rolled her shoulders back and down like her yoga teacher was always reminding everyone, no matter how advanced the class she taught. Holding herself up, putting on as confident a face as she could muster, she carried a box of boutonnieres through the gathering crowd then made a beeline across the foyer to get to the room on the other side.

Her heart beat rapidly as if she had just run the Music City marathon. *I can do this. I just need to make sure these get pinned on the other half of the wedding party, and that Liam gets the correct one.* Benny was already pinned as were his groomsmaids—she and Jessica), and his groomsman—his younger brother, Charles). Benny's reasoning for choosing her for this task was still a mystery other than to slowly torture her. *Stupid emotional sadomasochistic torture. He and Liam are probably both getting off on this. I really need to remind them to keep their kinks to themselves and not involve me. But today is their day and I grin and bear the crap out of it... and I will make a note to yell at Benny later, after the honeymoon.* She knocked on the door.

Liam was in this room, along with his groomsmaid—his older sister Lindsey—and groomsmen: his best friend from high school, Daniel, and *him.* Joy shut her eyes, sending up a quick prayer that he wasn't the one to answer.

It had been three months since she walked out on him, three months of utter confusion. He had called her several, respectfully distanced-apart times but she had only replied with a single text message saying she just wasn't ready to talk yet. She had been too confused with herself. *How can I tell him I miss him terribly but still don't want to be in love with someone who will one day die? What have I done? Why? Everyone dies. You're being ridiculous.* She tried to remind herself of her reasons. *Self-preservation? Out of fear of loss? Maybe we really had been drifting apart? Or did I just build a wall for no reason other than I don't want to lose anyone again? But I can't go back now. Right?* No, it wasn't right. *He deserves someone who isn't so emotionally befuddled. Someone who can be there for him. Someone who is strong enough...*

She'd known he would be here. Benny and Liam knew everything that had happened between her and Lucas, yet here they were, paired to walk down the aisle together. At the rehearsal, they had barely spoken—mostly just a friendly greeting—instead focusing on their friends, respecting their time. Then, the words came.

"I miss you."

Those three words were like daggers to her heart. He had told her in a quick moment alone, after the small catered rehearsal dinner in the basement of the church where the ceremony would take place. She had forgotten her purse on one of the pews and he had followed her.

"Joy," he had called to her, announcing his presence in the darkened auditorium. The full moon glowed through the dark stained glass, casting a warm wash of light on the white decorations. That's what the grooms wanted, a white wedding. "You look beautiful tonight."

"Thanks." She turned towards his voice. She could barely make out that he was standing in the open main doorway. "You too."

"Can we talk?" he asked softly.

"Um..." Her heart had caught in her throat. She threw her purse over her shoulder and started walking towards the exit, towards him. "Tomorrow? I can't tonight." She came to a stop several feet in front of him.

"Promise?" he asked, taking a step towards her. She nodded her head yes, keeping her feet firmly planted and locking her knees. The electricity in the air surrounding them threatened to knock her on her ass. *Would this feeling ever go away?* He took another step and the electricity intensified. She swayed and he reached out to help steady her. She felt the fire rush from his touch throughout her body, resting in her gut and her face.

"Too much wine with dinner." She smiled up at him.

He locked on to her gaze, his eyes speaking a million words that couldn't otherwise be spoken. He opened his mouth to speak then shut it again. He opened his mouth again and barely breathed out those three words. "I miss you." It wasn't just the words, it was his eyes. She could see his heart breaking and with it, hers shattered again.

Before thinking, she acted. Leaning up, she kissed him softly on the corner of his mouth. She wanted him to feel better. *She* wanted to feel better. She lingered and he turned just a fraction of an inch and kissed her back. She accepted and deepened the kiss, threading her fingers through his hair and pulling him closer. Then faster than it started, she let go. *What did I do?*

"Tomorrow?" he asked as she backed away, their eyes still locked.

"Tomorrow," she confirmed, "after the wedding." Then she walked out, leaving him probably too hopeful—leaving herself too hopeful.

Dammit Joy, what the fudge monkey were you thinking?

The door opened in front of her. Those dangerous eyes found hers quickly. *Dammit. After the vows, I am definitely moving up the yelling at Benny to the first chance I have, after the vows.*

"Wow," he breathed. "You're breathtaking."

Same, shit. She sucked on her lips and smiled. She tried to swallow and return her heart back to its proper place. "I need to pin you," she said. He raised his eyebrows and gave her a cheeky grin. She rolled her eyes and held up the box of boutonnieres.

"Ah," he said as he opened the door enough for her to enter but not enough for guests to get a good look.

She found Liam standing in front of the large mirror in a corner of the large room, messing with his expertly tied

335

bowtie. He was dressed in a white three-piece suit that matched Benny's. "You look heavenly," she said, trying to get his attention. "Are you ready for this?" she asked, pulling his succulent, eucalyptus, and white rose arrangement out of the box.

"I am so ready," Liam replied, his hands shaking. "And I am so nervous, can you do the honors?"

"I would love to." Joy stepped in front of him, lined up the boutonniere with his lapel and carefully placed the first pin. "Benny is the same."

"I just hope I can take care of him like he deserves," Liam said as she double-checked both pins were secure.

"That's what you're worried about?" She glanced over Liam's shoulder and saw Lucas helping Daniel with his tie. "If you take care of Benny half as well as you take care of Lucas, then you will have a wonderful marriage. But I have a feeling that you'll work harder for the one you're passionate about and love deeply. In fact, I'm so sure that you will take care of him, I'm going to skip over the obligatory best friend warning to not break his heart."

"Well, thank you." He gave her a glance out of the corner of his eye. "You know, if you gave me that speech, I'd have to remind you to be careful with my best friend's heart."

"I'm trying." She smiled, even though her eyes told a different story. "I need to do some more healing before I should handle anyone else's heart. I don't want to give him false hope, so please don't tell him. I started going back to therapy because I don't want to break either of our hearts."

Liam smiled at her, "Oh, hon, I know, Benny told me."

She rolled her eyes at him. "Of course he did."

"Don't be too upset with him. It's literally both our jobs to know as much as possible about the people and products we work with. Now that we're forming a union, we share our information with each other, but not others," he explained, giving her now empty hand a gentle squeeze. "So, is it helping? Do you think you'll get back together?"

"Well..." She stalled, her gaze drifting around the room until settling on Lucas again. "I think so, but no promises."

"Just tell me this." He leaned in close to her. "Think of it as a wedding gift of information. Do you still love him?" She sucked in her lips and nodded her head yes. "Do you want to work it out with him?"

She nodded again. "Eventually, yes. Like I said, I'm working on getting to that point."

"OK, thank you." He smiled at her then pointed to the floral box sitting on the stool next to them. "Can you take care of the rest of these?"

"Oh, of course." Joy glanced at the clock. Less than thirty minutes before places. She picked up the box and handed the

337

small bouquet to Lindsey who was on her phone. "Here," she said.

"Thanks," said Lindsey, barely looking up to grab the flowers.

Next was Daniel, who had made his way over to talk with Liam and check out his reflection in the mirror. "Y'all look fantastic, I promise," Joy snipped as she pulled the last arrangement out of the box.

Lucas was standing alone by the window, his hands in his trouser pockets. "Your turn," Joy said as she approached him slowly.

He turned to face her, warmth radiating out of his eyes. "I'm all yours," he said, conveying a deeper meaning while making sure his jacket was straight.

"Hmph," Joy grunted at his loaded remark and focused on lining up the flowers correctly. She leaned forward on her toes to better angle the pin. "There, I think that did it." She stepped back to take in her work. "All done. Looks great." She couldn't stop from checking him out. He raised an eyebrow as he caught her eye on the way back up and smirked. She rolled her eyes and headed for the door.

"Wait, Joy." He grabbed her naked hand. No jewelry adorned her hand except for a simple gold bracelet. His hopeful eyes searched hers.

"We'll talk later," Joy reassured him. "I promise."

He nodded and placed a gentlemanly kiss on her knuckles.

The ceremony was the epitome of an enchanting white wedding. White and green floral arrangements tastefully adorned the pews. The sun shone through the mostly red stained glass windows and cast a warm rosy glow on the bridal party accentuating the radiance of the couple proclaiming their love. The groomsmen and maids separately led the way up the outer aisles, lining the way for Benny and Liam to follow suit. The grooms met in front of an elegant wall of cascading flowers. Hauntingly beautiful piano and a violin duet filled the air, wrapping everyone in their romance.

Time stood still as Joy witnessed their commitment made binding. After what seemed only a moment yet a thousand years , they were announced Mr. and Mr. Lejeune-Calmes. Joined together, they led the way down the center aisle.

Lucas met Joy in the middle. "It's after the ceremony," he reminded her as she slid her arm in his and they started their journey.

"I consider this part of the ceremony," she replied curtly behind her smile. "We still have to do pictures."

"I am here when you're ready" Lucas leaned down and whispered in her ear. "And might I add, I have thoroughly enjoyed walking down this aisle with you." Her toes curled in her high heels.

The photoshoot was entertaining. Joy did her best to focus

on what was required of her and enjoy the moment but her heart felt like a hummingbird the entire time. Lucas didn't say another word to her, yet his mere presence was overwhelming. He was placed near her in almost all of the photos where they were both present—so much so she became suspicious that someone tipped the photographer to do this just to annoy her. With the way Benny kept winking and wiggling his eyebrows at her when he caught her eye, her suspicions rose. She just hoped they enjoyed their wedding day entertainment.

The ensuing reception presented an epic feast amongst tables that walked out of a fairy tale. Similar white and green floral arrangements adorned the tables graced with crisp white tablecloths and fairy lights. The fairy lights were everywhere. More cascading flowers and greenery adorned the walls and intertwined with sheer drapes. Everything gave the ethereal ambiance reminiscent of *A Midsummer Night's Dream*. The whimsy swept over her, utterly consuming her.

She sat next to Jessica and they barely spoke, gorging themselves on the decadent delicacies. Bacon-wrapped dates with a honey-balsamic goat cheese dip and stuffed grape leaves drizzled with an apple tzatziki sauce battled for runner up as the fish and pheasant entrée—sustainably and locally sourced, of course—stole the show.

"Did you know that the grape leaves and the wine are both from a sampling of different local wineries and vineyards?" said Jessica in between bites. "Benny could not stop talking about it for the last month. I couldn't tell if he was more excited about all the indie local businesses he could support or that Liam went with an alliterative main course."

"It's not too surprising." Joy licked the dip that had fallen on her finger. "Liam is super bougie and what's more bougie than pheasant and alliterations? Mmm, this is sinful." She took another bite of the salty sweetness of the date and bacon mixture with just a touch of a bite in the dip.

"You can say that again," Jessica chuckled, leaning into Joy. Joy watched as Jessica ate a grape leaf in almost one bite and held up the last bite to the vase in between them. "Even the food matches the décor. You know what, these kind of remind me of something but I can't remember what."

"Huh, it does now that you bring it up," Joy agreed, cocking her head and leaning forward in her chair to inspect the symmetry in its shape despite it being so wild and free.

"Didn't Liam do a magical job with the décor?" Benny stood smiling proudly behind them, a hand on each of their chairs. "He actually put together the sample bouquets for the florist to truly understand his vision."

"How did we not know this?" Jessica asked, leaning back away from Benny in order to see his towering face. "You should get him to come and revamp the store."

"He will be needing a new job soon." Benny brought his hand to his chin and stroked it contemplatively. "He might be interested. I'll feel him out."

"Oh, you'll be feeling him out all right." Jessica gave him a knowing wink and giggled, raising her hand to him.

"You know it," he said proudly, completing the high five.

Joy was bemused at their interaction but was slightly confused. "What do you mean he'll be out of a job soon? I thought he and Lucas were on good terms? Did something happen?" She leaned forward and quickly glanced down the long table to see Lucas and Liam chatting at the other end.

"That's a bromance if there ever was one," he replied lowering his voice. "No dear, the love is strong with that force. Lucas is almost finished taping and Liam is staying."

"Oh, that's right. Huh." Joy looked at her hands in her lap. "Never mind. What's next, Mr. Groom?"

"We're about to cut the cake then have our first dance. Then I better see you both out on that dance floor."

"Roger that, chief." Jessica saluted him. "Terry is around here somewhere and mom is home with the kids for the night so I am planning on dancing until I can't feel my toes... then take off my heels and dance some more! This mother is free tonight!" She did a little jig in her chair.

"Knew I could count on you, beautiful." He nodded to Jessica then turned to Joy, pointing a stern finger in her face. "You better dance your ass off too. Groom's orders. No mopey shit at my reception. I will not have those vibes tainting my atmosphere."

Joy raised both hands. "No moping and all the dancing, got

it." She smiled at him reassuringly. "I promise."

"Hey, ladies, sorry to barge in but I need this handsome stud to come with me for a minute." Liam had come up behind Benny and placed his hand on the back of Benny's arm.

Benny turned and planted a kiss on Liam's cheek. "Anywhere with you baby."

As Joy watched Liam lead Benny to the dance floor, her eyes wandered over to find Lucas. He was leaning on his elbow turned towards and talking with Daniel, a huge grin on his face. He looked relaxed, happy. Good. She let her gaze linger a moment too long as Lucas looked past Daniel and locked onto her. She gave him a closed-mouth smile, trying not to look too guilty. He held up a finger to Daniel and stood up.

"Crap," she whispered.

"What?" asked Jessica, who only had eyes for the dancing newlyweds.

"I promised Lucas I would talk to him after the ceremony, and now I think he's coming over here," she whispered frantically. Lucas looked like he was finishing a conversation as he started slowly walking towards her. The butterflies in her stomach and heat flushing through her body were worse than the first time she had seen him in her store.

"I still don't understand why y'all broke up, did y'all even have an argument?" Jessica turned her head towards Joy but only gave her a fleeting look.

"Depends on your definition." Joy rolled her eyes. "At a minimum, it was all too good to be true from the get-go."

"Hey now." Jessica grabbed Joy's hands and squeezed. "Joy Elizabeth Moore, you are a gem. J-E-M *and* G-E-M. You are priceless and worthy of getting what you want. You are worthy of doing the right thing for you, whatever that means"

Joy squeezed Jessica's hands in appreciation as Lucas stopped where Benny had been just a few minutes before. "Good evening ladies." He nodded to both of them. "Joy, would you care to dance with me?"

"Um…" Joy hesitated. Jessica nudged Joy with her toe. "Actually yes, that would be nice. If Jessica doesn't mind me leaving her?"

"Nah, I'm good. I see Terry making his way over to me." She winked at Joy. "He won't leave me alone if I beg. And sometimes I do." She wiggled her eyebrows then batted her eyelashes. "I do have the darndest time remembering our safe word," she added with a deep southern belle drawl.

"Frankly my dear, that is exactly why I didn't want to stay with you," Joy said while standing up and straightening her dress.

"Milady," Lucas held out his hand. She accepted it as he led her to the dance floor. Just as they stepped out, 'Perfect' by

Ed Sheeran came on. She froze. "Perfect," he said softly as he took the hand still holding hers and gently spun her into his arms. He fixed her hold on his arm and started leading. She followed quietly, afraid her voice would shake. How she had missed his embrace...

"Joy, I..." he whispered about halfway through the song but sighed and stopped when his eyes met hers. She looked away, her heart pounding. He took a deep breath then said, "I'm moving in about two weeks."

"Oh." Startled, she quickly glanced back up at his face. "So soon? Where?"

"Filming wraps next week and I've got a part in a movie that will be filming mostly in Canada."

"Mm," she hummed. "When does that start?

"Not till January." He hesitated. "However, first I'm going back home for a short visit, then I have training in California."

"Oh." She sucked in her lips and chewed on them. Snow swirled in her thoughts, a good deep, lasting snow, something she hadn't experienced since moving to Tennessee. Frozen mystical beauty crunched underfoot and laced the trees. "Canada is beautiful. I hope you have fun. I wish you all the good luck... or should I say break a leg?" She raised an eyebrow as he pulled her in tighter as they made their way slowly across the dance floor.

"There's only one thing better than luck from you," he mused, his gaze intensifying.

"What is that?" she asked, her brow furrowing. Her mind and heart battled, thoughts and desires thrashing around and clouding her brain. Simultaneously, she hoped it was her and that he wished he'd never met her.

"Do you think you could ever be happy with me?" He was smiling but his eyes, his piercing eyes looked as though he'd just witnessed a puppy being shot. "Do you think you'll want me again?"

"I want you, now." Joy spoke the words rapidly and without thought, her heart taking over at his words. "I do, Lucas. I want nothing more than to be in a happy and healthy relationship with you but right now, I can't."

"What does that mean for us then?" He spun her out then back in so she was tucked in his arm. It wasn't fair the way her body instinctually reacted to his touch. The shiver and the heat distracted her from what she knew she needed to hold on to. "What can I do? Anything?"

"No." She shook her head. "No, not at all. It really isn't you, it's me. But I also don't want to hold you back, so if you find someone else, you can forget about me, OK? I'll be OK. I just need some time to work on, well, me."

"I think you're quite wonderful just the way you are, for what it's worth," he commented, raising his hand from the small of her back to gently tuck a loose hair behind her ear, slowly grazing his finger across her cheek and down her neck. "What does working on yourself entail? If you don't mind sharing?"

"It means I'm working on my issues with my therapist." She looked down at his chest in front of her as they continued to dance as the song changed. "It means I don't know if we'll work."

"Does anyone? Really?" he asked, leaning his forehead on hers, swaying their bodies to the new tune. Joy was unsure if he was being rhetorical or not.

"No, I suppose they don't," she said, relaxing into him.

23. changing dreams

J oy sat on her favorite velvety sofa and waited for Benny. He and Liam had returned recently from a short honeymoon and he had asked for a meeting with her, alone. *He sounded so ominous.* She curled her legs up beside her, a mug of hot tea warming her hands, and shivered. It was eerily chilly for a southern mid-October. She studied the steam swirling in front of her. *I wish I could evaporate like that.*

She groaned as she stared at the folders now laying stacked neatly on the table in front of her. *This is terrible. I hate all of this.* She took a sip of tea and stared daggers at the stack. She had just been pouring over her personal and business financials, trying to figure out how to make ends meet. The number-crunching was giving her a headache. While she had been able to get her house fixed, it looked like she was going to have to sell it unless she had a repeat boom like she'd had in the spring. She sighed, pulling out her phone to look up the price of storage units. *I wonder if I can fit everything into a storage locker.*

348

"Boo," said a deep honey voice behind her.

"Bee!" Joy squealed, setting her mug and phone on the table as she stood to hug her friend.

"There's my girl." Benny swept her in his comforting embrace.

"I missed you! How are you? Ugh," she groaned as he squeezed her tightly enough to pop her back and lift her an inch or two above the ground before relinquishing his grip.

"You're welcome." He winked at her. "You needed it."

"Actually," she said as she rolled her neck from side to side and stretched out her arms, "that feels a lot better, thanks."

Joy sat back down into criss-cross applesauce as Benny did the same opposite her. Benny rested his elbow on the back of his seat; his posture, though relaxed, gave an air of dignity. Joy's gave an air of 'she had too much caffeine' today. He caught her up on all the adventures he and Liam had embarked on their journey to the Florida Keys; going to Hemingway's home and deep-sea fishing were Benny's favorite. He was absolutely horrified when Liam dragged him to the creepy doll museum. After much teasing from Joy, Benny dragged out Joy's drama non grata.

"Not much happened after your day," she explained as she shrugged her shoulders. "I pretty much told him we were on pause indefinitely, that if we happened to both be single and

349

meet again and I was in a healthier place then I'd be up for rekindling things, but as of now, I want to set him free. It was the right thing to do, right? I mean, I don't want to hold him back but I know if we had stayed together, I would lose what was left of my mind every time I knew he was doing a stunt and it would spiral to every time he traveled and then to every time he rode in a car." She shrugged again.

"Did you think about doing couples counseling?" He cocked an eyebrow inquisitively at her.

"Shut up." She stuck her tongue out at him. "That would make too much sense and besides, maybe I just want to deal with my neurosis by myself, OK?"

He squinted his eyes at her. "Sure, that's totally it." His gaze locked on her, sending shivers down her spine. "I mean, your feelings are valid if that's what you're actually feeling. Are you sure it has nothing to do with you being scared to love someone besides Ryan? Perhaps even more? Perhaps you were even happier with him than you were at the end? Before you knew it was the end."

Joy stared back at him, feeling as if she'd been hit by a ton of bricks. "I've never thought of it that way," she said, her eyes closing. "I thought I was just scared about possibly losing him."

"I think there's that," he agreed, nodding. "I just think it runs deeper. And if you love him more, then it would hurt more if you lost him." She looked like a deer in headlights as he continued. "You probably have heard this, but I need you to know this: love is not finite. When you love someone new, whether it be a friend, or a lover, or a child, it doesn't negate the love you have for other people. When a parent has a second child, they don't all immediately stop loving their first, right?" She nodded, following his words. "Their love grows to include the new child. They have a favorite first child, and now they have a favorite second child. One is not greater than the other. They're different and can even make the first one better or deeper. "

"That makes complete sense." Joy wiped away the tear that dripped down her cheek. She shrugged again. "Well, there's nothing I can do now. He's gone already, I believe, and I doubt he'll have a reason to come back here again."

"Well, if you do meet again," he brought his hand to his chin and tapped his pointer on his cheek then pointed it at her as he continued, "either by chance or by choice, if you're still in love with him, you should get out of your own way and tell him. Let him decide if you're too big of a mess for him. And if you are, then you'll know."

"How did you get to be such a sage?" Joy chuckled while wiping away another tear.

"Pssh, I've always been excellent counsel." He grinned. "But, it's your life, your choice, you do, you boo. Only you know deep down what's right for you."

Joy rolled her eyes. "In other words, don't blame you for my choice?" Benny shrugged, "Well, it's getting late, let's talk about why you wanted to meet up. You sounded like there was a very professional reason."

"It is." He shifted so he was no longer facing her, and placed both elbows on his knees, clasping his hands together. "This is just a proposal, and if you don't like it, then you are allowed to say no." He looked over his shoulder at her.

Joy nodded. "OK, I'm listening. Is this about the prison product project? You didn't give me any details."

Benny leaned down and pulled out his laptop from his stylish black leather messenger bag. "Not exactly. Now, as your friend and your employee, I am well aware that you've been having some extra financial constraints." He pulled up his presentation.

"Very nicely done," she said, leaning in to get a better look. "I really like your font and your bar graphs."

"Liam advised with the aesthetics, he's so good," Benny said with the back of his hand held to his mouth. He put his hand down and cleared his throat. "I will cut to the chase, then explain several different scenarios and options, and after that I'll take questions." He held his hand back up. "Sound good?" She nodded and gave him a thumbs up.

He took such a deep breath that it shook the couch. "Liam and I both have a dream of owning our own business and would like to buy the store." He proceeded to present their offers—buying their way into some form of partnership with her. He expressed their immediate desires and future ideas of how to grow and handle the business, then answered her questions in great detail.

"Wow, it sounds like you've thought of everything, when did you have time to do this?"

"It may or may not have been what we worked on when we weren't otherwise disposed," he replied with aloofness. "What can I say, when you and your partner catch the dream together, it makes things a lot more fun."

Joy tapped her cheek and pursed her lips together. *THIS IS PERFECT. HOLY SHITEMAS! PLAY IT COOL PLAY IT COOL.* She coyly tucked a lock of hair behind her ear. "Would you be interested in buying the store outright? Not a partnership?"

"Yes!" he exclaimed while pulling up a rougher-looking proposal. "This is what we actually wanted to present to you originally but then we thought maybe starting with a partnership would be easier."

"OK, let's do it," she immediately replied with certainty after looking over the new figures.

"You're not going to take time to think about it?"

She shook her head. "I don't need to. It's time for a fresh start. This was truly an answer to a secret prayer. And I was letting this hold me back. I need to move forward, for me."

"Wow, OK, I'll tell Liam and we'll iron out the details."

"Sounds perfect!" She grabbed his hand to shake their deal. "Just do me a favor and let me tell Jessica, OK?"

"Like I'd want to wrestle that possum." He placed a hand on his hip. "That pleasure is all yours."

"Thanks." She smiled. "Well sir, it was a pleasure doing business with you, but I think it's time for me to call it quits."

"And I've got to get back to my nice pre-warmed bed." He wiggled his eyebrows at her suggestively.

Joy gathered her paperwork and straightened up as Benny left. She pulled out her phone and saw three unread messages, one from Jessica, and two she hadn't had the heart to open even though they were several days old now. She opened the one from Jessica—just the normal daily evening check-in text, catching her up on all of Jessica's goings-on. She clicked to type a response but as the line blinked, waiting eagerly for the next letter, she was drawing blanks. She backed out and her thumb hovered over Jessica's number. "I better just rip the Band-Aid off," she coaxed herself then pressed the call button.

"Hey! What's up?" Jessica picked up, her tone perky then dropped. "Everything OK?"

"Actually, everything is great," Joy replied. She was nervous and excited. *But this feels right.* "Do you think you could get away next month for a week? I was thinking we could finally take that road trip out west we always wanted to."

"Ah," Jess cleared her throat. "Are you ready for something like that?"

"As I'll ever be." *Which is not really, but sometimes we have to do things scared, right?* She placed a hand over her heart. *Right.*

"Then um, let me think about it." She paused for half a second before exclaiming, "Yes! I mean, Terry and my mom should be able to handle the kids but I'd have to check with them and my boss."

"Cool," Joy said evenly.

"So, boss, do you think I could have a week off to go on a road trip with my best friend?"

"Sorry, I'm going to need you to ask your future new boss that one," she said in her best customer service voice.

"Hold the phone. What do you mean?"

"I'm also calling to tell you that I'm selling the store." She paused, listening to the silence on the other end. "I got an offer I couldn't refuse and the new owners are fantastic and promised to take care of you."

"What?!" Jessica shrieked into the phone. "Who did you sell it to?"

"Benny and Liam." Joy proceeded to fill Jessica in on their previous conversation, then explained how she also wished to sell her home and use this opportunity to get it ready and list it. "So I'm planning on leaving on the road trip right before I list it so I don't have to vacate for every showing. I can just have fun with you and write during our downtime. "

"What are you going to do after you sell your house? Live in your bike?" Jess shrieked. "How much have you thought this through?"

"I was thinking that after I closed on the house, I could travel for a while first. Cross things off my bucket list—you know what? I've never been skiing. I've never been out of the country. I've never been camping where there wasn't at least a latrine. I could backpack through Europe or something."

"Whoa... OK, OK." Jessica spoke slowly, absorbing everything she'd just said. "OK, so do you think you'll settle back here? When you're done?"

"I honestly don't know." She shrugged her shoulders despite knowing Jessica wouldn't see her. "But I have a few ideas. I really want to write more and I can do that just about anywhere."

The women circled their conversation back to their road trip and brainstormed ideas about what they wanted to do along the way and what they'd need, like passports, just in case they decided to take a detour and visit Mexico. As they talked, Joy piddled around the store, fiddling with displays and silently starting to say her goodbyes. While the store had been her dream for so long, it no longer held the place in her heart it once had. *Sometimes dreams change, and sometimes dreams die altogether.* She ached to let it go and dive into figuring out what actually made her tick now.

Joy pulled her sweater tighter around her to block the November night air as she locked the store. A couple of weeks had passed; Jessica had gotten the all-clear from all parties to be gone for ten days after Thanksgiving. She had contacted a real estate agent and was in the process of listing and packing her house. *Those who move around the holidays tend to need to move quickly so all the better to be ready to be out,* she reminded herself with every piece of packing tape slapped on a cardboard box.

Benny and Liam not-so-subtly stepped up into the owner responsibilities despite closing not being for another three weeks. Joy didn't mind—one less thing she needed to worry about. Things were looking brighter than they had in a long time. She felt lighter, like she could just take off on the wings of the chilled night breeze sending goosebumps down her spine.

She dropped her keys into her bag and rewrapped her scarf around her neck more securely, then proceeded to trip over air and stumble down the brightly lit steps. The porch light was a beacon spitefully contrasting against the seasonal darkness, a spotlight on her mishap. She caught the railing right before she would have completely bottomed out and laughed at how close a call she'd been to face planting. *You can be such an airhead! At least I didn't fall going up the steps this time. Sheesh woman. Mom put you in ballet classes as a kid for a reason. To learn how to balance. UGH.*

"Uh, are you OK?" a concerned male voice interrupted her self-deprecating thoughts. She looked over to see a man standing in the shadows dressed in a dark sweater.

Whodilally is that? As he stepped out of the shadow, she started to recognize his features, though he seemed out of place. He was holding his arms behind his back. He looked oddly confused, or perhaps it was concern draped over his features. Then it dawned on her.

"Oh, hey, Chuck! I'm fine, just wasn't paying attention apparently. Wow, don't you look spiffy!" Joy complimented him, shifting her bag to her other arm and subtly smoothing out her ruffled sweater. "What's the occasion?"

"Ah, well you see..." He stumbled over his words then held out a small pot of deep purple mums. "Here, I wanted to give you these, and ah, I wanted to, um, wow, you think this would get easier after college." He blushed. "I wanted to see if you would go out with me?" His voice rose to a higher pitch as her fingers brushed his while accepting the pot.

"Oh, wow. These are lovely, thank you," *Wow, well I can't say this is unexpected but what do I do?* Out of the corner of her eye, she watched as he ran his fingers through his wavy hair while she inhaled the flowers' sweet aroma. *Well, he is kind and pretty cute and you really don't know anything about him,*

Joy, other than he's punctual and very good at tending to his uh, packages.

Shit, Benny, why'd you put that innuendo in my head? Maybe he is what you've been looking for...

Or maybe not. You don't owe him anything.

One date is not the rest of your life! It's OK to get to know someone, it's OK to open your heart to the possibility of love again. And it's OK if you find out if he's not... She gazed into his hopeful dark brown eyes, so different than *his* but just as caring. She felt her heart flutter. *No more making choices because I'm scared.* "Um, what were you thinking? Like getting coffee or something?"

"Or something," then quickly added, "but coffee works for me."

"OK, well, when were you thinking? I'm free now actually," she shrugged nonchalantly, "if that's good for you?"

His eyes grew wide and the grin he wore spread from ear to ear. "Ah, wow, um, I was thinking later this week, but totally now, yeah, yeah, I'm free."

***

Joy's hands gripped onto her mug as they sat across from each other. She sipped quietly, nodding along as she listened to him drone on about something. She wasn't really paying attention anymore... *What was he talking about? Something about intramurals maybe? I am too distracted.* She had accidentally noticed what one of the young ladies at the table next to her was looking at on her phone. *Lucas.* Her heart was all aflutter. It was taking so much energy and effort not to look back to try and catch another glance. *This isn't fair. I am supposed to be moving forward.* She gazed into Chuck's eyes and the flutter calmed. He seemed perfect on paper, but there was just nothing happening: no spark, no chemistry. She drained the last of her coffee and set it on the table.

"Do you want something else?" he asked eagerly.

"No." She shook her head. "Thank you, I'm fine."

"Can I ask you something?" He leaned in and propped his elbows on the table. "Something kind of personal?"

"Sure, though no promises I'll answer." She crossed her legs and the top foot started bouncing rapidly despite her casual tone. "What is it?"

"You're not feeling this, are you?" he asked melancholically, his finger gesturing between the two of them. "You're still in love with him, aren't you?"

Her foot stilled. She hadn't expected he'd been so perceptive. "Um, wow, OK, we're doing this." She bit her bottom lip and shook her head. "No. I mean, don't get me wrong, I think you're a great human being. It's just... it's just me. And as far as the second question, I... I don't..." She glanced at the table next to them where the young ladies were giggling and she saw a glimpse of a different photo of *him.* She shut her eyes and shook her head. "No, yeah, if I'm being honest with myself, I'm not completely over him yet."

"Then why aren't you with him? He obviously cared for you deeply." He leaned back. "He made you happy."

"How do you know?" She cocked an eyebrow.

"I have eyes." He shrugged his shoulders. "And ears."

"Mm-hmm." She tilted her head at his cryptic statement.

"Look, I think you're absolutely incredible, but if you're not feeling it with me, then I respect that." He shrugged his shoulders again. "You're missing out, but I respect that. "

Joy snorted at that. "You're right, I am. It's all on me."

"So, I'll be around if you change your mind." He reached across the table, slid his hand in hers, and gave it a comforting squeeze. "But I want you to be happy, even if it's not with me. So, are you?"

"Am I what?"

"Happy?"

She squeezed his hand in return and nodded her head slowly. "I think I finally am."

24. beach brave

"Are you sure you're ready? Got everything?"

"Let's see..." Joy went through her list as she pinched alternating fingers on her opposite hand. "Clothes and shoes, check; toiletries, check; laptop and chargers, check; bike on the rack next to yours and secured, check; household items stored in POD, check; sign everything for the house and the store, check; and snacks are right here." She patted the tote bag she had just placed in the rental car's back seat then stood up and rested on the open door. "I think that's it. You?"

"Terry has the kids, Benny and Liam assured me they can live without me for a while. If I've forgotten something, I can just buy a replacement."

"What about your license?"

"It's right here." Jessica pulled her wallet out of her purse and flipped to her license. She held it out for Joy to see. "You?"

"Wallet, purse, license, phone, and lip balm are all right here." Joy patted her newly downsized purse. "Let's do this!"

"And you're sure you can do this? No flaking out on me an hour out of town, right?"

Joy nodded her head determinedly. "I am 500 percent sure."

"Woot!" Jessica hollered as she jumped in the driver's seat. "Hop in bitch!"

Thus began their long-awaited journey westward. Their first stop was Memphis. Despite not being far, Joy had never been there and Jessica had only been once for a cross-country meet. Next was Little Rock, then Oklahoma City, Amarillo, and Albuquerque before reaching the south rim of the Grand Canyon.

The chilly dry air brushed against her skin as she stepped out of the car. They made it—the fricking Grand Canyon. The women walked the short distance from the deserted parking lot to the lookout. The magnanimous view was slightly disappointing.

"Huh, I thought it would be bigger." Joy pursed her lips and rubbed her arm as she hugged them to her chest.

Jessica slowly turned her head and tilted it, staring at Joy with one eyebrow raised incredulously. "Are you serious?"

"What?" Joy shrugged. "I didn't say I didn't like it, it's

beautiful, definitely grand... I just thought it would be bigger."

"First of all, that's what she said," Jessica said sternly as she turned back to the view. "Secondly, I think you're just in a mood."

"What makes you think that?"

"Gossip columns." Her voice danced lightly as she threw her hands in the air and started to spin slowly. "Just remember, they are just that, gossip."

Joy rolled her eyes. "I know." *How dare she allude to that stupid online magazine plastering photos of Lucas with some other new girl with presumptuous headlines. His body language screams she was just a friend. But then why did my gut twist so hard when I saw the newest pic during my newly developed habit of researching... no, stalking... let's call it researching the internet for news about him on a semi-daily... OK fine, semi-hourly basis. I'm not trying to be creepy, it's just because I'm concerned. Not at all because I don't have the courage to pick up my phone and text him, dammit.*

Jessica stopped spinning for a moment. "Do you?" She placed her hands on her hips and mustered up a serious tone. "If you miss him so much, why don't you do something about it?"

"I never said I missed him."

"You didn't have to," Jessica sang-song while spinning.

"Am I that obvious?"

"Yes, miss pouty face, you are." A sinful smile crept across Jessica's face. "You know, if you're just missing him in the bedroom sense, you could totally add some citrus or spice to your evening reading repertoire."

"What is that supposed to mean?" Joy furrowed her brows.

"Oh, dear lordt." Jessica facepalmed with her right hand. She sighed dramatically then assumed a standing in a zen-like pose, holding her thumbs against her middle finger. "Fan-fiction lemony goodness, child," she exclaimed dramatically, shaking one of her hands in Joy's face suggestively. "Smut!"

Joy cackled. "You should see your face right now," she snorted. Jessica intensified her face, exaggerating her pursed lips and jerking both hands now and doing a little shimmy.

"Nothing wrong with having a little harmless fun," Jessica deadpanned before breaking out into a silly yet beautiful dance.

"I can only handle closed-door romances right now!" Joy's phone rang then, harshly interrupting the mood. She looked at the screen. "I'm sorry, I need to take this. Hey!" She turned her back on Jessica and pulled her notebook out of her bag, "Yes... Uh-huh... Yes, I can make that work... Yeah, um... yes, that works for me... Great! I'll be on the lookout for it. Thanks!" Joy scribbled a few notes then hung up.

"Who was that?"

"It was my editor. I sent her my final pages for my current book and a couple of rough pitches for my next project. She wanted to schedule a time to go over her notes after I read them."

"Cool!" Jessica nodded. "So you finished it then?"

"Finished is a complicated term." She smiled at Jessica as they started down the short trail. "I don't know if I'll ever be finished, not even this round of edits, or even if it does get published. I'll always want to go back, to fix it, to tweak it, and make it better than before. But I won't. It'll be out of my hands so I'll write another story—hopefully, better than the last."

"But still, you have completed one step in the journey you've decided to take."

"I guess I have."

They continued in silence on the smoothly paved path. The sun warmed their exposed skin despite the frosty air. They paused on a ledge, staring off into the view. Joy spoke casually, breaking the silence. "I don't think I ever told you this, but you saved my life. This part of my journey wouldn't be possible without you."

"What are you talking about?" Jessica asked, coming to stand beside Joy.

"After the accident, I didn't just lose my family, I lost my identity. Everything that I thought defined me. I had been a wife and mom for so long and I had let it take over, let it utterly consume me." She sat on a nearby boulder jutting out from the path. Jessica crossed her arms over her chest and stood, watching her.

Joy avoided Jessica's gaze, staring at the dusty ground in front of her, took a breath, and continued. "The first time I was home alone after they had all gone... I had my first real shower in weeks after my cast was removed. I didn't realize I was so numb emotionally and when the cast was removed, it was like it took away my blockade... like a switch went off while I was standing under the hot water. Every feeling was hitting me like a bullet with every drop. I was the one left alive and it didn't make sense. It was unbearable. I wanted to escape the pain. I thought about ending it all. I sat there with the razor in one hand hovering over my wrist, wondering if that would work. I don't know how long I was there. I don't even remember sitting down. But you came over. You had let yourself in and knocked on my bathroom door, just letting me know you were here with me. So I put it away. I didn't so much as touch it to my skin. Because of you. Because of your friendship."

"Wow." Jessica paused for a moment, thinking, then shook her head. She walked closer to Joy and stood directly in front of her. "I don't think I saved your life. That's not the way I see it. I only showed up—you're the one who stopped. You're the one who fought it. Own your strength, Joy. Each and every moment that you've lived since then, you've won another

367

battle. Every time you laugh, every time you cry, every time you breathe, every time you love. "

Jessica swung her arm out and gestured to the breathtaking view. "Do you see this? Do you see where we are? Don't you see how far you've come? Six months ago you wouldn't have sat in a car if your life depended on it. Now we're here, at the Grand frickin' Canyon, checking off our road trip bucket list we made in college! Do you see how much you've grown? You inspire me, woman!"

"I do?" Joy asked, wiping away a single tear.

"Yes!" Jessica replied, running her fingers through her hair. "Why do you think I haven't run away screaming from my family?"

"Because you're an amazing human being and you love them?"

"No! I mean yes, of course, I'm amazing, but no, not just because of that or because I love them." She shook her head, her curls falling out from her loose ponytail. "This may sound terrible, but I watched how miserable you were without them, and before that, I watched how much effort you put into making your relationship work. You never gave up. You wore yourself out, yes, but you never stopped. Not completely. You inspired me to take better care of myself and better care of my relationships, just by being you." Jessica slipped her arm around Joy's waist and gave her a squeeze. "I'm proud of you."

"Well, when you put it that way, I guess I'm proud of me, too," Joy reciprocated and slung her arm over Jessica's shoulders. "I think I'm finally figuring out who I am again, and it feels really good. I only wish I could've figured this out sooner when they were here. I think knowing who I am without those titles would've made me better at those titles."

"It's amazing how that works," spouted Jessica. "What titles are you looking to be now? Any chance of a reunion with anyone in particular?" She wiggled her eyebrows at Joy.

Joy rolled her eyes. "Did I tell you that I recently read Joan Didion's *The Year of Magical Thinking*?" asked Joy lightheartedly. "That was the first time I realized I wasn't truly alone in my grief. However, I pitied her. I pitied myself. And pity is not empowering. How long did I punish myself for living? Life is hard enough as it is. I don't want to punish myself like that anymore."

"Yeah?" asked Jessica. "What are you going to do about it?"

"I'm thinking we need to finish our road trip out west and maybe see if kismet is in my favor," Joy replied, grabbing Jessica's hand and pulling her back towards the car. "Come on, I have an idea. We need to call Benny."

***

Joy's heart thudded deafeningly in her chest as she stopped in front of the double doors. "Stop breathing so fast, you'll hyperventilate and pass out," Jessica whispered, nudging her in the ribs.

369

Joy gulped in a deep breath and nodded her head and muttered, "Thank you. Benny confirmed this is the place, right?"

"Yep, he just texted. No problem, sister." Jessica rubbed Joy's back soothingly. "Are you sure you want to do this?"

"One thousand percent." Joy looked Jessica dead in the eye. "I don't want to live with regrets, even if this doesn't work out the way I want... I have to try."

"Well then, go get 'em, tiger." Jessica grabbed the door handle with one hand and started pushing Joy through with the other. "Rawr," she purred as Joy walked in front of her. Joy threw Jessica a confused look over her shoulder but kept walking. "I'm going shopping so just call when you're ready to be picked up," Jessica said, letting the door shut behind Joy.

Joy took a minute to gather her bearings. The coffee shop she had just entered was very sleek and modern, yet rustic with its raw wood accents. The divine smell of freshly roasted coffee gently caressed her nostrils and instantly calmed her heart. She looked around; the place was busy, but not overflowing. She stepped aside as she heard the door open behind her and let the two extremely fashionable women entering lead the way to the stainless steel counter. She did her best to chase all feelings of being underdressed and inadequate in her mom jeans out of her brain as she stood in line. *Kristen Bell wears mom jeans and looks amazing, and so can I. I need that mantra on a t-shirt.*

"Hi! What can I get started for you today?" the brunette

cashier asked sweetly at a million miles per second. Someone was either an innately fast talker or very caffeinated. Her long hair was swept back and a ponytail trailed down her back. A few strands fell over her shoulder highlighting the "coffee queen" sticker on her name tag.

"Um, hi Julia, can I get a medium mocha?"

"Sure can," she replied. As Julia focused on the machine in front of her, Joy felt a warm breeze signaling the door had been opened. "What's the name?" she asked as Joy started to turn her head, but stopped before she turned completely around. She closed her eyes; she recognized the sound of his gait, the smell of his aftershave. "Ma'am, what's the name?" Julia asked again.

"Lu..." Joy started to say then processed what had been asked. "Joy—and can I add a medium Earl Grey Latte?" Joy handed Julia her card and shoved some loose change in the tip jar.

"Sure thing," Julia replied, swiping her card and handing her the receipt. "It'll be right up over there."

"Thanks," Joy said, shoving the card and receipt in her bag, not taking the time to put them in her wallet. She zipped it closed and turned around.

"Joy?" His sweet voice hung in the air like melodic notes on a bar graph. The one and only Lucas E. Worthington—leading actor, devilishly handsome, and who also happened to be her ex-boyfriend who was actually real and not a fantasy that she had feared she'd dreamed—was actually standing in front of her. His smile, as white, sparkly, and charming as ever, made her knees just as weak as the first time she'd met him. Yet she stood strong.

"You're here," Lucas said, more of a statement than a question.

"I'm here," she confirmed, nodding her head and getting lost in his ever-warming and comforting gaze. "I asked Liam to help me find you," she confessed. "Well, technically I asked Benny to ask Liam. He's very protective of you, you know."

"I'm aware," Lucas chuckled.

"Jayce, your order's ready," shouted the barista. "Mocha and Earl Grey Latte."

"I think that's ours," Joy said as she walked to the end of the bar.

"Hey, wow, I love your work, man," said the hipster barista to Lucas as he handed them their drinks. "Hope she's *worthy* of you, ha ha" he added, giving a suggestive wink to Lucas.

"I just hope I'm worthy of her," Lucas responded, smiling, his eyes never leaving hers.

"That was never the question." Joy spoke the words with as much earnest sincerity as she could muster. "Do you have time to talk?"

"For you," he said as he led them away from the barista still staring at them and towards comfortable seats in the corner, "I have all the time in the world."

"Same," she said, sliding into the armchair facing him. "I just need to text Jessica and let her know I'll be busy for a while."

"Is she here?"

"She dropped me off." She ran her finger along the rim of her cup. "We're on a road trip."

"You *drove?*" he asked incredulously. "To L.A.?"

"Yep." She nodded, biting her lip as she sent Jessica a quick text who immediately responded with a tiger gif. *What is that supposed to mean? 'Go get 'em, tiger' or 'I'm the tiger king'?*

The former couple sat in silence for a few minutes, letting the awkwardness wash over them and recede like the tide. They caught up on all the happenings in each other's lives the previous few months. They finished their drinks and continued their conversation as they wandered out of the restaurant and down the street.

Joy followed his lead, noticing none of the scenery other than the palm trees interspersed along the buildings. Somehow they ended up at a beach. They fell in step next to each other, the salty air fueling the natural electricity between them. Joy paused when she realized they were walking so close they were practically touching, all but a hairbreadth between them.

She tossed her tied-together sneakers over her shoulder and rolled her jeans up. She walked to the water's edge, letting the frigid waves lick her ankles. He stood behind her watching, not sure if he should interrupt.

OK, Joy, you CAN do this. You're scared but that's OK. You got this. Suddenly Joy turned to face him. She looked into his gaze and determinedly marched to where he was standing. He raised an eyebrow inquisitively. "Look, I came here not just because I wanted to apologize and talk to you. I came here because I'm still in love with you and if you'll take me, I want you back."

"Really?"

She nodded her head.

"You have no idea how long I've been waiting for you to say that." He brushed her wild windblown hair out of her face. "I love you," he said, rubbing his thumb along her cheek.

Joy leaned up, standing on her tippy toes, and kissed his bottom lip. He leaned further down, wrapping his arms around her as she entwined hers around his nec, and fiercely reciprocated her kiss—until his phone rang loudly interrupting their passionate embrace.

"It's Liam," he said, looking at the screen.

"It's fine, you can take it," she said, breathing heavily, her forehead on his chest. "I need to check in on Jessica anyway."

He answered as she pulled her phone out. She had several missed texts from Jessica. The latest said, "How am I as a paparazzo?" Joy scrolled up to see picture after picture of her walk with Lucas. A new message popped up with the loading image icon. "Does this mean you're good?" Joy looked around, trying to see if she could spot her friend as the image continued to load. *Ding.* She looked down, and there was a beautiful picture of her and Lucas kissing.

Joy quickly texted back, "Wow, your stalker skills are better than I realized. 10/10 would recommend... and yes, I'm excellent." She added a few smiley face emojis for emphasis.

Jessica replied, "I stan you."

"Always and forever, same" Joy texted before putting her phone back.

Lucas glanced back at her and smiled. *I'm very good indeed.*

Epilogue

A few months later, Joy went to visit Peter and Ryan's graves only to find Lucas standing there in front of their stones. His head was bowed slightly, hands in his pockets, shifting his weight back and forth and swaying with the wind. She hid behind a tree, not wanting him to notice but wanting to see what he was doing there. Obviously, he had never met them. They weren't his to mourn. If they were still alive, he wouldn't be in her life. But there he was, seemingly in conversation with them. After a few minutes of observing his behavior, she slunk a little closer and heard him say something about not being a replacement.

"Lucas," Joy called, not wanting to hear any more without him knowing she was there. "What are you doing here?"

He turned and smiled at her. "I know you talk to Peter here and I wanted a chance to talk to him as well."

"That's really sweet." Joy walked over and wrapped her arm around his waist. "And he would've really liked you."

"Ryan too?"

"Oh, no, he probably would've hated you." She laughed,

shaking her head. His arm that draped over her shoulders slid off and grabbed her hand. They started walking to a paved pathway in the shade of the trees lining the park. She was glad they'd never met. She felt like both of them complimented her and helped her be better in different ways. Each man had their strengths and flaws, as did she, but she was essentially thankful she never had to choose between the two. While it was easier with Lucas, Ryan had given her Peter, and grieving the loss of them had helped her find her voice.

"Or, he would've at least been envious of you. Good heavens, I don't know, maybe he would've loved you more than I do for all I know. But I hope he loves you now, and I hope he's OK with me loving you, although I haven't really thought about it... much."

He squeezed her hand. "Well, I am most certainly more than OK with you loving me and I hope you are with me loving you."
  "Absolutely," Joy replied.

"Yeah? I want to ask you something then..." Lucas hesitated, looking up at the mostly blue sky above, dotted with a few white clouds. The leaves were beginning to turn but the weather was still hot.

"Ask away," she responded, suggestively raising her eyebrows.

"Will you start wearing this for me?" he asked, holding out the emerald ring he had given her all those months ago.

"Oh, of course! I didn't know you still had it!" she exclaimed, putting it on her right hand, back on the finger it felt so right on. "Thank you, I love it just as much this time if not more."

"Oh, actually, that was the wrong one," he replied, smiling slyly, pulling something else out of his pocket. "It's for your other hand," he said casually as they continued to walk. He handed her a smaller but statelier diamond ring.

She abruptly stopped and stared at the ring in her hand. "Is this what I think this is?" She looked up to find him kneeling in front of her. Her breath caught and tears filled her eyes.

"Joy Elizabeth, with every fiber of my being I love you. Would you please..."

"Yes!" she interrupted, leaning down and pulling him into a passionate kiss.

"Make me the happiest man alive and give me the greatest honor of being my bride?" he finished asking as they pulled away, foreheads resting against each other.

"Only if you promise me you'll kiss me at least fifty times for every kissing scene with another person."

"I promise." He took the ring back from her and slipped it on her left ring finger.

"Good, let's start banking those now," she said, pulling him back into her embrace.

378

About the Author

Becca Bilbo Dorris is me, hi. I wrote this. I enjoy creating and oscillate mediums frequently- writing, painting, knitting, consulting, and I recently took up guitar and writing lyrics. I currently live with my family, cats, dog, chickens, and ducks. I hope to be a fiber farmer when I grow up. One day, I also hope to be organized enough to form a newsletter and website. You can currently follow me on Instagram- @rebilbo and @redbilbo and at least for now, I'm on Tik Tok- @beccabilbodorris

Also by Becca Bilbo Dorris

Adorrisable Poetry Edition: Muses & Fuses
A short book of poetry describing the frustration of being distracted from the intended project by writer's block, lack of inspiration, fatigue, and parenthood..

Made in the USA
Middletown, DE
15 July 2023

35137854R00234